PRAISE FOR
WICKED AS YOU WISH

★ "A truly original novel. A deftly executed melding of folklore and reality grounded in contemporary issues."

—*Kirkus Reviews*, Starred Review

★ "An enchanting story that is both a feast for the senses and a unique spin on the hero's journey."

—*Publishers Weekly*, Starred Review

"Rin Chupeco's marvelously magical *Wicked As You Wish* is a great read for fans of fairy tales, myths, and legends. In fact, avid fans will want to read it two, three, or four times just to catch all the twists, updates, and Easter eggs, as nearly every chapter is loaded with delights. Come for the adventure, stay for the sassy jerkwad firebird."

—Kendare Blake, #1 *New York Times* bestselling author of the Three Dark Crowns series

"Readers looking for a vibrant, Harry Potter–esque fantasy full of secrets, spies, magic, monsters, and mayhem need look no further."

—*Booklist*

"Wildly creative, with myriad references to folklore and fairy tales, this alternate-reality adventure will surely appeal to modern fantasy fans who can keep up with a complex plot that unfolds at a breakneck pace."

—*Horn Book Magazine*

PRAISE FOR
THE BONE WITCH TRILOGY

★ "*The Bone Witch* is fantasy worldbuilding at its best, and Rin Chupeco has created a strong and colorful cast of characters to inhabit that realm."

—*Shelf Awareness*, Starred Review on *The Bone Witch*

★ "Mesmerizing. Chupeco does a magnificent job of balancing an intimate narrative perspective with sweeping worldbuilding, crafting [their] tale within a multicultural melting pot of influences as [they] press toward a powerful cliffhanger."

—*Publishers Weekly*, Starred Review on *The Bone Witch*

"*The Bone Witch* is a fantasy lover's fantasy, with a rich history and hierarchy of its own. The secrets and workings of its magic are revealed slowly in a suspenseful novel that is sure to appeal to those with a love of serious, dark fairy tales."

—*Foreword Reviews* on *The Bone Witch*

"Readers who enjoy immersing themselves in detail will revel in Chupeco's finely wrought tale. *Game of Thrones* fans may see shades of Daenerys Targaryen in Tea, as she gathers a daeva army to unleash upon the world. Whether she is in the right remains a question unanswered, but the ending makes it clear her story is only beginning."

—*Booklist* on *The Bone Witch*

★ "Rin's beautifully crafted world from *The Bone Witch* (2017) expands in this sequel, which joins dark asha Tea on her crusade of revenge... Dark and entrancing with a third volume to come."

—*Booklist*, Starred Review on *The Heart Forger*

★ "In this spectacular follow-up to the rich *The Bone Witch*, Tea's quest draws the reader further in, setting them on a more dangerous yet intriguing adventure."

—*Foreword Reviews*, Starred Review on *The Heart Forger*

ALSO BY RIN CHUPECO

The Girl from the Well
The Suffering

A HUNDRED NAMES FOR MAGIC SERIES

Wicked As You Wish
An Unreliable Magic

THE BONE WITCH TRILOGY

The Bone Witch
The Heart Forger
The Shadowglass

THE NEVER TILTING WORLD SERIES

The Never Tilting World
The Ever Cruel Kingdom

AN UNRELIABLE MAGIC

RIN CHUPECO

sourcebooks
fire

Published by Sourcebooks Fire, an imprint of Sourcebooks
P.O. Box 4410, Naperville, Illinois 60567-4410
(630) 961-3900
sourcebooks.com

Cataloging-in-Publication data is on file with the Library of Congress.

Printed and bound in the United States of America.
VP 10 9 8 7 6 5 4 3 2 1

Kian delos Santos
Danica May Garcia
Raymart Siapo
Leonardo Legaspi Co
Roman Manaois

Say their names.

1

IN WHICH TALA FALLS DOWN A MOUNTAIN

On a bright spring morning in Avalon, Tala Makiling Warnock stood at the peak of the kingdom's tallest and most terribly cursed mountain and prepared herself to fall off it.

It was much more difficult than it sounded.

Simeli Mountain had a reputation long before Avalon had succumbed to the frost. Every two weeks since Alexei Tsarevich, the seventy-fifth king of Avalon, had established a working government, a retrieval crew swept through the mountain's base, searching for ducks that barked instead of quacked or geese that cried instead of squawked. Simeli was a popular attraction for parkour aficionados, ninja warrior wannabes, and people who were certain that the high of a spell-induced adrenaline rush trumped the risks of transforming into temporary magical poultry. Social media was rife with videos of disgruntled-looking ducks and foul-squawking geese taken by their disrespectful so-called friends, so reputations were at stake. Mountaineers and climbing enthusiasts avoided the place entirely.

Climbing Simeli was easy enough. Paths had been carefully carved into the mountainside by terrain engineers and forest ecologists. The more impatient could opt for a forty-five-minute ride in spelltech-powered cable cars to carry them to the annex.

The trick wasn't in the ascent but in the drop.

More specifically, a thirty-thousand-foot drop.

Even more specifically, an obstacle course *built* into the thirty-thousand-foot drop.

People called it the Simeli gauntlet. It was called the lemming challenge among the locals who knew better.

"Friends don't let friends fall down Simeli on their own," Kensington Inoue informed her loftily, as if he'd been jumping off the mountain his whole life instead of starting a couple of months ago, shortly after Alex's official coronation. The boy had made it look so easy. Everyone but Tala had completed the route. The failure rankled her.

It didn't matter that she'd lived all her life in Invierno, where nothing ever happened and the closest she'd ever gotten to a proper adventure was arnis sparring sessions with her father.

It didn't matter that her friends had undergone grueling physical training for years in comparison. It didn't matter that the others had trained to join the Order of the Bandersnatch and serve as King Alex's honor guards by the time they could walk. Loki had given her a crash course in parkour, and she'd proven a quick learner but was nowhere near the same league as the others. Her mother had been training her to dispel wards and defensive spells too, but the magic in Simeli was so expansive that not even Lumina Makiling at her strongest could override it.

Tala was now an official member of the Order of the Bandersnatch just like the others, but some days, she still felt like she wasn't good enough.

All the other Banders had successfully completed the Simeli gauntlet—Ken and Loki and West and even Nya, though the latter had lived most of her life in an isolated village and had never even been on a mountain before. Lola Urduja and the Katipuneros had finished it so many times they could do it in their sleep despite their advanced ages. Running Simeli had been a favorite pastime in their youth, long before the Snow Queen had blanketed Avalon in frost and sent Alex, Tala's family, and countless other Avalonian refugees into exile.

No. That wasn't right. It was Alex who had, in an ironic twist, caused the frost, to prevent the Snow Queen from causing more damage to his kingdom. And he'd done it using the Nine Maidens, a massive monument of a spelltech so incredibly powerful it had taken twelve years to find their off switch.

"It's been a while since we've been gallivanting around like this," Tita Baby said, sounding far too excited to jump off a mountain when she'd complained about her rheumatism only the day before.

"Yes," Tala echoed, staring down at the sheer vertical drop.

"Took eighteen tries for me, you know." Tita Baby said cheerfully. "It was then I learned I needed glasses pala."

"Twenty times for me," Tita Teejay sighed. She pursed her lips, using them to point in Tita Chedeng's direction. "She made it in only thirteen."

"Twelve," Tito Boy signed.

"Punyeta," General Luna swore, although Tita Chedeng assured Tala he actually meant *fourteen.*

"Took me a sixth try to get it right," Ken admitted. "What about you, Loki?"

"Three."

"Show-off."

It had not occurred to Tala to count, but she knew she was well into the late twenties at this point.

"Took me six tries too," Nya commented, her curly hair whipping around her as she stared over the edge.

"Bet I can finish this round faster than you can, Rapunzel." Ken had a glint in his eye, as he always did whenever he was in the mood for playful pestering. Ken had pulled off his infamous Yawarakai-Te prank on the Ikpean girl only the week before—pretending to lop his leg off with the sword, knowing full well that the blade could only cut the nonliving— and had received a punch for his efforts while in midswing. His left eye still looked a little swollen. As far as Tala could tell, he'd had the world's worst crush on Nya ever since.

Nya raised a questioning eyebrow. "What do I get for winning?"

"Dinner at your favorite restaurant, my treat."

"And what happens if I lose?"

"Dinner at your favorite restaurant, my treat."

"What's the difference, then?"

"My level of smugness."

Nya's lips quirked up. "You're impossible."

"What's impossible is you beating me, so be prepared for me to be absolutely insufferable at—"

Nya calmly stepped off the cliff with the same ease she might have had strolling through a park. Suspended in air for a few brief seconds, she only had time to flash Ken a bright grin and flip him the bird before gravity took control, and she was soon lost amid the rising mist.

"Is that a yes?" Ken yelled down, cupping his hands as if she could hear him better that way. "Should I take that as a yes?"

"Smooth," West complimented him.

"No, it wasn't," said Loki, who took things unironically.

Ken shot them a wide grin. "She likes me," he said happily before he, too, was jumping.

"We're wasting time," Lola Urduja said crisply. A flock of birds tried to sweep past, but all it took was a glare from the old woman for them to change course, breaking their vee formation to carefully swoop around her instead. "Shall we wait until we run out of decent air, or shall we begin?"

West bowed to her, then obediently pitched himself forward. The other Katipuneros followed suit, tottering briefly into the space where rock met air before toppling out of view. Though frail-looking on solid ground, the elders dove down swiftly with surprising grace, twisting effortlessly to avoid the incoming rush of wind.

"Are you gonna be okay?" Loki asked.

There was an obstacle course built inside the Simeli visitors' center, a rudimentary facsimile of the lemming challenge, and Tala had trained there constantly under Loki's watchful eye. But even without the added practice, she'd gone through the drop enough times to know that she was more than capable of the physical aspects of the course. The problem was that there was more to the Simeli gauntlet than just strength and agility.

"I'm good," she said. Loki was officially joining the Fifth Honor as a cadet that day, and she couldn't be prouder of them. Unfortunately, that meant they wouldn't be around as much to help her practice. Which meant she would have to look to someone else for further instruction.

Like her father.

And she wasn't ready for that just yet.

"I'll meet you at the bottom, then." Reassured, Loki flashed her an impish grin as they spread their arms out on either side and let themselves fall backward off the peak.

As Ken had said, *show-off.*

"You go ahead, hija," Lola Urduja said. She always insisted on being the last one off, to be in a better position to spot and head off accidents.

Tala suspected she was the reason for the elder's precautions. "Right," she said, taking a deep breath. She stared down at the fog coalescing below her like a hazy blanket. *I'm going to beat you today,* she thought, trying to psych herself into believing exactly that, and jumped.

The first obstacle was the four winds themselves. North, east, south, and west were at constant war with one another, and the result was a vertical labyrinth where you had to spin and twist to keep from slamming hard into gusts that blew in all directions, using trajectory and your own momentum to springboard your way through. Tala could see airflow from the north wind rising up to greet her and flung herself to the right.

She avoided the eastern wind that would have slammed her into the mountainside and clung tightly to the southern gale instead, the only one pushing her in the direction she wanted to go. Riding the south had its own dangers; to prevent fatal mishaps, a sturdy net was stretched underneath all that magicked space.

Tala kept her eyes peeled for the telltale glitter of spells that marked the second part of the course. They were easy enough to miss and then easy enough to dismiss even if you didn't. There were eleven steps total, suspended in thin air and spaced five feet apart. They were called swanshirts after Avalon heroine Princess Elisa's swan-cursed brothers.

Tala let go of the southern wind and launched herself onto the first of the swanshirts. She bit back a grunt of pain as her hands came into contact with the rough, abrasive surface. Swinging her legs, Tala focused on the next nearest ledge below her, angling her body so she could swing herself down.

A densely packed whirlwind of boxed air spun a thousand feet below the eleventh and final swanshirt, and it served as a trampoline to reach the next stage. If you didn't leap high enough, you hit a pack of dense bespelled air that you came out of sprouting feathers and a beak.

Beyond that was a jumping spider platform that required her to brace her legs against two nearly translucent walls set four feet apart, forcing her to hop forward along its length in increments while hoping she didn't lose her balance. Tala's arms were sore by the time she'd muscled her way through, bringing her to the last and final course, which was where she kept screwing things up.

It didn't *look* like it should be difficult, which was the most frustrating part. It was a warped wall made from a dense, naturally occurring wave of wind; you had to run up the steep incline and grab at the edge to pull yourself up. From there, it was another thirty-foot fall.

Tala scaled the warped wall with little effort and dropped to the ground beyond it.

Long, thorny brambles now encircled her from all sides. The base of Simeli Mountain was overgrown with these invasive species. They called this area the Labyrinth; most participants spent more time here than they actually did falling down the mountain.

This was the part everyone hated. People had tried cutting their way through in the hopes of a shortcut, only for the brambles to entrap and keep them immobile until Simeli staff arrived to extricate them. The admin had been very explicit about banning offenders for life; not only were the thorns from some species of endangered plant that flourished only in Avalon, the overabundance of it here meant that one would have to slash their way through at least fifty miles of thorns before any visible exit presented itself.

There were already a few chickens and ducks waddling about, eventually tottering out of view underneath the thorns. Tala's agimat, her inherited magic-negating curse, had protected her from this fate, which was the only good thing she had going for her each time.

The internet was full of tips and tricks on how to overcome Simeli, save for this part of the gauntlet. The area was cursed to forbid anyone from revealing its secrets, lest they be hit with a forgetfulness spell.

Her friends had been particularly stubborn about not telling her. Tala could respect that. They didn't want her to cheat. *She* didn't want to cheat. She couldn't count it as an accomplishment if she had.

Except she also maybe *wanted* to cheat. She'd done this over twenty times by now. She'd free-fell the required thirty thousand feet to say that she had, in fact, finished Simeli. She was *literally back on the ground*, for crying out loud.

But *no*. She had to get out of the bramble maze on her own. The only tip regarding the Labyrinth that wasn't under a sealed indictment was that it was constantly shifting and changing, which meant any map of the place was rendered useless in a matter of minutes.

She hated escape rooms. The last time she'd been in one was three years ago, when a short-lived mystery maze had opened in Invierno. Her mother enjoyed it; she'd been the brains of the team and was extremely competitive. In contrast, her father had lolled around, cheerfully admitting he was a lazy arse and that Lumina would be better off without him getting in the way—

No. She wasn't going to think about her father right now. According to Simeli's hall of fame board, Lumina Warnock was the seventh-fastest person to complete the lemming challenge in recent memory. If her mother could do it, then so could she.

Tala was still at it over an hour later, five minutes past the personal time limit she'd allotted herself because she always hated making the others wait and still nowhere closer to getting out of the maze.

"I give up," she announced resignedly.

There was a cheerful, thrumming sound behind her.

A golf cart puttered into view. It was full of geese.

Its driver, an old lady who Tala had unfortunately met several times by now, leaned out to squint at her. "Had enough, little miss?" she asked, not without sympathy.

"Yeah," Tala mumbled, shamefaced.

"Don't worry, dearie. You'll do it at the next try." The old woman said that each time, but Tala had stopped believing her after the tenth attempt. No doubt she'd said the exact same thing to all the fowl now clustered around her.

Scowling, Tala climbed into the cart. A pair of mallards scooted out of the way to give her space.

Her friends were waiting for her. A private room had been allotted for them—knowing the Avalon king had its perks—though it was early enough in the morning that there were few other people around. West was still holding up a banner he'd made that spelled *Congratulations* across it, like he did every time despite evidence to the contrary.

But something was different this time. Nya was twisting nervously at the sleeve of her shirt, and there was a slightly apologetic expression on Tita Chedeng's face, like the one she'd worn when she'd offered to dog-sit for a neighbor and Sparkles had snatched Tita Baby's freshly laundered underwear off the clothing line.

Tala hopped off the cart, and golf cart lady continued merrily on toward the medical center.

"It took you only fifteen minutes to reach the warped wall, compared to the twenty from last time," Loki said, eyes on their watch. "This is excellent, Tala. You're only ten seconds behind the general."

"Talentado," General Luna added affectionately.

"I'm sorry." She didn't know what she was apologizing for. That she wasn't good enough to finish? That they had to wait so long for her in each instance?

"Don't ever be sorry," Nya chided.

"Walang iwanan," Lola Urduja said.

"What does that mean?"

"That we won't leave anyone behind. That we're all in this together, no matter what."

Ken mulled that over, a grin breaking over his face. "Walang iwanan. I like that."

Tala smiled sheepishly at them and then froze. A man stood a few yards away, oversize hands stuffed down the pockets of his coat. His dark eyes watched her carefully.

It was her dad. He'd offered to move out to give Tala the space she needed to process their situation, but she'd thought even that was a step too far, a decision too hasty. Still, they barely talked at home despite her mother's determined efforts, and it almost felt like they were living apart anyway.

No. That wasn't accurate either. She'd been the one to refuse to talk, went out of her way not to be there when he was. She knew he didn't like it but had honored her reasons and let her be.

Her mother had been more vocal, urging Tala to forgive him, pointing out that he was still her father no matter what. Lumina was a Filipina, and she subscribed to the view that nothing was more important than family. But Tala was petty and hurt and also someone who prized being honest with the people she loved and expected the same thing from them. She'd already gotten into several arguments with her mother about her dad. It wasn't fair to pretend like this was just some typical problem they could resolve as a family.

Most families didn't have immortal fathers who'd been responsible for the genocide of at least a million people. Most families didn't have fathers who'd once been the consort of the Snow Queen before he'd grown a conscience that was several hundred years too late in the making.

"Dad." Tala had tried to say as little of it as possible to her friends, but she knew they were aware of the ongoing tension between her and her father.

Kay Warnock's eyes now looked tired and worn. Tall as he was, his shoulders were slightly hunched, like he would shrink himself down if the world would pay him little notice that way.

Her father took a step forward, faltered when Tala didn't do the same, and remained where he was. "I wanted to talk to ye," he said gruffly, his Scottish brogue more pronounced than usual. "Something's happened."

Tala froze. "Is Alex…?"

"No, His Majesty's fine. But the king wants all of ye back at Maidenkeep."

"We have a thing to do with Zoe first," Ken said, slightly evasive. "Alex knows about it."

Kay nodded. "He gave that a mention, aye. He'll give ye an hour, two at best, and then you're all to assemble at mission control. But he'll be wanting tae talk with the Katipuneros right away, Urduja."

The others were already peeling off their air patches, running off to grab knapsacks they'd stored in the center's lockers for safekeeping.

"Is it bad?" Nya asked worriedly, voicing their unspoken concerns. Alex wouldn't have sent Kay if it had been something of little consequence.

"I'd rather not say things out here in the open," Tala's dad said carefully. "We've got a looking glass on standby. Alex gave me five minutes, and I'd appreciate a little more movement on the lot of ye."

While the others made ready, Tala stared at him. He turned and met her gaze with a steady one of his own, and it was she who had to look away.

I wanted to talk to ye. He knew she didn't want to see him. His understanding and his quiet compassion were the only constants she'd always known about him, which was why the truth of his past had hit her like an oncoming truck.

"I know ye don't want to, love," he said softly, "but it's important. I'm sorry."

She could think of only one reason why he would seek her out now, and it had everything to do with the sword. That was a secret only they knew and shared, and it tied them together in ways that neither wanted.

And Tala didn't want to think about the repercussions of that either.

2

IN WHICH EVERYONE IS TALKING ABOUT THE FIGHT CLUB

Tea-ta was full of customers when the Banders entered. Maidenkeep's gardens were open to the public, and among the food establishments there, it was the boba café that often received the most visitors.

Inside, Tita Teejay waited for them, a tray of their favorite drinks on hand. "No," she said firmly when West reached down to retrieve his wallet.

"I feel bad about not paying." He said this every time, though her response was always the same.

"The work that you are doing *downstairs*"—Tita Teejay said the last word in an almost theatrical whisper, as if there was someone listening in—"is all the fee we require. In the meantime, you must hydrate, hijo."

"Thank you." West accepted his drink.

"Good luck." Tita Teejay handed Tala a large plate of chocolate chip cookies bespelled with anti-lethargy magic. "And this one is for everyone else below."

"What are we going to do without you two?" Tala asked her fondly.

"Go hungry, probably."

There was another exit leading out of the kitchens that brought them to a small veranda, where a large cedar tree loomed above them.

Nya pressed her hand against the tree bark. There was a faint click as a portion of the spell detached itself from part of the trunk, revealing a small wooden door carved on its surface. Ken pushed it open. "After you, ladies," he said gallantly.

It was Ken who'd first discovered the tree's secrets. He'd christened it the Utsubo—the Hollow Tree, or the Hollows for short—after a story his father had told him as a child, of a famed musician and ancestor of theirs who'd been raised inside a cedar tree.

The Hollows was located inside a magnificent specimen of a tree that graced the royal gardens, bespelled with ancient magic that was still going strong several millennia later. It was said to be among the oldest planted within the castle grounds and so ancient it had borne witness to the legendary Queen Vasilisa's reign. It was a popular spot to visit among tourists and locals alike, which made sneaking in an impossibility, until Tita Teejay and Tita Chedeng had calmly proposed a solution and applied for a business license. Both twin sisters had degrees in food technology and potions development, something Tala was unaware of, which explained Tea-ta's success.

While the cedar was only twenty or so feet in diameter, the room inside it was as long as half a football field, with mobile AC units set up in all four corners. Couches and pullout beds lined one side, with a small refrigerator nearby for emergency snacks. A small area had been set up for gym use, complete with a punching bag and a few weights. Rows of tables made up the other half of the Hollows, with the laptops and workstations there ready for use.

Several wide-screen TVs encompassed another quarter of a section of wall, showing different news channels. One of the screens was hooked up to a security feed inside the east tower, where the Nine Maidens were housed. Maidenkeep's most notorious spelltech was intimidating even from this vantage point, the circle of black obsidian stone monuments a reminder of how they'd been able to reclaim Avalon in the first place. Alex was banned from entering its premises, a precaution he had agreed to. Wielding the Nine Maidens was addictive, and no one wanted to risk it.

Dexter Gallagher was fiddling with a looking glass at the center of the room, his hands skating across the polished surface with deft, confident skill, loading some fresh spellware. Cole was helping him.

A small jewel was suspended in the air above the prototype, sur-rounded by a heavy barrier to prevent its theft. The Ikpean priestess had given them a bag full of those spellstones as thanks for bringing Nya safely to Maidenkeep. Alex had given each of the Banders one as a reward for saving him, and Zoe had placed hers there at the Hollows, to remind them, she said, of what they were still fighting for. Tala had very prudently handed hers over to her parents for safekeeping, not really sure if she even wanted to use it.

Zoe was watching the screens, a scowl on her face. "Hey," she greeted them, eyes still focused on the screen as she took a sip from her own glass of antifatigue rosemary black sugar tea.

"…called the conditions within the site 'appalling' and a 'blow to what America stands for,'" the reporter was saying as the camera panned to what appeared to be a government facility under obvious heavy guard— the Touchstone detention center in Texas, according to the scrolling news reel. "Secretary Karen Delkimov has denied all claims that other similar facilities have been breached over the last few weeks or that detained children under their care have been taken. To date, the Department of Immigration has continued to ban all but official staff from entering the Touchstone correctional facility…"

"The Touchstone concentration camp," Zoe corrected the woman with a growl. "Say it, you cowards." She finally turned to them, raising an eyebrow at Tala.

"No," Tala confessed with a slow flush.

"You'll do it next time," Zoe said reassuringly. "It took me over twenty times to figure it out too."

"Does that mean you're going to tell me how to beat the Labyrinth?"

"Nope."

Tala sighed.

Ken squinted at the screen. "Please don't tell me we're going to crash one of these ICE-holes. Not that I *don't* want to, but that's gonna be a lot of people to fight in the daytime."

"Of course not. Against the rules, remember?" Zoe didn't look particularly happy about it, though. She gestured toward the heavy jugs of water lined up against one of the beds. "We're only going to be leaving water out in the desert. Think these are enough?"

Ken let out a dramatic sigh. "You know, Zoe, the reason I was all gung ho about joining your fight club was because I thought there would be someone to punch."

"I thought you of all people would be tired of getting punched out," Zoe said dryly.

Ken's eyes wandered to Nya. "It depends on who does the punching, I guess."

The looking glass Dex was working on was currently the only one of its kind, a prototype his father called the Red King—two looking glasses built into one. Determined to keep the spelltech a secret until it was ready to be unveiled to the public, Alex had turned it over to Zoe for unofficial testing, and she had roped the others into helping her.

Zoe's idea of what constituted testing had been very on-brand for the Order of the Bandersnatch. Still, Alex had some key rules. Wear face scramblers at all times to avoid detection. Use earpieces. Call no one by name during the missions. Don't get caught; if you do, say nothing to anyone but the lawyers Alex would be sending their way. Fortunately, no one had needed to test out that last rule just yet.

Last month, they'd given cornucopias and medical supplies to relief workers in Burundi, though it took a while for Loki to find doctors willing to give them malaria inoculations without asking too many questions before they could even enter the country.

Before that, West had pulled some connections to get them cheap insulin. They'd even gone almost viral a couple of weeks ago after secretly replacing the Worldenders' handmade slogans berating licensed medical spells as the work of demons with actual facts about magic, biology, and women's rights. Unsurprisingly, the Worldender rally had been short.

Tala had pointed out that the latter was close to skirting the rules Alex had set down for them, but Zoe hadn't seemed bothered by it. "As long as they don't know we did it," she had assured Tala, "and as long as it can't be traced back to us, we should be fine. I'll make sure of it."

"Got an email from Jennifer," Nya said. "They've managed to give out the insulin without anyone the wiser. But she wants to know if it's possible to put together another drop soon, this time in Chicago." She shook her head in wonder. "Avalon's only been functioning for a few months. Why is our insulin a hundred times cheaper than theirs?"

"I'm sure you know why. Is there enough in our CashMe funds for a second round?"

"Barely, but the donations should be on the rise now that word is spreading and people are linking back to Jennifer's own account."

"I'll pay for it, Zo," West said earnestly. "I know you don't want me to keep footing the bill, because this is supposed to be a self-suffragette organization—"

"Self-*sufficient*, West. Though I appreciate the compliment."

"That too. But at least let me get this one. Dad does stuff like this a lot. He calls it seed funding."

"You're a treasure, West. Thank you, but only for this one time. I don't want you making this a habit." Zoe glanced at Dex. "Are we ready?"

"I've set the coordinates near the Texas border," Dex said promptly. "We can go whenever you say the word. We found a good spot away from their sensors. We can keep the port up indefinitely if we want to."

"Why Texas specifically?" Loki asked.

Zoe pointed to the television screen. "It said that they're expecting an influx of immigrants any day now. We'll be deep enough in the desert that we shouldn't attract attention but near enough that anyone passing through should find our stash easily. Hopefully."

"How many trips have we made this week?" Cole asked abruptly.

"Two, counting this one. The first with those Worldenders, and—"

"There are five locations listed in this looking glass's backup directory, all activated within the last seven days."

Dex turned red. "It m-might be an echo," he stammered. "I-it's safe to travel, but there are s-some features that require constant c-calibrating and this is one of—"

"If it's a bug that won't compromise this mission, then I'm sure we can take a look at it again later," Zoe said calmly, studiously avoiding Cole's gaze. "Everyone ready?"

There was a chorus of yeses. Everyone moved to grab a couple of water jugs to carry.

"Just a few reminders. American Border Patrol now carry spelltech called the Spark-64 in lieu of their usual firearms," Zoe told them. "Their bullets dissolve on impact."

Nya made an angry sound. "No bullets, no accountability, huh?"

"The bullet's a clear con on my list." Zoe smiled at Tala. "But the pro is that their spelltech is now susceptible to magic. Should the worst happen, we have hexbombs to temporarily negate their guns. And then we've got Tala. Be on your guard at all times."

"I really wish we can get through one of these briefings without needing a pro and con list," Ken sighed.

"Not while I'm in charge, no. Fire it up, Dex."

The looking glass glowed; Tala could see the desert in its reflection. Zoe was the first to hop through, then Cole, who was still frowning, and then the others. Unlike the standard looking glass, which required a physical device also stationed at their destination to work, the Red King only required one at its starting point. Dex had tried to explain the mechanics to Tala before, rambling enthusiastically about chirality and enantiomorphs. She still didn't know what any of those words meant.

Tala hadn't been back to the Royal States of America since they'd left Invierno. She didn't miss it. She remembered the scorching heat and didn't miss that either. From this end, there was only a hole suspended in the air where they'd jumped out, and she could see the Hollows shimmering from within its center, Dex peeking nervously through it at them.

"Find a good place, hide your stash, then return here," Zoe ordered crisply. Her features were blurred by the face scrambler, as were everyone else's. "Buddy system as always, and don't stray too far. Don't bury the water too deeply."

"Yes, Mom," Ken teased.

"If you spot any border agents, stay out of sight and inform the others as soon as you can," Zoe continued. "No contact. Twenty seconds to hide the water and return," Zoe instructed. "There may be trouble, and we'd best be out of here before it arrives."

The group spread out. Tala lugged her containers over to where a large rock outcropping lay, kicking dirt away with her shoe to dig up a shallow hole, deposit the jugs, and rebury them.

Just as she was finishing up, a familiar tingle tickled at the back of her neck, and her head jerked up, suddenly hyperaware. There was magic here, and none of it was coming from within their group.

"Wait," Loki could also detect some forms of magic, albeit not through an agimat like Tala. They met her eyes. "You sense it too, right?"

"There's a lot more spells here than there should be," Tala agreed. "Too strong to be anything natural."

Loki growled low and signaled frantically, thumbing toward the west where a cloud of dust was rising up.

There was a screeching of tires, and then a woman screamed.

West snarled, nose twitching. "We can't leave. This is trouble, but it's trouble we can't look away from, Zo."

He and Loki were already running ahead toward the noise, but Tala already knew what they were going to find.

There were arrests in progress. She could see several people face-first on the ground, agents handcuffing them down the line. Tala didn't know how many children there usually were in these cases, but she could count at least eleven. The older teens were being roughly handled like the adults; when one made a cry of protest at their mistreatment, an officer responded with a kick to his shins.

"Bastards," Ken hissed.

"No contact, Ken," Zoe muttered to him, though she sounded torn. "I promised Alex."

"There's something else." The strange electricity Tala could sense in the air wasn't coming from the agents. She could feel the magic practically vibrating in her bones from the force of it.

An agent walking toward the captured immigrants paused in his step and then never moved again. A block of ice sprouted up from nowhere, trapping him within a frozen prison in seconds.

There was more shouting and more cursing as the others drew weapons, casting about frantically for someone to shoot at.

It was then that Tala saw him. The boy stood almost out of view, half-hidden behind a small knoll. A ball of ice manifested in the palm of his hand; he lobbed it at another border agent, encasing them in ice in the same manner as he had the first.

The move had not gone unnoticed. Someone yelled out an order, and the cops opened fire.

Solid, translucent ice walls formed up from the ground in front of the boy, and he laughed as their bullets lodged deep within the frozen barrier and melted away, protecting him from their worst.

He wore a scrambler too, his features like an overly pixelated image. But Tala knew who he was. It felt like someone had reached into her chest and squeezed painfully at her heart.

Several cops fled toward a waiting truck, and others struggled to open several large crates that were stacked atop the vehicle.

Tala was already running, ignoring Zoe's yells to stay put, gathering her agimat around her.

She knew what was in those boxes. She could *sense* what was in those boxes, because she'd encountered them before. West had already shifted, his face scrambler now useless. The black hound tore past her, making straight for the crates. It was no surprise to see Cole catching up next.

Cole and West knew what was inside those container units, same as she did.

Three of the crates sprang open.

With a roar, ice wolves came tearing out.

One of the agents held a control device, but from the look of panic on his face and the way his fingers kept constantly jabbing at it to no effect, Tala knew the creatures were not following his orders. Which was why the first of the wolves turned toward the nearest target—another border officer—jaws clamping onto his leg. The man went down, his colleagues yelling for backup as they emptied bullets into the beast, which shrugged off the assault and continued to chomp.

The second wolf turned toward the cuffed immigrants, baring its teeth. It was promptly knocked down by West, who jumped atop it to rip out a huge chunk of hide, ice glittering against the sunlight. The wolf roared and tried to get off a bite, but the black dog dodged and snatched at a hind leg, tearing it off with a vicious howl.

The last freed wolf moved to attack West, but Cole reached it in time, slamming a knife into its body. Tala saw the telltale branch-like shadows swarm out from its hilt, burrowing into the wound. The wolf stiffened, and then backed away when Cole withdrew the weapon. With it now fully under *his* bidding, it was West's opponent it attacked, savaging its brethren.

Zoe and Ken had taken charge of the asylum seekers, guiding them toward the others. "I *said* no contact," Zoe groaned.

"Hands up!" Another cop leveled his gun at Tala. "Don't move, don't move, don't move!"

He was shooting before he'd even finished the sentence. Tala flung up an arm. Her agimat instinctively activated, and the bullet dissolved the instant it passed through the natural barrier around her. Seizing the advantage, she put herself in between the agents and their previous prisoners, determined to shield them as best as she could.

The man didn't get a second chance to fire; another ball of ice turned him into a statue in moments. Ryker skidded to a stop beside her. From his bunched shoulders and clenched fists, she knew that he was furious.

At *her*!

"Stop putting yourself in danger!" he snapped.

"Pot, meet kettle!" Tala shot back. "You've been attacking all those concentration camps these last few months! You can't tell me not to get involved when you're up to your eyeballs in it!"

"This isn't your fight!"

"My decisions aren't *yours* to make!"

All the crates were now open, and five more ice wolves came bounding out. If they were supposed to recognize Ryker, they didn't show it. The agent with the remote had figured out the spelltech. "Kill them!" he hollered.

"We have everyone!" Zoe shouted. "Let's go!"

West abandoned the maimed ice wolf and retreated, Loki snatching up the clothes the boy had shed. Cole followed, his eyes on the remaining wolves milling before them, the wolf he'd possessed still under his control and facing off against the rest. But Tala refused to budge from Ryker's side.

"You don't have to stay," Ryker said quietly.

"I'm not doing this for you." She'd known that he'd survived their fight at Maidenkeep. She'd hated the relief that had swept over her when she realized that. She knew he'd been responsible for the previous break-ins in Arizona and Texas, knew he had rescued the children imprisoned there. She could find that almost admirable, except she knew he'd brought those kids to the kingdom of Beira, where they would be raised to serve the Snow Queen and fight against Avalon.

Still, she felt lighter and giddier, seeing him alive and well with her own eyes. "Aren't the ice wolves supposed to be on your side?"

"Not with that asshole controlling them with some kind of thrall spell." He took a quick glance at where Zoe and the others were waiting.

"Get out of here. They're waiting for you. Surprised the scrambler even works on you."

"I've got better control of my agimat than the last time. And these are terrible odds, even for you."

He laughed. "I like that you're worried for me."

"Shut up. I'll deal with the cops if you deal with their wolves."

"Fair enough." The ice wolves crept closer, but Ryker was ruthless. More ice sparkled at his fingers, and when he flung them outward, the ice had transformed into sharp spikes that neatly bisected two of the closest wolves.

Some of the agents were raising their guns again, but Tala pushed out with her agimat. It was exhausting work, to keep her sphere of influence wide enough to encompass the patrol standing several yards away, but as she'd told Ryker, she was a lot better at this now. She watched the weapons glow like beacons, spells warping around them.

One of the officers attempted a shot. Nothing happened. Tala summoned up all her strength, reached out with her mind, and deactivated the spell. It was like her previous training with the cellphones all over again, practicing for accuracy but without a Carly Rae Jepsen song for accompaniment.

The ice wolves stumbled forward, free of the agent's control. All immediately turned on the now unarmed agents, snapping and snarling.

"That's our cue to leave," Ryker whispered.

"You're not taking these people with you."

"Does Alex know he's getting a fresh influx of immigrants, then?"

"I know him. I know he'll do the right thing."

"And you're going to stop me from taking them?"

There were a thousand reasons why she couldn't trust him. A thousand reasons she couldn't like him, whatever he was to her in the past. "Yes."

"Tala, you have to know that—I want to—" Ryker paused. She couldn't see what he was thinking, doubted she could even without the scrambler. "I wish I could see your face," he finally said softly. "I miss you."

The spurt of joy Tala felt should have horrified her. She pushed it back down, packed it into the part of her that knew she shouldn't care. "That isn't my fault either."

"I know." He gave her a light push, back in the direction of the others. "Go. And thank you."

She ran into the portal without another word, expecting the safety of the Hollows, only to find herself in the chambers at Maidenkeep, the ones allotted for the government's administrative offices.

Zoe tapped at her right ear. "Dex, shut it down."

The portal disappeared immediately.

"Why are we at—" Tala began.

"We couldn't very well bring them to the other place, now can we, being a secret and all? I told Dex to redirect us here. I know there aren't a lot of people at this time of day, and this room hasn't been put to use yet." Zoe looked at the worried-looking immigrants and sighed. "Alex is going to kill me. What do you propose we do with them?"

"Process their papers," Loki supplied quietly. "Give them a hearing. See if they're eligible for asylum under Avalon law. Maybe we weren't their first choice, but wherever they decide to go after this, they'll be safer here than where they left."

Zoe nodded, the scrambler blurring with the movement. "They can't know who we are either. You all better scatter and lie low, before somebody gets suspicious. Let's meet up again tomorrow." She winced. "If we still have a place to meet up by then. Does anyone know any Spanish? I want to tell them to stay here, that someone else will bring them food and water shortly."

"Estás a salvo aquí," Cole told the men and women. "Te traeremos comida y agua."

"Gracias," one of the women whispered.

"We'll need to tell someone from the immigration department," Nya said, petting West. The black dog sat on his haunches and wagged his tail.

"I'll handle that," Zoe promised. "I just don't want them waiting and afraid."

"Would have been easier if we could have brought our segen to use," Ken groused.

"Yes, and in two hours, they'd have known who you were. There's a reason Alex forbade it."

"Cole brought his."

"I know, and I'll deal with him later," Zoe said, glaring.

"It wasn't my official segen."

"We're going to argue about more than just the semantics, Nottingham."

One of the asylum seekers stood up and said something else, to murmurs of approval.

"He said he wants to stay here and help," Cole translated. "He wants to make sure that other people coming through the borders are safe too."

Everyone looked at Zoe. "Avalon's got a history of helping resistance fighters," she said calmly. "Queen Talia once said everyone deserves the chance to fight for their own freedoms. But he'll need to talk about that with Alex first."

"You do know we're already in trouble, right?" Cole asked dryly. "You don't need to add to it?"

"Yeah, but they have every right to want to save their own. These are their families. And as much as I empathize, they *should* spearhead this particular fight. They would know where the routes are. They know the spots to avoid. Again, they'll still need His Majesty's permission, but I won't be the one to say no to them." Zoe's eyes blazed. "Everyone deserves a chance to go for what they believe in, don't you think? Avalon's supposed to be the land of fresh opportunities. Let it be that for them."

Cole gazed back at her, frowning, but said nothing.

"The agents were going to deploy ice wolves to hunt down asylum seekers," Tala murmured, still shaken by the thought. It didn't seem like Ryker knew that either. His anger had been real.

"Why so surprised at this point? If anything, they're exactly as cruel as I imagined them to be." Zoe sounded odd. She sounded…satisfied somehow. Then her expression grew rueful. "Alex is going to kill me," she repeated and sighed again.

3

IN WHICH A SWORD IN THE STONE GOES VIRAL

Dex was already waiting by the time they'd gone through the numerous security checkpoints needed to enter Avalon mission control, located at Maidenkeep's most heavily guarded wing. Normally cheerful if a little excitable, Dex's face was now a study in exhaustion, like the last hour had aged him by two years. "I'm s-so glad you're all here!" he blurted out. "You're only supposed to take three Wakeful potions a day, and His Majesty is already on his fifth."

Tala groaned. "I told him to ease up on those. Let me talk to him. Who's he annoying this time?"

"He's done with the insurance companies. He's with the ministers now."

Alex had commandeered one of the largest chambers in Maidenkeep for mission control, which he'd coined his Round Table. While most of Avalon's departments were located on the east side, this was the only government office located at the western end of the castle. Four widescreen televisions were mounted on the wall, each tuned in to the 24/7 news channels of four different kingdoms. Several computers had been set up, all attended by techmages: men and women selected and vetted for both their loyalty to Avalon and their brilliance in spelltech security. A group of Avalon's ministers, ranging from natural resources to defense, occupied a cluster of armchairs on the right side of the room, watching the news.

As always, the firebird was never far from the king's side. It waddled to and from the support beams overhead, occasionally letting out a throaty warble to remind everyone it existed.

"How are you holding up?" Tala asked softly, stepping up beside him, watching his gaze flick back to the television screen.

"Surviving, somehow. Thanks." He grinned faintly back at her. "How was the Simeli gauntlet?"

Tala scowled.

"That bad?"

"You ever tried it yourself?"

"Not even the least bit interested."

"Might help you destress. Watching four different news channels at the same time won't do that."

"I have good reason." He pointed at the screens, all displaying different headlines.

Environmental Protection Agency Head Says Climate Change Is a Hoax.

Royal States' Yemen Raid Yielded Multiple Casualties, No New Intel.

King Repeals Toxic Waste Restrictions.

"I expect a final proposal for government hiring guidelines so we can recruit the exact opposite of these people," he said to his ministers.

"You're still pushing yourself too hard, Your Majesty." Patrick Fasshagh, Avalon's minister of the interior, rose from his armchair. He was a man in his sixties, with a shock of cropped white hair and worried brown eyes. He'd previously served King Ivan, Alex's father, as one of his trusted advisers in the royal council, and he was now serving Alex in the same capacity, reemerging from Austria, where he'd been languishing in exile.

"You cannot seek to do everything. Allow the other ministers to shoulder some of your burden." He stopped short, blinking at Tala's father, who'd emerged from behind the group and shut the door quietly behind him.

The minister of trade rose, a faint sneer on his face. "Why is the Scourge here?"

"The Katipuneros insist on keeping guard over it, Alex," Kay said calmly, ignoring the man. He was taking great care not to look at Tala either, though she could feel herself tensing up all the same. "No sense in arguing with Urduja once her mind is made up, so I've returned alone."

"Thanks, Uncle Kay." Alex had taken to calling Tala's father that more often as of late, mostly to emphasize to the rest of his officials that he wasn't going to tolerate their dislike of the man.

"He's a criminal, Your Majesty," the man seethed.

A blaze of fire shot down from above, inches away from the man's beard, cutting him short.

"Be nice," Alex chided the firebird gently. "Minister Ancilotto, Uncle Kay and I go way back, and he's saved my life on at least three occasions. He can call me anything he pleases." He turned to the Bandersnatchers. "We've been getting reports of unusual activity near Wonderland. My Fianna are still busy mapping out the rest of Avalon, adding anti-infiltration spells to the looking glass ports we've been setting up. Wondered if you guys might want a look at this one."

"Yes," Loki said eagerly, immediately.

"They're only kids, Your Majesty," the minister of defense protested.

"Technically, so am I, Lydia. They saved my butt and helped me win Avalon back when no other adult could. Uncle Kay, I was hoping you'd tag along too."

"I don't think," Minister Ancilotto growled, "that we should be allowing the alleged Scourge of Buyan to be participating in any official—"

The firebird positioned itself on a small stool by the man's elbow and let out a cheery *wark*. Ancilotto stepped away from it, looking alarmed.

"Cartographers have already tried mapping the area. They believe what's left of the forest is still salvageable, despite the wild magic still lingering there," Lady Gannyroot, the minister of natural resources, explained. "I'm tempted to investigate the place myself. There could be rare species growing there that would be beneficial to study."

"Loki's ability to sense magic will be an important asset," Alex said. "Tala too, if you'd like to go."

"I would," Tala said, because while she understood the importance of Alex establishing best practice policies now while his kingdom was still young, she didn't exactly qualify for any government positions.

"May I accompany them as well, Your Majesty?" West asked timidly. "There was a branch of the Eddings family living in Wonderland when the wars took place. I'd always been curious about the area."

West probably had a family branch in every known corner of Avalon and beyond; the Eddings lineage was just as old as Alex's. The young king nodded, a faint ghost of a grin stealing across his lips. "Dad always said that the Tsarevichs had never been able to tell an Eddings what to do, and I don't intend to break with tradition now."

"I'd like to join too," Nya chimed in.

"I was thinking of a different mission for you, Lady Nya," Alex said. "Minister Farioke has been pinpointing locations around Avalon that may be vulnerable to attack from hostile agents, and she includes Ikpe on that list."

Nya stood up straighter. "My village successfully fought off the frost, Your Majesty. I'm sure they'll be more than capable of defending against anything else. My grandmother would make sure that—"

"Be that as it may," Alex interrupted gently, "I'm sure they'd be happy to have some help from us. We're putting up more looking glasses throughout Avalon for easier traveling. We also want to shore up our defenses, and a direct port to Ikpe would be beneficial to us both. My tourism minister has been planning a citywide enchantments fair to attract more visitors to Avalon, and I want to make sure they'll be protected. Your grandmother is a formidable woman, but you know neither she nor the village is invulnerable to spells."

Tala felt her face heat up. When they'd taken cover in Ikpe and met Nya for the first time, she'd accidentally breached the village's magical barrier, allowing Deathless to infiltrate and attack.

Nya nodded. "I haven't been back there in months."

"I'd like to volunteer as well," Ken said quickly.

Nya scowled. "Why? I don't need your—"

"Thanks, Ken," Alex said smoothly.

Nya groaned quietly.

Alex gestured toward another inner chamber. "Before all that, though, I want to talk to the rest of you here. Alone." He glanced back at Kay. "If you don't mind waiting for a while?"

Zoe, who'd been uncharacteristically silent this whole time, winced.

"Aye, I'll do that. Tell one of your techies to bring up the most recent map of Avalon. I'll show them any vulnerable terrain I can remember, let the other Fianna honors know to bolster defenses there too."

"But you've been at Maidenkeep all these months. How would you know where to..." Alex trailed off, eyes widening. "Oh."

"Aye," Tala's father said quietly. "My mind's not what it used to be, but I've fought your ancestors enough times in the past to remember the parts of Avalon we always liked to focus our attacks on."

Unexpectedly, Alex laughed. "Thank you." He glanced back at the rest of the ministers. "His knowledge is invaluable. I want you all to put that to good use."

There were nods all around, a few more reluctant than others.

Tala, Zoe, Cole, and Dex followed the king into a smaller chamber that served as a meeting room, complete with a table, several chairs, and a whiteboard at the ready. More thought had been placed into its design than it appeared at first glance; Tala knew, for instance, that the room was heavily soundproofed.

The firebird selected a secluded corner of the room and promptly settled down for a nap.

Still very calmly, Alex closed the door. "Dexter," he said, tone relatively mild. "Can you take a quick sweep for any planted bugs around?"

"Bugs?" Tala exclaimed. "This is the most secure part of the castle."

"I trust my ministers to do what they're supposed to do, but I can't trust all of them just yet. The Dame of Tintagel foretold a traitor. Until we know who that is, I'd rather make sure."

Dex fished out a small portable device that looked similar to a mobile phone but wasn't, and swept it over the room. "Nothing I can detect, Your Majesty."

"Tala, any spells within the vicinity?"

Tala focused. "Nope."

"Good." Alex rounded on Zoe and promptly exploded. "Would you care to tell me why there are currently *thirty-seven asylum seekers* in my Department of Immigration offices, all of whom are of the mistaken belief that they are still in the Royal States of America? When I lent you the use of the looking glass prototype, we agreed on no contact!"

"And I will take full responsibility for that. But believe me, Alex, we didn't have much choice. We couldn't leave them with the Border Patrol."

"Well, those same Border Patrol are likely aware now that we have the technology to port into their kingdom without requiring a second looking glass on-site. There's every chance they're going to demand these refugees back to save face, and they're going to spin it as an attack by us on Royal States soil."

"It was the right thing to do, Your Majesty."

Alex scowled at her. "I know. That doesn't mean there won't be repercussions, Zo. Those refugees' statuses are in limbo, because like hell I'll be handing them over. You could have compromised the Gallaghers' prototype too!"

"It's my fault," Tala spoke up. "I didn't listen to Zoe. I stayed behind longer than I should have to fight them. But they had *ice wolves*. I think they're going to start siccing them on anyone attempting to cross their border."

Alex stilled. "Nobody told me about the ice wolves. Cole?"

"Looks that way," Cole said shortly. "They had spelltech on hand to collar them. With the wolf that I…" His lip curled, a grimace. "I could sense that it hadn't been in the Royal States long. It had been taken out of Beiran forests."

"Which means the Americans are either poaching on Beiran land or they've been given permission to by the Snow Queen. Or she gifted them the wolves herself." Alex frowned, thinking. "That changes things. They won't want to advertise the fact they've got ice wolves on their borders. Not yet. There's a huge enough outcry about how those concentration camps are set up as it is."

"You place far too much faith in their decency," Zoe grumbled, "given what a lot of them are already willing to ignore."

"I'm expecting a lot of good things with the Red King looking glass, Zo. It can create portals for two different locations simultaneously. It can be left open almost indefinitely without requiring more energy. You were supposed to help me test it, not reveal its existence to the Americans."

"They're not going to get the Red King, Alex," Zoe insisted. "You have my word on that."

Alex glowered some more, then turned away. "We have the sword."

"What?"

"The Nameless Sword. That's what I wanted to talk to you about. The ministers don't even know yet. Someone found it in the courtyard this morning. Lola Urduja and the Katipuneros have been guarding it ever since they came back. I knew you already had a mission planned for the Hollows, which was why I delayed telling you till now." Alex sighed. "People will know soon enough anyway."

"Are you sure?" Tala sounded calm. Too calm, when what she really wanted to do was start screaming.

"It's a sword buried inside a damned stone, and no one's been able to lift it out so far. Every government leader and their godmothers are going to want to attend the summit. And everyone else with delusions of being the next great Avalon hero." Alex was back to scowling. "Dexter, how has the Red King fared so far?"

Dex beamed. "Purring like a kitten every time we use it. Great sensitivity, fast recoil, and very nearly instantaneous spell switching. No errors that I can detect. Dad's working on an optional add-on that would set up defensive spells around it, so we could toggle the additional shields on and off—mainly to protect it from the elements but also in cases of vandalism or willful destruction."

"Tell him that once it's been thoroughly tested by Zoe and her group, I want it implemented at every government portal we're installing. And I'll want to talk to you again after we take a look at the sword."

"We're taking a look now?" Tala croaked.

"But of course," Alex said with a cynical smile. "It's gonna be a madhouse soon enough. May as well see it while we've still got some peace and quiet left."

It was exactly as Tala had remembered. Dull and rusting, its hilt and what was visible of its blade robbed of their original shine, it didn't look like anything to boast about, embedded in at least three feet of solid rock. It was the kind of oddity an enterprising picker might find at a rummage sale, polish up, and sell for a couple thousand nimues to an eclectic buyer.

But in her hands, it had sung.

In her hands, it had blazed to life with the light of a thousand fires, had given her the courage of a thousand warriors.

In her hands, she had beaten the Snow Queen.

It took everything Tala had not to tremble, looking at it now. She hadn't wanted it then, and she still didn't want it now.

A series of ropes were stretched around the stone. Techmages were already on-site setting up wards around it, overseen by Severon Gallagher, Dex's father and a large hulk of a man second in size only to Kay Warnock. As if adding barriers would be of any help, Tala thought, since the sword would never budge unless it had claimed an owner. Lola Urduja and the Katipuneros were still stationed around it, none of them looking particularly happy.

With them was another group of Filipinos, and it was clear that neither group were friends from the hostile looks each were throwing the others' way. The newcomers wore dresses made of takmon shells similar in style to what she and her mother wore to official Avalon ceremonies. A woman in her sixties, obviously the one in charge, drew near. "Lumina," she said coolly. "It's been a long time."

"Nay," Lumina greeted stiffly.

Tala bit back a gasp. Nay? Did Tala's mother just call the woman *Mom*?

"Fifteen years almost. Far too long to never have seen my own granddaughter beyond a few photos on the computer."

"You could have visited us in Invierno, Nay. I've asked several times in the past."

"Not while you still live with the criminal, Lumina."

Tala's mother froze, anger in her gaze, but remained silent.

"Is he here today?" The older woman scanned the area. "Or is he still hiding, like the coward he's always been?"

She was talking about Tala's father. Kay was still with the techmages, but Tala felt emboldened to defend him. "He's not a coward."

The old woman turned to her, and her eyes softened. "Tala. You cannot be anyone else but Tala. My apo." She smiled. "It is good to finally meet you."

"Corazon," Lola Urduja said sweetly, coming up behind them before Tala could say anything, with General Luna at the rear. "How nice of you to drop by."

"I am here to represent Philippine interests, Urduja. An opportunity no longer available to you, now that you are Avalonian."

"It is possible to be both, but that requires a higher level of intelligence."

"You are nothing," General Luna said, warming up to the fight, "but a second-rate, trying-hard, copyca—"

"Thank you, Heneral," Lola Urduja said. "That will be all."

One of the men was idly twirling an arnis stick in his hand. The tip glowed briefly, seemed to fade from view like a chameleon blending into its surroundings, only to reappear. He spotted Tala looking and winked. "We could teach you if you like."

"I…" Tala looked back at her mother, but the latter was too focused on the mutual hatred between the two elders to notice. "Why would you even offer?"

He chuckled. "We are Makilings too, and of the same clan descended from Maria. But you must ask your mother for permission first. We do not want to offend, and she's not very happy with your lola."

"I didn't even know any representatives from the Philippines would be here."

"We offered our services as soon as we learned you had thawed Avalon. King Alex accepted our offer. We only just arrived today." He gestured at the sword. "Looks like we are right on time. Once the world knows about this, it will be chaos."

Tala turned to Alex, surprised.

"The Philippines has always had close ties to Avalon," the king admitted. "They didn't mention they were from the Makiling clan when they first contacted Minister Jiang."

The man laughed. "I suppose your father never told you. The Filipino delegates who come to Avalon are always led by the Makiling clan. We owe Avalon much after sheltering us during the outbreak of the Filipino-American wars. The Snow Queen might still attack the kingdom. Our agimat will help fight her off."

"You have changed far too much, Urduja," Tala's grandmother said. "You have forgotten our ways."

"The real tragedy, Corazon, is that you haven't changed at all."

"Constancy is not the vice you believe it to be, *mare*." Corazon bowed to Alex. "Your Majesty. Pasensya po. It's been a while since I've last seen my family, and my emotions got the better of me."

"No offense taken," Alex said, more curious than affronted.

Her grandmother turned to regard Tala again. "Look at you now, hija," she said fondly. "So beautiful. And a close friend of the king, no less! I understand you have many responsibilities, but I would like it very much if you can find the time to visit your lola while we are here. Shall we set a date? We can teach you many things about wielding an agimat."

"Nay," Lumina warned.

"It is her decision, Lumina. She is old enough. Perhaps a week from now? We should have finalized arrangements with Avalon by then."

"I…" Tala floundered. "I would like that?"

"Mabuti naman, hija. Please excuse us, Your Majesty. It's been a long journey, and my bones are not as good as they used to be."

"I didn't know she was your grandmother either," Alex said quietly after the Filipino delegates had left.

"Neither did I. I didn't even know she was working for the Philippine government."

"Officially, she's the head of cultural affairs," Lola Urduja said. "Unofficially, she's in charge of all spelltech development within the Philippines. I shall go and talk to security to ready themselves with buckets of water, just in case."

"Water?" West asked.

"It is the easiest way to melt witches like her," Lola Urduja said and walked away.

"Lola Urduja and my mother were rivals, for the longest time," Tala's mother said and sighed. "You should take your lola up on her offer."

Tala paused. "But…"

"We might not see eye to eye on many things, but she is your grandmother. She was right. It's not my place to prevent you from meeting her."

A *honk* from the firebird. It sat on top of the hilt of the Nameless Sword and sniffed, clearly not impressed.

"It was already there by the time anyone else noticed," Lola Urduja said. "A guard on his first day of duty in this case. Rotten luck. The security cameras on-site saw nothing. It simply appeared out of thin air."

"Doesn't look like much, does it?" Alex stepped through the partition, seized the hilt with his hand, and gave it a hard tug. It didn't move. "That's a relief," he said, letting his hand drop. "Want to take a stab at it, Zoe? Tala?"

"I'll be honest," Zoe confessed. "It's extremely tempting to try."

Tala froze.

"We can't keep this a secret," Kay Warnock said, stepping out from the shadows. "Else someone'll cry foul."

Lumina exhaled. "I'm glad you waited till they were gone."

"Aye. I think my avoiding them while they're here will be for the best."

"He's right," Lola Urduja said. "Let those who are worthy pull out the stone while the cameras watch. We have little choice, hijo. Avalon laws decree that all who wish for a chance at the sword do so and that no one can be turned away."

"We're gonna have swarms of tourists who think they're the next Arthur or Alice." Alex groaned. "Can we handle those, Severon?"

"We'll need to," the man said dryly, taking off his pince-nez and wiping one of the lenses with the hem of his shirt. "It's a good thing porting up more looking glasses was one of the first things we prioritized. We won't need to limit accommodations to the capital, and some of the other cities could use a boost in capita. Minister Grenshaw should have more accurate numbers, but we should meet the minimum standards for safety."

"That's not enough. You're telling me I'm going to have more strangers in my kingdom than it's ever had in decades, some with their own agendas. Minimum standards aren't enough. I'm not going to lose my kingdom a second time. Get your team on Ministers Grenshaw's and Silverknot's cases and come back to me with a more concrete plan."

"Yes, Your Majesty."

"To get those answers, we might first need a better idea of how many tourists we're expected to receive." Lumina Makiling Warnock said. "I think it's about time you announce the sword to the world, Alex."

The king frowned. "I'd been hoping to wait a few more days."

"That might no longer be possible." Tala's mother took out her phone. A quick flick of her thumb, and its screen was projected out into the empty air before them, where a video was playing.

"Fuck," Zoe muttered, watching as West, in his shifted canine form, took down an ice wolf. Tala and Cole barreled past, their faces thankfully blurred and unrecognizable, but the camera stayed on West, who turned his head briefly to snarl at an agent attempting to move in on him.

"This was posted less than an hour ago," Tala's mother said. "By the Royal States' Department of Immigration account. I presume the dog is West Eddings."

"Yes," West said. "It makes me look kinda like a badass."

They watched the rest of the thirty-second clip in silence. To Tala's relief, the refugees didn't appear in the video, and neither did the other members of the Hollows.

"I was wrong. They're not even hiding the fact that they're using ice wolves." Alex's jaw was clenched.

"Like I said," Zoe muttered. "Optimistic to think they have any decency left. Glad we were far enough away that they didn't detect the port."

"That they've released the video themselves is clear indication that they think they can use ice wolves and get away with it, without any sanctions," Lumina continued. "In fact, they're positioning this as a *reason* to use ice wolves—to defend both incoming asylum seekers and their Border Patrol from rabid dogs used by drug cartels in their human trafficking. Frankly, given who's in charge, I wouldn't be surprised if they get away with it. But one of the allegations coming out is that Mexican traffickers are supposedly using advanced looking glass spelltech to get past the border." Lumina frowned. "If they'd caught the Red King on film, they would have shown it, so I think we're safe there at least. But I'm worried about how they'll spin it back to us."

Alex's mouth quivered. "And you're suggesting we announce the sword's discovery to keep attention away from their video."

"There is a sense of the romantic and the adventurous that is linked to the Nameless Sword," Lola Urduja said, looking like she would very gladly push romantic adventure into traffic had it come courting. "The legend fires up the imagination. It's a tragic history, but very popular."

"Let us be your social engineers, Your Majesty," Tita Chedeng piped up.

"My what?"

"Social engineers," her twin sister, Tita Teejay, added. "We'll take over your social media accounts, find the best way to present the information. We are quite good at it."

Lola Urduja wrinkled her nose. "The way you both have your noses stuck to your phones at all hours, I shouldn't be surprised."

"We have a hundred thousand followers on our personal account," Tita Teejay said primly.

"H-how?" Tala asked.

"With our pictures of Miss Philippines and her siblings, of course." Miss Philippines was a thoroughly malignant hell beast currently housed in the body of a perfectly manicured and well-groomed Pomeranian. The twins had adopted her along with several other cats and dogs after settling in Avalon. Tala breathed easier.

"And, of course, the occasional tasteful nude," Tita Chedeng added cheerily and ignored the strangled chokes in the wake of that statement. "Charot, my loves. I am only kidding. Give me access to the Avalon account right now and let me try."

Once the relevant passwords were provided, she crouched down before the stone and took a careful, practiced shot of the sword. The firebird chirped and batted its eyes at her.

"I don't actually have an official statement yet," Alex pointed out dryly.

"We won't need one. A picture is worth a thousand words. You can break the news in your own time and on your own terms. But let this picture percolate for a bit."

Alex considered that for a few seconds. "All right. Post the picture. Let's get it started."

It was a lovely picture. Tita Chedeng had caught the light perfectly, lending a strange, almost ethereal glow to the Nameless Sword, even despite its obviously decrepit condition. But it was the firebird, still sitting on the blade's hilt, that made the whole photo. It was looking loftily down at the camera while its beak remained jutted up in the air, haughty and somehow mysterious looking. It clearly knew its best angles.

Tita Teejay posted it. As they watched, the likes and reposts started rolling in, the numbers climbing with increasing frequency. Excited OMG and Is this real??? comments began popping up.

"You see?" Tita Teejay said smugly.

"I can't tell him," Tala said softly, while the others were distracted and her father had inched closer to where she remained unmoving, unable to tear her gaze away from the sword. "I can't tell them."

"Ye're gonna have to soon enough, lass. This isn't something you can hide forever."

"Maybe someone else will pick it up. There'll be thousands who'd want to try. Tens of thousands."

"Sometimes it only takes the one, Tala."

"Please don't tell them. Not yet."

Her father was silent. Slowly, his hand inched toward her. Without even thinking, Tala reached out to him. Her mother turned, spotted their linked hands, and smiled happily. The lump in Tala's throat grew.

"Not even yer mum, lass?" Kay asked gruffly.

"No. She's serving on Alex's royal council, and she's bound by law to tell him. I don't want to put her on the spot like that. Please, Dad?"

Kay closed his eyes. Tala knew he was morally bound to tell Alex too. But he only gave her hand a squeeze.

"Aye, Tala," her father said. "That much I can do."

4

IN WHICH HORSE IS
NOT A HORSE

K en blinked up at the sky for several seconds before slowly rising into a sitting position. "Bloody hell," he said.

The cause of his frustration stood several feet away, no doubt pleased by its impudence. Horse snorted, cast a baleful look his way, and then stomped one hoof back down on the ground for good measure.

"You said you were an excellent rider," Nya said. She still hadn't completely forgiven him for the Yawarakai-Te trick he'd pulled on her, but her natural propensity to be kind overrode her huffiness. Already she was by his side, assessing him for injuries.

"I am. He's just an arsehole." He groaned, cricked his neck, heard and felt a satisfying pop. "I'm all right. He's being a prat because I didn't bring him along to Invierno."

Horse trotted up to Nya.

"Be careful!" Ken struggled to stand. "He doesn't take very kindly to strangers who—"

Horse bowed his head low before Nya, begging for a petting and nickering eagerly.

"Hell," Ken said, staring. "He likes you. He doesn't like anyone. He sure as hell acts like he doesn't like me half the bloody damn time."

"He's all right," Nya said, sounding strangely hesitant. "It's because... um, I don't know. I just knew he wouldn't hurt me."

"And you arrived at that conclusion after seeing him throw *me* off?"

"Grammy said I had a way with animals sometimes. Didn't you say he was *your* horse, though? Horses generally tend to respect their owners."

"See, that's where you're mistaken. First of all, I don't own Horse. It's just that he lets me ride on his back at a greater frequency than he would allow anyone else. Second, he's not technically a horse, as you can probably already tell. Third—I did mention that he's an arse, didn't I?"

The arse in question snorted again. Its mane and tail floated around it, like it was perpetually swimming through some invisible sea. Its mane, in fact, was made of a gelatinous, shiny substance that flowed and trailed in the air the way hair buffeted in wind might move, similar to maybe a jellyfish. Strands tickled at Nya's cheek, making her giggle. Its eyes were a bright, intelligent red, and there were hints of fangs every time it drew its teeth back. It was a magnificent specimen, even by its species' standards. Unfortunately, it knew it.

Ken had a hell of a time completing the paperwork needed to bring Horse to Avalon, since nobody wanted to touch it for fear of getting bitten, and also because Horse was something of an endangered species. He hadn't been home in over a year, which meant no one had taken Horse out riding in all that time either.

The bastard must have really missed him.

"Have you ever stopped to consider," Nya began, "that maybe he's an asshole because you gave him a ridiculous name, like Horse?"

"I was trying to name him what I wanted him to be more like."

"And did it work?"

"Huh. Touché." Ken stood. His butt was a little sore, but he knew how to fall without getting hurt, and Horse knew how to throw him off without harming him…too much. He marched over to where the kelpie was still glowering. Nya stepped back, and Ken grabbed its ear before Horse could try to bite him.

"I didn't know I was going to land myself in the middle of Avalon, you little runt," he growled, tugging hard enough that he would get all its attention, though never enough to hurt. "We were supposed to sneak into Invierno, snag the prince, then hightail it back out. It should have taken us a day, tops. I didn't think I was going to spend a couple of weeks—well, fine, technically *half a year*, but that wasn't my fault either—fighting my way to Maidenkeep, with ice wolves nipping at our heels and ogres trying to turn us into mincemeat pies. If I'd known *that*, I would have taken you with me. But I didn't, so it's no use sulking over it. You're here now, aren't you? And we've got more places to explore, don't we?"

Horse grunted and flattened its ears back.

"I can't bring you to places where there's gonna be lots of civilians. You caused a panic the last time, plus you're not exactly legal to keep. But if I'm gonna be off looking for trouble, I'm at least gonna ride you into it. All right?"

Horse whinnied.

Ken stroked its neck. "I know. I'm glad you're here too, you oversized snot."

"You're both ridiculous," Nya said, amused.

Ken grinned at her, then swung himself up Horse. This time, the kelpie bent its head and let him clamber up without fuss.

"I don't know about bringing it to Ikpe, though," Nya said worriedly.

"I thought rescuing the prince was going to take us a few hours at most, and look where that got us. I'd rather not take any more chances. Plus, I promised Horse it could go. I guarantee that it'll be on its best behavior. Plus, it can spot nightwalkers and Deathless from a mile away."

Ken scratched the creature behind its ears fondly. "Can't you, you mangy mutt?"

Horse whinnied cheerfully.

"But are you sure you want to go back with me? Mama might blame you for me leaving, you know."

"It's been months since then. I'm sure everyone's put seeing you married out of their heads by now. Horse's asking if you'd like a ride, Rapunzel."

Nya's fingers tightened on the broomstick she'd been carrying since the day they'd met. "I don't know much about kelpies, but I do know the only riders they accept are humans they've saved. The rest lure people into the water to drown. So, uh, I'd like some confirmation first."

"That's right," Ken said lightly. "I saved its life, and it saved mine. And that's a myth. Once they've been bonded to someone, they'll accept anyone they like. Even girls who lose Simeli gauntlet runs to their owners."

"Wait, what? I won our bet! I finished first!"

"You started several minutes ahead of me!"

"I was only seconds in! And even so, my time was a lot shorter than yours!" She stopped again. "I think."

Ken paused as well. They'd been too busy worried about Tala that they hadn't checked their official times at the Simeli visitors' center, and Kay Warnock's arrival had soon put that out of their heads.

"We could head back to Simeli after this and try again," he said. "See whether I'm gonna treat you to dinner or whether I'm going to treat you to dinner, as per our previous bet."

He knew he'd won *this* fight when Nya shot him a much more genuine smile. "All right. If that'll keep you quiet." She shot one last nervous look at Horse but then held out her hand. "Help me up, will you? I'm still not that good a rider yet."

48

"It's good that you're cautious." Nya sounded more nervous than Ken thought as she settled herself above the kelpie.

"I'm not sure how anyone in Ikpe's going to react to a kelpie," she confessed worriedly.

"You hear that, Horse?" Ken asked. "You're going to be the center of attention, you adorable bastard."

To the Ikpeans' credit, they didn't look worried at the sight of Horse cantering toward their gates. What did look worrisome was the beginnings of a tall metal fence that encircled Ikpe. Soldiers clearly not from the village patrolled the perimeters, armed to the teeth, looking more like mercenaries at home in a war zone.

One of the women keeping vigil by the gates, clearly the one in charge, relaxed when she caught sight of them. "Your grandmother has been expecting you, Princess," she greeted.

"Princess?" Ken echoed. He supposed she was, now that he thought about it. Lola Urduja had told him that the Ikpean leader was descended from royal blood and that some of Nya's ancestors had been joined at one point in marriage or similar to the royal houses of Avalon, making Alex a very distant relative. Nya only flushed.

"Your mama's been huffy since you left, Nya. Would you like to visit her first?"

Nya was shaking her head. "I want to talk to my grandmother and then leave as soon as we can."

"We have time," Ken offered. "It's been a while since you last saw her, I'm sure we can—"

"Absolutely not, Ken. Not right now. Taci, does Grammy know I'm here?"

"I believe so, Princess," the Ikpean admitted. "She said she was expecting you here this week."

There was nothing surprising about that statement, since Nya's grandmother was also a seeress.

"And how is she, Taci?" Nya asked.

"As well as can be expected, considering the property developers that have come knocking."

"The what now? Someone's been building here for months and you didn't tell us?"

"Not months. *Hours.* They are attempting to beanstalk the land."

"Beanstalk?" Ken asked. "What the hell is that?"

"One can construct a building, distill it into a spelltech, and then erect it at another place almost overnight. An Avalon patent, I believe, that lapsed after the frost. We have halted their progress for now, but their leader has been threatening to resume operations."

"I think I can make an educated guess as to who'd laid claim to it," Ken said darkly, catching sight of the stylized hot-air balloon logo embroidered across the soldiers' chests.

OzCorp was a spell technology corporation founded by Ruggedo Nome, long considered one of the most brilliant minds on the planet. They specialized in consumer spelltech, ranging from electronics and software to online services, and were the largest company in the industry. Alex had reluctantly allowed them to set up shop in Avalon, having found no reason not to grant the same permissions he had done other interested corporations in his kingdom. Ken had assumed it was because they were direct competitors of Avalon spelltech. Now he realized it was maybe because they were giant arses.

"They're wearing the OzCorp brand, and I sincerely doubt that Alex, of all people, would have allowed them to do this. Don't they already have their main headquarters at Marooners' Rock? The one along the outskirts of the city? That's the only one His Majesty approved, right?"

"You're gonna ask a multinational conglomeration why it's doing its best to expand before the rest of the competition find traction in Avalon?" Nya asked wryly. "Or why they've just decided to build right next to the biggest spellstone mine in the kingdom?"

"You two best come in first and see to the priestess," Taci said. "She would know more about this than we do."

The village was the same as Ken remembered it—the same cozy-looking houses, the same well-cobbled paths, the same statue of a woman at the village's center, the absence of a hand on one arm not discounting the presence of a sword on the other. There were the same kind of butterflies too, glowing in and out of view as they flew above their heads, weaving and reweaving the defensive spells that had protected Ikpe from the frost. With Tala gone, they had reverted back to their golden glow.

"I am relieved that the Makiling girl did not accompany you," Ema, another Ikpean with them, said dryly. "We had quite the difficulty, reworking the enchantments she unraveled during her short stay here."

"It wasn't her fault," Ken protested.

"This is not a barb at her expense. If anything, it has taught us to be humble. The Makilings are not to be underestimated, and we can do much to learn from their talents at dispellment."

"I'll let her know." Ken watched several trucks roll by, loaded with boxes. "Looks like business is booming, despite the new neighbors."

"Ah, yes. Ayanti's ekwang is once more in demand, and we are making a killing with our medicines." Before Ikpe had become known as the village that had survived the frost, it had been famous for being the potion capital of the world. Small wonder Nya was so good at making them.

Ken took a deep breath. "And how are the... How's Iniko? And the others who were with her?"

The corners of Taci's mouth turned down. "Still suffering, I'm afraid.

There is no known cure for the Deathless curse, but we have tried our best to ease their pain." She gestured at a small clinic they were about to pass. "They are housed here indefinitely."

"Until the day they die," Ken said bleakly.

"Were you acquainted, milord?"

"A little. Can I see her? Just for a minute." Ken could feel Nya's eyes burrowing into the back of his head, but he refused to turn around.

Taci conferred quietly with Ema and another Ikpean. "Only for a minute," she allowed. "But you must be warned, milord. They will not recognize you, and their behavior will not be their own."

They left Horse secured to a tree by the monument and entered the building housing the victims. The inside of the clinic was clean and sterile, painted a pristine white. Ema led them down one corridor and bid them to stand behind a glass partition that separated onlookers from the people inside. If they could still be considered people.

The woman pulled back the curtains, and Ken saw dark eyes against a pale white face, lips bared in a permanent snarl, face bearing the marks of bruises, though the walls were carefully padded. She'd been fitted in a straitjacket for her safety, and she was roaring and rolling on the floor in a desperate bid to free her hands, shrieking expletives at times and shouting praises to the Snow Queen for the rest.

"The Snow Queen and her ice maidens use pieces of an enchanted mirror to invoke thrall spells on the Deathless to control," Ema said. "But without their guidance, their victims become...less focused."

The glass was one-sided, Taci said, but Iniko must have sensed their presence, for she immediately scampered over to where they stood, laughing maniacally. Even this way, Ken realized with a pang, she was still beautiful.

"Have you come back for me, milord?" Iniko taunted. "Are you here to kiss me again, drive me mad with longing? Will you meet me in dark alleyways and dance with me underneath the night sky? Release me, milord, and present me to the Queen, and she will reward you with everything." She cackled. "Free me, Lord Inoue!"

Maybe it was a mistake to have come here. If Ken had been hoping to spot some remnants of the girl who'd lured him into dancing with her at this village all those months ago, he could see nothing of that before him now.

Iniko's face changed abruptly. Her tone shifted, from mocking to strident. "You will wed a daughter of the deep, boy," she whispered, "one whose scales shall run through her veins, one who shall carry the taste of the sea in her tongue. You will drown in her sorrows, and she will dance in her agony for you. Take the blade, Lord Inoue, and aim it true. Aim it true! Aim it—"

"That is enough," Ema said crisply, drawing the curtains shut. "She is only one of many housed here. If their souls remain within their bodies, it is not they who speak through their mouths."

"What was that?" Nya asked. "Those things she was saying… I don't understand."

"That was my doom," Ken said, ice in his gut. "Word for word the exact same prophecy foretold when I was born."

"What?" Nya was pale. "You told me that you were fated to marry a sea creature, the first time we met. This was the prophecy talking about it?"

"Pretty much. Also pretty sure no one else beyond my family knew about this. Do Deathless foretell dooms too?"

"No," Taci said. "But Iniko herself was descended from more than a few seeresses, though she had shown no inclination for the ability before."

"Fat lot of good that did her, huh?" Ken resisted the urge to howl with frustration. It was his fault. If he hadn't singled her out back then, she wouldn't have been a target.

"I'm sorry," Nya said quietly, features now carefully composed, though there were tears gathering in her eyes too. "But we must talk to my grandmother as soon as possible. Perhaps in the future, we can learn how to help her and the others."

"I'm surprised you guys aren't blaming me and the king for this," Ken muttered.

She smiled sadly. "We're the guardians of a spellstone mine, Ken. One of the richest deposits in existence. It's a responsibility we all take seriously. If there's anything we do know, it's that it's easy to blame but harder to forgive. And that there is nothing about you or His Majesty that requires our forgiveness."

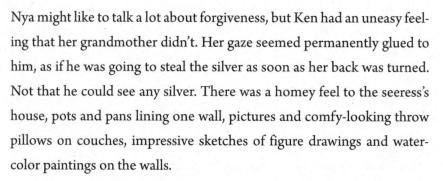

Nya might like to talk a lot about forgiveness, but Ken had an uneasy feeling that her grandmother didn't. Her gaze seemed permanently glued to him, as if he was going to steal the silver as soon as her back was turned. Not that he could see any silver. There was a homey feel to the seeress's house, pots and pans lining one wall, pictures and comfy-looking throw pillows on couches, impressive sketches of figure drawings and watercolor paintings on the walls.

"You were at the village a few months ago," she said, every word sounding like an accusation, "but you never accompanied the Makiling girl to see me."

Of course not. He hadn't gone to see the priestess. He'd spent a good part of their last night at Ikpe taking part in their village celebrations, dancing with girls like Iniko and accidentally turning them into Deathless. Ken cleared his throat. "Given the circumstances, I should have, in hindsight. We weren't expecting to leave your village so suddenly."

"I knew of your arrival. But my visions are stronger when I see the people for myself. I wish I'd known then what I know now." The priestess turned to her granddaughter. "King Alex must be busy, if he is now leasing land to foreign developers so close to Ikpe. While tracts of Avalon are his to redistribute as he wishes, I question the wisdom of offering contracts to companies with a poor record of sustainability."

"He wouldn't." Nya sounded incredulous. "OzCorp is the last corporation he would allow free rein here. Surely there must be some mistake."

"They appeared overnight. Morning came, and a new facility stood. To protect the mines, only Ikpe is allowed to possess land in this region. We asked to see the permit granting them access, and they were quick to supply us with a copy. As far as we can see, it is a legitimate document."

Nya accepted the paper and skimmed quickly through it. "Oh no," she groaned. "Ken, Alex didn't sign this, but Minister Ancilotto did."

"It may be that His Majesty was unaware of the minister's approval," the priestess said grimly. "Is it possible to break the contract without consequence?"

Her gaze was back on Ken. He found it more than a little disconcerting. It felt like she could see every mistake he'd committed from the time he'd stolen and lost his mother's favorite saddle when he was nine years old to the trick he'd pulled on Nya. Maybe *that* was why her grandmother seemed to disapprove of him.

"It will be difficult to demand that they move immediately. If their papers are genuine, they must still be given a requisite number of days to relocate by law." She paused. "There is also a very unhappy kelpie standing at the center of the village."

"I'm sorry." Ken didn't even bother to ask how she'd known, despite her cottage having no direct line of sight to the plaza.

"It was a good decision to bring it. You will need it before long. Kelpies are a rare sight this far inland, though you do not seem particularly fond of the sea."

"Uh, yeah. I can't swim to save my life. Literally. In fact, that was how I wound up with Horse." Ken paused, but they were waiting for him to continue, both looking oddly expectant. "When I was twelve, a band of poachers tried to sneak through our lands. Security was on alert for them along the nearby coasts, so I guess they avoided those routes. They'd caught a kelpie foal and were trying to meet up with a buyer from China who'd paid a lot of money for it." Ken's lip curled at the memory. "I'd just been given ownership of Yawarakai-Te by my dad, and I was feeling pretty cocky. Nobody knew what I was up to, because I was sneaking out at night and roaming the countryside. The kelpie had bitten through its muzzle and was making enough of a racket to wake the dead. They stuffed a new one on it pretty quickly, but I was close by. They thought they'd tie me up and gag me, leave me for the stable hands to find."

He grinned. "Anyway, I left them unconscious, called emergency services, and rode out with the kelpie before the team arrived. The poachers already had warrants out, so that wasn't a problem. I knew foals were endangered and that animal control was going to stick it in some lonely cryptozoo up north. So naturally, being a twelve-year-old genius, I decided to hide it out at my mother's stable. Thought I was smart enough to keep it there indefinitely."

He saw Nya trying to hide a smile, but the priestess was just as intimidating as before. "What I didn't know was that the guys I'd beaten up were only half the gang. They tracked the foal to my barn the next day, tried to smuggle it out through a portable looking glass they had. Like the fool I am, I fought them but got thrown through and into the Pacific Ocean, where they'd been planning to escape by ship. The kelpie jumped in after me, saved me before I could drown."

That had been a horrifying experience. Ken had managed to shut out most of his memories of it, but he could still taste the water, the salt in his lungs, and shuddered before he could stop himself. He did remember the sudden weight underneath him, bringing him back up to the surface so he could take in a much-needed gulp of air, and the soothing whinny by his ear. He could deal with small rivers and streams, but the thought of the ocean made him start sweating profusely. "We managed to flounder our way back to the ranch, where I got a nice commendation from the Queen herself but a three-hour lecture from a very shouty mom. Was grounded for a month. Everyone knew kelpies can't be returned to the wild or to a conservation site once bonded." Ken shrugged. "So Horse and I have been best buddies ever since."

Nya was looking impressed, and he couldn't help a twinge of pleasure. It wasn't something he'd planned on boasting about, but...

Her grandmother was harder to win over. If anything, she actually looked...pitying? "Do you remember your own doom, Nya?" she asked.

Nya seemed puzzled by the change in subject. "Yes. You said I was to marry a corpse."

"*Rise, daughter of Mami Wata,*" the older woman quoted. "*Unbind yourself from the earth around you. The firebird shall show the way to the corpse-husband. He shall come to you without shadow, and the ivory shall embrace the night. But even in death, he lives. You shall make your vows over the ghosts of the past. Rise, daughter. Take the dagger, and aim it true.*"

Ken was staring at her, a sudden sinking feeling in the pit of his stomach. "What are the chances," he said, "of Rapu—of Nya and I having that sort of similar wording in our dooms?" *Take the dagger, and aim it true.* Surely that was just a coincidence?

"The same chances," the priestess said softly, "of my granddaughter being fated to marry a corpse-husband and of you being fated to marry a daughter of the deep. Several months ago, my granddaughter was to be wedded, though we had no idea of who the husband was to be. Today, we have found our answer."

A large shattering sound broke through the air. It sounded like someone was jackhammering through stone.

"Ken?" Nya asked worriedly as Ken rose with a grunted apology, making for the door.

"Alex wouldn't want them destroying ground too close to the spell-stone mines, Rapunzel!" Ken wasn't very knowledgeable about a lot of Avalon laws, but he did know that the main reason people were forbidden from building in this part of Avalon was because drilling *through* the ground could harm the spellstone mines. This could all wait till later. There was corporate ass to kick first.

Horse must have sensed his intentions; it was neighing with glee long before it caught sight of Ken. One quick nudge at the flank was all it took to send the kelpie thundering down the path, the gates leading out of the village already beiung pulled back to let them through by Ema, who wore a wicked smile on her face.

Ken had two sword segen. Yawarakai-Te was a notoriously kind blade; it only cut down anything that wasn't sentient. His other sword, Juuchi Yosamu, was a different story, with a reputation for inflicting madness on those greedy enough to use it. Ken rarely ever brought it out to use, even if his bloodline was unaffected by that particular curse. It didn't seem right to use something that history had always associated with evil to do good.

Yawarakai-Te was more than enough to cut through the metal fence, though. It was a nice, clean cut, if Ken did say so himself. The whole upper portion of the bisected wall slid to the right, sending clouds of dust rising up as it crashed heavily into the ground.

This did not sit well with the soldiers, who were aiming weapons at them.

"Ken!" Nya screamed.

One of the men opened fire.

Both kelpie and boy rippled out of view. They reappeared in front of the startled soldier, and one swipe from Ken's sword cut his gun in half. The other OzCorp mercenaries swiveled, but Ken and Horse were gone again, blinking back in front of another guard and disarming them in the same way.

The soldiers paused, realizing that the Ikpean warriors were rushing to Ken's defense, and raised their hands.

"What's the meaning of this?" The man who came stomping out of the building was clearly the one in charge; he had a construction helmet on, was not in combat fatigues as the others were, and was also wearing a lab coat. He looked about ready to give another order to fire despite his men's capitulation, raising his own gun, but Ken took that decision away by reappearing before him, blade leveled calmly against his throat before the other could blink.

"You're on the king's land," Ken stated calmly.

"I am Alsaid Corvington, OzCorp's CFO. We have a permit from the minister of trade himself."

"A bureaucratic error, I'm sure. This area is not for development. I'm sure Minister Ancilotto will be all too eager to extend his apologies."

"You don't speak for the king—"

"Did I fucking stutter?"

"He could well be," one of his colleagues standing behind the man murmured, clearly the bigger brains of the two, since he'd been smart enough not to piss Ken off. "That's Kensington Inoue, from the Order of the Bandersnatch."

"Good to see I'm famous. Send your complaints off to the ministry, but none of you are to dig here until matters have been settled with King Alex."

The first man glared, but the other was signaling hastily for the other soldiers to do as Ken ordered. "I will make the call," he said, "but you must give us an hour to at least secure our research."

"This isn't over," Corvington threatened.

"When is it ever?" Ken waited until they were escorted away by the Ikpean warriors, then reached down to scratch fondly at Horse. "See? I bring you to the best places, don't I?"

Horse nickered.

Ken turned, blinked at the furious look Nya was shooting his way. "What did I do?"

"Exactly what you did last time!" she exploded. "Not only were you being reckless, you keep treating this like it's some kind of game! Did you ever stop to think how I—or anyone else—would react, seeing you try to cut off your own leg? Or think about how I would feel seeing you put yourself in the line of fire? You're not always going to be this lucky. One day, someone's going to swing a sword at you, and it's not going to bounce off your head like last time." Nya stopped, a little overcome.

Ken inhaled noisily. Their brush with the last ice maiden at Maidenkeep all those months ago, it seemed, still frightened her more than she'd cared to admit. Heck, it frightened *him* whenever he thought about it, so he chose not to. "Yes. About that. I'm sorry. I, uh, wanted to impress you because I—"

"I do wish you'd told me earlier that you were coming, Nya," came a slightly miffed voice. A pretty older woman who looked too much like Nya not to be related to her strode up to them. She studied him carefully, like he was a specimen under her microscope. "I suppose he isn't my first choice for consort. I still think Laroquai would be a good match for you, Nya, but let it not be said that I would stand in the way of fate."

Nya stiffened. "Mama—"

"This isn't the time for arguments, my dears," the Ikpean priestess said calmly, walking up to Ken and laying a hand on Horse's nose. The kelpie grunted and nuzzled at her.

Ken froze. The last time he'd been in Ikpe, Nya's mother had been determined to wed her off to anyone in the village to circumvent the prophecy of Nya marrying a corpse. She was no longer looking at him like he was an interesting bug but like he was a choice slab of meat on sale at the butcher's.

"Do you like my daughter, Lord Inoue?"

Ken knew it was a trick question, but that didn't matter when he didn't know the right answer. He cast Nya a panicked look, but the girl appeared horrified herself, unable to muster up the words to make a protest. She hadn't wanted to visit the rest of her family. She hadn't wanted him to go with her to Ikpe. The reasons were now suddenly crystal clear.

It occurred to Ken that OzCorp was not gonna be the biggest threat he was going to face that day, and that he was going to be held responsible for Nya's lack of wedded bliss all those months ago, when she decided to escape her marriage and accompany them to Maidenkeep. Her grandmother was silent as well, her gaze steady on him. He wanted to point out that the priestess had given Nya permission to leave and that it wasn't his fault that the old woman appeared to have changed her mind since, but he was still a little too scared of her to voice his dissent. "Well," he floundered instead, "we've never even gone on a—"

"You spirited her away from the village. You have compromised her honor."

"But I wasn't the only person in the—"

"It's so much better than the actual corpse we'd been fearing, don't you think, Mama?" Nya's mother said happily. "Nya, my love, let me plan this wedding. Imagine—perhaps if you hadn't left the village like you did, this nice young man would have been my son-in-law by now. Really, Nya, your impulsiveness gets you into all sorts of trouble. You must have gotten that from your father's side. A month should be enough time to prepare."

5

IN WHICH LOKI BREAKS
THEIR TOOTHPICK

W ould you rather be attacked by a hundred spider-sized ducks," West asked idly, thumbing through his phone as they walked, "or by a duck-sized spider?"

It was clearly a difficult question, because Kay Warnock mulled it over for several minutes before venturing, "How big exactly would a spider-sized duck be? Because let me tell you, I've seen a lot of those huge eight-legged bastards."

The Tangled Woods, the dense forest that straddled the edges of what remained of Wonderland, had been deemed safe by techmages to travel to, but only for two miles past the initial barrier the Department of Defense had set up. "There's no guarantee what the effects of spells would be on any of you beyond that," one of them had warned.

True to form, Loki and their friends were already four miles in. Nothing out of the ordinary was showing up in their hex detectors. They caught the occasional flashes and blips of magic fizzling in the area, but none were of the intensity or the range required to cause them worry.

"The spiders are the size of your palm," West explained.

Kay squinted down at his large, meaty hand. "A duck-sized spider," he decided. "Ducks are angry wankers."

"Loki," West said. "Same question."

"A duck-sized spider isn't as bad as people think. I've traveled all over the outback with my folks. They've got two-footers out there."

"Tala?"

"A hundred ducks," the girl responded promptly. "Anything is better than spiders. Are these questions Loki's expected to answer for their upcoming ranger test in a couple of months?"

"I hope not." Loki was set to join the Fianna rangers' Fifth Honor, the same division his father had once led. Mykonos Vasilakis had taken over after Anthony Sun-Wagner had been forced to resign, and Loki had been worried about making a good impression as their test date drew nearer.

"Cole," West said. "Would you rather be a reverse centaur or a reverse mermaid?"

Zoe choked back a laugh.

A sudden shimmer of wild magic, a larger concentration than they had encountered so far, sparkled to their left.

Two throwing daggers sliced through the air, embedding themselves in two separate tree trunks on either side of the wayward spell. Both blades sparked, and the charms inside them fizzled into view, a glowing net shooting out to trap the magic between them.

"Does the reverse mermaid still have a supersonic scream, like a regular mermaid?" Cole asked calmly, lowering his arm. They'd all been given warding daggers by the techmages for the expedition, to deactivate any wild magic still in the area and ensure a safer journey.

"Yes," West decided.

Cole shrugged. "Reverse mermaid."

"Zoe?"

"Reverse centaur," the brunette said calmly, lowering her arm as well. She retrieved the daggers and tossed one back to Cole. "No way I'm gonna spend the rest of my life looking like a fish. You'd look ridiculous as a mermaid, Nottingham."

Ruyi Jingu Bang felt hot in Loki's hands, responding to the traces of Wonderland spells still around them. "Let's not get too complacent," they said. "Any signs of the surges His Majesty mentioned?"

Tala shook her head. "We might have to go even deeper into the woods to figure that out." She was keeping her distance from her father, much to the latter's obvious dismay. Loki didn't want to pry, though they knew their friend still hadn't completely forgiven Kay for not telling her about his past.

West was still staring at his phone, wearing the most ridiculous grin on his face.

"What are you doing?" Loki muttered, keeping an eye on the trees around them. There were no documented fauna in the Tangled Woods. That didn't mean there wasn't anything here.

"A good boy," West whispered.

"What?"

West tilted his phone so Loki could get a better look. It was a video of their foray to the Texas border earlier that morning. West was in his shifted form, happily tearing a chunk of hide off an ice wolf. There were multiple videos of this circulating at this point. *Good Antifascist Boy*, this title proclaimed.

"I'm a very good boy," West said proudly. "Four million views and climbing. Do you think this would be good PR for Zoe and the others?"

"Does the video capture anything else about the 'dog' or say anything about where it came from? Did they film the looking glass too?"

"Well, it only shows me in it and the wolves." West turned pale, switching briefly to Avalonian in his sudden worry. "Oh, *non utinam*. What if my mom sees this?"

Loki paused. Their gaze had caught sight of something odd that lay a few meters ahead of them, and they frowned. The larger concentrations of wild magic like the one Cole and Zoe had dispelled could be brought back to the spelltech outpost established at the Avalon side of the border for the techmages to analyze.

But this one was different. Loki was seeing higher concentrations of magic here, but against all expectations, it wasn't showing up on any of their spell detectors.

"Tala," they said urgently.

The girl gulped. "Yeah. I can feel it."

Kay Warnock's eyes flicked down to their recorder, though Loki knew it wouldn't be registering there. "Describe it to me, both of you," he ordered grimly.

"It's a lot like a looking glass, only there's no frame or structure or anything else holding it up, sir," Loki said.

"Only the glass itself is suspended in the air, and it's shining," Tala added.

Kay growled low. "Don't move, any of you. That sounds a lot like a Dormouse spell. But that's impossible. I thought there wasn't enough magic from the Wonderland ruins to still generate anything that big. The Fianna gave us some shielding wards but nothing strong enough to contain this kind of enchantment."

Loki tried not to visibly gulp. Bomb spells had been responsible for wiping out most of Wonderland during the war. Dormouse bombs were the weakest, followed by White Rabbits, then Mock Turtles. When Queen Elizabeth XXIV, the Mad Queen of Wonderland, had, in a final fit of madness, set off a Mock Turtle, none within its blast radius had survived. It had taken out nearly the whole kingdom and a small area of Avalon besides.

It didn't matter that the Dormouse was the weakest of the bomb spells. If they didn't get out of there immediately, there may not even be anything left of them to bury.

West had pocketed his phone, his features creased with worry. "I smell trouble," he whispered.

"We need to retreat back to Avalon, West. We can't dismantle this bomb on our own."

"Are we bringing the others along too?"

"What others?"

Sunlight grew more limited the farther they ventured into the forest, and West was gazing steadily at the darkest part of the woods. His nose was twitching like mad. "I can smell someone in there. But I can also smell *something* else too. Something large. Something that stinks."

"Nightwalkers?" Zoe asked.

West frowned. "Yes and no. I can smell fear. There's someone else here, and they're human."

"We'll need better equipment before we can push forward," Kay said, "and we're gonna need one of the mages tae disarm this Dormouse without it literally blowing up in our faces."

A hideous roar broke through the woods.

"Guard the Dormouse," Loki said promptly. "I'll go take a look."

They were already moving, skirting past the bomb still glowing in the air to plunge deeper into the woods, leaving Tala's protests behind them. It was darker in these parts, but the sparks of magic flashing before them lighted their path as they drew closer to...well, whatever the hell had made that sound. Ever the loyal friend, West was already by their side, shedding his clothes to assume a lion's shape, loping effortlessly beside them. Wordlessly, Loki slid onto his back, and West promptly switched to maximum speed, trees flying past them.

Wonderland had been utterly destroyed decades ago; what remained was too saturated with wild, uncontrolled magic to be deemed safe for exploration, even by experts. The few to buck authority and common sense and try had never returned. Loki could feel the air grow thick and cloying, warped by unseen spells. The trees were gnarled and misshapen here, twisted limbs looming over them, and while there were no animals, Loki thought they could hear noises all the same, except they sounded like whispers.

A clearing lay ahead, and Loki saw the clash of magic against magic again before they saw the girl. She'd set up a shield spell that was holding against the blows battering against it.

But the attacking jabberwock showed no signs of letting up. Again and again, its crudely curved talons struck at the shield, which was already showing cracks along its sides—a good indication that it would not hold up against the assault for much longer. The jabberwock was an immense, ugly thing, with a snout too thin for its boxlike face, red eyes large as dinner plates, and large wings like a bat's.

The girl wasn't alone. There was a group of soldiers with her, battering at the jabberwock. A swipe from the monster was enough to take many of them down despite the fire guns they were shooting at it, which were having little effect.

Sizzling bolts of electricity lanced through the clearing, but they were not caused by the girl, the soldiers, or the jabberwock. The wild magic was simply reacting to their spells, making their situation even more dangerous than it already was.

"Aim good, buddy," Loki muttered as they took out Ruyi Jingu Bang from behind their ear. The staff said nothing, as staffs were wont to do, but Loki knew it heard them. "Aim good," they repeated and threw as hard as they could.

The blunt end of the staff hit the jabberwock square in the face...and kept right on hitting, battering at the startled creature until it grudgingly backed away. West snarled, carefully circling the beast and trying his best to distract it. "Be careful!" Loki shouted at the lion. Jabberwock claws were tipped with a particularly potent poison; one successful swipe, and West could be dead in minutes.

The girl had frozen, watching him with amazement. "Sun-Wagner," she said.

"How do you know who I am?" And then Loki took in the whole scene. Faint magic still hovered in the air, the residue of which felt similar to the Dormouse bomb they'd left behind. Several pieces of equipment were on the ground. Loki had seen similar-looking machinery at the Gallaghers' laboratories. Loki was no expert in spelltech, but these looked like equipment for containing volatile magic spells—the same kind Kay wanted the Fianna to bring for the Dormouse. But these bore a different company logo: an embossed hot-air balloon, rising into clouds.

This was all guesswork on their part, but it looked awfully like the girl was smuggling a bomb spell out of the Tangled Woods.

"Guess I've been found out," she said. She had yellow hair and trimmed bangs, and her brown eyes were openly mocking.

"You're from OzCorp."

"And you shouldn't be here." She wasn't attacking. Ruyi Jingu Bang was still keeping up its furious assault, batting at the jabberwock's attempts to cut at it, flashes of electricity following in its wake. That left Loki defenseless. The girl could very easily use that to her advantage.

Instead, a javelin spell formed in her hand, and she threw it hard at the beast. The jabberwock bellowed, its wing punctured. The creature's poison was more than Ruyi Jingu Bang could bear; to their horror, Loki saw telltale streaks of black staining the wood, the jabberwock's venom corrupting the surface.

Loki didn't own Ruyi Jingu Bang, technically. It was one of China's most significant cultural artifacts, and the only reason it was in their hands instead of in a museum in Beijing was because unlike most other segen, the staff chose its owner and would break itself out of any exhibit to be with them. Having been bespelled without ties to any one family bloodline, it had decided first on their father Anthony Sun-Wagner and then on Loki as its most recent possessors. Even the Chinese government knew better than to restrict its wishes.

And now, not only were their fathers going to kill them if they wound up destroying a thousand-year-old artifact, the Middle Kingdom would have their head for it.

Loki took a running jump and leaped for the closest tree, scampering from branch to branch until they were almost on top of the beast. They leaped, flipped through the air, and landed a flying kick right at the monster's face, sending it toppling down to earth. It lashed out, and Ruyi Jingu Bang blocked the slash—and splintered as the beast's claws split it in two.

Braying, the jabberwock tore out of the clearing and deeper toward the Wonderland ruins.

Breathing hard, Loki and the girl faced each other. West returned to Loki's side, eyeing the stranger balefully.

"I should have known," the girl said thoughtfully, almost to herself. "Of course there would be two of those creatures."

"You have the right to remain silent," Loki said. They weren't technically a ranger yet, but out here, they were the closest thing to it. "For both our protection, keep your hands away from all spelltech within your person till I say otherwise. You have the right to a lawyer—"

"We're getting a little ahead of ourselves, aren't we?" the girl asked, batting thick eyelashes at them. "You're outnumbered. You didn't even ask me for my name yet."

"We've got time for that later."

"What are the charges?"

"Smuggling a bomb out of Avalon."

"Was I really? Or maybe this was all a sting on the Fianna's part, and you're setting me up?"

"Fianna don't do that."

"All cops do that. You can *try* to arrest me, but I don't think you'd want to. Wonderland magic still lives on here, and I think it would be extremely painful for us both for you to make the attempt." The girl gestured around them. "Do you see any bombs there?"

"I would if I investigated your equipment."

"Which you can't without a warrant. I know my rights. You're not even a Fiann."

"Are you planning on attacking Avalon?"

The girl threw her head back and laughed. "Of course not. This is only research."

"But why?"

"That's for me to know and for you to find out, isn't it?"

"Miss Fey."

A portal fizzled into view, and Loki ducked another barrage of lightning. They raised their broken staff instinctively, but the other soldiers had also regrouped, standing in front of the girl.

"Loki." Tala, Zoe, and Cole had arrived, all of them breathing hard. "The Fianna's arrived," Tala said. "Dad's talking to them, and…" She paused, taking in the scene, her eyes narrowing.

"Take the equipment, gentlemen," the girl from OzCorp said. "We're done here. Something strange is going on in these woods, and I'm very glad to leave. I suggest you do the same, Sun-Wagner."

"You can use a looking glass without a second gate," Loki said, stunned. The Red King was not yet available to the public. The Gallaghers said it was the only one of its kind. Avalon was also quick to detect any unauthorized ports coming from outside the kingdom, so it was hard to believe they wouldn't have noticed this one…

…unless, of course, it was an unauthorized port already within Avalon.

"I really feel," Zoe said, "that we should intervene somehow."

"We haven't attacked you," Miss Fey said. "And you'll be hard-pressed to justify attacking us. Avalon hasn't officially announced this place as being off-limits. I'm told you're all very smart children, but I doubt any of you are familiar enough with spelltech to accuse us of any kind of sabotage."

"Crap," Tala said, sounding mad. "Something's jamming my phone. I can't access video recording, and I can't override it."

"Avalon does not have the monopoly on spelltech breakthroughs. Or spell negators." Miss Fey watched them as the men carried the rest of the devices through the looking glass. "I really wouldn't pursue this if I were you."

"Then it's a good thing," Loki said, "that you aren't me."

She laughed again. "Better luck next time, kiddo. I'm sure we'll meet again."

She stepped through the portal. The looking glass flickered out behind them.

"This is bad," Loki said. West nudged at their hand and whined.

Cole had already moved, circling the area where the portal had been. "Alex will need to know about this," he said tersely.

"We can call them out," Zoe said, sounding coldly furious. "We just let them go! We could have done something!"

"Not this time. We don't have anything to show for it beyond our testimony. She was right. We don't have the expertise to confirm what they were doing here." Loki looked down at their staff, careful not to handle the parts still coated in poison. This looked bad too; if the venom had succeeded in leaching into the wood, the chances of repairing it were almost nil. They felt sick.

"We may not have anything to formally accuse them, but at least Alex knows who to guard against." Slowly, Tala touched the tip of Ruyi Jingu Bang. For a moment, the toxin staining the staff there seemed to lighten, only to fail and resume its inky color. "Can it be fixed?" She looked as stricken as Loki felt.

"I don't know." Years of meditation had taught Loki how to appear outwardly calm. Inside, they were a shaking mess. Was it possible to actually kill a segen? "I really don't."

They made it back to the Avalon side of the border, where Kay and the Fifth Honor waited for them. From the looks of it, they'd just finished containing the Dormouse. The equipment they'd brought along looked pretty similar to the OzCorp tech the girl had brought along. Loki was in trouble, and they knew it.

"Lord Eddings," Mykonos Vasilakis said stiffly. He was a tall, burly man, clean-shaven with a buzz cut. He was looking down at West, whose ears were lowered. "My apologies. Any Fiann worth their salt would know better than to put your lordship in danger. Any recruit hoping to join our ranks knows this."

Loki swallowed. "Sorry, sir."

"Did you ask Kay Warnock for permission before exploring further?"

"I...no, sir."

"Do I have reason to believe, judging from the state of your segen, that you then proceeded to act recklessly?"

"There was a jabberwock, Lord Vasilakis," Zoe argued. "We couldn't have foreseen—"

"Sun-Wagner should have. There are no lone wolves in the Fianna. Everyone works together to ensure no one is left behind. Not only has Sun-Wagner shown a blatant disregard for their companions' safety, but they went against the commanding officer in charge of the mission and acted without thought. Frankly, I'm not sure if that's Fianna material."

Loki froze.

"Technically, I'm not the commanding officer," Kay said calmly. "Ain't got an official title in Avalon, and you know that, Mykonos."

"The lack of a formal title doesn't mean you don't rank high in the chain of command, Kay, and you know it. You outrank me even without a position to your name." Mykonos glared at Loki. "I will be asking you to write a report about this incident," he finally said, "and you will present it to the Wake himself. The decision regarding your status is his to make."

Loki knew a reprieve when they saw it, but it was a blow all the same.

"Gorio, send word immediately to Jasper and the other techmages that we've got both an 11–20 and a 20–30 situation here. They need to investigate for other wild magic as soon as possible before more Dormice blow up twenty miles of Avalon land, and we'll need to radio for a couple more honors to search for the jabberwock. You may go, Sun-Wagner," Mykonos finished curtly. "Your segen will be needing repairs."

Loki nodded, schooling their face to hide their distress, and saluted before taking their leave.

"But that's not—" They could hear Zoe start to protest.

Cole, a Nottingham with a military upbringing who knew how these things went, laid a hand on her shoulder. "This is out of our hands," he said.

West and Tala moved to follow them, but Loki shook their head, wanting to be left alone. They glanced at each other; Tala nodded reluctantly, and Loki strode back toward the forest entrance, fighting staff cradled carefully in their hands.

A black mark by the Fifth Honor leader *before* they'd even become a cadet—that must be some kind of record. Just not the one Loki had been hoping for.

6

IN WHICH ZOE LOSES HER TEMPER

Alex had really done it.

Alone in the Hollows, Zoe stared at the television in front of her. "...we are, of course, prepared to welcome anyone who might choose to visit Avalon, in light of this new development." Alex was a natural on camera, calm and composed and looking very regal. He'd insisted on making the proclamation in lieu of a spokesperson, and it had been the right call. The young royal had both the good looks and a boyish vulnerability that appealed.

Zoe glanced at her phone. "Nameless Sword" was one of the hottest topics online, second only to "Sword in the Stone." The video with West was still going viral, but people had mostly jumped on it with "good boy" and "antifa dog" tags and comments to cheer the shifter on, so she wasn't in trouble for that at least.

A sudden beep told her she'd received a text. She frowned when Tristan's name flashed on-screen, and she thumbed the message aside. They'd broken up, as far as she was concerned. They hadn't talked in months. They had yet to even be on the same continent since taking back Maidenkeep. Tristan's father had just been appointed Royal Britain's ambassador to Avalon. He'd said it wasn't a good time to talk, though that seemed more of an excuse to avoid her.

They'd had one phone call, three days after securing the palace. The castle had been turned into a makeshift hospital in the days after while Alex began the slow, painstaking process of putting the rest of his kingdom in order. Zoe had been tired and cranky when Tristan had contacted her, with only a few hours' sleep a night. Suffice it to say, the conversation had not gone well, and they hadn't talked since. And in the whirlwind of activity during the weeks that followed Alex's coronation, she'd been too busy to think much of him.

He'd still been mad that she hadn't told him about the mission to rescue the king, but his anger faded when she'd told him she knew about him and Alex. She'd asked him if she'd only been his rebound. He'd balked at responding to that, which was an answer all on its own. They'd ended the call with no resolution on either end, but she already knew it was over.

Zoe wanted to rage. She wanted to cry.

But she could only do one of those.

Another quick check of her phone revealed over seven hundred thousand likes on the photo of the Nameless Sword. A cursory search turned up nothing substantial about the border patrol, though West was still getting a lot of attention.

She'd received messages from her family as well. The first had been her father, worriedly asking if she was all right. As an architect living in New York City with no claims to nobility, he had no ties to Avalon beyond her and her mother, but they had always been close. Alex had told her that the Cheshire had visited him numerous times, always at the risk of getting caught, to comfort and reassure him during the months she'd been trapped inside Avalon. Zoe was grateful to the Wonderland noble for that. Her father understood her Avalon heritage and had never kept her from her responsibilities to the kingdom, despite his fears for her safety.

He'd planned to visit, but it was still chaotic enough in Avalon that

Zoe had demanded that he wait. Plus, people still insisted on calling her Lady Fairfax instead of Lady Carlisle, no matter how many times she'd tried correcting them. Her father would be overlooked quite easily here.

As for her mother... Well, nobody really told Felicity Fairfax what to do, as she'd proven in the one and only email Zoe received from her two days earlier, proclaiming in elegant French that of course she would *come to the summit to see you, my little poppet, but has the castle been renovated to modern standards yet? The rooms could get quite drafty. The horrors it does to my hair!*

Felicity Fairfax had used her official royal email, signing off with the Fairfax crest: a deer running on a field of green, a throwback to an ancestor who'd spent years enchanted as one. No inquiries as to how Zoe was doing or feeling. No questions about her time in Avalon during the frost.

It was like she hadn't even noticed that her daughter was missing for nearly six months.

Not really wanting to think about her mother, much less write her a response, Zoe stared at the Red King looking glass. The mirror activated easily at her touch, loading up and running through its standard diagnoses before the reflection cleared, to find herself staring back at it.

"I didn't have a choice," she said aloud.

"Didn't you?" came the droll reply.

Zoe spun. Nottingham was leaning against the closed door with his arms crossed, watching her in that careful, guarded way he often did that told her he was quite annoyed with her despite his lack of expression.

She hadn't even heard him enter, despite having equipped the Hollows with spells that would alert her to anyone coming in. That annoyed her. Knowing how much she'd come to rely on him annoyed her even more. He was organized, had quickly learned how to work the Red King proto- type, and had a talent for details. Zoe had nearly blown a fuse when he'd gone missing the month prior, sending only a terse "family business" in response to the worried texts she'd sent him. Sure, he had bad taste in books, and he could still be terribly condescending, but sometimes he would sit with her here at the Hollows and they would watch old movies like *Somewhere in Time* or *Some Like It Hot*, and he didn't even argue when she told him she hated *Roman Holiday* despite adoring Audrey Hepburn and how she would much rather never watch it. It was nice, not having to find something to fight him about.

"I was hoping for some privacy." The Banders had their own rooms at Maidenkeep, but Zoe didn't want to rage there. "Or are you going to rat me out to Alex?" Adding Nottingham to the group had been one of Alex's demands before he would let her test the looking glass. Zoe was going to invite him anyway and so had acquiesced easily.

"Depends. Are you planning to take more trips without telling anyone?"

Of course he knew. She'd cleared the looking glass's data record cache yesterday, but doing the same to the backup directory had required Dex's passcode, which she figured didn't matter because she had already sworn Dex to secrecy.

She hadn't known he would be so inquisitive about it. Nottingham didn't seem interested in looking glass technology beyond traipsing in and out of them.

"It doesn't matter if you wipe it now. I remembered the coordinates from this morning."

"Oh, so you have an eidetic memory now?" Zoe spat, yanking her hand away.

"Only with you." He pressed his finger against the surface, and the looking glass obediently called up a series of locations. "There were two planned trips this week. One port was opened near the medical center in

Virginia and the second at the Texas border." He shifted to another block, and a different map popped up. "Except there are three more listed here. One in Namibia and the other at two more locations in Alabama, the Royal States."

"Dex said it was a recalibration error—"

"Dex is a terrible liar."

"I really don't know why you're harping on this."

"There was some news to come out of Alabama recently about the man who'd been found guilty of assaulting a woman. The one who'd gotten a slap on the wrist because the judge said he was *too nice to be jailed*."

"I remember seeing some of the headlines. So?"

"The latest ones said he'd been found beaten up in his cell. There weren't any working cameras. Their forensics suggested it might have been a hexbomb."

Silence. Zoe focused her gaze back on the television screen, where Alex had just ended his speech and was being escorted off the platform. It was easier to look at him than at the boy beside her.

"The judge responsible is now up for recall. He'd been arrested too. They found child abuse materials on his computer."

Zoe pursed her lips. "Wow. What a scumbag."

"Red King coordinates show someone activating a port into both the county jail and an address near that judge's house."

It was hard to fake a smile with her teeth grinding against each other. "Coincidence, I'm sure."

"The Namibia port opens into a national park. A couple of hunters have gone missing, presumed attacked by lions. One of them had also been in the news recently, boasting about his travels and the game he acquired."

Something snapped inside her. "Not game hunters. Trophy hunters.

They were *trophy* hunters. If they can only feel powerful from killing animals, then maybe they shouldn't use spelltech guns to cheat. Spelltech guns, mind you, that have been *banned* inside the park that they bribed the officials into letting them bring anyway. I didn't kill them, if that's what you're implying. I just threw a hex spell at them before they could shoot, and they ran. They'll probably be found soon, cowering under a bush somewhere.

"Yes, I punched Brandon Tusker, but only once. Trust assholes like him to exaggerate and pretend like *they're* the victims. No, I didn't plant anything on that judge's computer. It was already there. I-I was so angry. So *angry*. He made his own choices. The only thing I did was make sure everyone knew."

Zoe stopped, suddenly aware that her hand was clenched tightly around her phone and that the protective case had actually cracked in her grip. Nottingham didn't say a word. A picture of the Nameless Sword, the very photo Tita Chedeng had taken, was now featured prominently on the news channel.

The hunters hadn't bothered hiding their location, and it was easy enough to track them with the looking glass. She'd been reckless enough to follow.

But then she'd seen the heat scans of their bespelled guns, realized they were entering the protected area of the park, and the frustration had built up, higher and higher until it had burned, white-hot and blinding, until she could see nothing else but her own rage.

She'd seen the photos in the judge's hard drive. She'd unleashed that same anger on Tusker.

"I didn't mean to," she finally said.

"Right," said Nottingham, in a tone suggesting he could be made to suspend disbelief once the right alibi presented itself.

"I didn't kill anyone. I only really meant to yell at Tusker. He accidentally fell into my fist."

"Right."

"I suppose," Zoe said stiffly, "that you've already snitched to Alex about this, and that's why you're here."

"I didn't tell him."

Zoe kept waiting for him to append a *yet* at the end of that sentence, but it never arrived. "Why not? Weren't you supposed to keep an eye on me?"

"I didn't tell him. And I'm not going to."

"But why?" It didn't make sense. He didn't approve of what she'd been doing, so why risk getting in trouble *for* her too?

"You handed Alex the spellstones Nya's grandmother gave you after we took back Maidenkeep."

Zoe nodded warily, not sure where this was headed. The Ikpeans guarded one of the richest spell mines in Avalon. The spellstones she'd gotten from their priestess could have outfitted a small island.

"You counted them out while traveling to Maidenkeep. You said there were thirty of them. But when Alex made his tally, there were only twenty-nine."

Zoe forced her fist to unclench. "Maybe I'm just bad at math."

"I didn't remember much, after we escaped the swamps. I dragged you as far as I could, then collapsed. I'd been injured, and I was cold, and there was no way we could have made it out of there without hypothermia setting in, or worse. But when I woke, you were treating my wounds. There was no fire, but I was warm."

"Nya's grandmother gave me medicine to—"

"And then there was something Dex mentioned a few days ago. He'd suspected we were all trapped in Avalon but only confirmed it after detecting high magical energy from within the kingdom, perceivable even through the frost. He thinks it was someone using a spellstone. He said that it was dangerous to use one that way, without any of the safety buffers that spelltech has."

"Dex's a genius. I would never have imagined he could find something so—"

"What did you wish for, Carlisle?" Nottingham was usually in perfect control of his emotions, but he was angry now. "You've placed the spellstone in this room not because you want people to remember what we're fighting for but because you've *already used one up*, and you feel guilty about using another. Tell me the truth, because I *will* tell Alex everything otherwise."

"Fine," Zoe shot back. "I wished for us to be warm. That's it. The spell gave me options, but they all asked for too much. Choices I couldn't live with if I accepted. So I asked for warmth, and all it wanted from me was my—"

"What?" Nottingham's hand was on hers, his grip tight but not crushingly so. "What did you give up?"

"Tears. That's all it wanted. I could live without tears, so I said yes. I've watched movies like *An Affair to Remember* and *Up* and every sad movie to ever exist, like, a billion times since then, and I've never cried even once, so as far as I'm concerned, that's a win for me. I don't use up as many tissues." His fingers were warm. It reminded her of that terrible night, the bolt of happiness and relief when he had no longer been cold to the touch or a heartbeat away from dying. "That's all it wanted. Tears. It's not something I need your pity for."

"You don't have my pity," Nottingham said, still watching her. Some of his fury had ebbed. "If anything, I should be thanking you."

"You already thanked me back at—"

"It was piss-poor thanks, knowing what I do now."

"You hurt yourself trying to save me, if you recall. I was only return-ing the—"

"Carlisle," he growled. "Shut up and take the compliment."

"You wanna know how to thank me?" Zoe challenged him. "Don't stop me from doing this. I *need* to do this. I swore to Alex that I wouldn't get the others in trouble, but I didn't make any promises about me." She placed her free hand against the mirror's cool surface. It sparked at her touch, triggering a collage of photos, videos, lives, that spread from one side of the looking glass to the other. "Look. You can't have some-thing powerful like this, where you can port to almost anywhere in the world nearly unrestricted, and not figure out a way to do something good with it. I know it's a huge advancement. I know it should never fall into the wrong hands. I understand why Alex doesn't want it for private use. But I have it, right now. I'm not going to use this for personal gain. I just want to help. As much as I can, for as long as I can. I'm not going to change the world, but I can at least change bits and pieces of it for the better."

It was wild, unreasonable, and ridiculous, this urge of hers to want his approval all of a sudden. She didn't want him to have access to this secret part of her that felt so maddeningly illogical. She was the queen of pro-con lists. She planned and preplanned for unexpected eventualities. She wasn't supposed to be this vigilante who snuck into corrupt judges' houses and punched rapists without a ten-point agenda on a PowerPoint presentation first. But here it was, and there he was, and for some reason, he wasn't trying to put her in her place the way he'd always tried to over the years.

"I have some conditions," Nottingham said.

Zoe already hated them, but she didn't have much choice. "Shoot."

"You need to tell me beforehand what you intend to do before you get into another damn expedition."

She hadn't expected that; she'd thought he would nix them altogether. She'd wanted to lie low after the last one anyway. She nodded.

"And for every mission you've already gone on, you have to accompany me on another."

Zoe's mouth fell open at that one. Not only was he *not* stopping her, he was *volunteering* to be a coconspirator? "Didn't you say you wanted to dissuade me from doing this?"

"Do you agree or not?"

"I agree. What else?"

"That's it."

"What?" He had the upper hand. She knew he knew that. "Are you sure?"

"Are you this terrible a negotiator that you want me asking for more concessions from you?"

"Of course not. Fine." Fine. Maybe he had a vigilante streak in him too. The Nottinghams were the black sheep among the who's who of Avalon society, so it wasn't like they were the epitome of good behavior either.

But behind that expressionless face, Zoe could sense that he was a little too pleased by this arrangement, which irked her enough to respond with pettiness. "It's not like you've been aboveboard this whole time either. You brought your segen to the Texas border."

"It wasn't Gravekeeper."

"Yeah, and the ice wolf obeyed you only out of the goodness of its heart—wait. You're right. You were holding a knife then. Are you saying you've got *another* segen?" The Nottingham scythe was the only one of its kind, the only known weapon capable of possessing and controlling nightwalkers. Zoe had heard enough rumors suggesting that the family's symbiotic relationship with those unnatural creatures went beyond just thralldom; a few prominent ancestors in their history had affiliated themselves with the Beiran ruler more than once. It only contributed to their infamy.

The Nottinghams were barely tolerated as it was, and they were always a step away from being denounced as traitors. If it went about that they'd kept a *second* segen that could possess nightwalkers…

Wordlessly, Nottingham picked up a pencil and held it to the light. As they looked on, telltale strands of magic wound themselves around the lead, with the same shadowed mist that often accompanied his scythe segen. "Gravekeeper was forged to focus the spell better. But we can do it with most weapons as a last resort."

"That means your family magic isn't tied to the weapon itself. It's tied primarily to your bloodline." It made sense in hindsight. Even a segen couldn't host something as powerful as demon control. The Nottinghams had made a pact the same way the Makilings had, then: with their own bodies, forcing their descendants to endure the same curse down generations without their consent. It made the spell more powerful, but always at a terrible price.

"It hurts worse if I don't use Gravekeeper, though."

"Hurts worse?"

Nottingham pulled back a sleeve, picked up a pencil. The scars that riddled his arm looked red and angry, like they'd been inflicted only recently, though she knew otherwise. The last time she'd seen him without a shirt on, she had paid little attention to those marks, more concerned with saving his life than anything else. But now she took note of the way it seemed like they were shifting with those black tendrils of magic as he forced the spell to the core, fully wrapping around the pencil, at the fresh sheen of sweat on his brow, the gritted way he forced his next words out. The magic he wielded didn't come from the scythe. It came from being a Nottingham. "Pain's more tolerable with a segen."

Zoe grabbed his arm. "Then let go!" She gasped. "Stop it!"

And even as he did, it occurred to Zoe what he'd been doing. He'd seen her rage, a side of her she had never wanted anyone else to know—not even her understanding but very law-abiding father, and definitely not her rule-breaking, self-centered mother. He certainly was not her choice of confidant, but he'd seen her all the same. Even stranger, he'd accepted her. And now, in a peculiar, roundabout way, *he* was deliberately showing *her* a side of him that perhaps no one else outside his own family knew.

He was honorable. Cole Nottingham was an honorable man. Or rather, that he was honorable was something Zoe had already learned during their time trekking through the Avalon frost, but now she knew he was also fair.

She was still clinging to his arm. He towered over her, but gone was his usual intimidation. And he felt warm, too warm—not in a feverish way but in the nice, comfortable way a coat felt on windy days. When had she ever thought he was cold?

She looked down at her hand on his arm. *He* looked down at her hand on his arm. The pencil had not shown signs of demonic possession for a few minutes now, but somehow, that was no longer important. "Thank you," she said and gave his bicep a light squeeze.

The anchorwoman cut in between them, her voice suddenly unexpectedly loud when the room had grown quiet. "We're coming back to you live with breaking news, where the Royal States of America has just announced plans for a state visit to Avalon. Royal spokesperson for King John, Samantha Sacks, at the state briefing."

Zoe and Cole spun to face the screen as it switched to Sacks's unsmiling face. "The Royal States is committed to peace within the greater Pacific region, and we hope to put aside any past differences between our kingdoms to engage in discussions about our future. This is all I have to say at the moment, beyond the fact that King John congratulates King Alexei Tsarevich for all the work he's done in revitalizing Avalon's economy and hopes to personally deliver his felicitations."

"He shouldn't," Zoe said. "The only thing Alex would accept from the American king is his boot up that madman's ass. And besides, aren't kingdoms supposed to ask host countries first before they make these plans? I'm pretty sure Alex doesn't know any of this."

"I'm not sure the Royal States cares," Nottingham said. "This is all about them wanting access to Avalon spellstones at this point."

But the anchorwoman wasn't done. "The announcement follows upon the heels of Avalon's discovery of the Nameless Sword. The number of tourists is expected to increase in the following weeks as those hoping to raise the sword from its stone travel to the kingdom. Ambassadors from other nations have already stated their intentions to visit, including those from Royal Britain, Japan, Norway, and the Philippines, all with historical ties to Avalon. While the—"

But Zoe had stopped listening. "Royal Britain," she muttered.

Nottingham had followed her train of thought. He dropped his arm, his face carefully shuttered.

"I'm going to break up with him," Zoe said, not sure why that came out guiltily. "We haven't been working for a while now. I don't think we'd been working almost from the very beginning. I just thought I could fix it. My mom's probably gonna come eventually. My dad too. I can already feel a migraine coming on."

"So's my family."

Zoe cast him a concerned look.

He smiled thinly. "We'll manage."

"You're all going to take a stab at the sword too?"

"We've got enough headaches with the segen we already have."

Zoe nodded. "I'm going to break up with him," she repeated more firmly. As soon as Tristan arrived. One less trouble to deal with.

"Right," Nottingham said, his voice curiously nonchalant, and suddenly Zoe was annoyed with him again.

7

IN WHICH NYA TEMPORARILY LOSES HER LEGS

They made for a gloomy group, sipping disconsolately on milk teas at the Hollows. Tita Teejay occasionally popped down to replenish their orders—mostly Dex's, who in his anxiety had already consumed two cups—and to add in a plate of brownies or cake slices, but she generally let them be. Tala knew the bad vibes were real if normally inquisitive Filipino aunties were voluntarily leaving them alone.

The news was on, and one screen was tuned to a news channel dedicated to coverage of the Nameless Sword. Tala could see the long lines that filled Maidenkeep's courtyard, where everyone was waiting their turn, hoping to draw the blade from the stone. Everyone who'd tried had been unsuccessful so far, and the reporters were busily interviewing a rueful few who'd failed in the attempt.

The other screen showed Ruggedo Nome, talking to reporters and defending his decision to build a new facility near Ikpe. The man was stocky in build, with carefully combed hair, dark eyes, and a perpetual grin on his face, like he was in on a joke no one else was. The man had tried out the Nameless Sword himself only an hour earlier and shrugged good-naturedly when the sword refused to budge. "I suppose I'll make a difference in the world some other way," he said philosophically.

"You just cut the ribbon on your main headquarters in Marooners'

Rock a few weeks ago," a reporter persisted in asking. "Why so quick to build another?"

"Beanstalking isn't illegal, technically," Nome pointed out. "And I had no idea about the land restrictions in Ikpe. And besides, who wouldn't want to lead the spelltech industry in Avalon, the birthplace of magic? It's no secret that I've always been fascinated by Avalon legends. The myth of Buyan had always imbued my imagination as a child—"

"Close display," Ken growled at the screen, which promptly turned off.

"I have a meeting with that ass tomorrow," Alex grumbled. "I'd rather boot him out of the kingdom, but apparently I have to exercise *diplomacy*."

"Speaking of diplomacy," Tala said, "I can't believe that you actually agreed to a state visit from King John of the Royal States of America. The worst king to ever king in the history of kings. That's the first foreign dignitary you're choosing to welcome. Here. In Avalon. Why are you starting at rock bottom?"

Alex rubbed at his eyes. "I didn't have a choice. I'm not looking to start a war with another nation so soon after Beira. If I can use this visit to ask them—nicely—for the Avalonian patents they've been hoarding over the years, I'll take it."

"And you really think they're gonna give them up, just like that?"

"No," the king admitted. "But I owe them. I told them I would be providing care for the people who were injured in Invierno. We have the facilities and the experts to make that happen. They sure as hell won't be getting any kind of decent health care in the Royal States."

"The people who…" Tala swallowed. "Oh."

The people the ice maiden had transformed into Deathless, when they'd still been in Arizona. Her classmates. So many other innocents.

"That wasn't your fault, Your Majesty," Nya said gently.

"But it was. If I hadn't been there, they wouldn't have been caught in the crossfire. And knowing they won't ever come back from that, since there isn't a cure…" Alex sighed. "Their news channels are already broadcasting hate pieces on Avalon. I'm mitigating as much of the damage as I can right now. I've tried reaching out to the Royal States through official channels, warning them about the thrall spells being used in their kingdom, but they're deliberately ignoring our communications, which doesn't bode well. It's also partly why I called for you all here. I think it's about time you all knew about what Avalon's end goal is moving forward."

"The end goal," Tala said, "is to lift *both* the frog curse and the Nine Maidens spell on you. Everything else can take a back seat."

"You sound like your mom," Alex said, grinning weakly. "And the Cheshire. There's a few things we need to do before that can happen, though."

"And one of those things," Ken said, pointing at the letter splayed out on the table, "is this?"

They all looked down at it. The paper wasn't bespelled or cursed, and it wasn't even anything as terrible as a death threat. It was written in a cursive, looping handwriting and contained three sentences:

> *Maidenkeep's too stodgy for the likes of me, but I'd appreciate a visit to your fair lady. Chin up, Your Majesty. You are worth more than the crown and the Maidens combined.*
>
> *B.Y.*
>
> *PS: Bring your Bandersnatch friends.*

Ken let out a loud slurp from his matcha boba and sighed. Tita Chedeng had helpfully added perk-me-up spells in their drinks, but so far, they weren't working. "How sure are we that this isn't a scam?"

"Choosing to con the king of Avalon, of all people, takes some guts," Nya said quietly. Something had happened between Ken and Nya since Tala had last seen them; neither were too keen on meeting each other's gaze.

"This isn't a scam," Alex said.

"As unlikely as it is, we can't rule out the possibility that it could be," Loki pointed out. Ruyi Jingu Bang was noticeably missing from their person. Tala had accompanied them when they had handed it over to the Gallaghers for repairs, but even the techmages couldn't promise it would work the same as before.

"I still don't get it," Ken said. "What is it about this letter that makes you think it was written by the real Baba Yaga?"

"Because this is exactly what the Baba Yaga said to six-year-old me back at Maidenkeep, right after the Snow Queen killed my parents. *You are worth more than the crown and the Maidens combined.* She found me, brought me to the Nine Maidens, and then cast the frog curse on me for good measure. Told me she had to if I was to survive."

"That's the part I still don't get," Zoe said. "How would hexing you with a frog curse save your life?"

"That's what I intend to ask her, except I don't know how to find her to begin with." Alex sounded frustrated.

"*I'd appreciate a visit to your fair lady.* Do you think she's planning on gatecrashing the festival that the minister of tourism is setting up next week?"

"Could be." Alex groaned. "Why did the sword have to show up now? Why couldn't it have waited until *after* we'd processed most of the citizenship and naturalization applications?"

"Wark," the firebird said wisely.

"How did you get the letter?" Tala asked.

Alex pointed up at the firebird, not minding at all that it had settled itself on his head like a crown, beaming down at them. "Came flying to me with the note tied to its leg. Aunt Lumina ran through our security cameras but couldn't find anything."

"Do you remember what she looks like?"

"She had short black hair." Alex closed his eyes. "Long lashes, dark eyes. She was younger than what the stories usually say of the Baba Yaga. She was dressed all in white. She carried something in her hand. I thought back then that it was a weirdly shaped two-by-four, but looking back, it could have been a pestle."

Loki frowned. "If she's got a pestle, then she's got transportation. She could be anywhere in Avalon at this point."

"So you think the Baba Yaga can tell us more about lifting the curse," Zoe said. "Is that the only reason we're here?"

"No, there's more." Alex cleared his throat. The firebird was slurping as much of his milk tea as it could take into its beak. "You guys up for another stroll through the woods?"

Loki groaned. "I'm already in enough trouble from the last time."

"This is different. We need to look for someone. His castle, specifically."

"Define 'someone,'" Zoe said warily.

"His name is Agenot Charming."

"Who's that?"

"Only one of the f-foremost experts on Avalonian history!" Dex piped up, stuttering in his excitement. "H-his ancestor invented the opticron—you know, the f-first ever video camera—and they've got the world's oldest collection of footage too! He'd know everything about the Nine Maidens and their curses!"

"He's also missing," Alex said, "though I suspect he's actually hiding somewhere in Albion, putting up wards to keep out of our radar. My techmages think they've found Villeneuve Castle, his home, but we'll be needing confirmation on the ground."

"Why would he be hiding from us?" Tala asked.

"Because Agenot Charming, aside from being one of our best scholars, is also a notorious asshole. He'd have wanted to keep the frost going if it meant he could do his research in peace."

"Great," Ken said. "And when do you expect us to roll up for that?"

"I was hoping after we'd finished our bobas." Alex checked his watch. "Ten minutes sound good?"

"You've gotta be kidding me."

"We could delay it for a couple of hours if you'd like. I've just received news that your parents have arrived from Royal Britain, Ken. Loki's and West's folks are here too. And I believe the Nottinghams are expected within the hour." There was a glint in Alex's eye. "Lady Margrethe was talking my ear off in her excitement during our last call."

All four Banders looked at one another. Tala didn't know why Cole would prefer to delay meeting his parents, but Loki had just been reprimanded by the Fifth Honor leader, West had just gone viral, and she'd heard enough about Ken's mother from Ken to be intimidated by the woman.

"On second thought," Ken said, "best make the trip now and see what Lord Charming's got to say about a curse."

***

"I can understand why we're here," Tala said. "But why are *you* tagging along?" she asked Alex.

"Because Agenot is already a jerk at his best, but he knew my father and he respects the crown. My presence should help convince him to come out of isolation."

"He really should take better care of his gardens, though," Ken said moodily, hacking futilely at the overgrown branches with Yawarakai-Te. "I think I've got ivy down my butt."

"Thanks for the visual, Ken," Zoe said.

"No charge."

Alex's techmages had pinpointed Villeneuve to be somewhere within the Hercyiman Forest, which lay between the mountainous Altai regions and Albion. It was an incredibly dense wood; at times, it was hard to see in front of them for all the heavy foliage blocking their path. It was no small wonder that the castle was hard to find.

Ken's kelpie, Horse, trotted closely behind him, Alex and Nya riding on it. West had already shifted into a bloodhound and was snuffling at the ground, pausing every now and then to whine. The firebird had soared on ahead, ostensibly to scout the rest of the area.

"West says he can't smell anyone else around but us," Loki said.

The kelpie neighed.

"Horse tells me it can smell water nearby, though," Ken translated.

"Water?" Nya asked nervously.

"Could be the castle moat," Alex said. "Or booby traps. Villeneuve Castle's notorious for them. Dex, can you find any water sources close by?"

"Not yet," Tala's earpiece crackled. "The wards around the area are still interfering with our scanners. Give me another minute to adjust."

"This better be worth it," Zoe grumbled. She shot a glance back at Cole. "Bend over," she commanded and started picking a few twigs out of his hair. "You look ridiculous, and it's annoying," she murmured grumpily.

Cole's eyebrow arched up, looking almost like he was about to smile. "Thanks," he said instead.

"Gravekeeper not acting up? No signs of nightwalkers around? Nothing you have to possess another dagger for?"

"None that I can sense."

"Take the dagger," Ken muttered, "and aim it true. It's gotta be a coincidence."

"Ken," Nya began apprehensively.

"I just don't get it, Rapunzel. Your grandma seems to know more about my doom than she's letting on. Is that why she's not stopping your mom from marrying us? Like if we're married to each other, it'll prevent our prophecies from happening?"

Nya was wearing the look of one who couldn't quite believe someone could be this much of a dumbass yet was also glad that he was. "You could have asked her at the village," she said weakly.

"That's the problem. I'm too terrified of her to ask her anything."

"Wait a minute," Tala said. "Are you guys getting married?"

"Of course not!" Ken said, turning red. "It's just some weird idea Rapunzel's mom cooked up. No one's getting hitched."

"Yes," Nya said, a bit more faintly.

"I'd normally climb a tree to see what's up ahead," Loki said, "but they're all too close together, so I doubt I'd spot anything. Dex, how good are those Avalon maps you've got?"

"The coordinates should be accurate. He's warding the castle, not teleporting it elsewhere. You should be right on top of it by now."

"There isn't anything here that even remotely resembles a castle. The woods are too dense for any kind of building."

The firebird returned, settled on Alex's shoulder, and let out an aggrieved grunt.

"Nothing?" the king asked.

It spread its wings out and shrugged.

"West, got something?"

The bloodhound whined again and gave a little shake of his head.

"I can *feel* something here," Tala said, frustrated, "but there's too much for me to push back." Her mother had taught her how to find the weak spots within most defense spells, but whatever was warding the place felt too...expansive. "I might be able to figure it out if you give me a few days to map out the perimeter first."

Up ahead, Loki stopped. "Um," they said.

"Is this an *I've finally found the way in* um, or a *crap, we're so screwed* um?" Ken asked warily.

"It's more of an *I don't know what this is doing here* um."

It was a pail, hanging from a low tree branch. It was empty, save for a long stick. *Don't strike this pail twice* was written on one side of it.

"Is this supposed to be some kind of test?" Alex finally asked. "Dex?"

"I have no idea what that is."

"I want to hit the pail," Ken said.

Nya sighed.

"I don't think Agenot Charming was ever described by anyone as having a sense of humor," Alex said. "But I'm not sure we have a choice. Tala and Loki can't find it, and neither can West or my firebird. Go do the honors, Ken. Everyone else, stay on guard. We don't know what's about to happen."

"All righty." Ken got off Horse. He strode up, took the stick out of the pail, and, after a deep breath, whacked at it twice.

Tala had been expecting creatures to fight. A sudden flood was not what she was expecting.

It had appeared out of nowhere, and before it could even register in Tala's brain, she was already somersaulting through the rush of water, quick reflexes the only reason she'd clamped her mouth shut before it could get into her lungs. It wasn't even a river; it tasted too salty to be anything else but the sea.

Kicking her feet, she worked her way back up to the surface. But there was no halt to the rushing rapids, and she only barely managed to grab at a tree trunk to keep her from getting swept away.

The others were faring a little better. The firebird had dug its talons into Alex's shoulders, dragging the king to another nearby branch above water level. West had shifted into a dolphin and was buoying Loki, Zoe, and Cole to safety.

But Ken and Nya were nowhere to be seen.

Ken couldn't swim.

Before Tala could succumb to a full-blown panic, a large fishtail flopped out of the water, then disappeared under the surface. Because West was clearly two dozen feet away, it couldn't possibly be his.

It reappeared, and then Nya was skimming through the water, far too quickly for an average human. Behind her was Ken's kelpie, and it was carrying a bedraggled, dazed-looking Ken on its back.

Nya opened her mouth and screamed.

It was a metal pail, but under the force of that shriek, it shattered all the same.

The waters receded just as quickly as they had arrived, leaving Tala on wet muddy ground, still clinging to the trunk. The firebird set Alex back on his feet, and West blurred back into West, crouching, with the most bewildered expression on his face. Zoe sat beside him, still shocked, her dark hair sticking in clumps to her face.

"What," she said, "the hell."

Nya was sitting on the ground too, her face all red, and Ken was gaping at her like she'd just sprouted gills.

And she might have, Tala thought, because underneath the skirts she wore, there was a very silvery tail peeking out.

"Nya?" Zoe asked. "What…"

"It was salt water," Nya mumbled.

"You were hoping it was fresh water," Ken said, finally shocked into some sense. His face still looked gray, and he sounded like there was a fish lodged in his throat. "Because salt water causes you to change. Into a mermaid. Mami Wata's descendant, right? That's what your grandma meant. And I was too much of a fool to realize what she was implying."

"Ken—"

"I've been worried about my doom all my life. That was the reason I've always been terrified of the ocean. I wanted to ask you out, because hey, there's no way you were ever gonna be some sea demon. But you knew all along. That's why you turned me down. And you would've kept hiding it from me. Guess my peace of mind didn't matter much, huh?"

"Ken…"

"No, it's okay. I'm cool. We're cool. You had the right not to tell me, and I had the right not to know. Does anyone have a towel to spare?"

"You're a mermaid?" Tala asked, a few thought processes behind everyone else.

Nya's broom was lying nearby. The Ikpean girl flopped the required several feet needed to reach it. It shimmered, and her long tail along with it. The latter then split itself into two separate lengths, transforming into legs.

"I'm sorry," she whispered. "My whole village was sworn to secrecy. I couldn't tell any of you. I wanted to, but…"

Ken said nothing and turned away. The look on Nya's face was heart-wrenching.

"Uh-oh," someone said from behind Tala. "I probably owe you guys an apology too."

The thing that had spoken was covered in black shaggy fur, with fangs as large as Tala's hands protruding from its upper mouth and immense paws that ended in sharp claws. It seemed capable of causing small earthquakes as its furred feet strode across the ground, kicking up heavy clumps of wet dirt with every step. But for all its brutish appearance, it wore massive robes dyed a deep purple, the fur on its head had been carefully slicked back, and the eyes that settled on Alex looked alert and highly intelligent…and embarrassed.

"No," Alex said sharply when Zoe reached for her whip and Cole his Gravekeeper. Loki was already reaching behind their ear, only to drop their hand with a resigned look after remembering there was nothing there. "He's a friend."

"Sorry, Your Majesty," the beast said in a calm, soothing voice that sounded nothing like he looked. "Should have deactivated the spells my father had set up around the castle, but with the jabberwocks still haunting the woods, I'd be screwed without them. Father imported this spell all the way from Sizhou—bought it from some Water Mother sect in China, pretty rare. You only needed to strike the pail once. Your dad knew the secret. Didn't it say *not* to hit it twice?"

"My father never told me," Alex said dryly, "and I'm not sure this is the successful reverse psychology that you think it is."

"Alex," Tala said, speaking slowly because she was still trying to deal with all the shocks she'd already been subjected to for the day. "Who is this…person, and why do you know him?"

"He's Lord Agenot Charming, the Duke of Suddene. I might have forgotten to mention that he's got a hereditary family curse." Alex paused, scrutinizing the hulking creature more carefully. "Wait. You sound a little too young to be Agenot. But he had a seventeen-year-old son."

"Real nice that you could even tell," the man-beast said drolly. "But I'm eighteen now, and my name is Aidan Agenot. Or the Beast of Suddene which, I gotta say, I kinda like better than just the *Duke of Suddene*. My father, Lord Agenot, didn't make it through the frost. Almost a blessing, really. He was really out of it by the end."

The heaviness in the air disappeared; Tala felt the spells around the place lessening, and in a blink of an eye, a castle stood before them where it hadn't before.

"Welcome," the Duke of Suddene said, "to my humble home."

8

IN WHICH PARENTS NEED TO SIGN WAIVERS SO THEIR KIDS CAN SAVE THE WORLD

The members of the Order of the Bandersnatch may have saved the kingdom of Avalon and were capable of looking after themselves, but that didn't mean crap to their parents. A horde of them were set to converge on the recently discovered Villeneuve Castle via the looking glass Alex's techmages had just set up, and Lord Charming looked slightly at a loss at having to entertain several dozen guests all at once when he'd had none for close to twelve years.

Lumina and Kay were the first to arrive through the port. Tala's father looked tense, more anxious than she'd seen him in the last few days. "Aidan," he greeted the beast tersely. "I'm glad to see you."

"Glad to see you've survived the years, sir." That Lord Charming knew her father didn't surprise Tala. She'd learned early on that there were many people in Avalon who didn't look at her father the same way people in other countries did. What shocked her was the clear sympathy in the young duke's tone.

"Glad to see you well, Aidan," Shawn Sun-Wagner told the Duke of Suddene. He was a good-looking man with Alex's blue eyes. It was easy to see that they were related and even more astonishing for Tala to learn that he was currently seventh in line to Avalon's throne but had given up all claims to marry the man he loved, even officially taking his mother's maiden name as proof of his break from the family. "Couldn't have been easy, a year in the frost while we waited twelve outside it, and with no one but your father for company."

"I guess you knew him," came the wry response. "It *felt* like a dozen years instead of just the one. Still. It's not every day you get to see a real live mermaid so far from the ocean. Did you know that people used to hunt them for their tails, for their supposedly medicinal properties? Dumbass superstition, though."

"No," Ken said, looking a little sick. "I didn't know that."

"I'm not really all that good with being hospitable, so I'm gonna go prepare some stuff His Majesty wanted to see. If you're hungry, you can… you know, order takeout or something. Coming, Sir Kay? I kinda think there's someone here who'll be glad to see you."

"What?" Tala asked, startled. She'd been under the assumption that Aidan Charming was the castle's lone occupant.

Kay glanced at Lumina, who nodded reassuringly at him. "I'll tell you later," she promised Tala, watching her husband follow after the duke.

"Not much of a host, is he?" Anthony Sun-Wagner murmured after the beast was gone. "The irony of having Charming as a last name."

"He's holding up well, considering," Shawn chided. "Agenot would not have made the best companion for anyone, even for his son. And how is my wonderful nephew?"

"The throne's still yours if you want it, Uncle," Alex offered.

"Over my dead body." He bowed to Kay and the Makilings. "Lady Makiling Warnock. So nice to finally meet you. And this must be Tala!"

Tala curtsied.

Alex couldn't keep in his snicker, and she glared at him. "You don't curtsy to me," he pointed out.

"Yeah, and your smugness is exactly why I don't."

"My Ken!" came a shriek from the direction of the portal. As if sensing the chaos to come, the firebird squeaked once and then soared out past the doors.

"Where's it going?" Tala asked Alex.

"Probably restless. It's been doing that a lot more recently. I think having to deal with the ministers is driving it bananas."

"More like it knows what's coming." Ken was groaning. "Oh no."

"All these months, and you never even bothered to call?" A striking brunette around Tala's mother's age stomped into view, looking none too pleased. "You sent for Horse but didn't even bother to send us a hello? Your father and I spent months worried about you! You couldn't even bother with *one* phone call?"

"I sent you several texts," Ken protested weakly.

"Texts? Your poor mother doesn't deserve texts! Like you haven't been trapped in Avalon for half a bloody year already!" His mother wrapped Ken in a tight hug. "How could you put me through all this waiting? When I learned you'd fought the Snow Queen on top of everything else, I thought I was going to have a conniption!"

"I'm fine, Mum," Ken grumbled, embarrassed. "Just not in front of everyone, will you?"

"I tried." The man following his mother bore many physical similarities to Ken and was dressed in ceremonial wear that would not have been out of place in a Japanese period play. "It's a wonder I got your mother to wait this long. Have you been practicing?"

Ken stood up straighter, his hand straying to the hilt of Yawarakai-Te strapped to his back. "Every day, Touchan."

"Good." It was clear that Kazuhiko Inoue wasn't as expressive as his wife, but his tone was warm. "Your Majesty, it's an honor."

"I'm glad to see you well too, Lord Inoue."

"Your Majesty," Margrethe Inoue greeted happily, wrapping Alex up in a hug as well, which he returned. "You had us worried for a while back there."

"I was pretty worried myself," Alex confessed.

"Let's not make it a habit. My son is enough to stress me out."

"Mum!" Ken protested.

"And who's this?" Lady Margrethe smiled prettily at Nya, who was lurking shyly nearby. She shot the woman a nervous smile, then turned her attention back to her grandmother. They'd sworn to keep her secret, but the girl still looked a little distressed. As far as Tala knew, she and Ken still weren't on speaking terms. "You've been sneaking glances at her when you think I'm not looking."

Ken turned beet red. "I wasn't!"

His father turned to nod at Loki's fathers. "Anthony," he greeted. "Shawn. It's been a while."

"Your son distinguished himself very well during the fight to reclaim Avalon, Kazuhiko," Anthony said.

"So did your child. Young Loki's due to serve in the Fifth Honor soon, aren't they?"

Loki looked a shade nervous. Shawn Sun-Wagner cleared his throat. "We're very proud of them," he said sincerely. "It's not an easy feat, to do the right thing."

Kazuhiko looked confused, but Loki relaxed and beamed.

"Merriwick, you old bat!" Shawn said next at a new couple emerging from the looking glass. With them were the Earl of Tintagel and, to Tala's trepidation, his mother, the Dame of Tintagel. "Last I heard, you and your wife were taking up sanctuary with the king of Denmark. Good morning, Hiram, Dame."

Merriwick Eddings, who looked too much like West to not be related, only grinned and signed.

"We've been traveling to and from Avalon the last couple of months," his wife translated, pausing long enough to scoop West and then Alex into embraces. "We've been helping finalize an official map of Avalon based on old family documents of ours." She turned to Lumina. "How are you and your husband?" she asked, embracing Tala's mother as well. "It's been more than a dozen years since I last saw you both! Where have you been hiding all this time?"

"In Invierno, Arizona!" Tala's mother laughed. "It's good to see you too, Madeleine."

The Dame sighed loudly. "I am very tired, Hiram," she said. "I knew the young Lord Charming would make an ungracious host, but the amount of collected dust in the air is more than even what I can predict. Is that a comfortable armchair I see over there?"

Zoe, who was in the process of settling herself on the aforementioned chair, winced and stood back up.

"I am sorry about the Dame, Lady Fairfax," Lady Madeleine Eddings apologized. "She isn't fond of traveling."

"We've met before," Zoe said dryly.

"This must be young Tala." West's mother extended a hand out to Tala, which she took. "Thank you for taking care of His Majesty."

"I didn't do much," Tala said, a little overwhelmed. They were all Alex's family. She was happy to see him surrounded by people who cared so deeply for him and at the same time also envious that she was somehow still the newcomer in his life despite being best friends.

"Almost like old times, isn't it?" Anthony Sun-Wagner murmured. "Feels like only yesterday that we were fighting off ogres and shades at the Scandinavian border. I miss being young."

"Times are changing," Lady Madeleine murmured. "Have you heard that the Duke of Eléve is at death's door?"

"Good riddance," Kazuhiko grunted. "Though I would have preferred him living long enough to stand trial and be convicted. Those girls deserve to see that at least."

"You'll have to make do with the Bluebeard trial instead," Shawn said. "Glad his daughter is starting fresh with the Locksley boy."

The looking glass flared up again, and Dex and his father stepped through. "Lady Felicity Fairfax isn't responding to our calls," Severon Gallagher told the king. "I told the techs to try again."

"S-sorry, Zoe," Dex bleated.

"That's all right," Zoe said heavily. "I knew that was gonna happen."

"We did find your dad, though," the young boy added, and the looking glass brightened a second time to let Jonathan Carlisle through.

With a happy cry, Zoe flew to him. Her father gathered her up, laughing, and spun her around. "I know you said not to come while things are still hectic here," he said. "But when they invited me, I couldn't resist."

"Ignore everything I told you before," Zoe said. "I'm glad you're here."

"The Nottinghams have been slightly delayed but will be arriving in a couple of hours," Severon continued.

"Is something wrong?" Cole asked, suddenly alert.

"None at all. Didn't mean to worry you. They just didn't want to hurry your great-grandmother."

"What have you been doing, Alex?" Lady Margrethe exclaimed. "The news has been a nightmare the last few days. You've agreed to a state visit from the Royal States? Ruggedo Nome's here? And the Nameless Sword's been found?"

"Ruggedo Nome?" Tala exclaimed. "The OzCorp CEO?"

"Trying to smooth out all the litigation surrounding the Ikpean property they bought here in Avalon," the king sighed. "But there are good reasons why I asked you all to come here in the first place, Aunt Margrethe."

"Really don't see why you gotta call all our parents for this," Ken grumbled.

"When I didn't have a kingdom, I was fine with letting you all get away with that, but now that I'm king, I've got laws to follow. You're still minors."

"So are you," Tala pointed out.

"Yeah, but I don't need permission from my parents to be king. I need your parents' permissions for this, though." Alex looked around at the adults. "And that really is what I need from you. Permission. Your kids saved my ass more times than I can count. But now I need their help for something else entirely. I am currently assembling a team working on creating a portal into Buyan. I asked you all here because Lord Suddene has access to everything we know about the place, and I would like you all to help him piece out the path that would lead us there. And I need your permission to have the Banders help me."

Some of the parents erupted promptly into protests.

"That's too dangerous, Alex!" Lady Margrethe gasped.

"There's a reason no one's gone so far as to try," Anthony said. "We could be looking at something even worse than the Snow Queen!"

"My apologies," Zoe's father said, a bit hesitantly. "But I'm not all too familiar with the details regarding Buyan or why finding a path to it could be deadly."

"Buyan founded Avalon thousands of years ago," Lumina Makiling Warnock said quietly, "in the same way the British forces created colonies in North America. Like them, they fought each other and split into independent kingdoms. Centuries ago, Avalon defeated Koschei the

Deathless, its last king. To prevent Buyan from falling into their hands, the dying ruler placed a curse on Buyan, closing it off permanently to the rest of the world."

"The Nine Maidens were originally Buyan technology," Madeleine Eddings added. "But Buyan had far superior spelltech than even Avalon. There are stories of the Alatyr, a much more perfected version of the Nine Maidens, that was said to cure even untreatable sicknesses and bring people back to life. The Snow Queen's apparent immortality was said to have come from the Alatyr."

"Which means there's a chance the Alatyr could lift the curse binding Alex to the Nine Maidens," Kazuhiko Inoue said. "I don't see any problems with helping him look for it."

"Kazuhiko!" His wife whirled to him, looking horrified. "The legends say reopening Buyan would be catastrophic to everyone! It's not just about Avalon. The whole world could be affected too!"

"The alternative is to do nothing and watch Alex die, Margrethe. Kings and queens have not lived longer than three or four years after using the Nine Maidens. His Majesty is only alive now because the frost kept him away all this time."

"There are safety measures in place. The Gallaghers made sure of it."

"We've built locking codes to ensure His Majesty can't enter the Nine Maidens tower on his own," Severon Gallagher said wearily, "but it may not be enough. There is an inevitability to this curse that even we cannot mitigate."

"The Snow Queen is also seeking Buyan," Anthony Sun-Wagner added. "Koschei the Deathless was her father. After his passing, she occupied Beira and forged an alliance with Avalon, but reneged after she accused both Arthur and Merlin of attempting to steal her father's secrets. She blamed us for the loss of Buyan. If we do not find the way in, then she will, eventually. And if Buyan technology still exists within, it is our duty to destroy it."

"Destroy?" Lady Margrethe exclaimed. "But why? If it can cure the dying, then shouldn't it be our responsibility to bring that to the rest of the world?"

"You just said we shouldn't be finding ways into Buyan only minutes ago," her husband chided her lightly.

"Yes, but if the technology becomes available, then *shouldn't* we think about being more altruistic?"

"And have the non-Avalonians come with their greed and take it away to enrich themselves at everyone's expense?" Merriwick Eddings signed. "Just like they have done with so much Avalonian spelltech already? It has been twelve years, and those patents have not yet reached the people they were designed to help."

Lumina sighed. "I don't know," she said, "if we will ever have the answers to that. But what we do have are our oaths to protect His Majesty, come what may."

The adults all glanced at one another, still uneasy.

"If you think that finding a new path into Buyan is what it'll take to save Alex, Lumina," Shawn Sun-Wagner said, clearly making the decision for them all, "then that's what we'll do."

"Thank you, Uncle," Alex said, relaxing.

"But where to even begin? There's a reason no one's been able to find it all this time."

"It's why I was looking for the Duke of Suddene in the first place. If anyone would know about finding Buyan, it would be Agenot Charming."

"Unfortunately, I am only his son." The Beast of Suddene was back. "But I'd say I know almost as much as he does. I can point you in the right direction at least. *The Book of Divergent History*, please."

There was a heavy thump from somewhere outside the room. A book came sailing through the door, levitating all on its own, and made a beeline for the beast, who caught it easily.

"Thanks. My father collected a whole bunch of folklore and oral histories in Avalon before we had to hide from the frost," he said, thumbing through the pages with great care despite his large, furred hands. "I was writing a dissertation on this to while away the time, cross-referencing against Avalon history and firsthand sources to see if I could verify the stories. If I ever get to go to college, I'll at least have my thesis ready. This poem in particular was popular back in Esopia. My father had photocopies of fragments of the only historical writing to come from Buyan, and it's almost word for word the same exact text as this one. Let me translate:

Three main paths to Buyan lie,
To claim what death can ne'er die.
The first of witches nine may sing
With fowl and sword, at cost to king.
The second brings with dragon's fires
The lands unburnt from mortal pyres.
The third shall wilder magic take
To World's End seven wonders make.
Gaze into the Alatyr,
And lay claim to your heart's desire.
Know thy heart and gird thy mind
For woe betide what you may find.

"I've heard of that before," the Earl of Tintagel said quietly, coming up from behind them. The Dame of Tintagel was already snoring on the armchair. "From my own research. It was believed to have been penned by Koschei the Deathless himself. The text was taken from documents he possessed."

"What does all that even mean?" Lady Madeleine complained. "It sounds rather like a prophecy to me. Wasn't Koschei a seer himself? As was his daughter?"

Tala shuddered. The Snow Queen's words came back to her, cruel and mocking: *The firebird shall find the consort's child, but she shall find it twice. The sword shall seek her out, yet she shall seek it twice. Twice she chooses and twice she falls and twice she rises. She is fire. And all shall burn.* The Snow Queen had been thrilled, thinking she had predicted the birth of her own child with Kay Warnock—only to be enraged when Kay found happiness with another woman and had a daughter with *her*.

"We've pledged to help you in this endeavor, Your Majesty," Kazuhiko said. "But I'm not so sure about our chances. It's a riddle, and I'm not sure we can solve it."

"I've already solved it," the Beast of Suddene said cheerfully and was subjected to a round of stares. "Well, if you're familiar enough with the history of both Avalon and spelltech, it's not that hard to figure out. The *witches nine* in the first path are obviously the Nine Maidens, but it suggests we'd be losing our king in the process, so I don't recommend it. The second talks of dragons from lands *unburnt from mortal pyres*. That's Esopia."

"Esopia's been inaccessible since long before the frost," Loki spoke up. "There's a wall of fire blocking us from entering. The Fianna have been slinging magic at it ever since Alex reorganized them, and nothing's worked."

"Which, I admit, would be the difficulty with that option. The third, though, talks about wilder magic and the Seven Wonders. That's more promising."

"Not really," Anthony said. "The Seven Magical Wonders are a myth. No traces of them ever existed."

"Nope," the beastly duke said. "Lots of sources from all over Avalon talk about the same places and the same descriptions, with few contradictions among them. Plus, they're all firsthand accounts from the time periods when the Wonders were said to exist. They weren't myths. We just gotta find out where they *used* to exist, and I've already got some ideas as to where. This isn't a fool's errand, guys. I've got centuries' worth of ancestors who'd been doing the research on this. It's, like, a thousand years' worth of work. Toward the end of his life, this was all my father raved about."

Lumina sighed, running fingers through her long, dark hair. "Be that as it may, it still feels like a long shot."

"Do you remember His Majesty's doom?" the Ikpean priestess asked unexpectedly. She drew nearer to the group, Nya trailing after her and doing her best not to look at Ken.

"Of course. Why?"

"*In shifting ice a prince you'll kiss, and the first shall be forgiven. The sword rises twice from palace stone, and the second shall be forgiven. Pledge your love to the blackest flag, and the third shall be forgiven. And then, my dear, and only then, shall you lift that which was forgiven.*"

Tala saw Alex wince. She knew he hated hearing it said aloud.

"*Pledge your love to the blackest flag.* What other kingdom has flown such a banner?"

Tala's mother froze. "Only Buyan has ever used a black flag to represent its kingdom."

Lady Margrethe gasped, a hand flying to her mouth. "So we really don't have a bloody choice after all but to find it?"

"There is more. *Only when those that were missing shall fly again, when those who were dead shall rise again, when that which was cold offers warmth again. That is how your curse shall be broken.*" The priestess smiled. "Was that not what you told the king when they visited you, Elspen?"

The Dame of Tintagel cracked open one eye. "Why yes, Udeme. I believe I did. But don't look at me to explain what all that means. I'm just a humble seeress."

Shawn brightened, flexing his fingers. "Well, looks like we've got more information than we expected to have. If we put our heads together, I'm convinced we can find the answers in no time. There's a reason fate has gathered us all here, ladies and gentlemen and nonbinaries. Let's not let her down."

"Is your dad always like this?" Zoe asked Loki.

"Why? How else is he supposed to be?"

"This is also why I need to find the Baba Yaga," Alex added, quieter so that only Tala could hear.

Another shimmering light from the looking glass, and Tala turned to look. The first to step out was a severe-looking man with a hooked nose and bushy eyebrows. He wore a uniform that had the crest of two scythes crossing against a field of white emblazoned on its front. A pretty woman with golden hair and a girl several years younger than Tala followed after him, the former assisting another older woman who looked to be in her late eighties. Cole had frozen at the sight of the older man, though he lost some of that stiffness upon seeing the women.

"Nicky!" the young girl sang out, racing toward him and throwing herself into his arms.

"Nicky?" Zoe asked, eyebrow raised and trying to hide a grin.

Of course. This was Cole's family. There was severe scarring on the right side of William Nottingham's face. The pretty woman—Tala could only presume that this was Lady Sarah Nottingham, Cole's mother—had scars too, though they were fainter and not as deep as her father's. There were no marks on the younger girl's face that she could see.

"Udeme," the old woman Lady Nottingham was assisting called out. She could be no one else but the Dowager Nottingham, Cole's great-grandmother. "Elspen."

"Anastacia," the priestess said. "It's been a while."

The dowager moved toward the other two seeresses, reaching out to grip both their arms.

A sudden wave of magic wrapped around them. No one else seemed to sense it but Tala and her mother; she nearly stumbled backward from the force.

"What?" Lumina asked. "What is going—"

"It comes." The low moan came from the Dowager Nottingham. "The fires come again. Burning. The kingdom is burning."

"A great kingdom will fall." This from the Dame. "When the sword rises from the stone shall the beginning of the end come. Winter arrives once more to these shores."

"A great kingdom will fall," Nya's grandmother echoed. "Before summit's end, that which was once thought lost shall be seen again."

"Only when the unending fires have been quenched shall we be saved," they chanted as one. "Only when the skies fill with the hope of Esopia shall we be saved. Only when that which cannot be cured is finally healed. Only when they return from World's End shall the true battle begin."

For a moment, all three stood, arms still locked together as if bound by some unspoken, horrific spell that only they could see.

And then, again as one, all three collapsed.

9

IN WHICH IT'S NOT TALA'S FAULT FOR EAVESDROPPING

And this is why," the Beast of Suddene said mournfully, "we don't invite visitors to the castle."

To his credit, the young duke had been quick to act, ordering his castle enchantments to prepare three separate bedrooms for the seeresses to recuperate in, and in ten minutes, all were clean enough to house royalty. If their parents had initially been reluctant about Buyan, they were all in at this point. The dooms the three old women had just prophesied had been pretty convincing. They had definitely convinced Tala.

"You think they can tell us what all that actually means?" Ken asked nervously. He had stayed on the sidelines, watching the adults shuffle in and out of the rooms as they checked on all three women, but lingered close to the priestess's bedroom, where Nya was currently tending to her grandmother. The firebird was flying back and forth, making a show of trying to help but in what Tala suspected was only a bid to get attention.

"Probably not. If you're worried about Nya, you could just go inside."

Ken scowled. "I can't. I mean, I'm worried, but..." His voice trailed off. "My doom scared the hell out of me the first time I heard it. That hasn't stopped as I got older. She knew that. She was the sea creature in my prophecy, and she never said a word. She could have eased my fears at the outset, but she didn't. If she's the girl I'm supposed to marry"—and here he paused, looking both giddy and terrified at the thought—"then why didn't she just tell me if we were gonna be in this together?"

"Well," Tala said carefully. "When we first met her, she was willing to do anything to get away from her marriage, even if it meant getting into the thick of the frost and helping us retake Maidenkeep. Her fears may not be as phobia-specific as yours is, but that doesn't mean they're not valid either. Just because she likes you doesn't mean she's not afraid of her doom coming true."

"You're saying she's worried about me? Because she doesn't want me to die like her prophecy implies?"

"Wouldn't you be?" Tala had promised herself she wasn't going to get involved, that Ken and Nya were just gonna have to work out—well, whatever else they had up their butts. The sight of Zoe marching toward Dowager Nottingham's room, armed with a pile of hot towels and a tea tray, spurred her into action, and Ken was quick to follow.

"Thanks," Zoe said after they'd relieved her of the towels. "They're all doing fine now, but Nottingham's still worried."

"How can you tell?" Tala asked, but they were already entering the room. Lady Anastacia Nottingham was propped against a stack of pillows, wide awake and looking rejuvenated. William Nottingham was elsewhere, probably talking to Tala's mother and the other parents, but Cole's mother was there with him, and so was his sister, Adelaide, who smiled shyly at them as they entered.

"Nottingha—Cole said you like Darjeeling tea," Zoe said brightly.

"That's very nice of you, my dear." The dowager wasn't as intimidating as Nya's grandmother, nor was she as vague as the Dame of Tintagel. She was what Tala expected great-grandmothers to look like, with a peaches and cream complexion and bright blue eyes. She didn't look like a seeress either, or even capable of giving birth to someone as imposing as William Nottingham. "Cole's told me a lot about you."

Cole, who had been standing near a window, managed to look faintly alarmed.

"And you are Tala Makiling Warnock, are you not? And Kensington Inoue." The old lady accepted the cup and breathed in the aroma. "Oh. Just like what my own mother used to make for me."

And then she said, like it was the most natural thing in the world, "The consort's child and the corpse-husband."

Ken was far too keyed up to take that calmly; he was already on his feet, trying to run to the door without looking like he was. "I think I should, um, check on the others. I'll catch you guys later." He was out the door before anyone could get another word in edgewise.

"Grandmother." Lady Sarah Nottingham was a lovely woman, and her voice sounded reproving. "You know better than to scare them like that."

The old woman let out an actual giggle. "He's going to have to accept it sooner or later. Sooner, preferably. There's a lot riding on his young shoulders. But you, Lady Warnock—I *cannot* see your destiny. A black cloud hangs about you like a fog, preventing me from looking too clearly. It would require someone stronger than me to read your fate. And you, Lady Carlisle..."

Zoe's head snapped up, the surprised look on her face giving way to pleasure at being referred to by *Carlisle*. It didn't last long, though.

"You will take the shire over the gest and the chaff over the grain. They will laugh at your foolhardiness. But it is you who shall laugh long and loud, for in the end, the dead shall rise for you. You shall lose your tears and you shall lose your way and you shall lose your heart, but if you will learn to trust outside yourself, then the dead shall rise."

Zoe froze. Cole had stepped away from the window, toward the bed. "Great-Grandma," he warned.

"I am sorry. But that is your doom, is it not, Lady Carlisle? I know it has always unsettled you, but I do not mean to say it out of spite."

"I'm sure you don't," Zoe said, sounding a little shaky. "Excuse me. I need to serve tea to the other seeresses first." She turned and strode briskly out of the room. Cole immediately took off after her.

"Oh no," the dowager sighed after Zoe made her hasty exit. "I made a muck of it again, didn't I? I'd hoped I could talk to her about this. My husband always did say I could be rather blunt."

"She doesn't want to talk about it at all, Grandma," Lady Sarah reminded her. "Cole and I discussed this with you."

"But we have very little time, my dear girl. She must come to terms with what the fates have decided, or we will not have much of a future. If she runs away from the words, then she will not be strong enough to withstand the reality when it comes."

"So *she's* Zoe," Adelaide said, sounding awed for some reason. "But you really were rude, Great-Grandma. Almost like how Grandpa would have said it. She was rude, wasn't she, Lady Makiling Warnock?"

"I will have to hand out more towels to the others as well," Tala said diplomatically. She didn't exactly understand what was going on with the Nottinghams or why the dowager was so interested in Zoe, but with the exception of their patriarch, the family did not live up to their dark reputations. She'd taken a liking to them instantly, Anastacia's frankness notwithstanding.

The adults were still busy, and Tala didn't want to interrupt them. All the other seeresses were being well taken care of, so she took the opportunity to explore the place instead. Villeneuve Castle was as stark and as featureless as Tintagel Castle, though unlike the latter, the previous lords here had not turned down modern spelltech, even if they were a dozen years obsolete. There were a few television sets, and the kitchen even had toasters and refrigerators. Most of the rooms were dusty and unaired, though, and Tala was prepared to return when the last one at the end of a row of corridors attracted her attention.

The room itself was bare; only a large mirror adorned one wall, and it was practically sparkling with magic. Tala had very bad luck with mirrors in unfamiliar castles, and the only reason she had let curiosity override self-preservation was because the Nameless Sword had already been found and was not likely to appear before her again like it had at Lord Tintagel's castle.

It was only when she'd drawn nearer that she spotted several rings hammered into the wall beside the mirror, resembling tiny door knockers. The spells contained in them tasted like both lychee and the rosé wine Tala had secretly tried when her mother had left a glass lying about when she was eleven.

Tala didn't exactly disrupt the magic when she reached out to touch one of the doorknockers. But she jerked back when the mirror hummed, the reflection switching abruptly to static before reforming again.

"I don't like it, Your Majesty," her mother's unhappy voice said from the glass. Instead of her reflection, Tala could now see her mother and Alex standing outside the door to the priestess Umede's room. There must be another mirror mounted near there, serving as a conduit. Neither noticed her. "I know you're obliged to welcome them, but my mother is not the type to offer her assistance without expecting something in return."

"We can't turn away any kind of assistance at this point," Alex said wearily. "The rajas of the Philippines have always been allies of Avalon, and it would offend them if I withdrew my invitation for them to stay. I'll do my best to keep them out of your hair. They're patrolling with the Fianna anyway, finding the weaker spots in Avalon that might be exploited."

"No, don't give me any special favors. This is between me and my mother, and I don't want to add to your problems." Lumina sighed. "Urduja will not be happy to hear this. She despises my mother."

Tentatively, Tala reached for another knocker.

The mirror's image changed abruptly; now it was of Loki and their fathers. "I'm sorry." The ranger recruit sounded so downcast, and Tala's heart went out to them. "First Mykonos's reprimand and then breaking the staff. I don't know if I can protect Alex if I keep making a mess out of this."

"Ruyi Jingu Bang protected you, as it was supposed to. You are far more irreplaceable than it is," Shawn consoled him.

"Mykonos is right, though," Anthony grunted. "What possessed you to venture out into the Tangled Woods on your own? I thought your time in the Order of the Bandersnatch would have improved your teamwork."

"Now's not the time to scold them about this, dear," Shawn remonstrated.

"This is exactly the time, because I'd rather they not make this same mistake again. Mykonos isn't known for his leniency, but he gave you a pass on this one, and I would hate to think it was out of deference to me."

Loki hung their head. "I know. When I heard the scream, I just ran without thinking."

"And then it turned out to be someone from OzCorp, of all people." Shawn sighed. "You can't put yourself in danger like that, Loki."

"I know. Sorry."

Anthony wrapped Loki up in a hug. "I know it was rough in Avalon during those six months. I can't begin to think about the strength it took to survive that with your friends, and I'm proud of you. I'm sorry we couldn't look out for you then, but I want you to remember that you can count on us *now*."

"Thanks, Dad." Loki's eyes were watering slightly. Hastily, Tala tried another knocker, hoping to find a way to close the damn thing.

She found Zoe and Cole instead. "You don't have anything to apologize for," the girl said, sounding irritable. "I'm just not very comfortable when it comes to strangers talking about me like they know who I am is all. Is your great-grandma always like this?"

"Yes," the boy admitted. "I asked her not to say anything, but sometimes she thinks she knows best—"

"Asked her not to say anything?" Zoe folded her arms. "Don't pretend like you know me either! You're the one who never wants to talk about your family or your past! You don't get to act like you know anything about me when you've never been able to meet me halfway! We've spent a lot of time together these last few months, and I still don't know anything about you!"

"Zo—"

She tried to push past him, but he was blocking the way. Angry, she shoved at his chest, but he grabbed her hands and refused to budge. "What do you want to know about me?" he asked.

Zoe looked up at him. Cole looked down at her. Her expression flickered from angry to suddenly unsure, an unexpected blush on her cheeks. His face changed too, from closed off to suddenly resolute.

It was when Cole bent his head lower and Zoe lifted hers up to meet him that Tala realized she was absolutely *not* supposed to be watching this and began tugging frantically at the metal rings again.

The mirror flickered again. This time, she saw the firebird perched on one of the castle's open windows, staring moodily out into the sky. It was warbling sadly to itself, and it took another minute for Tala to realize it was actually *crying*.

As if sensing it was being watched, the firebird's head snapped in her direction. With an angry screech, it leaped and slammed into the surface.

Tala jumped back, grabbing onto another knocker as she did. The firebird's angry face changed, and now it was her father, standing in a slightly darkened room. He was looking at a mirror as well, but not at the one Tala had been using to inadvertently eavesdrop.

"Are you this desperate, Anneliese?" he asked heavily, using the name the Snow Queen had presented to the world. "You've been tracking all the unsecured channels into Avalon all this time, hoping to find me?"

Tala's blood ran cold, just as she spotted the image of the Snow Queen illuminated inside the reflected surface. "I was successful, wasn't I?" She didn't sound like the intimidating, angry queen who Tala had always encountered in the past. Now she sounded quiet and sad. "You shouldn't be worried. I still cannot overcome the wards the Tsarevich boy had woven around his kingdom, but I can, at least, finally talk to you again. Kay…"

"What will it take for you to end this war? Everyone who's ever hurt us has been dead for centuries. You're fighting nothing but the dead and gone."

"I still fight their descendants, Kay. For as long as their bloodlines contaminate this world, I cannot stop. Arthur and Merlin betrayed us, my love. I will not stand to have them celebrated as heroes."

"Alex is neither. He is innocent in this."

"Why do you care for them this much? You know they only use you."

"It's called friendship, Anneliese. I am afraid you have been so long without that, you no longer recognize it if it stares back into your face."

"You're right, Kay. It's been so long since I've had anyone I could call a friend. You were the first friend I ever had, after Father died. Don't you remember? You used to visit me, sing songs underneath my tower. You would take me rowing across the Hintersee, long before any other human discovered it. We had the lake to ourselves for years. We would spend nights there, just us and the moon. You told me you loved me for the first time there."

"I remember," her father said quietly.

"You knew I spoke the truth about Merlin. They left you to die at Camlann because of it. Why would you take their side now, after we were together for so long? Did you finally tire of me?"

"Arthur was guilty, but his descendants are not. I loved you, but you were willing to burn down the rest of the world to get to them. I waited for as long as I could, hoping you would see reason, but in the end, I couldn't stay. Not even I could change your mind."

"What will it take to end *this* then, Kay? Come with me. Promise to remain by my side, and I swear I will put an end to my war with Avalon."

Kay froze. *He's considering it,* Tala thought, horrified. *He's actually considering it.*

"It's too late for us, Anneliese," he finally said.

"There are others who seek to harm Avalon, my love," the Snow Queen said mournfully. "What if I promised to help the Tsarevich boy? What if I swore to take down his enemies? Will you change your mind then, and come with me?"

Her father hesitated again.

"You will," the Snow Queen said joyfully. "You will, won't you?"

"What are you planning, Anneliese?"

"It would not be a surprise if I told you." The Snow Queen leaned forward and pressed her lips against her side of the mirror. "We will talk again, my Kay. And I will prove my love for you when next we meet, beyond all doubt."

Her image faded. Kay continued to stare at his reflection for several seconds more, and Tala watched him, heart pounding.

"Did they get rid of all privacy laws in the rest of the world during the years that Avalon was under siege?"

Tala spun, flushed. The Beast of Suddene was standing behind her, arms folded and with the smug air of someone threatening to tattle.

"I wasn't intending to overhear!" she spluttered.

"Sure," said the Beast of Suddene. "But now that you did, you couldn't look away. Sir Kay is your father, right? The Scourge of Buyan?"

"Don't call him that!"

"Kinda hypocritical to say that and still think he might possibly be cheating on your mom with the Snow Queen, right?"

Tala felt her whole face turn beet red.

"Look, I don't even want to know. I *will* be asking your techmages to reinforce the obviously outdated communication ports within the castle. If you've got a beef with your dad, I'm not gonna meddle. That's always been the Charming motto: *non sumus snitches*. Ironically enough, I'm here because your father sent me. He said he wants you to meet someone. Thinks it'll help you understand him better."

"Who?"

The duke's massive paw reached past Tala and settled on one of the knockers. Her father faded from view.

"A ghost," he said.

126

10

IN WHICH TALA WATCHES A HIGHLIGHTS REEL OF HER FATHER'S PAST

Tala's mother and Alex were now both on the couch, the former idly flipping through channels on a large-screen television on the wall when Tala and the beast arrived. The firebird was already atop Alex's head and gave no indication that it knew it was Tala who'd been eavesdropping on it.

"The pirates?" her mother asked, pausing at an Avalon news channel that showed a large ship idling at what appeared to be an Albion port, a skull-and-crossbones flag flapping at its mast. The Pirate Republic of Neverland Docks at Lyonesse, the headlines read. "Are you serious, Alex? You're opening your doors to the Neverland pirates?"

"They've always been Avalon allies, Auntie—after Hook died and they elected someone actually competent to lead them anyway—and we could use more friends around. And they're a humanitarian organization. Have I ever told you guys about the time they smuggled me out of Luxembourg?"

"I'm not against them, per se. But I am against having to host that terrible spelltech ship they like to sail in on."

"I think they're all right. Anthony Sun-Wagner vouches for their leader, Captain Mairead."

"I hope so. That's a horrifying weapon to have within our borders. There you are, Tala. The seeresses are doing well. Let's go meet your father at the castle's recreation room."

"This castle doesn't look like it's got a recreation room," Tala said. True to his word, the Duke of Suddene had made no mention of her spying on her father, but that didn't alleviate her guilt. She was anxious for her mother. Did she know? Would her father tell her? *Was* this cheating?

"My father had a one-track mind. Money was no object when it came to installing anything that would help advance his research. He didn't think much about buying things for comfort or fun for himself, much less for his family."

"I'm sorry."

"Yeah. But thanks for the concern. I'm considering constructing a swimming pool in the backyard as a giant middle finger to his memory, once I've solved the logistics of fur and drains. Shall we?"

"What do you know about the opticron?" Alex asked Tala as they followed the beast and Lumina down a long, carpeted hallway where small gargoyle-like creatures sculpted from stone glared down as they passed.

"Not much, actually."

"The Lord of Suddene's ancestors invented it in the late 1600s, toward the end of the Final Renaissance period, though they were pretty secretive about it till the early 1800s. The Charmings have served as videographers as well as historians over the centuries."

"I intend to turn over most of my collection to the national museum that His Majesty intends to build," the beast rumbled. "Excluding some footage that, I believe, is a little too personal for public consumption."

Tala's mother stopped in midstride, and Tala nearly crashed into her. "Is that what my husband is doing, Lord Charming?" Lumina asked softly. "I suspected it when he asked for some privacy, but I wasn't sure."

"Call me Aidan, ma'am." The beast inclined his shaggy head. "Over the course of several millennia, my forefathers and foremothers have captured moments on film that your husband experienced firsthand. It is not unusual to want to be left alone with your past at times, to remember."

The recreation room was pitch-dark when they entered, the only source of light an oval automaton that resembled a cross between a projector and a UFO. A heavy tarp covered a spot on the wall where the mirror her father had used to talk to the Snow Queen had been, and Tala could feel her nerves fraying all over again.

The device hovered in the air, its lens trained on a wall where a video was playing. Tala saw the tall figure of her father behind the opticron, silent, unable to tear his eyes away from the scene before him.

It was a video of a man, handsome but stern-looking, with an ascetic, military air only bolstered by his smart haircut and neatly pressed uniform. "A mechanical device that could capture my voice and my movements for posterity," he was saying. "What will the Avalonians think of next, Warnock? Perhaps they can one day transport my physical body through one of these little oddities with no one the wiser, yank me out through it to wherever you are."

He paused. His eyes contradicted the rest of his appearance; they looked soft, creased at the corners, and kind. "But I can't leave this place even if I wanted to, Kay," he said. "Too many are counting on me. And I'll be damned if I leave them to die alone."

Tala's father reached for the whirring opticron, stopped the video. "About time you got here," he grunted, voice rougher than usual.

"Kay," her mother sighed.

"S'all right, Lumina. Did me a little good." Kay smiled tentatively at Tala.

She forced herself to smile back. "His Grace said you wanted to show me something?"

"Yeah. You and the king too. Got it loaded up." He stopped, suddenly self-conscious. "Er. Feel like I ought tae tell ye that I'm in this one. No wrongdoing or anything like that. Just that it might surprise ye a wee bit."

"I've seen videos of you doing karaoke. I can't be any more trauma-tized than that." *Any more than already knowing you're almost a thousand years old*, she wanted to add but didn't.

"Here we go," the beast said after they'd found chairs to sit, and he pushed down on a button.

The video shifted to a young, startlingly beautiful woman. Her skin was as dark as Tala's and her mother's, and there was something famil-iar about her dark eyes and the slant of her nose, the stubborn chin and ringlets of dark hair, even the way she cocked her head to one side, like Lumina sometimes did.

The woman began speaking rapidly in a language that Tala didn't understand but that sounded at certain words and phrases like Tagalog. The beast adjusted something on the opticron, and subtitles popped up below the video. "...afraid we have no time," the woman said. "We have no choice. In another hour, the Americans will break through our bar-riers, and we will be overcome. We are too few and they are too many. These are my final orders. You are to take these spellstones that we have saved"—she gestured behind her, where other warriors stood with heavy sacks thrown across their backs—"and bring them to Avalon. Queen Fa Tien will know what to do, and she will grant you all sanctuary. One way or another, we will save this village and everything it stands for."

"No, Maria." Another man stepped in to view, and the woman turned to confront him. He was white, perhaps in his very early twenties, and handsome. He wore the same brown breeches that the others wore and was bare chested like them as well. "You can't do this," he said, his strong accent making it obvious that the language he spoke wasn't native to him. "*You* need to flee with the others. Once the Americans realize you're gone, they'll pull back."

Maria laughed. "You know that isn't true, Kay," she said, and Tala's jaw dropped. "They say they're after my head, but what they want is our mines. We have taken every stone we possibly can from it, but I am the only one who knows how to destroy it completely. We are a small village. There is nothing else of strategic importance here. You've fought in battles all your life, sir. You know what I say is true. If they know it is destroyed, they will not risk their lives any further. And so it must be, come what may."

"You'll lose your magic," the younger Kay choked. "You could die."

"A life sacrificed for another day of the republic to live. I accept those terms. My mind is made up, and you know nothing will change it. I protected it from the Spaniards, and I will protect it from the Americans. I place my people in your hands and at Avalon's mercy."

The young Kay's shoulders drooped. "I don't deserve much of Avalon's mercy, Maria. But I'll fight to make sure you've got theirs."

"Go, friend. And may Bathala go with you. Mabuhay ang rebolusyon! Mabuhay ang tribo!"

The video ended. Tala's hands remained clasped against her mouth.

"It's one of the few films anyone's got of Maria Makiling," Kay said quietly. "She thought the opticron was an expensive piece of junk, that carrying it around would make us look more suspicious to the Americans. Practical lady, even till the end."

"We sent a copy to the Philippines a few decades ago," Aidan Charming said. "To the Makiling clan. Thought they would welcome it. They didn't."

"Because they think Kay was responsible for Maria's death," Tala's mother murmured.

And more than that, because her mother had married Kay. It explained why she was estranged from Lola Corazon and the other Makilings.

"It's always been complicated," her father said. "They thought I should have destroyed the mine, not leave her to do it. Or that I should have forcibly dragged her back to Avalon. Sometimes I still think that's what I should have done."

"Maria saved us," Lumina said. "Imagine what could have happened if the foreigners had gotten their hands on that mine. Imagine what the Japanese army would have done years later, had they gained access to that."

Tala stared down at her hands. So many choices, she thought. So many decisions she had no say over, yet she was here, dealing with their repercussions all the same.

But was she any better? She'd rejected the Nameless Sword…

"But doesn't this weird you out, Mom?" she asked, trying not to think about it. "Watching Dad talk and work with an ancestor of ours who'd lived over a hundred years ago…and then marrying him?"

Her mother chuckled. "I was well into my twenties when I first met your father, and I knew of his work with Avalon, years before that. My only mistake was not telling you sooner about him, and for that, I will always be sorry."

But would I have done the same? Tala wondered. *Would I have gotten used to him if I'd known earlier about everything he'd done before he married Mom?* Her mother hadn't done anything wrong by loving someone who Tala knew sincerely wanted to change. The decision had worked for her.

But she wasn't her mother.

Her father was right. It was complicated.

"Lord Charming," Alex said. "Would you mind if I watched the Wonderland footage you said you had?"

"But of course." The beast loaded up the next video. The firebird approached the screen, its beak practically nudging at the wall it was displayed on.

It was a short video, no more than fifteen, twenty seconds. Tala watched a large mushroom-like cloud bloom over the horizon, similar in appearance to a nuclear detonation.

"That's when the firebird went missing," Lord Charming said. "It was at the center of Wonderland when the explosion happened. Glad to see you're doing well, little one."

The firebird said nothing. It continued to gaze at the screen long after the video was over. It cooed sadly.

"I don't know how it even survived. Wonderland had its share of powerful creatures far from that epicenter, and even they didn't make it."

The firebird laid its head on an armchair, looking guilty.

"That's all you have?" Alex asked.

"Unfortunately so. It's still sparking debates among historians, figuring out what really happened. Weren't you there, Sir Warnock?"

"Not at the thick of it, no."

"Mother told me that the Mad Queen Elizabeth blew up Wonderland trying to open a portal to Buyan," Alex said. "The riddle you told us triggered that memory... I was hoping there would be more information."

"I'm sorry, Your Majesty. I can only offer theories. We've always had little to go on regarding Wonderland's demise."

Her father turned back toward the opticron. Another video started up, and it was the same one of the stern-looking man as before.

"Kay," her mother said, surprised.

"It's all right. I want them to see this."

"And I'll be damned if I leave them to die alone," the man continued. "You know it's hopeless. I know it's hopeless. But I won't leave. I can't leave." He paused, closed his eyes, and took in a long breath. "I think you'll find this after I'm dead," he said, so very calmly, "if they don't destroy it first. I can hear them calling for my blood outside. Would have enjoyed one last adventure with you, eh? On days like this, all I think about is what would have happened if I'd taken you up on your offer, gone into hiding with you. We could have been…happy, maybe. But then that weakness passes. You know me. In two months, I'd be itching for something new to fight, and you'll get drawn into my mess all over again. I told you I'd die before I'd let them blacken your name any further. Well, old chap, looks like I'll be keeping my end of the bargain."

There was a series of loud bangs against wood. The man stood, straightened his collar. "And now if you'll excuse me," he said, "there's someone at the door."

The video ended.

"He died there, in Khartoum," Kay said, a catch to his voice. "He was the maddest bloke I'd ever met. We were enemies first. He was working for the Belgian king then, and I was a…free agent. Wound up resigning his position and fighting the Congo's Force Publique harder than I did. I couldn't get to him in time. Couldn't even find his…"

The firebird hopped toward him, cooed sadly.

"Aye. You were right in the thick of it too, weren't you? You and Queen Caroline, Gordie, and Pasha."

"Gordon," Alex repeated, and then he sat up straighter. "Charles Gordon. The hero of the Congo, former governor general of Sudan. The forty-fifth wielder of the Nameless Sword. He called it Pasha."

"Aye. One of your foremothers fought with him there. Avalon always had bad blood with Belgium. In the end, we took King

Leopold II out and avenged Gordie, but the worst in the Congo had already been done."

"If I remember my history right," Alex said, "King Leopold II died of natural causes."

Kay looked at him then, and an odd smile flickered on his lips; for a moment, it made him look like a stranger, more in keeping with the Scourge that so many people had said he was.

"Aye," he said. "Of natural causes." But then the look disappeared, and her father returned. "Tala…"

"I would like to take stock of the catalogs you have planned for the museum," Alex said calmly to the beast. "How many would your lordship be willing to part with?"

Lord Charming was quick to take the hint. "I've got lots of old footage of the Balkan Wars and at least one where your ancestress, Queen Talia, made the famous Hundreds speech to the soldiers. And then there's the treaty with the French in…"

His words faded as they made their exit, and Tala felt gratitude to Alex again, for allowing them privacy. "I know that you worked for Avalon after you left the Snow Queen," she said. "But in what capacity did you work for them exactly?"

"An unofficial one."

"You were an assassin."

"What choice did he have?" her mother pointed out quickly. "Other countries who would have gladly made use of him would have been just as bad as the Snow Queen. Only Avalon was willing to work with your father, but even they could not claim him publicly. It was his way of making amends. He could not—" She broke off. "I'm doing it again, aren't I?"

"Mom?"

"Defending Kay, even when he didn't ask me to. Or want me to." Lumina looked down. "You're not the first person to ask this or to question just how much redemption your father deserves. It's become a habit of mine, to be a bit prickly on the subject."

"Your mum's got a soft heart for hard-luck cases," Kay said with a faint smile, taking her hand. "Even after I've gotten old and ugly."

Tala understood what they weren't saying. In a lot of ways, they'd both been alone and only had each other to fall back on. "I'm sorry I'm asking too many questions."

"No," her mother said. "This time, we *want* you to ask."

"I was good at it," Kay said quietly. "And for a while, it made me feel like I might even be able to make up for some of the things I'd done in the past. But then we lost Gordie, and I started to wonder if I was worth all this. He'd refused to give me up to his British masters. That was one of the reasons they pulled back reinforcements, and it led to his murder. Leopold's death wouldn't bring back Gordie and the millions of Congolese, but I thought it would be easier, knowing the bastard wouldn't be sleeping warm and safe in his royal bed either. But it didn't give me the satisfaction I thought I would have felt. And then I started wondering if killing them was just the same thing as what I'd been doing before that and if I had the right to decide if they deserved it."

Tala looked down at her parents' clasped hands. She almost didn't ask the question, but her mother's gaze was reassuring, as if she already knew. "Were you and he…"

"Lovers?" Kay chuckled, though the laughter sounded forced. "No. Not in any physical sense. You can imagine that that sort of thing was frowned upon then, and Gordie was too…religious, I'd say. Harder on himself than he was on anyone else. He was the bravest man I'd ever met, but even he was afraid. Afraid that he was growing old and that I wasn't.

Afraid he wouldn't make that much of a difference before his time came."
He reached out with his free hand and laid it gently on Tala's, questioning. After a moment, Tala turned her palm upward, linking her fingers through his, then did the same to her mother's with her other hand.

"Uncle Kay! Aunt Lumina!" Alex burst back into the room, looking harried. "I have to leave!"

Kay rose, startled. "What is it? Another attack?"

"Not on us. There's been a breach at one of Texas's detention facilities."

Tala's eyes widened. "How many children did he take this time?"

"He?" Lumina echoed. "Tala, how do you know—"

"He didn't," Alex broke in. "The border agents managed to trap him inside their camp somehow. And if we don't do something, they're going to catch him this time."

11

IN WHICH PIRATES MAKE EVERYTHING BETTER

Y ou need to let me go after him," Tala panted, running to keep pace with Alex as they strode into the Hollows, West, Loki, Ken, and Nya at their heels. Zoe and Cole were already inside, in the middle of an argument as always. Dex was already fiddling with the controls of the Red King, the coordinates logged in and the location "Southern Front Texas facility" displayed beside the system's parameters.

"It's too dangerous," Alex said, scowling.

"You don't know how many more traps there are inside it," Tala said. "I can negate most of the spells in there. I'm the best chance at getting him out."

"And I think you could use some backup," Zoe offered mildly. "We're all already here. But why are we going through this trouble for someone working for the Beiran queen?"

"Do you want to help or not?" Alex demanded crabbily.

Zoe sighed. "We would like to, Your Majesty."

"Dex, patch us through to Maidenkeep control."

"Done, Your Majesty."

"Good. Put me through to Severon. See if anyone can scan the facility and see the defense spells they've got installed in there."

"So this is what you've been busy with, Tala?" Tala's parents had followed them into the Hollows, her mother not looking amused at all. "Alex, you said that they were doing social outreach programs for NGOs."

"They're still doing that. Technically speaking."

"I'm not going to let you bring Tala in there without—"

"Mom!" Tala burst out. "I can do this!"

"What I was going to say was that I'm not going to let you in there without me. Two agimat should be more than enough to dispel their spelltech."

Tala looked at her father, who had somehow snagged a chocolate malt beverage from one of the twin titas at the café en route. "Listen to your mother" was all he said, with a loud slurp.

"You're not coming, Sir Warnock?" Zoe asked.

"Not the best idea, as I'm wanted in several dozen countries, and those numbers are climbing."

"New face scramblers," Zoe ordered sharply, tossing Tala that and a couple of small packets. "It'll throw up a screen connected to mission control."

"And those are my recipes for temporary invisibility," Nya said. "They work better than what the Fianna's got."

"We've got a basic layout of the place, and we've detected the areas with high concentrations of body heat, which I'm assuming is where they're imprisoning the refugees," Zoe continued. "Loki, take the lead. West, follow after him. Would be good if you shift now instead of later."

"Yes, ma'am," West said and promptly shifted into his familiar blood-hound shape.

"Based on what we've seen, their spell dampeners are configured toward individuals and smaller groups instead of over a wider area," Cole continued briskly, to Tala's surprise. "Seems like the agents aren't used to heavy resistance within their own compound, so any security measures in place are usually to reinforce the barriers outside. Lady Makiling Warnock and Tala should concentrate on taking down as much of the spelltech as possible. The rest of us should take care of the refugees."

"How long have you been studying this place?" Zoe asked, one eyebrow raised.

"Noticed you watching it the last few days. You said there were higher levels of activity there than in others, and this proves you right. Just figured I'd come prepared."

Their gazes met. Then Zoe turned away, reddening slightly. "They may have added more spelltech in anticipation of capturing Cadfael," she said. "But I'm guessing it'll only be concentrated at wherever it is they have him hostage."

"Dad's sending me a more updated layout of the facility," Dex reported.

"Kay and I can help guide you through it," Alex said, handing Tala an earpiece that she hurriedly put on. "Their bathrooms look like the best place to port you in. They've got the least security, and we can override it." He pointed at a screen where the map to the place had already been laid out. "You're going to travel along this corridor and down these stairs. The highest concentration of heat energy is here. That said, ICE still outnumbers you."

"That's never been a problem before," Ken said bleakly.

"We're bringing enough spells to make up the difference," Zoe promised. "As long as Tala and Mrs. Warnock can deactivate the tech."

"All right." Alex turned to the looking glass, where a portal was now forming. "Good luck, and don't get caught."

There was only one person using the toilets in the men's room when they popped into view. The man turned with a yelp, his pants still down, but it only took one hard punch from Cole to silence him completely. Lumina caught the falling man and dragged him into an empty cubicle. "Keep us moving, Your Majesty," she said, and a floor plan flickered into Tala's vision.

"I'm highlighting the area where we think they're fighting Ryker," Alex replied.

Following Zoe's lead, Tala tore open the packet the girl had given her, and a thick lavender scent assailed her nostrils almost immediately. The world turned hazy, darkened for a couple of seconds, then returned to normal. Tala stared at the mirror across from them, which reflected no one else in the room but the unconscious agent. "Cool," she said.

"So," Tala's mother murmured as they filed down an empty passage, trying to be as quiet as they could. "Alex called him Ryker. That's the name of the boy who ambushed us in the desert."

"This isn't the time, Mom," Tala muttered. Loki, who she assumed was still in the lead, uttered a terse "Stop!" from in front of them, seconds before several ICE agents raced down the hallway. The cops stopped before a sealed door, the leader hastily inputting a code to allow them inside.

Once the doors slid shut behind the men, Lumina narrowed her eyes at the entrance. There was an audible click, and it slid open easily. "I'm not sure you'll be willing to talk about it later. You didn't tell me he's been responsible for all these break-ins. He also seemed quite concerned for you all those months ago, despite everything."

"He nearly killed us, and you think he was *concerned*?"

"Am I wrong?"

"I promise we can talk about this after we get back. *Can* we talk about this *after* we get back?"

Her mother nodded thoughtfully, like she'd discovered something important. "Hmm."

A little annoyed, Tala directed her frustration at the electronic camera mounted on the ceiling. She forced her agimat down on it, caused it to overheat, and watched as it stopped recording.

"Looks like it's gonna be two doors ahead," Ken reported.

"We can detect large amount of heat patterns on both," Alex said. "Can't tell which one Ryker's behind."

"Throw the dice and make a guess," Kay's voice said. "Keep a couple of ye outside just in case ye'll need a quick getaway. Clear that room first, then move to the next if it ain't what you're looking for."

Tala had assumed that the barrier defenses blocking them from entering the room were state of the art and the best that could be bought, but between her and her mother's agimat, they may as well have been inferior replicas. The door opened. Tala heard Cole take a quick intake of breath. "Shit," he muttered. Then she heard Zoe gasp.

Tala saw why they were horrified the moment she stepped in. There were children, twenty or thirty all huddled in an enclosure that didn't seem large enough to accommodate them all, with nothing but metallic blankets for beds, the warmth spells in them barely detectable to Tala. A bucket in one corner served as their toilet and was already close to overflowing. Most of the children were far too young, six to eight years old at a guess, but it was hard to tell because they all looked frail and hungry. As they approached, a strong odor drifted toward them, and Tala realized that none of them had bathed in days.

Ryker wasn't here, but she knew they weren't leaving until *these* kids were safe.

Some of the children rose to their feet, but most remained where they were, watching them approach with fright. Tala looked down, saw the outlines of her hands coming back into view. The invisibility potion was wearing off.

"Oh my god." Zoe was horrified. "Oh my god."

"You've seen the news," Cole reminded her, though even his voice carried with it an angry snarl as he took in the state of their clothing, their obvious exhaustion.

"You still never get used to it. I don't want to get used to it." There was a snap. Zoe's Ogmios went flying, the whip snapping the locks off the cage with ease.

"You said we weren't supposed to bring our segen."

"I'm sure these kids won't tell anyone. Go guard the exit."

"Oh no." Nya was already by the cage entrance, offering her hand to the children, who shrunk back, unsure of how to respond. "We have to get them out of here. A few of them are in bad shape."

Tala curbed her own anger, focused on taking out every recording device in the room that she could find. ICE had relied far too heavily on spelltech, which worked to the Banders' advantage. Even their light fixtures were coated with heat magic that she could easily override. It raised the question of just how long ICE had been using magic while restrictions had been placed on civilians.

She clapped her hands twice, and the room plunged into darkness.

"Nice," Zoe said.

"Alex," Tala's mother said, her voice tight. "We've taken out every kind of spell we can find in this room. Is it possible for you to send a portal at these coordinates so we can take these poor children out of here?"

A murmur of voices as His Majesty and Tala's father conferred with each other, but it was Kay who finally spoke up. "Ten seconds. Any longer and they're gonna find it."

"We've disabled their spelltech. They probably already know. It's all right," Nya said comfortingly to the wary children. "We're going to take you away from this place, help you find your family."

"Trust her," Ken added, standing a little awkwardly beside the girl. Nya shot him a surprised glance. "We want to help."

"Te ayudaremos a encontrar a tu familia," Lumina said reassuringly. "Lo prometo."

The kids glanced at one another, then back at her.

"Lo juro," Cole added quietly.

One of the older kids stood up and walked toward Nya, accepting her hand. The rest followed her.

The portal winked into life before them. Dex was a genius; he'd adjusted the looking glass so that the more comfortable-looking beds in the room were in their direct line of sight, and that was all the motivation the kids needed. Many raced toward the portal without further prompting.

"Tala!" Alex's voice was loud in her ears, and she flinched. "Heat energy in the second area just tripled. But energy is up all over your floor too!"

"What?"

A screen blinked into view before her eyes. Dex had hacked into the ICE facility's video feed, and she saw a group storming through the corridors. She had no idea who they were. A tall woman with long, brown hair led the way, wielding a rapier. She was followed by an eclectic group of people: a balding man with suspenders and a bow tie that screamed accountant, a few teenagers with ripped jeans and punk haircuts, a drag queen in five-inch heels, even a monk in traditional Buddhist robes.

"Pirates!" Alex exclaimed in her ear. "The Neverlanders!"

She saw agents rushing out to confront them, only to be knocked off their feet without any of the Neverlanders even touching them. As she watched, the woman with the rapier gestured, and her shadow rose from the floor to quickly punch out one of the defenders before sinking back down to the ground.

"They're using their own shadows for weapons," she heard Alex mutter, impressed despite himself. "Pan did that a lot."

"More shots!" she heard Dex cry out. "They're all coming from the second room!"

No.

Tala took off, racing out of the room before her mother could yell at her to stop. She unlocked the doors leading to the second area with little trouble, enough fury and fear coursing through her that the security spell melted from the force she'd brought to bear on it. She shoved the doors open, discovered it led farther down another corridor, and wasted no time tearing through it, hoping she wasn't too late, feeling sick at the thought that she might be.

She stopped only to tear open the second packet of Nya's invisibility spell, then pushed her way through another set of doors.

And stopped when she saw the row of agents before her, *firing* into a cage of children, and her horrified screams were lost over the sounds of gunfire.

It took her another moment to discover that they weren't firing at the children but at Ryker, who was wearing his own face scrambler. The shield of ice he had created was riddled with countless bullets, though none had penetrated. The children behind him, mainly teenagers, were clinging to one another as they watched, horrified.

It looked like every agent in the vicinity was there, doing their best to empty their guns into Ryker, whose sudden stagger told Tala that he was rapidly weakening.

Tala did a quick sweep with her agimat; the guns weren't spelltech, but their ammunition was coated with high-impact magic. The smoky metallic taste was strong in her mouth, and she knew the spell made them deadlier, allowed for maximum spray for a likelier chance to hit their targets. So she directed her curse, along with her anger, into the nearest gun, trying to prevent it from going off.

Much to her surprise, it exploded.

It knocked at least half of the agents off their feet and rendered a quarter of them insensible. The rest started to turn, startled by the fresh threat behind them, only to find nobody standing there. Ryker took the opportunity to push his shield through the cage barriers. It shattered, sending sharp icicles hurtling toward the agents, and still more went down.

Tala had reached the cage amid the chaos. "Ryker," she panted.

The boy's head snapped toward her voice. "Tala? What are you doing here?"

"Rescuing you! What are you doing here?"

"Do you really need to ask that?"

"You got careless."

"I wasn't. They set a trap, and they were waiting for me." Ryker generated a fresh set of shields as the agents who could still fight began shooting again. Tala could hear their calls for backup and knew that wasn't a good sign. Her earpiece was dead, which meant there was still enough working spelltech in the room that was cutting off her communication to Alex.

"How were you expecting to get out of this?"

"I didn't have a clear idea until you showed up."

More yells from the agents, but suddenly Alex was back in her ear. "What do you think you're doing?" he yelled.

Tala watched as the guns in several agents' hands exploded, one after another, and knew her mother was in the room with her. "Did you get all the children?"

"Yes, and we retrieved the other Banders too. Your mother stayed to find you. Whatever possessed you to—"

"You told me you heard gunshots. I was expecting the worst. What did you think I was going to do?"

"Who are you talking to?" Ryker asked.

"Alex."

"Alex?" She couldn't see his expression but knew he was stunned. "He's helping you save me?"

"Tala!" Her mother's very angry voice sounded beside her, much closer and a lot more threatening than Alex's. "We are going to have a very long talk once we get back, anak." This was followed by several Tagalog epithets as Lumina directed her ire at the rest of the agents. More guns violently malfunctioned, and more screaming commenced.

"Ahoy, you fucking mateys!"

The pirates came bursting into the room. Agents attempting to stand kept getting knocked down again as the Neverlanders' shadows did their work.

"Alex," Tala said, "can you change our coordinates and port us somewhere that isn't in Avalon?" Alex might be helping them, but they both knew he couldn't let Ryker back into the kingdom, even unofficially.

"Got anyplace in mind?"

"I do, actually." She could see the outlines of her fingers again, saw her mother's silhouette taking shape beside her, even as she was taking out several agents at a time, even as more continued to pour into the room. Their face scramblers might hide their identities, but once ICE figured out they were using agimat, it would only be a matter of time before they deduced who they were. "You said the prototype could open portals into two different places at the same time. Is it possible to open one into Avalon for the other teens and the other wherever I specify?"

She could feel his glare through the earpiece. "I'm only giving you ten minutes alone with him before I'm personally intervening."

"Tala," her mother said.

"I promise I'll tell you everything. Just please give me this time."

Lumina glanced over at Ryker, who had stiffened once he'd recognized the older woman coming into view beside Tala.

"All right," her mother finally said. "But again, our turn to talk later."

"What's happening?" Ryker asked.

"We're getting out of here." Tala directed her focus upward, toward the light fixtures, and then clapped twice again.

In the ensuing darkness, Tala spotted the two portals forming inside the cage with them. One clearly led to the Hollows, and she could see Dex's worried face looking back out at them. "Hurry," Loki yelled from somewhere off-screen.

The teenage refugees needed no convincing. Lumina's mother guided them through the looking glass, casting a wary glance at Tala and Ryker, but said nothing. "I trust you," she said quietly.

Tala's eyes filled with tears. "Thank you."

Her mother let go, and they both jumped through their respective portals at the same time, with the pirates close behind.

***

"She recognized me," Ryker said. "Why didn't she attack me?"

"That's not the kind of person Mom is." Tala could still see the traces of the bonfire they'd had the last time she was at Elsmore High, though it had been over a year since then. Any evidence of the ice beasts that had interrupted the festivities were long gone, though.

"I thought you were bringing me to Avalon to arrest me."

"I'm sure the thought did cross Alex's mind."

"Then why didn't you?" Ryker looked out over the Arizona desert. "You have every right, and I wouldn't have been able to stop you."

"Young love is rough," the accountant-looking pirate said nostalgically, squatting down between the two. "Why, when I was your age, I fell in love with a beautiful girl who rejected me for a—"

"Look," Ryker interrupted, sounding strangely worried. "Can you, uh, give us a minute here?"

"You pirates were supposed to go through the other portal with my mother," Tala said, irritated that her attempt at a private talk was long gone.

"How were we supposed to know?" their leader asked. She was dressed more like she was about to hit a heavy metal concert than fight ICE agents. "But that's so very rude of us. We haven't been properly introduced, have we?" She stuck out her hand. "The name is Mairead Tattercloak, current leader of the Pirate Republic and captain of the *Jolly Roger*. These are my crew. The man with the bow tie is Langsworth, the girl with the big do is Seraphina, and these young'uns are Universe, Goblin, and Trevor."

"Tala." She accepted the captain's hand.

"Tala Makiling? The spellbreaker! What an unexpected pleasure!"

"You *know* me?"

"The Bandersnatchers who helped thaw Avalon? We were part of the search team looking for you and your friends!"

"I think it's right for Mr. Cadfael to be concerned, dear," said Seraphina. She'd fought in her heels and boa and now remained gracefully upright despite the uneven sand around them. "And of course we would follow after you two. We look out for our own."

"And what the hell does that mean?" Tala demanded. "How do you know Ryker's name?"

"Captain," Ryker said nervously, in a manner more subservient than Tala had ever known him to act. "I'd appreciate it if you can allow me the chance to explain it myse—"

"I think you've been hiding enough secrets from this young woman long enough, Sir Cadfael." Captain Mairead pointed to Ryker's wrist. Something glowed there, and Tala's mind only just registered it as a low-level camouflage spell so faint she didn't even pick up on it, just as the skull-and-crossbones tattoo inked there glittered to life. "We cannot keep this a secret from the Avalonians, dear, now that we have accepted their hospitality. Why did you think we came to the Texas facility in the first place? He was in danger." She held out her right arm, wrist turned outward, and her crew did the same, revealing identical tattoos. "The *Jolly Roger* calls on us to look out for our own, and he is one of us."

"What?" Tala screeched.

She hadn't needed to pull out her arnis sticks in the Texas camp. Now she drew them and closed the distance between her and Ryker.

"Wait!" the boy protested, scrambling back as she swung them at him.

"I don't believe you!" Tala shouted at him, showing no signs of stopping. "Is that how you're planning to get into Avalon? Alex had an agreement with the pirates that grants them entry into his kingdom, and *that's* how you're going to bring your Beiran army in, is it?" Alex had already given the pirates sanctuary. That gave Ryker access to the kingdom without needing Beiran spelltech. She felt betrayed.

"Do we intervene, Captain?" Langsworth asked.

"What do you think, Bankei?" Mairead asked the Buddhist monk.

The man looked thoughtful. "Let's give her a few more swings."

"I wanted to help you rescue refugees," Tala snapped, "but you've been plotting this whole time to go behind our backs and assault the—"

"No!" Her sticks collided with a shield he'd set up, though it shattered easily. Ryker was undeterred, creating more with every blow. "Mother— the Snow Queen—doesn't know that I'm with the pirates!"

"Then why join them in the first place? What did you have planned for that?"

"Not to use them to infiltrate Avalon! I've been with them for nearly two years! Long before I was even in Invierno!"

Tala paused at that, sticks still raised.

"He helped us save refugees on the verge of drowning along the Pacific," Captain Mairead confirmed. "Kept right on helping us after that. The *Jolly Roger* practically purred whenever it saw him. That's our spell-tech ship—a bit like your Nine Maidens, I'm told, though not quite as powerful. Doesn't suck out our life force either, since there are enough of us to share the load. That's our whole citizenship process—we offer membership if the *Jolly Roger* takes a liking to them. We were just as surprised as you are when it wanted him to join our roster."

"But he works for the Snow Queen!"

"As I've said, I don't decide who joins up. The ship does."

"But I've never seen that tattoo on him before."

Ryker turned red. "I had to hide it."

"Part of the agreement," Langsworth confirmed. "More than a few people out there who don't like us—can't imagine why—and we've had to keep it hidden a time or two."

"I never told Mother." Ryker hesitated. "We're not on good terms right now. She thinks I've been spending too much time with the asylum seekers and not enough time helping her seek revenge."

"And you have no other ulterior motive?"

He stared hard at her. Now that they'd turned their face scramblers off, he was just as handsome as she'd remembered, just as angry as when she'd seen him last. "What kind of question is that? I don't want you hurt.

Mother doesn't know I can get in. I swear." Ryker's eyes met hers. "I do want to protect you."

"I don't know if I should trust you," Tala said softly.

Ryker sighed. "I know I don't deserve that from either you or Alex."

"Alex's heart is a lot bigger than he lets on. Why do you want to protect me so badly?"

Ryker looked up at the sky. "Because right now," he said, "I need something I know is worth protecting. You saved my life today. You saved my life the last time too. Whatever faults I have, you of all people know that I always pay my debts. If you can't believe my affection for you, then at least believe that. I swear that whatever schemes Mother's involved in, I'm not a part of them. I just want to help those kids. Please."

"Your mother won't be happy."

"Mother doesn't need to know. I haven't even been back to Beira for months." He opened his eyes, took her hand. "It's not just the border, you know. Horrible things are happening to children elsewhere. Unsavory adoption agencies. Children being kidnapped from other countries. I have my hands full."

"And she isn't helping you?"

"She wanted me to stop. Said her goals were more important than a few children." He looked so sad and bitter and confused. "I don't understand. I was one of the unimportant children she'd been so adamant about saving before."

"Maybe that was just a ploy to sway you to her true cause?" Tala suggested, more gently now. He wasn't lying. He looked far too heartbroken for that.

Ryker stared at her. "You don't know her, Tala. She's not what everyone thinks she is. It's... I can't believe that. It's just that her priorities are different now."

"You can always join us."

"What?" Ryker looked like the thought had never crossed his mind before.

"You joined the Neverlanders. You can join Avalon too. Help us set up a network where we can do all this legally. Where you can save more kids on a national scale. You'll have more support that way, more resources."

Ryker looked at her like he wanted to say yes. "After everything I've done?" he asked. "You'd still welcome me in?"

"It's not too late."

"You have the biggest heart I've ever known in anyone." He looked away. "But I... It's complicated."

The sound of a materializing looking glass made them both draw back.

"I guess that's my cue." Ryker stepped back, turned away from her, and walked toward the desert. "Thank you, Tala. I owe you again."

"Wait!" Tala exclaimed. "Do you even know where you're going?"

A faint laugh was her answer. "I always do."

"Let him," Mairead said. "He's fond of disappearing like that."

Tala watched and waited until she could no longer see him against the sand. And it took a light tug from Alex, who was now standing beside her, before she finally turned away.

⁓

Tala and her parents sat on the veranda looking out at the great cedar tree that contained the Hollows. Her mother had chosen a sour plum tea, and her father was already on his second Milo dinosaur drink.

"Why is he still so committed to her?" Tala said, staring at her rock salt and cream cheese boba. "He knows the Snow Queen isn't being truthful with him. He knows the Snow Queen will destroy Avalon if she gets the chance."

"Because it doesn't sound like he's ever had stability," Kay supplied quietly. "And that's what the Snow Queen symbolizes for him. A parent who's never abandoned him, a home when all he's known is constantly being shuttled from place to place. The only reason he's even questioning his place with her right now is because of you."

"Me?"

"You didn't abandon him, either," her mother explained. "You keep saving him at great cost to yourself, and he can't completely understand why."

"And then there's the Snow Queen making contact with me today," her father said offhandedly.

Tala's mouth fell open. She wasn't sure if he would actually tell them. It wasn't like she really believed her dad would cheat on her mom, but now that he'd said it, she felt glad. "Oh."

"Told yer mom first chance I got. Suddene promised to overhaul their tech, update their spellware, make sure she doesn't get in again. A shame that Ryker doesn't know what she's cooking up."

"She must have been monitoring all ports in and out of Avalon if she could find Villeneuve Castle so quickly," her mother sighed. "Tala, it might take Ryker some time to realize that what the Snow Queen is promising him is a lie. But he's questioning it now. That's a good sign. And that the Neverlanders are looking out for him is even better. He's right at the cusp of figuring it out."

"How sure are you two about all this?"

Her parents looked at each other. "Sure. Because that's how I did it," Kay said simply and took a mighty slurp of his drink. "Though I'd say he won't be taking as long as I did."

12

IN WHICH ZOE BECOMES A COMMUNITY PLANNER

When Zoe decided that the best way to help people was to supply them with the necessary spelltech to fight back against their oppressors instead of carrying out dangerous solo missions on her own, she thought arming the refugees they'd saved at the Texas border with some nonlethal but very useful spelltech would be the extent of it. The unexpected benefit of the Avalon patents being stolen by numerous foreign corporations was the plausible deniability—who was to say that someone else hadn't supplied them with all this knowledge?

Except someone from the refugees must have said something, because she'd wound up receiving an email from the Water League, asking for help in distributing water rods to Ethiopia.

Alex had approved of the endeavor when she'd checked with him, and she'd sold the rods at the lowest price she could possibly give, just enough to pay for the raw materials and labor. This was for a good cause, she decided. This was fulfilling Alex's objective of using Avalon spelltech for good. Plus, she still had to go on three of Nottingham's own absurd missions as punishment for punching a rapist and trolling trophy hunters (which wasn't *fair*, really; she was doing society a favor), but doing this ensured she wouldn't have to go on more.

Thinking about Cole Nottingham brought more heat to her face.

She'd nearly *kissed* him. Stood on her tiptoes and nearly put her mouth on his, and the only reason she could think of for the lapse was because she was in a castle in the middle of nowhere and the lizard part of her brain that'd spent too much time watching sappy movies and reading love stories thought that was romantic. She must have swallowed more seawater than she'd realized.

What especially hurt was that he'd rejected her, and not the other way around. She'd been all too willing right until he'd turned pale, lifted his face away from hers, and said hoarsely, "No. I can't." And then he'd apologized and left, and Zoe was suddenly glad she couldn't muster any damn tears to spare.

This was fine. She'd acted aloof when she'd seen him again, and he was clearly just as willing to pretend that nothing had happened, which was great. She had a hundred other more important things to organize. She was in touch with a bazillion communities that deserved more of her time than Nottingham and his stupid face and his stupid mouth and his stupid life.

For instance, another nonprofit had reached out to her that day. They were Amazon rain forest watchdogs, so Zoe had sent them an introduction letter to the Swedish minister of technology, who had a hydrospell large enough for their purpose, and an invoice for the required parts they needed to fabricate. Three hours later, she was mediating between another organization and a law firm specializing in civil liberties for an Avalon patent that could hunt down trafficking rings with greater efficiency. And then she'd gone and had an excellent lunch with her father and mentally patted herself on the back for being awesome and unflappable.

A nagging part of her brain, probably the lizard part again, told her she was still dissatisfied. She'd done the best she could without actually getting physically involved, maintaining enough pretext so as not to land

Alex or Avalon in trouble. So why did she still feel frustrated, like she still needed to do more?

No. This was fine. *She* was fine. Not only was she doing good, she was also circumventing the ridiculous concessions Nottingham wanted to impose on her. She hadn't cried for nearly 130 days now. She didn't need tears. Helping other people was almost as cathartic. She was gonna be okay.

She maintained that sunny outlook right up until she received an email from Tristan Locksley.

His family had arrived a week or so ago, without her knowledge. She had no desire to meet him or his parents. But his father was Royal Britain's ambassador to Avalon, which meant she had no choice but to grit her teeth and bear his presence occasionally. What she really wanted to do was to tell him in person that things were officially over.

Unfortunately, as his email explained, that was no longer going to happen.

They met the next day. Tristan was prowling around the reception area that Maidenkeep had set aside for visitors. His bow segen, Robin, was slung over his back. He had a habit of carrying it everywhere, and Zoe had never been sure if it was because it gave him some sense of security or because he wanted to show it off.

Didn't matter. She'd promised Nottingham she'd go on whatever harebrained scheme he'd planned that day, and she didn't want to spend too long with her ex on top of that.

Wordlessly, she pointed to one of the empty rooms. He followed her, then waited until she'd closed the door behind them. "You didn't have to go through all this trouble," Zoe began bluntly. "You told me all I needed to know in your email."

"Zoe." Tristan didn't sound like his usual self. Tristan didn't even look like his usual self. His clothes were rumpled and unkempt, and there were dark circles underneath his eyes, like he hadn't been sleeping well. Which was all very strange, because Tristan liked looking perfect. Despite all that, he was still impossibly handsome.

"You all right?"

"I've been better," Tristan said gruffly, and it was only then that Zoe spotted the piece of paper he was holding, the gilded edges bristling with magic.

"Goddamnit, Tristan! I told you I'd do it! You didn't say we needed a contract!"

"I had to be sure." The boy sounded desperate. "You know how important this is to me."

"Yeah, I'm sure pretending that we're still together so you can hide the fact that you hooked up with the current king of Avalon is very important to you."

Tristan flinched. "It's not just about me. We can't cause another scandal. We've already gotten enough of that when Lance married Alyssa."

Ah, yes. His older brother, Lance. He'd married the heiress to the Bluebeard fortune despite the family's less-than-savory reputation and alleged connections to the Mafia. It didn't help that their patriarch was locked away in Belarus, facing execution. The newlyweds were no longer on speaking terms with their parents, and it seemed Valentina Locksley had placed all her hopes and ambitions on her younger son instead.

None of which, Zoe knew, involved Tristan coming out of the closet.

"The contract was written in your favor," Tristan said. "No one's gonna know. I know you agreed and I trust you not to tell, but I have to make sure, cover both our asses anyway. I can't let my parents down."

Zoe looked at him. That had always been the problem with Tristan, she supposed. He was a people pleaser. He wanted his parents' approval, and it didn't matter that he'd always been a doting son, a model student, a brilliant archer, and a worthy successor to Robin Hood's segen. It never seemed to be enough for them, but he kept trying all the same.

"Just give me the damn paper," she snapped.

"You'll sign it?" Tristan looked hopeful.

"I'm not doing this for you. I'm doing this to ensure Alex's safety." She glanced through the agreement. Tristan was right; this was written in her favor. No expectation on her end, absolution for any blame that may arise from their pseudo relationship while it lasted, leeway for her to break the contract at any time she wished after his parents left Avalon, an offer to compensate her for any financial expenses…all in exchange for pretending to be his girlfriend for the next two weeks while his family was here, while he was in close proximity to Alex. And she was to tell absolutely no one about it.

"You could have your pick of any girl back at Cerridwen to do this."

"They would never agree to pretending."

Zoe should have felt bitter, was surprised that she felt…nothing, really. Maybe she was just too stressed to be angry. "Lucky me, I guess."

"I'm sorry, Zoe." Tristan sounded genuinely earnest, and that somehow made things even worse. "I did…do care about you. Immeasurably. I didn't ask you out just because I was on the rebound, like you think. I thought we could be happy together."

No, Zoe thought. *You asked me out because you wanted to please your parents more than you wanted your own happiness.* She finished scribbling her name on the dotted line, watched it glow a bright red before settling back down into inky black.

"I hurt Alex, I know," Tristan said. "I wouldn't be surprised if he never wants to talk to me again. But I'm trying to protect him in my own way too. I don't want to get him in trouble, and I'm trying to take command of my own feelings for a change."

"No, you're not. You're still in denial." Zoe handed the paper back. "If you were really in control, you wouldn't have asked me to do this in the first place."

He nodded. "Be that as it may, you're still my girlfriend now."

The door swung open.

Zoe spun around just as Tristan did, the latter drawing his bow.

Nottingham didn't move away from the line of fire, only stared coldly back at his old rival. "They said you were here, Carlisle," he said evenly.

How much did he hear? His face gave nothing away. "We're just finishing up."

"You didn't tell me you were working with Nottingham," Tristan muttered.

"No, I didn't." Zoe started to move past him, but Tristan caught her hand.

"There's a party I'm supposed to attend tonight, at the Schaffers' manor," he began hesitantly. "I know it's sudden, and I know one of the stipulations is that I give you a heads-up, but…"

"I'll be there. That's what girlfriends are for, right?" She squeezed his hand before releasing it and striding off back toward the Hollows. "And shut up," she said over his shoulder.

"I didn't say anything." Nottingham said, and his voice was infuriatingly calm.

Nottingham must have visited here in the past, because he'd known to choose a secluded spot to port to. A couple of people picking up trash nearby watched them arrive, waved cheerfully, then returned to their work.

As it turned out, they weren't the only ones. The beach was full of volunteers collecting garbage and gathering up driftwood. "You brought me a quarter of the way around the world to clean up a beach?" Zoe asked.

"Not quite as glamorous as fighting fire in the Amazon, unfortunately." Nottingham rolled up his sleeves and tossed her a small tube. "There's sun protection spells in it. You can sit here and watch, or you can come help out."

Zoe cracked her knuckles. "Of course I'm gonna help out. What I'm mad about is you making me think we were going to do something equally..." She trailed off. Equally *what*, exactly? Reckless? Illegal? Nottingham's choice was as safe as it would ever get. "Now what?" she asked instead.

"Separate the cans and bottles. Some people from ScythiaTech will need to analyze them with some scanners they've set up, see where they originally drifted in from."

"Beach cleanups won't be as effective if we don't know *where* people are throwing their trash from and why it washes up here," one of the volunteers called out cheerfully.

"That's pretty smart," Zoe admitted. "All right. Tell me what you guys want me to do."

For nearly an hour, she and Nottingham worked side by side gathering up soda cans and plastic rings, content with a comfortable silence. Occasionally, someone would take a guitar and break out into song, others singing or humming along. At some point, the heat was enough for Nottingham to strip off his shirt before resuming the work, and Zoe kept her eyes on the ground, refusing to let them wander to his broad chest and shoulders. She'd already made that mistake once, and she wasn't foolish enough to go down that road again, now that she had a working brain again and was a safe distance away from mysterious drafty castles and seeresses who knew more than they should.

It was just—the scars. She knew he had them, knew that was a by-product of the terrifying segen his family owned that he currently wielded. She'd seen them in the thick of the frost, when she thought they were both going to die. But now he was healthy and fit, and the scars stood out more than ever, and Zoe felt a sudden rush of sadness for what he'd had to endure, and she was disturbed at the thought that they in no way made him any less attractive. And his family had them too.

"Yes. Except my sister."

Shit. She'd been wondering out loud again. "I'm sorry. If you don't want to talk about it, I understand."

"I don't mind. It's something we have to live with."

"But should you?" Zoe scooped up a handful of candy wrappers, adding them to her pile. "I mean, is your segen that important that you're all going to risk actual bodily injury for it? Can't you just, I dunno, find another one? One that won't eventually kill you?"

"This is not what's going to kill me," Nottingham said calmly.

"You don't know. It could."

"It's not something you can throw away just as easily. You know that it's bonded to our bloodline. It's atonement."

"For what?"

"You know our history. I've got worse ancestors than just the sheriff of Nottingham."

"You can't be expected to pay for the sins of your forebears."

"As long as we live off the riches they ruined peoples' lives to get, I'd say it's almost a fair trade."

But you didn't want to, was what Zoe wanted to say. *Your grandfather is as rich as sin, but you told me you lived in the Bronx with your mother and sister.*

"I like your family. Even if your grandfather's kinda terrifying and I'm still nervous around your great-grandma. Your sister is adorable."

A smile tinted the corners of his mouth. "She is." A frown took its place. "Carlisle, I'm sorry about—"

"Your great-grandma?" Zoe burst out, not really wanting him to refer to what happened at the castle again, especially when they were almost back to normal and everything. "She's right, in a way. I *should* come to terms with my doom. I just don't like having to hear it spoken aloud. Dad doesn't really understand, and my mother just dismisses it as nonsense."

But it wasn't. *The dead will rise for you* wasn't really something even a random prophecy would throw around lightly. It still frightened her.

"Is she feeling better?" All three seeresses had been discharged from Villeneuve Castle the day before. Unfortunately, none of them had a clue as to what the prophecy they'd foretold in unison had meant.

"She is. This isn't the first time it's happened. Your dad doing well?"

He was choosing to change the subject himself. Zoe relaxed. "Yeah. Dad's holding up pretty good, despite not understanding anything that's going on. My mother won't be here till next week. I'm not even sure she realized I was missing when we were stuck in the frost."

"Sorry."

"We've never been really close. I love her, but I wouldn't trust her to be responsible for anything, least of all me. Dad's the one I usually spend most of my time with." Zoe admired the pile she'd accumulated. It wasn't as high profile as an Amazon rain forest, true, but it felt oddly satisfying. "Thank you for bringing me here. Although I highly suspect your objective is to wear me out so I don't go off on more reckless missions on my own."

He shrugged. "Or maybe it's just something fulfilling you can do that you won't need to feel angry about doing."

Zoe wanted to correct him, then didn't. She *had* been angry, hadn't she? She'd wanted to make a difference. It was why she'd been talking to all those nonprofits, all those organizations. But sometimes thinking about the things they still couldn't change only added to her anger.

Zoe looked down at her watch and took a deep breath. "I have to go. I've got somewhere to be tonight."

"That's several hours away."

"Yeah. But it's a formal function, and I..." She sighed. "I promised to look my best."

She didn't want to admit out loud that she was going to a party with Tristan to pose as his girlfriend, but Nottingham had always been good at figuring out nuance. He nodded, a shade less friendly, a bit more aloof.

"Will you come back with me?" she offered.

"I'm going to stay a little longer. Close the port off on your end. I can find my way back."

"Okay. I... Really, thank you. This wasn't what I was expecting, but I liked it."

He finally smiled then. "Get going before Alex finds out we've left the looking glass running for over an hour."

Nottingham hadn't asked about Tristan or the status of their relationship. And it was only after she'd returned to the Hollows that Zoe realize she'd *wanted* him to. She wanted to explain. Telling someone else went against the terms of her agreement with Tristan. But she could have probably figured a way to if he'd asked.

But he hadn't. Because he wasn't curious about her and Tristan. At all. Despite almost kissing her.

And she hated that it was bugging her like hell.

13

IN WHICH THIS ABSOLUTELY *ISN'T* A DATE

Ken and Nya most definitely, absolutely, were *not* going to crash the party at the Schaffers' manor tonight.

It didn't matter that the OzCorp CEO himself, Rackety Gnome, was rumored to—

"Ruggedo Nome," Nya corrected him. "Technically, Ruggedo Nome VIII."

"The numbers after his name make him sound even more insufferable. Catch me calling myself Kensington Inoue XVII."

"I'm not sure you know how names are supposed to work."

"I'm trying to sound cool here, and you're harshing my vibe."

She rolled her eyes. "Fine. Whatever. Carry on."

It didn't matter that the OzCorp CEO himself, Rackety or Ruggedo Nome or whatever the hell his name was, was rumored to be attending the celebration, which was to honor the Royal States ambassador to China's birthday. Ken found this highly suspicious. Why the ambassador to China? Was Nome smuggling in contraband spells from the Middle Kingdom? On Avalon soil? That was tantamount to treason.

"It's only treason if they're Avalon citizens," Nya said. "It could also be that they're just, you know, friends. Rich people mingle regardless of political affiliation."

"What did I just say about harshing?" They were most definitely not following Dexter Gallagher down the corridor to the lab where his family oversaw and trained other techmages, set up in the castle basement with restricted access. Alex most definitely did not give them the necessary clearance, which was why Dex was *not* quickly buzzing them in through the various checkpoints without any interference whatsoever. It helped that everyone else was focused on the security around the Nameless Sword, which was on its fourth day of people lining up to try and pull it out of the stone.

"Dad and the others are still working on some upgrades for the Nine Maidens, to mitigate them siphoning off Alex's life force should he use them again," the young techmage said. "In the meantime, I'll be the Q to your B."

"Your what to my what?"

"The Q to your B. You know. Q, brilliant MI-5 inventor? And then B, world's greatest spy?"

"Have you ever watched a James Bond movie before, Dex? It's *Bond, James Bond.* Not *B, James B.*"

"Really? Am I misremembering it again?"

"You're fine, Dex." Creating spells had corresponding curses. For the Gallaghers, it was memory loss. Sometimes they forgot pop culture references; sometimes they forgot their own names. It was a big reason why Alex had added therapy as essential Avalonian health care. Ken couldn't even begin to think about living that kind of life where you could possibly forget even your parents, as Dex had that one time.

"Ken would make an excellent love interest for a spy," Nya said mischievously.

"I'd make an excellent love interest for anyone," Ken said without thinking, then regretted it immediately when her smile dimmed.

"I know," she murmured, quieter now.

They were most definitely not going to talk about the mermaid incident either. Ken *wanted* to, but he also *didn't* want to. She'd lied to him! But it was for a good reason. But he deserved to know, especially if their prophecies were linked! But maybe dooms were just bloody ridiculous and Nya was just as interested in him as he was in her, and some gormless, most likely spurious prophecy shouldn't come between that! But what if they came true, and he was fated to become some kind of walking dead where he would be decomposing and would no longer be, at the very least, hot?

He tried to imagine Nya choosing to be with him for his mind instead of for his body. It was impossible. Without his looks to distract her, she would realize he'd had only one functioning brain cell and dump him in two seconds.

And that was also his problem. Ken couldn't hold a grudge to save his life. He'd tried his best to stay mad at Nya for not telling him—for all of two hours. All it took was her grandma getting sick for him to toss that resolve out the Beast of Suddene's drafty window and reach out. He was still mad at her. He also wanted to *not* be mad at her. He was trying to figure out how to do that and still stress how genuinely hurt he was. An apology would help, but he couldn't demand that from her if he wanted something genuine; Nya was gonna have to work that out on her own.

But they were most definitely not going to talk about *that*.

The lab was cluttered with glowing orbs and strange mechanical tools that not even Ken at his bravest would have thought of touching. "I feel like we're in the opening scenes of an alien disaster movie," he said as they passed a table that had an impressive-looking cobweb-like contraption that slowly contracted and expanded, seemingly on its own.

"That still needs further testing, but it's made to capture spells in action," Dex said. "Snatch and trap, before the magic can do damage. The Fianna have been trying out the prototypes for us."

"Lucky them." Ken shuddered. "Looks like a robotic deranged squid that could snatch me up from underwater."

"That bad?" Nya asked tentatively. She looked a little guilty.

"I can't even stand looking at seafood sometimes," he said and changed the subject. "Hey, isn't this Loki's segen?" Ruyi Jingu Bang was on the table, broken in two.

"Yeah. Loki had a spellstone, and they wanted to see if we could repair it. Shouldn't be a problem, though I can't guarantee if it'll work just as good as before. But that's not what I want to show you guys." Proudly, Dex gestured at his own worktable with a flourish.

"Well," Ken said after a pause. "I was expecting something a little more...awesome-looking."

"They *are* awesome," Dex said, looking hurt. "They're amazing. I figured that since you already have two sword segen, it would be useless to make another. So I made support tech to complement them instead."

"I like them. Thank you." Nya picked up an earpiece made from some kind of alloy so transparent that it was nearly invisible. "What's this for?"

"They'll be completely undetectable upon wearing them. It's automatically linked up to Avalon control, so they'll hear you no matter where you are. Unless someone blocks the frequency we're using, which is almost impossible, since we encrypt communication on both ends."

"Is there something else that won't make me look like I'm a teenage bouncer for some club?" Ken asked.

"I've got a small piece of rope that can lengthen up to a thousand feet, with a curve on the end to cling to cliffs and building edges. I'm going to call it the Captain." He paused, looking delighted. "Because it's a grappling *hook*, right? So it's Captain *Hook*, like in the—"

"I like it," Ken said sincerely. "Sounds like something Rapunzel here would enjoy. Get it? So she can climb up walls the way Rapunzel climbed up her own hair when she was fighting the—"

"Please," Nya groaned. "No more, the both of you." She pointed to a small pouch. "What does this do?"

"You can fit anything in there, no matter its size," Dex explained. "But it's limited to about half a dozen objects, because this kind of spell requires more memories than I'm prepared to give."

"I hope making all this extra tech for us isn't affecting you or your family's well-being."

Dex turned pink. "Yeah, thanks for the concern. We all went through the mental training, passed the required health tests needed. Plus, Alex gives us excellent benefits. Therapy whenever we want, spa sessions, leave for downtime... It's a big help."

Nya pushed the handle of her broom down into the tiny bag. It went in easily, disappearing into the impossibly small space. "Oh, cool!"

"I made this especially for you, Ken." Dex produced a pair of heavy boots from under the table.

"Seven-league boots?" Ken asked, perking up. "Now we're talking."

"Not exactly. I'm calling them obscuras. His Majesty instructed us to make all your spelltech as low key as possible. There's going to be a lot of magic detectors and dampeners at the party, and anything flashier would put you guys on blast. And, uh, it has a lot to do with Juuchi Yosamu."

"How?"

"We've been doing research on the potential of harnessing shade spells. Their effects on life spans, Schlemihl's work on their potential life-saving properties, things like that. Shades aren't technically good or bad on their own; they just are. It's people like the Snow Queen who enthrall them and give them a bad name, really. The main obstacle is, well, unless the spelltech is sound, most people eventually go mad with constant use of shadow magic. There've been hundreds of case studies documenting that. But Juuchi Yosamu is unique in that its bond with your family line means it shields you not just from itself but from other similar spells."

"So you're saying I'm the best person to test out these obscuras because I'm the least likely to go mental?"

"Pretty much, yes."

"Fair enough." And they were good boots too, sleek and comfortable. Ken took a few minutes to stomp around in them, then clicked his heels together just as instructed. The shadow underneath his boots expanded outward, slowly climbing up the shelves before them. "Sick."

"Captain Mairead and some of her pirates use shadow spells too," Nya said.

"*Jolly Roger* spelltech, probably. I'd like to have a look at that ship one day. Imagine all the spelltech on board that. But right now, I'm supposed to patch you guys through to the king once we're done."

"Thanks. We've got some reports of our own to make."

"I trust Dex's briefed you?" Alex asked once they'd secured the connection. The Nine Maidens made for an intimidating background on the screen behind him. Ken could see the Beast of Suddene and Dex's father circling the magical monstrosity, monitoring the stones and conferring quietly with each other.

"He's a genius, Your Majesty," Ken said, and the boy reddened slightly. "These are all gonna come in handy for tonight. And incidentally, wanna know what we found out about the Gnome guy?"

Alex nodded. "Out with it."

"A few whistleblowers working at OzCorp have reached out to our social media. Tita Chedeng and Tita Teejay brought them to our attention, helped us verify them. They can't give us details because the contracts they signed before getting hired on were extremely restrictive, and they can't get too specific without breaking them. They *were* able to tell us that some of their employees had gone missing, though."

Alex frowned. "That would be highly illegal. Any names? Official positions within OzCorp?"

"A marketing head, a PR guy, a couple of spelltech programmers, and one more in sales," Nya said. "One of the people we're talking to is a lawyer for a missing employee who'd managed to get their hands on an email between a couple of OzCorp higher-ups. Unfortunately, it was in a bespelled server. The client only had the file for several minutes before it self-deleted, but he managed to take a snapshot on his phone. We still don't have a paper trail leading back to them. The lawyer swore his client gave him the go-ahead to share this with us before he lost communication, though." Nya scrolled through her phone. "I'll put it up on-screen."

What popped up was an email that made just as much sense to Ken as Zoe's terrible drawings did.

Hey Caoire,

Few things still missing from the Blessed Isles list.

- We've tried plotting out a full map of Nibheis, but our scanners aren't penetrating completely. Malcolm says it's haunted. No sign of World's End, but we might have to drop in at some point to verify coordinates since radar isn't cutting it.

- We keep losing people at K. mountain. Earplugs don't work.

Plotting out the 7w's at the moment, though still think the board is pushing it. If historians can't find it, we won't either. Don't care how much money Corvington throws at this.

Talking with our contact in Shenzen, will let you know more at the Schaffer briefing. How many investors will Corv pull in, you think?

- Sloan G.

The room went silent. "Blessed Isles was another name for Buyan," Alex said grimly. "I take it that's why you're so keen on crashing the Schaffer party?"

"Yep. We gotta know what OzCorp is up to before we get eight hundred more of their facilities popping up around Avalon."

"Seven. They have land for seven more sites, not including the one in Ikpe and their main headquarters at Marooners' Rock."

"What?"

"My minister of trade was a little too trigger-happy when it came to signing permits. I've spoken to him already. Your confrontation with the border agents had me thinking. Care to make a guess at who won the bidding to supply them with those firearms?"

"OzCorp," Nya said bleakly.

"It's likely that OzCorp created those thrall collars used on the ice wolves as well. And we now know they use shardstones from Beira. I want to know how far their relationship goes." Alex paused, an odd look crossing his face as another message came through on his end. "Ken, Nya, good luck. Dexter, keep up the good work." He hesitated. "You guys don't mind that I'm putting you two on this assignment, right?" he asked, sounding oddly awkward. "I can always—"

"Of course not," Ken said.

"Everything's fine," Nya said, though her voice was a little shaky.

Yeah. They were absolutely not gonna talk about *that*.

They were most definitely not supposed to attract attention at the party. They would absolutely go incognito, maybe pose as waiters working for the Schaffers—whoever the hell the Schaffers were.

His mother offered them an unexpected, easier solution.

"Your father and I were invited," Margrethe Inoue informed them gleefully, handing Ken the invitation cards, handcrafted in special gold calligraphy and smelling of very expensive perfume. "And I was all ready to turn it down. But if *you're* interested, then perhaps you can go in our stead. Farrah Delacourte has been after me to talk about her so-called prize-winning Endelwean hogs, and I'd rather eat a cactus. Have you even anything to wear? Lord knows you've given me enough palpitations in the months you were missing, but I won't have you showing up at the Schaffers' looking like you've been fighting your tux."

Ken was well aware that he'd gotten his gift of gab from his mother. He just didn't like being on the receiving end of it. "I've met Farrah Delacourte. I imagine she'd talk about her hogs to anyone."

"Why do you even want to go? You used to hate it when we dragged you to stuffy black-tie events."

"I'm, uh..." Ken scrambled for a reasonable explanation. Margrethe Inoue could smell a lie the way pigs could sniff out truffles, but if the lie contained some sliver of truth, he might be able to wing it. "Alex asked me to go? To represent him in an unofficial capacity?"

That was the wrong thing to say.

"I'm calling Louise! Whatever suit you've decided to wear for tonight won't be enough! I know your taste in clothes, young man, and it is *appalling*! In fact, I think your father and I should go as well, to make sure you don't accidentally bespell someone there. The Westfields and the Beiruts still haven't forgiven us for that last stunt you pulled at Cerridwen's, sweet Vasilisa. You will be shaming neither this family nor the king!"

She turned to Nya, all sweetness and light when she was a terrifying cyclone only seconds before. "My dear, a very renowned seamstress will be coming, and I would be delighted if you could choose a dress from her repertoire. At our expense, of course."

"Thank you for your generosity, ma'am."

"Please, no gratitude necessary. Anything for my son's date."

"Oh, I—I'm not—"

"Please keep him out of trouble. Check his pockets at intervals for any pranks. He'd stuff a whole bullfrog down the prime minister's pants if he thought it would make a girl laugh."

"Mum!" Ken protested.

"I really like that your mom was fine with you potentially making a fool of yourself at the party, right up until she realized you were going on the king's behalf," Nya murmured several hours later. Before them loomed Schaffer Manor, one of the most expensive residences in Avalon. It was constructed in under three months, using a type of magic that only the very wealthy could afford.

Ken scowled and fiddled with his tie. "Are you sure you can get around in that?"

Nya was wearing some kind of yellow cloud. The intricacies of women's fashion were lost on Ken most of the time, up until she smoothed down the hundred ruffles on her skirt and revealed a breathtakingly elegant shoulder to his line of sight, and for the first time in almost eighteen years, Ken briefly lost the power of speech. He was used to Nya in burlap sacks. It wasn't fair that she looked as fine as the weather was tonight, the clouds of which, coincidentally, were as fluffy as what she was wearing.

But he wasn't going to tell her that. She'd been obviously trying to banter with him like she used to, and as much as he missed that (and missed her, if he had to be honest), Ken felt like he deserved an apology first.

And that was hard when she was standing there looking like sexy cotton candy.

"If I'm to believe your mother," Nya said, shifting to accidentally expose a bare leg, and Ken's heart started beating twenty times faster, "this dress costs as much as an Andalusian thoroughbred, which I assume is a very expensive horse. I spent ten minutes fighting my way into this dress, and I don't have the energy to fight my way back out. So I've decided that I'm going to live inside this. Forever."

"Hmrugh," Ken said.

"What's that?"

"Nothing."

"Do nothing in there that will upset your mother," Kazuhiko Inoue told his son just as they stepped through the archway leading into the manor. "I don't think His Majesty wants you to do anything that would make her unhappy, even if he wants you to snoop around."

Ken grinned. "I'll do my best. Were we too obvious?"

"King Alexei's father sent me on similar missions before." His father eyed the throng of people chatting among themselves. "Any more problems with Juuchi?" he asked quietly in Japanese.

"Iie." Ken had told his father about Juuchi Yosamu and Yawarakai-Te temporarily fusing together that one time they'd been fighting ice wolves during the frost.

"Both blades have always been about yin and yang. Light and dark. Two blades molded into one, that could cut the nonliving yet control the dark. Few people have been able to fuse them like you have, and I think it's promising. If you are to protect His Majesty, it is good that you can tap into their fullest potential."

"I don't know how to do it again, though."

"Time will help that along. Let me know if it happens again. I've talked to the Gallaghers and a few other spellforgers, but so far, we're drawing blanks. In the meantime, be careful. Suits and ties hide fangs in here. Take care of Nya-san. Your mother will be upset if she doesn't see you two dancing at some point."

Ken blanched. "Is she trying to set me up with Nya?"

"You don't like her that way?"

Ken did. Ken very much did. He hated prophecies. "It's kinda complicated."

"Uncomplicate it long enough for one dance, at least."

Farrah Delacourte made a beeline for them as soon as they passed the foyer. Margrethe groaned visibly and fled to one of the smaller, private rooms. Kazuhiko soon followed after one last wink at his son.

"I have a problem," Nya said. "I know nothing about mingling with wealthy people. How are we gonna find a rich old white guy among all these rich old white guys?"

"Let me do most of the talking."

"You always do most of the talking anyway."

"Shush and let me do most of the talking." With Nya's hand firmly hooked under his arm, Ken began to stride across the room, greeting people at random. "Nice evening, isn't it? Great food, love the music, how've you been? Really like your dress, brings out the blue in your eyes." The other guests appeared confused at first but then smiled and nodded, some even clasping his hand briefly like they knew him before moving on.

"Do you know them?" Nya whispered.

"Nope. It's always been about faking it, really." Ken's focus was on Alsaid Corvington, OzCorp's CFO. He was milling about the refreshments table, chatting with a few American emissaries. Ken was fairly sure any secret meetings weren't going to start without him on board, which meant they'd arrived in time. Unfortunately, the man would recognize them if they got too close.

"You should try some of the canapés," Ken said out loud. "They're imported from Spain."

"Why, thank you," one of the ladies they passed said, pleased. "I shall."

"Have some of the escargots too. They're fantastic." Ken snatched a couple of flute glasses from a passing waiter. "How am I doing?"

"As much of an ass as I know you're being," Nya said, amused.

"We're standing in a room full of multimillionaires. Assery is required. Would you…" Music was starting up. It was nowhere as elaborate as the dances back in Ikpe, but Ken was already talking before he could shut up. "Do you want to, ah…dance? Just to make it look legit?"

Nya stared at him, wide-eyed, blushing. For a moment, Ken thought she might actually say yes.

"Ken," Nya said. "I…I'm really—"

"Ken," Dex's voice warbled through his earpiece. "I'm detecting some weird energy upstairs."

Ken liked Dex, but at this moment, he wanted to strangle him. "Anything specific you can make out?"

"Could be all the high-profile guests with their own warding spells, but this one's a little stronger than usual. Not a lot of OzCorp people around actually, unless those photos you sent over aren't up to date. Got into their security cams. I see some of the Elroys, a ton of Chinese businessmen, some European royalty like the Windsors and the Mavers and the Locksleys. Crap, is that Zoe?"

Zoe spotted them as well. She flushed, mouthed "Later!" at them even as she let Tristan Locksley draw her through the crowd.

"Shade," Nya whispered.

"She's not throwing shade. Zoe said she'd broken up with him, but maybe she's investigating something on her own—"

"I meant you should activate the shade spell." Nya inclined her head toward the stairs, where Alsaid Corvington was also now walking toward. A couple of guards blocked the stairwell after him, scowling at everyone. "Because I don't think they're going to let us up, no matter how much you tell them you like escargots."

Ken shifted his stance, nudged his boots together. His shadow grew, lengthened, and slipped upstairs with the rest of the men. "Hopefully nobody looks down at the floor and sees what I'm missing. And I gotta tell ya, Dex, this is *some* invention. Is this what an acid trip's supposed to feel like?" It was disconcerting to be in two places at the same time: standing with Nya by the hors d'oeuvres and also flitting along the ceiling above the OzCorp CFO as the man and a few others made small talk. It was like navigating a battery-operated toy car with a remote and also *being* the battery-operated toy car.

"You okay?" Nya whispered.

"Bit of vertigo. S'all right."

"Looks like everyone's here," Corvington said crisply as he stepped into a room where twenty or so people were waiting. "Alan, fire up security."

The whole room glittered and was soon cocooned in an anti-eavesdropping spell. Ken saw one of Corvington's aides drop to the floor unconscious, though it attracted little comment from the others in attendance. Possibly some repercussion stemming from the magic's use. Bastard even made other people take on the spells' punishments for him.

Fortunately, it didn't push out Ken's shadow, which still hovered at the ceiling above them, trying to blend in with the rococo borders.

"Anti-eavesdropping spells nullify sound from *outside* the room," Dex said, sounding gleeful. "Since your shadow's already inside, it won't be affected."

"Shall we expect Nome as well?" one of the men asked.

"Unfortunately, Mr. Nome is busy. He is a very hands-on CEO and is, in fact, currently working on the very reason I invited you all here. We'll keep this meeting brief. I'm thrilled that you are all interested in our latest project, but we require more than just that. My secretary here will be passing around waivers—ordinary clauses, mind you, stating that nothing you learn here must leave the room, with a forgetful spell attached if you break the agreement."

"You've been dangling this over us the last few months, Alsaid," one of the men complained. "We're not one of your lazy employees that we need to sign our silence over. We'll keep your secret, whatever it is."

"And if it's what we suspect it is," another said, "then you know we'll be on board."

"I do not intend to impugn your honor, but I would rather no one from the media catches wind of this until we're ready to reveal it to the world. If you are, however, uncomfortable with the thought of an NDA, I'll bid you good night and show you out, with my apologies. Well?"

No one moved to get up.

"Then if you will be so glad as to sign—"

"My dear boy!"

Ken's attention was pulled back into the ballroom, where he was being hugged by someone who definitely wasn't Nya.

"It's been ages since I last saw you!" A voice crooned by his ear. "Is your mother here? Of course she is. She wouldn't miss this for the world!"

The Duchess of Sunfolk's face beamed at him, Nya's rather apologetic one behind her. Beside her was her husband, Ralph Norweggers, not looking as happy as his wife. Ken felt the same; Danielle Norweggers was the worst gossip in Royal Britain, and she was constantly trying to set Ken up with the nieces and goddaughters she'd accumulated over the years. Her husband was a misanthrope and a bigot tolerated by the ton only because he was rich.

"How strong and tall you look now!" the woman exclaimed. "And so handsome!"

"It's very nice to see you again, Your Grace," Ken said weakly, meaning none of it at all.

"Thank you again, gentlemen," Alsaid Corvington said from farther away. "And let me be the first to say: congratulations. You've just received front-row seats to the next revolutionary step in spell technology that will change the world."

"I'm surprised you'd be at this little ol' party," the duchess said. "You've been staring at the wall with such a bored expression on your face, I knew I had to come and cheer you up. And who's this? How charming. I'm Danielle, and this is my husband, Ralph."

"My name is Nya. It's such a pleasure." Nya returned the woman's handshake, then extended another to the duke, who only grunted and pretended her hand didn't exist. Nya turned her winning smile back to the duchess. "Ken was very kind to invite me. I've never been to anything so grand before. You must know everyone here."

The woman preened. "My family goes all the way back to peerage at King George's court, and I know all the prominent families in the kingdom. Even the Countess Farlay-on-Waters; such a scandal!"

Ken looked worriedly at Nya. She flashed him a reassuring grin. "Please, tell me," she said eagerly. "That sounds so fascinating."

Thank you for your sacrifice, Nya, Ken thought as the duchess launched into speech. It took another couple of seconds to reorient himself and return to the secret meeting upstairs.

"Without giving too much away," the man was saying, "we have not only successfully captured one, but we have also been able to incorporate it with little difficulty into the spelltech we've created."

Startled murmurs among the men.

"Nearly three decades of research has come down to this. But unlike Avalon, we are committed to using ours to better mankind. Imagine the possibilities. The lives we could save. The people we could help."

"The wars you could fight," Ken muttered. "This is bullshit."

"As much as I share in your optimism," another man said cynically, "how certain are we that this is more than just vaporware? The quality of spellstones required for such an undertaking would be massive. None of the artificial mines we have in Chengdu could power anything of this scale, and I suspect Avalon would not be so willing to give up theirs."

"That is the beauty of it. It requires only half the spellstones you would expect."

The murmurs grew louder, disbelieving.

Corvington laughed. "Spellstones are only one of two methods for powering spelltech, as you know."

Ken's heart sank. Alex was right.

A pause as the others in the room digested this new bit of information. None of them looked surprised or protested. When another of the men finally spoke up, there was only speculation in his voice, pondering the possibilities. "It is true then, that the Queen of Beira is more amenable to sharing shardstones than Tsarevich is with his spellstones? But surely there will be some pushback once word gets around."

"Who's to say what is legal and what is illegal anymore? It would be prejudiced to hold on to obsolete opinions when the future can look so bright. I already have people working on government policy, gentlemen. Leave that to me. What I require from the rest of you is financial backing, in exchange for some very lucrative shares."

"And if Avalon protests?" the man asked.

Corvington's smile grew wider. "We may not silence Tsarevich completely, but he will be too busy to do more than complain. The Royal States army has already expressed interest, and we have begun prototypes along other similar veins. I guarantee, my friends, that profits will increase several times over. I've sent a kit to your emails with more details. This is on a first come, first served basis, unfortunately, and if I do not hear from you within forty-eight hours, I shall presume that you are no longer interested."

A man laughed. "Expect my signature in the next hour, Corvington. You make a compelling case. If I can get my hands on anything with even a tenth of the power of the Nine Maidens or the firebird, then I want in."

"You can always try your hand at the Nameless Sword," someone suggested, and everyone laughed.

"That will be all, gentlemen," Corvington said, checking his watch. "I suggest we pay our valets and leave early, if you value your cars—"

Ken was brought rudely back to his surroundings, startled, when the duchess screamed. Her husband was on the floor, bleeding from his mouth.

Nya was standing over him, looking mortified but still unrepentant.

"She punched Ralph!" the duchess shrieked.

"I might have been stuck in ice for a dozen years, lady," Nya said, red-faced, "but I know he had no right to say that about Ken!"

"Whoa, whoa, whoa, whoa," Ken said as a crowd began to gather. "What happened?"

"All I said," Ralph Norweggers snapped, managing to right himself again, "was that you were a lucky man, picking her, the cream of the crop from those southern American plantations, considering you're only a Jap. It was a compliment. I don't see how she—"

Ken punched him. The man went down again, and the onlookers gasped.

"You have no right to say that about Nya!" Ken snapped.

"Ken!" His parents were rushing toward him. "What are you doing?" his mother cried out.

"Ken," Dex's voice said. "What did he mean by paying their valets early? I'm running a quick scan of the area, trying to see if there's any spell activity within your location—"

"Your son is a disgrace!" Ralph sputtered as several waiters helped him to his feet. His eye was already sporting a faint bruise, though Ken wasn't sure if it was from his fist or Nya's. "How dare he put his hands on me!"

"Nya was defending my honor, and I was defending hers," Ken said. "He got off lightly!"

"Tell me what happened," Kazuhiko said calmly.

Ken repeated the insult to his father.

"Absolutely harmless jokes," Ralph gasped. "Certainly not deserving of the abuse that I—"

Margrethe Inoue punched him. The duke hit the floor again.

"I'm sorry," Ken said to Nya. "I knew he was the worst before all this happened. I should have excused us."

"I'm all right. He's not the first to try that on me."

"—something's deliberately nullifying the spells put in place for security," Dex went on, oblivious. "I think you need to evacuate everyone out of there before it's too late—"

Somebody else screamed.

"Crap," Ken said, because a hole had appeared in the air at the center of the foyer, growing larger with every second. Something big was forcing its way through the portal.

He was expecting shades. An ogre, even.

"Ken?" His earpiece crackled. "Are you out? Have you evacuated?"

Wordlessly, Nya handed him her pouch. Slowly, Ken reached in and drew out his swords, then handed it back to her so she could retrieve her broom.

"There is," he said, "a dragon in the ballroom."

14

IN WHICH ENTERS A DRAGON

The dragon appeared just as confused as they were. It sat for a while in the middle of the ballroom, tail and wings sticking out the windows it had inadvertently broken, oblivious to the streams of people fleeing and calling for help, until the only ones left behind were Nya, Ken, and his parents.

Finally, it shook its head and rose up on its haunches, steam hissing from its mouth as its wings tried to unfurl, the tips brushing against the walls on either side. Ken knew that the house, biggest mansion in Lyonesse or not, wouldn't hold it for long. At this rate, the roof wasn't going to make it out in one piece.

The dragon was also made completely of ice. What should have been scales were instead something that resembled hard textured diamond, and they shone and glinted under the lights every time the beast moved. Its ruby-red eyes opened and focused on them for the very first time. It grunted.

"Dex," Ken continued calmly. "Can you let Alex know that there's a supposedly extinct-as-hell dragon sitting inside the Schaffers' mansion, and maybe let the Katipuneros know so they can hightail their asses down here and help us?"

He could hear frantic movements coming from the earpiece. "I-informing him right now! I'm putting an emergency through to the Fianna too, and getting all the—"

The dragon raised its head, nostrils flaring like it was about to shoot out fire. Or ice, as the case was likely to be.

Its ears flattened. It reared back and opened its mouth.

And belched. It was a terrible, ungodly sound. The stench filled the room in seconds, and everyone keeled over, gagging.

"Holy bloody Koschei's stinkhole," Ken wheezed, already on his knees. "We surrender already."

The dragon belched again, but this time something rippled *through* it, like the whole creature was merely a reflection on water. It tried to raise itself up only to collapse, looking dazed.

"It's not used to its own weight," Kazuhiko observed clinically. "Almost like a foal."

"This isn't a horse, Dad," Ken groaned.

"It isn't, but that doesn't explain its current behavior. It's acting like it's not even used to its own body."

"We should probably leave while it's not attacking," Nya spoke up timidly.

They all looked at one another, glanced back at the dragon, which was still struggling to stand on all four legs, and started their retreat while it puffed and belched one more time. They were almost out the doors when bright lights flashed in through the windows, temporarily blinding them.

"Royal States military!" someone blared in at them with a megaphone. "Do not move!"

"Oh bloody hell," Ken's mother cried out. "Are they mental? They're going to make things worse!"

She was right. The dragon's tail whipped around, barely missing them by inches, as the creature turned to confront the men stationed outside, now snarling angrily.

"Dex!" Nya yelled. "If you've got contacts outside the mansion, tell them to pull back! They're going to escalate the—"

The windows exploded as gunfire rained through. Ken's father was already in motion, springing in front of his family just as he activated a barrier, the bullets slamming harmlessly into the shield spell he'd put up just in time. The dragon roared as fire bullets pierced its crystalline skin, shattering it in places. Angry, it extended to full wingspan and leaped straight up.

Ken was wrong. The roof survived the dragon's assault in one piece, because the beast took out the whole upper structure at once when it took flight, sending it crashing into the front yard still intact. It wasn't just the Royal States army firing at it, Ken realized. He spotted soldiers with the Union Jack pinned to their chests lining up beside the American troops, along with several contingents of Japanese, French, Spanish, German, and Chinese troops. There'd been much more security for the gala than he'd thought, given the different nationalities in attendance, but it was clear that none of them had any fighting experience against creatures this large, and they were simply relying on using as much firepower as possible.

"Hold your fire!" Ken yelled, but nobody paid him any attention.

"Reckless," his father growled. "None of them even stopped to consider if there were people inside."

"Ken!" Zoe was there, lifting the hem of her sleek white gown so she could move more easily. Tristan was with her.

"I'm not getting anything from the creature!" Dex sounded frustrated. "I'm not expecting body heat, since it's made of ice, but there aren't even any energy patterns. As far as the readouts here are concerned, it has about as much tangibility as an image on a screen!"

"I don't know about it not being real, but I can vouch for the authenticity of the damage it's wreaking." A blast of wind from the drag-on's mouth turned the police cars lining the driveway into blocks of ice, people scrambling out of the way and careening into one another as the ground beneath them grew slick. "Those are real spells coming out of its mouth!" Ken yelled.

"Oof. Now *those* I can see on my radar, yeah. But that's impossible. How is magic coming out of something my scans are telling me doesn't exist?"

A portal materialized, and Tala and Loki leaped out, eyes wide as they took in the sight. They were accompanied by a dozen Fianna. "Alex sent us," the Filipina said, tossing Ogmios to Zoe, who caught it easily. "The Katipuneros are protecting him, but we're here to help."

"Zoe," Tristan said. "There are secret service people from over twenty countries here. Let them handle this."

Zoe shot him a glare. "You said you wouldn't dictate my actions."

"Please, Zo."

"If it harms any of my friends, I'm butting in. Can you try and negate its powers, Tala?"

The girl frowned. "Not until it lands, or unless you can launch me into the air at it. It's flying around too quickly."

"Dex says he can't detect it."

"Can confirm," Loki said. "I'm not detecting any magic...uh, until it does *that*." A ball of ice the size of a fire truck had just slammed down on top of another car. "I don't understand. How is it able to—" They stopped abruptly, their gaze on a crowd of people made up of morbidly curious passersby and party attendees too foolish or too drunk to leave.

"Loki?" Ken asked.

Loki took off without warning, dashing toward the crowd. They grabbed the arm of one of the girls.

"You!" Loki snapped. "Fey!"

The OzCorp girl they'd encountered at the Tangled Woods blinked up at them. "Did I do anything wrong, officer?" she asked, a shade too sweetly to be innocent. "I was only here, enjoying the party like everyone else, before this dragon showed up. Goodness. Can you imagine that? A dragon? And the Schaffers were worried about the Vanderlusts one-upping their gala!"

"Loki, you have to let her go," Tala said, glaring hard at the other girl despite her words. "We don't have a choice."

Loki stared at her, teeth quietly grinding. They let go.

Fey rubbed her wrists. "I would suggest protecting the others from the monster before it harms anyone else."

"She planned this," Loki seethed. "I know it. It's too much of a coincidence that Corvington just happens to end their meeting and leave right before the dragon appeared. Didn't he hint as much?"

"Yeah, but we can't prove it yet," Tala said, sounding grim. "Contain the nightwalker terrorizing the citizens first, find evidence later."

The dragon swooped down, raking bursts of concentrated ice down on their heads. A few people were caught in the blast, frozen before they could even cry out.

The creature wasn't detectable by spelltech, but it felt pain. When the dragon completed another revolution and dove down again for another attack, Ken was waiting with both Yawarakai-Te and Juuchi Yosamu in either hand. So was Tala, arnis sticks raised beside him.

The dragon shrieked ice again, but Tala pushed her arms out. The cold blast hit the empty space in front of her and bounced away, like she'd turned some invisible force field on. As it swooped past, Ken lunged for it. His sword made a strange grating noise as the blade plunged into the beast's side and remained stuck, carrying Ken off along with it as it soared up into the night sky once again.

"What are you doing?" Dex's voice sounded panicked.

"I don't know!" Ken plunged the other sword into another spot along its flank, and the dragon bucked, nearly throwing him off. They were rising in altitude, so quickly that his head was spinning, but Ken grimly held on. Once the dragon had leveled off, he yanked Yawarakai-Te out with great effort and plunged it back in at a higher point above his head, pulling himself up the beast inches at a time and manhandling his way to a better position as the dragon plummeted back down for yet another assault.

He wasn't sure if anyone else was hurt—he had to cling on tightly throughout the rapid descent—but when he opened his eyes, the dragon was once more ascending into the night, and his father was now on its back with him. "What are you doing here?" Ken spluttered. "It's not safe!"

"Baka. I wore those swords longer than you've been alive." Kazuhiko clung, unyielding, to the icicles sprouting from the creature's back. "In the old lore, a dragon's head is its least protected body part. We must find a way to reach that and use the blades there."

"It's a huge dragon! That's gonna take some time!"

"I am in no hurry to land. Your mother will, unfortunately, be chewing both our asses off once we do."

Father and son looked at each other. Despite their peril, they both started laughing.

It took them five minutes. The Fianna had begun shooting cutting spells at the creature but only succeeded in tearing off part of its tail, a loss it didn't seem to feel. Zoe and Tristan had joined in, Zoe with her Ogmios and Tristan with his family's legendary bow. The latter shot at the dragon with unending accuracy, arrows of varying fire and light elements hitting but not penetrating. "Aim for the head!" Ken yelled as they sailed past again, not sure if he was being heard.

Tala and Nya were having better luck, the former negating the attacks the ice creature made whenever it dove back down to the ground, while the latter was trying to whack at its snout with her broom as it swept past her, much to Ken's irritation. "You're gonna need a stronger weapon than that!" he yelled down at her during another pass.

"I know what I'm doing!" was the equally irritated response. In retrospect, she was doing just as much damage as the soldiers, whose fire spells weren't even bothering to slow the creature down.

The dragon circled back and this time made directly for Tala, its jaws wide open like it planned to swallow her whole.

It flew directly into an unexpected snowstorm. Hail as large as rocks pelted at it, and Ken and his father had to duck down to avoid the worst of the attack. Thick icicles as long as the dragon's own forearms materialized within the storm and drove straight into the creature's eyes. Roaring, the beast veered away from Tala, temporarily blinded.

Ken's father had taken Juuchi Yosamu by the time they'd both reached the dragon's head. "Strike when the dragon's closest to the ground," Kazuhiko ordered, and Ken didn't need any further instructions, waiting until the beast swooped down one last time.

Both Inoues stabbed their swords into its head at the same time, hard enough that the blades went all the way in, with only the hilts sticking out.

The dragon squealed; for the first time since taking flight, its wings retracted. It staggered in mid-descent, then fell, tottering wildly from side to side. It tried to send out one last stream of ice as revenge, but Tala was there, turning all its attempts into smoke.

Below Ken and his father, Nya stood, holding her broom like it was a baseball bat. When the dragon drew close enough, she swung it with all her might, uttering a loud battle cry as she did, the sound shattering the windows in the vicinity that weren't already broken.

The broom hit the bridge of the dragon's nose. The whole creature shattered from the impact. Ken felt like his eardrums were exploding along with it. Bits and pieces flew out into a dizzying array of irregular mosaic, and the dragon literally *broke* apart, starting from the point of impact. Tala's agimat shielded both her and Nya from the blast, but Ken and his father had to jump away for safety at the last minute, ice shards cutting into their clothes and arms all the same.

What was left of the dragon promptly melted away after that.

"Where is he?" Tala demanded.

"Where's who?" Nya asked.

"Ryker!" Tala scanned the crowd, angrier than Ken had seen her in a while. "He summoned that hail."

"The hailstorm that helped us take down the dragon?" Zoe asked. "I thought he was supposed to be fighting for the other side?"

Tala glowered at her.

"Hey, just asking. Did you see him do it?"

"No. But who else could it be? We need to find him."

"Your pet is dead," Loki rasped to the OzCorp woman.

"It's not my pet," Fey said calmly. "That's quite the slander."

"I know you have something to do with this."

"If you had evidence, you'd say so, wouldn't you?" The girl stepped forward, placed a hand on theirs, and laughed when they drew back. "I'll even talk to the Fianna, answer any questions they want. But I'll still walk away after that, and you won't be able to stop me, will you?"

Loki could do nothing but glower, helpless.

"No one is to leave," said the Third Honor leader, who'd introduced herself as Sakima. Her Fianna had already taken charge, cordoning off the place and assisting emergency services that had arrived. "That's an order from His Majesty. We're going to need to take statements from everyone at the Schaffers' gala, but we'll try not to take up too much time."

"This is preposterous!" the duchess shrilled. "My husband needs medical attention!"

"Was he injured by the dragon, ma'am?"

"N-not quite," the woman hedged.

"I was punched!" the duke shouted. "By every single one of the Inoues! I'm taking you all to court!"

"And once people learn the reasons you were punched," Margrethe Inoue said with deadly calm, "I'm quite positive you'll earn a lot more sympathy."

The man paused. "Perhaps I wouldn't go so far as to file charges," he admitted, now cautious.

The Fianna leader sighed, clearly familiar with the duke and his reputation. "As your injuries don't seem to be life-threatening, Your Grace, I would suggest keeping quiet and saying very little until the EMTs see to you."

"Will no one apologize?" Ralph Norweggers sputtered as Kazuhiko Inoue helped him to his feet. "It's a matter of civility. I can talk about all the plantations in the world, and they still have no right to—"

Ken's father punched him. The man went down, out cold.

The duchess screamed again.

"Kazuhiko!" Ken's mother exclaimed, a hand coming up to her mouth to cover her snort of laughter.

"He said he'd been hit by *all* the Inoues. I may as well prove him right in one aspect."

"Was that really necessary, milord?" Sakima asked, only slightly reproachful.

"It was a punch a long time coming, ma'am."

"I'll still need your statements." The Fiann looked around at the frightened people, the destroyed mansion. "Bad business, this. Messy situation for His Majesty, and I don't mean the manor."

"Tell me about it," Ken muttered. His ears were still ringing from Nya's shout.

"Media's gonna have a field day with this," one of the warrior women said soberly. "They're going to spin it as our security not being up to par, just you wait."

"All the more reason to find out what's going on. Question all the guests, Hazel," Sakima ordered. "No exceptions. I don't care how rich they are."

"The OzCorp people aren't here," Nya said. "They left shortly before the dragon appeared."

"So you're thinking they have something to do with this?"

Ken and Nya glanced at each other, unwilling to explain just yet. "Just an observation," Nya finally said.

"Sun-Wagner, I expect you to stay with Michele, give us the full report. I know you have a hearing with the Fifth early tomorrow morning, but I can ask him to move the appointment to a later time if you wish."

"That's not needed, ma'am," Loki said. "I'll stay."

"And, Sun-Wagner. Good job."

Loki blinked, not expecting the compliment, then beamed, a little self-consciously. "Yes, ma'am."

"The Fianna's decision about your status?" Tala asked, temporarily forgetting her annoyance. "That's for tomorrow?"

The ranger novice flashed her a nervous grin. "Yeah. I'll let you know how it goes."

"Dex?" Ken asked, tapping his ear.

"I'm still trying to pinpoint the source of the portal, but it's slow going.

Signal's getting bounced all over the place, from here to Spain to Asia and back again. Whoever's responsible doesn't want us to trace it back to the original source. Give me a few minutes, see if I can ferret it out."

"You didn't need to do any of that," Nya told Ken.

"Of course I did. The dragon was making a wreck of everything, and I figured if it wasn't coming down, we were going up."

"Not that, though I have some thoughts about you climbing up that dragon without any protection, and you're going to hear more from me about that later. I'm talking about"—Nya indicated the unconscious duke—"this."

"Yeah, well. I'll punch a hundred of him any day without thought, and for the same reasons. He deserved it. I've been the punchline enough times myself to know a bigot when it smirks in my face. I know you can take care of yourself. You were the first to wallop him all but good. It's just that if you're gonna go fight someone, I wanna be there fighting alongside you, for any reason. For all the reasons."

Nya's eyes were shining. Despite their volume, her clothes had escaped damage during the fight, and under the moonlight, she looked lovelier than ever. Ken stepped closer toward her without thinking, until his pants leg brushed against her skirts. It would have been very romantic, if it wasn't for the crowd and the injured people and the remains of the melted dragon everywhere and the sounds of sirens approaching and his parents standing to one side, his mother pretending like she wasn't noticing anything going on with him and Nya while at the same time giving the impression that she very much needed to know, and also the mermaid incident.

Nya must have remembered that too, because she gulped and shuffled away, and that was enough to break the spell. "Thank you," she said softly.

"You didn't have to do it," Ken said, his voice even softer. "If they connect your screams to the dragon shattering, you could get in trouble."

"Maybe I'm trying to evaluate what secrets I should be keeping if it involves someone I care about."

Ken stilled. "Are you—"

"I found it!" Dex yelled, it felt like, into Ken's ear. Both he and Nya flinched.

"Damnit, Gallagher!"

"Sorry, so sorry. But I think I know where the portal is coming from." Dex sounded excited...and scared. "It's coming from right here inside Avalon. I'll send over the coordinates to His Majesty soon, but I think it's coming from OzCorp's main headquarters, over at Marooners' Rock."

15

IN WHICH LOKI
RESCUES A STRAY

The tide of gossip was rising: rumors that Avalon was compromised, that this was all a stunt to elevate the "irrelevant" kingdom, that King Alex himself was experimenting with his newfound abilities and was committing all sorts of human rights violations in the process.

Nya, Ken, and the Inoues had taken on some notoriety after the incident, and while they'd all turned down interviews from the press, Ken's social media following had swelled to nearly triple his previous number. Loki hadn't been identified yet as far as they knew, to their relief.

The dragon had done little to stem the tide of visitors still flocking to Avalon, where people continued posting selfies beside the Nameless Sword or recorded attempts to take it out.

The Fifth Honor had returned to the forest to hunt the jabberwock, but it had disappeared.

Loki's status was still in limbo. They were waiting outside the Fianna's head office, where the Wake, the elected leader of all thirteen honors, was to make his final decision. They kept turning the newly repaired Ruyi Jingu Bang over and over in their hands; Dex and the Gallaghers' lab techs had performed a miracle. That it was looking new and whole was all Loki could hope for, really. "There weren't any curses I had to deal with in exchange for fixing it," they remembered Dex saying. "It was almost like the staff itself had absorbed whatever the spell's repercussions were, like it had a mind of its own. Weird, right?"

Loki studied the staff in their hands. It *was* weird.

"Would you rather marry the Royal States king and have the strength of a hundred men," Zoe asked contemplatively, "or marry Aferstan Bluebeard and become immortal?"

The Bandersnatchers, all of whom had accompanied Loki, paused to consider both options. Since Bluebeard was a serial murderer and the Royal States king being what he was, it took a while to decide.

"Bluebeard," Tala finally decided, rubbing her shoulder. "He's already in jail in Belarus, and they'll probably execute him any day now, so it won't take that long to wait, I suppose."

West wrinkled his nose. "Barbaric practice."

"Would it require consummation," Nya asked, "or would this be a marriage in name only?"

"Consummation is necessary," Zoe decided.

"Urgh."

"Still Bluebeard," Tala said. "What about you, Loki?"

"The same," Loki said. "But I think at this point, we're all probably biased."

Ken chuckled. "Yeah, probably Bluebeard too. Cole?"

Loki had seen the tension between Ken and Nya last night but was glad that they seemed more relaxed about it today. Maybe they'd made up.

Cole shrugged. "Me too."

"Let's make it unanimous," Zoe said. "We're all marrying Bluebeard, which, given his history, is a bit ironic."

Chuckles all around. Loki stared at their staff.

"Hey," Tala said gently. "I know you're worried. And I know you've wanted to join the Fifth Honor for a long time. But I just wanna let you know that whatever happens, you're still gonna be a Bander. Walang iwanan, like Lola Urduja said."

"Are you okay?" Tala seemed more subdued than usual. Loki narrowed their eyes. "You keep holding your shoulder. Did you pull a muscle?"

"Ah, no. Just a bit sore." The girl winced. "I tried Simeli again this morning. You guys really can't give me a clue?"

"We'd lose our memories," Nya reminded her lightly.

"Ugh. I know. I just really don't know how to get past the maze."

Loki had a very good idea of why Tala kept failing at that last stage but kept their mouth shut. They had faith she would figure it out, though they felt bad about how torn up she was at not having succeeded again.

"You'll do it," Ken chimed in loyally. "You have no idea how close you are to the answer. And, Loki, I'm sure you'll be fine. Personally, I don't see the appeal in joining the Fianna. What if your commanding officer turns out to be a prat?"

"Well," said the Wake calmly from behind him. "Normally, the rules are in place to weed out the prats from taking charge in the first place, but I suppose we've had some rare exceptions in the past."

Ken coughed, looking a little red. "Didn't mean any offense, sir."

"None taken. Shall we, Sun-Wagner?"

Loki stood up nervously. Zoe patted them on the back. "We'll wait for you."

The Wake's office looked almost like a typical administrator's, if one discounted the numerous weapons, both familiar and grotesque, mounted on the walls like they were university diplomas. The man gestured at Loki to sit, himself occupying a high-backed chair behind a wooden, slightly scuffed table with a small name plaque that said *Bharat*

Keer, PhD, Rígfénnid on it. A laptop, deactivated hexbombs redesigned as paperweights, and an empty beer glass with a decal that said *World's Greatest Dad* rounded out the rest of the items. "Sakima informed me about last night," he began. "She was very impressed."

"Thank you, sir."

"You showed courage under fire and were quick to obey orders. This time around."

"Yes, sir."

"Your ranger test will continue as scheduled in a month's time. I suggest you stay out of trouble till then. His Majesty, however, has asked to bring you along on certain select missions of his choosing despite the fact that you are not an official recruit yet, and I've agreed." He leaned forward. "Lord Kensington and Lady Nya have uncovered accounts of people turning up missing inside OzCorp. I'm sure you've heard."

"Ken and Nya told me that, yes."

"This is at His Majesty's request, you understand. Other novices would be directing traffic. Your previous service to the king means you have the privilege of working on matters he deems to be of immediate importance. He has asked to keep you on for investigating key personnel at OzCorp. Vivien Fey was the name he mentioned specifically. You are free to follow up on her, on three conditions: that you do not directly go out of your way to confront the woman, that you conduct your investigation only through legal means, and that you must inform us immediately of any findings."

"I agree, sir."

"That said, your parents' history with the Fianna will not provide you any other special favors."

"I would never ask for them, sir."

"I've read the report you wrote on Mykonos's orders. Vivien Fey is working on a special Avalon visa as provided by OzCorp. Seems like she's one of their talents, and they'll be fighting hard to keep her here. Appearances can be deceiving, but we've taken a look at her background, and nothing's triggering any red flags beyond that incident of trespassing. No criminal record, graduated summa cum laude at MIT at only sixteen years old, double degree in biochem conjuration and mechanical engineering. Only dependent is a younger sister—Abigail Fey, fifteen years old. The Sixth asked her in for questioning, and she claimed she found the Dormouse bomb spells herself just as you arrived. Only thing we can get her for was an unauthorized port into the Tangled Woods, and OzCorp paid for that fine. We had to let her go. You're smart, Sun-Wagner. You know how the process goes. Tell me what happens when there's no concrete proof of any wrongdoing."

"It means there's no case, sir."

"Exactly. Cops the world over have a bad rep, Sun-Wagner. That's why His Majesty is very adamant about shaping the Fianna to be both disciplined *and* accountable for our actions. We're doing our best to buck against the trend, and that includes going down hard on any Fiann going rogue. I believe you. But we need more proof than just that."

"Thank you, sir."

"Keep out of trouble, Cadet, and you should have no trouble. Dismissed."

As they promised, the Banders were still waiting outside. "Told you it wouldn't take long," Zoe said, smiling.

"Thank you," Loki said. Their legs still felt like jelly. "You didn't need to."

"Of course we're here for support, Loki," West piped up. "That's what we do."

"Thanks," Loki said gratefully.

"And now I gotta go," Tala sighed. "Promised my lola I'd spend the day with her and the other Makilings."

"You really agreed to that?"

"Yeah. Hope it's not a mistake. They really don't like my dad."

"You don't need to go if you don't want to," Zoe pointed out.

"I think I should, if it can help soften their stance on him. Plus they seem to know some arnis tricks my folks haven't taught me yet."

"If you need someone to rant to later, I'm all ears," Loki offered.

Tala smiled at them. It brightened her face, made her look even prettier. "Thanks. I'll probably take you up on that."

Tala took her leave near Maidenkeep's entrance, and the rest were prepared to head back into the Hollows until West stiffened, nose twitching. "It's her," he gasped.

"Her?" Ken asked.

"The OzCorp girl. Fey whatshername."

"Hide!" Loki had already spotted Vivien Fey, strolling down the corridors of Maidenkeep arm in arm with the minister of trade, talking and laughing. Everyone ducked behind a wall, but neither noticed their presence.

"Thank you so much for vouching for us, Minister," Vivien was saying. "I'm sorry for telling you at such short notice."

"We child prodigies should stick together, I suppose," Minister Ancilotto chuckled. "I don't think it was fair for His Majesty to give you such a short time frame to relocate. Since I feel like this was my mistake, I just want to rectify it as best as I can. I hope this won't stop OzCorp from doing more business with Avalon?"

"On the contrary, we're even more interested. It's nice to deal with a government agency that's refreshingly free from corruption for a change."

"I didn't do much. His Majesty has already given you permission to transfer any equipment you've left behind back to your headquarters, so my letter is merely authorizing you to do what you've already been granted."

"We want to err on the side of caution, and we definitely don't want to antagonize His Majesty any further."

"I understand. His Majesty can have a temper sometimes. May I escort you back to the looking glass?"

"I'll be meeting some of my colleagues in Lyonesse, so that won't be necessary. I haven't had time to explore the city just yet."

"She's got some balls, doesn't she?" Zoe whispered. "Right out here in the open, where she knows we could see her."

"We need to follow her," Loki said.

"Loki," Nya said. "Hello? You just got out of a meeting with the Wake where, I presume, he told you not to get into *more* trouble."

That was true. "I can't just let her go like that! I'm pretty sure Ancilotto just gave her permission to go back to the Tangled Woods!"

"The Fifth Honor investigated the place and found nothing," Cole said quietly.

"I don't think they're there to destroy any evidence. I think they're gonna attempt to capture the jabberwock again."

"The Fianna have been searching for it this whole time," Zoe pointed out. "I don't think they'll find it in the course of one afternoon."

"I need to sniff her," West said.

"What?"

"I have an, um, photogenic memory, but for smelling."

"I think you mean photographic memory, West. Are you saying you remember every scent you've ever smelled?"

"I can. And I think I can track the jabberwock too. If it's still in the woods, I'll find wherever it's hiding before they do."

"We could tell the Wake," Nya suggested.

"He just told me they're no longer investigating Fey," Loki said. "I doubt they'll reopen the case on my say-so. He also told me to avoid confronting her, and that's not what I intend to do here."

"Loki, this might ruin your chances to join the Fianna again."

Loki knew that. And if they had to be honest, a part of their insistence was their frustration, that Fey was blatantly getting away with it and mocking them while she did it. But they couldn't wait for the Fianna to go through the process. "I know, but I think this is a lot more important. We'll tell Alex at least."

"What are you all doing?" It was Tita Baby, staring at them with her hands on her hips. By her side were Tito Boy and General Luna.

"Nothing," Nya said immediately, but it was too late.

The woman watched Vivien head off to the palace gates. "I see. You think there are some shenanigans going on with that girl. Well, none of you shall be gallivanting off into trouble without us to watch over you."

"I don't know what you mean," Loki began evasively.

"Don't play coy. Where are we going?"

They sighed. "To the Tangled Woods."

"That is being very sneaky," Tita Baby said disapprovingly. "You are going where they do not want you to go."

"If I was in their place," Tito Boy signed, "I would do the same. It seems there is more at stake here than just a place in the Fianna."

"Tangina," General Luna agreed.

"You're…siding with us?" Ken asked.

Tita Baby let out a long-suffering sigh. "That is a lot of risk to take when your career is at stake, Loki. But if the Fianna have no legal basis to spy on her—and they are spread out all over the kingdom as it is, trying to secure Avalon—then our presence can at least give you *some* legality. I only do this because I trust your instincts, Loki. But I must warn you. We will probably find nothing there to be concerned about."

"Santa Maria, ina ng Diyos," Tita Baby said, crossing herself fervently.

It was easy enough for West to find the jabberwock.

What they didn't expect was to find the monster on its side with its eyes closed, its wings folded to one side. It seemed to be asleep.

Plaintive cries sounded in the air, far too high-pitched and small to be coming from the massive jabberwock.

"Didn't you fight one of these in the past?" Loki asked Tita Baby.

"Yes. But in fairness, it was only a fledgling. Not one of this size."

"Patay," General Luna rumbled.

"Are you nervous, General? We're not as sprightly as we once were, but the three of us could still take one down, just like old times."

"No," Tito Boy signed, staring hard at the jabberwock. "He means *dead*. It's dead."

The general was right. The creature wasn't breathing.

Cautiously, Loki crept forward. The others followed their lead. "There are slash marks along its abdomen," Loki said quietly. "I didn't do that. So either there's something else in these woods that it encountered strong enough to kill it, or someone else found it after the Fianna left."

"Are we really gonna stick around and find out who did it, though?" Ken asked nervously.

"This doesn't look natural," Tito Boy signed, crouching down and laying a hand across the jabberwock's flank, where a series of burn patterns was evident. "These look like laser marks. Military-grade lasers, from the extent of the damage."

"Well, I doubt that the Fianna did that," Zoe said. "Nya, didn't you say that OzCorp had employed some soldiers when they were building near Ikpe?"

"Yeah. And the wounds look fresh. They might only be minutes behind us, if they found this jabberwock sooner than we thought."

There was another heart-wrenching cry. Loki circled the fallen monster and saw a small head poking up near the jabberwock's tail. It was smaller than his forearm and had large ears and a long snout. It blinked bright red eyes at them and then cried again.

"Tangina," General Luna breathed.

"A baby jabberwock." Even Tito Boy's fingers were trembling.

"We need to kill it." This from a grim Tita Baby.

"No!" Nya exclaimed.

"I'm sorry, but we don't have a choice. It's dangerous."

"We're not going to kill it, Tita. Please."

Tita Baby met their gaze and exhaled.

"Baby jabberwocks are harmless at this stage," Tito Boy signed. "It will need some sustenance with its parent dead."

The wockling paused in its crying and cautiously sniffed at Loki's extended palm. It purred softly when Loki slowly stroked its fur.

"What do jabberwocks eat again?" Tita Baby asked.

"Spells," Zoe said. "Low-level magic will do. I have something, for emergencies." She dug into her pocket and produced a small kit. She took special strips of candle paper, then struck her thumb along the edge to create some light. "It's just a bit of food for you. Here you go."

The wockling hopped closer, nuzzled at the thin parchment with its snout, and then promptly began to nibble at the flame it produced.

"This changes matters," Tita Baby said. The wockling was now curled up in Loki's arms, looking contented as it feasted. "You were right, Loki.

We can stretch the truth if it gets you into trouble, tell them *we* found it and that you were nowhere nearby."

"A nancy," General Luna grunted, also inspecting the corpse. "Babae to."

"He's right," Tito Boy signed. "Wockling's mother. Might be another jabberwock out here, and we won't want to be in the same vicinity as its dead mate."

"May tao," the general warned, stilling.

Loki heard it too: noises that told them people were fast approaching. The glints of spells from the distance suggested that they were armed with magic.

They reached into their own kit again and produced a round object that looked like a cross between a bath bomb and a hamster ball. "Move several feet back, and keep together."

Once they'd done so, Loki threw the ball at their feet. A cloud of smoke wafted up and passed through them. They watched as the Banders and the Katipuneros slowly disappeared from view, until there was nothing to see but the foliage behind them. They looked down at the wockling in their arms. They could no longer see it, but they could feel the baby's weight, hear its soft purring.

The noises grew louder. Loki wasn't surprised to see several men come into view, wearing OzCorp uniforms. There were other soldiers present, a different emblem stitched into their uniforms.

General Luna bit back another curse. "Alastor," he whispered bleakly. "Private security."

"That's the same one we saw near Ikpe," Nya whispered.

Alsaid Corvington, the CFO of OzCorp, led the group, followed by a couple of men in civilian wear.

"Heads of the OzCorp R & D department," Zoe murmured. "Henri Indra and Jacob Coval."

Loki looked past the two and bit down on their lip to prevent a gasp from escaping. Vivien Fey was there with them, scowling.

The firebird flew in after them.

"Why is it here?" Loki asked, shocked. From the muffled swearing from the Katipuneros, it was clear they weren't expecting it either.

"Maybe Alex sent it?" But Ken sounded uncertain.

The group passed them without a second glance; the soldiers drew their weapons at the sight of the fallen jabberwock. Their leader issued a terse order, but Loki couldn't hear what they were saying.

There was a popping sound as Tito Boy deliberately stepped out from behind the invisibility curtain Loki had set up.

"What are you doing?" they whispered at him, but the man ducked behind a tree to move closer to the group. He began signing rapidly.

"There's a spell around them, an anti-eavesdropping one," Tita Baby said. "But that is no barrier to your tito."

"The rich do not think of those with disabilities, and so we always find unexpected loopholes, no matter how richly paid their lawyers." There was a smugness to Tito Boy's gestures before he began translating the conversation for their benefit.

"Dead," one of the Alastor men reported, nudging his gun against the monster.

"My phone isn't working," Tala whispered, "and I doubt any of yours are either. They're really intent on hiding evidence."

Corvington swore and delivered a hard kick to the unmoving creature's hide. "Indra. How does this change things?"

"Perhaps we can reconfigure the project so that one will be enough to power both the prototype and the original," one of the men suggested.

"That will deplete its potential power by at least half, not to mention possibly kill it sooner than we want," his colleague argued.

"Shet," General Luna muttered, and Loki could only agree, because it sounded like OzCorp already had the other jabberwock. Did they know about the baby?

Their question was promptly answered. "Fey here said the jabberwock displayed visible signs of pregnancy," Coval said. "The wockling should only be about three, four hours old but still dangerous. Is it likely to survive on its own?"

"It won't survive your experiments," Fey said coldly. "It would need another three years before it could handle our prototype. You'll kill it without giving us any advantage."

"Ruggedo Nome doesn't want to wait three years."

"A dead jabberwock will delay the project by more than that. Your soldiers are far too trigger-happy with their guns."

"What do you expect from American mercenaries? You don't get the final say in this. Maybe if you hadn't been taking so many vacation days, the project would be on schedule."

"My sister's been sick! And I never asked for more days off than my job allowed!"

"Not my problem. I make the final decisions here. You're just another overpaid bitch."

"How dare you speak that way to me!"

"I'll speak however I want, to whomever I want." The man took a threatening step toward Vivien but was stopped in his tracks when the firebird hovered before him, blocking his way. It gave a little snarl.

"Fine," he said, retreating. "Everyone, spread out and search. It shouldn't have gotten very far."

The wockling in Loki's arms whimpered.

"Why aren't they worried about the firebird?" Zoe asked. "What's going on?"

"We must leave this place as soon as possible," Tita Baby whispered.

"Detecting heat signatures!" Indra announced. "And a unique energy pattern, two hundred meters south! It's...wait."

"What now?" Corvington snapped.

"It's an energy signature, but it's not from any of our equipment! Someone's cast a low-level spell in the area! Give me a few seconds to lock it down."

"Get ready to run!" Loki hissed. Already the scientist was turning in their direction.

There was a loud cooing noise.

Loki looked up, bit back a gasp. The firebird sat on an overhead branch, gazing down at them. It took in a deep breath.

The fireball it unexpectedly unleashed turned a nearby tree into a blazing inferno. It sprayed the ground before them, stopping the soldiers from drawing nearer to where they stood.

The little jabberwock screeched.

"I heard it!" a soldier yelled. "I heard the wockling!"

"That's our cue to leave," Loki ordered. They were already running, the rest not far behind. Already the spell was starting to wear off, and the soldier nearest to them jumped back when they appeared. He raised his gun.

There was a crack of a whip, and the firearm spun out of his grasp. Zoe was running backward, lashing her Ogmios out at any soldier within reach.

Loki grabbed at the toothpick tucked behind their ear, then realized it was no longer there.

The soldier's head whipped back when something came hurtling out from the woods to wallop them hard across the face. The man was unconscious before he'd even hit the ground, but Ruyi Jingu Bang was far from done. It latched on to the next nearest OzCorp mercenary, battering at his head and neck until one final thwack sent him flying into a tree.

The other soldiers opened fire on the staff, but it leaped out of sight, only to drive another soldier's face into the ground from above, then lengthened on both ends to take out another two men on either side of it. It ducked out of view when another group fired a fresh round, inadvertently shooting their comrades.

"Stop!" Corvington was screaming. "Hold your fire, hold your fire!"

Fey remained where she was, staring at Loki. She looked stunned to see them there.

Loki lifted a hand, saluted her briefly, and then was off.

It took no time at all to reach the Avalon border and find the Red King port they'd used to get there. A whistling noise hurtled toward them. Almost instinctively, Loki raised their hand and caught Ruyi Jingu Bang easily, though the momentum sent them tumbling into the portal, sprawling back into the Hollows.

"I smelled them all," West said a bit viciously. "American Templates One through Twenty-Two. If I meet any of them again, I'll remember."

"Well," Tita Baby said, panting slightly, bent over with her hand against her chest. "So it seems that the OzCorp personnel weren't just experimenting with bombs. They were planning to capture the jabberwock and use it for some kind of spelltech."

"Not any spelltech Alex approved, that's for sure." Zoe frowned. "I'm more interested to know what the firebird was doing there and why it was aiding them."

"And why OzCorp didn't seem bothered to find it there," Ken added.

Loki looked down at the staff. The question of whether the Gallaghers had fixed their segen had been answered, but it seemed like they'd fixed it far too well. "Welcome back. I think."

Ruyi Jingu Bang wriggled in their hand in response, then shrunk until it was back to the size and form of a toothpick without waiting, like it had been that all along.

"We need to talk to Alex about his firebird," they said, dread clenching in their stomach. "Did it send that fireball to help us escape, or did it do that to alert them to our presence? And why?"

Everyone looked helplessly back at them, but nobody had an answer.

***

Telling his parents turned out to be the easiest part of the day. Anthony and Shawn Sun-Wagner saw the wriggling jabberwock in their arms and began talking animatedly before Loki had even mounted an explanation.

"Brittany will know how to take care of it," Anthony said. "They've never had a jabberwock before, but they've got a government permit in Scotland to run a loch preserve with the Nessies. It'll feel right at home there."

"It's only a wockling," his husband reminded him. "Sam might be the better option. Remember, he just took in that nest of baby rocs? They'll help it socialize. He won't turn down the chance. This will be the first jabberwock to ever be cared for in captivity. Let me make a phone call."

Loki waited. Several minutes later, along with half a dozen documents drawn up to transfer the jabberwock to its new home, Shawn finally paused. "Wait a minute. Loki, how did you even find a jabberwock? We'll need to tell Alex about this! Oh, crap. We forgot to tell Alex!"

"In the forest," Loki said, being deliberately literal. "Alex already knows."

"But does the Fianna know? Let me call Bharat and see if we can—"

"I, um, wasn't supposed to be there. I think I could get into trouble, but I'm not sure."

Both parents looked at each other. "Loki," Shawn sighed. "You can't disobey orders just because you want to. Haven't you learned from your near expulsion?"

"I was technically obeying orders," Loki said cautiously. "Alex approved it."

"And that technicality is only going to save your ass if you confess immediately to Mykonos. Because if they find out—and I assure you, they will—you can kiss a career in the Fianna goodbye. Loki. What are you even doing, dear? Are you trying to sabotage yourself?"

"You both went against the rules too, because there was something you believed in more. I feel the same way about this. Plus, there's a chance that the firebird might be helping OzCorp, and I think it's important for Alex to hear that from me personally."

"Do you have proof?"

"We couldn't get any. But the Katipuneros would vouch for me."

"Will it hold up in court? It would be your word against theirs. Because OzCorp has a very good set of lawyers, and they will spin this quickly. They could argue that you brought the firebird there to harm *them*."

"I know," Loki said miserably.

Another look passed between their parents. "We trust you," Anthony finally said. "Promise me that you'll at least have the Katipuneros with you if you and your friends think you need to investigate further. Your father and I are civilians now, so this is all out of our hands. But you will have to fess up to Mykonos, Loki. And I can't say for sure how he's going to respond in light of this."

Loki nodded. "I'll accept any punishment they decide." They did the right thing. They were sure of it. But now all this was giving rise to a fresh onslaught of doubts. They'd always dreamed about joining the Fianna.

His parents had been so proud to learn they were following in Anthony's footsteps.

But it was starting to look like their duties there would often contradict the ones they had as part of the Order of the Bandersnatch. And should they finally be officially recruited into the Fifth Honor, Loki had a sinking feeling that they were going to have to choose one over the other.

"I'm glad you're being responsible about this at least. We'll watch over the wockling until our friends from the reserve arrive." Anthony wrinkled his nose. "In the meantime, take a shower. You stink."

16

IN WHICH TALA HAS THE BIGGEST AGIMAT

I can't believe that I'm saying this," Tala said for what felt like the hundredth time, "but this is way too much food."

She'd eaten at boodle fights before. Her parents and the Katipuneros had prepared one for Alex when he'd first arrived at Invierno.

But this was like the boodle fight of boodle fights. The table was at least a dozen feet long and half as wide, and every conceivable space was laden with heaps of food served on banana leaf plates: bowls of sour tamarind soup with okra and pork chunks, vegetables in coconut cream, beef and tripe in thick peanut sauce, grilled tilapia with tomatoes on the side, chopped sizzling pork innards with liberal sprinklings of crackling skin on top, and there were many others that Tala didn't even know the names of. Scoops of steaming rice were generously piled up beside the viands.

Her stomach was growling louder than a caged tiger. She had had misgivings when she'd finally accept her grandmother's invitation, even with her mother's blessing, but now she'd forgotten what they were.

Lola Corazon placed a large serving of adobo before her. "I was told this is your favorite," she said with a smile.

"It is. But this is all so…" The Philippine delegation to Avalon was comprised of thirty-five members. Most were also descended from the same tribe that Maria Makiling once led, making them all her kinspeople of a sort.

"You are a Makiling. More importantly, you are my granddaughter. You deserve the best that we have." Lola Corazon offered her a portion of rice that she accepted, while the others dug in with gusto. Tala enjoyed eating with her hands. There was something particularly satisfying about shoveling food into your mouth using only your fingers, like somehow food tasted better that way.

"The adobo tastes exactly how Mom makes it," she said.

"And who do you think taught her?" Lola Corazon asked. She was still smiling, but the corners of her mouth were pinched.

"Oh. I—"

"No, no. Do not concern yourself with it, hija. Your mother and I have always been at odds, even from when she was little. If she had not married the Scourge, she would not have had to hide away in America, and perhaps we would have known each other better. But I am very proud of you. I had no idea you were so close to His Majesty. Did you know that Makilings have married ancestors of his, long before Maria took the agimat onto herself? I would not be surprised to see history repeating itself soon."

"Really?" Tala took a big gulp of calamansi juice and ate another mouthful of rice with her sisig. "Alex's my best friend. But it's nice to know we have another connection."

"He says you saved his life."

"He did?"

"We worked with his father for years," another of the clan spoke up, who'd told her earlier that his name was Miguel. "Kawawa—his parents taken from him so soon. They would not approve his lifestyle."

It was true that the castle wasn't as opulent now as when they'd first discovered Maidenkeep. Alex had called most of the adornments excessive and had packed away some of the more sentimental items for safekeeping or sold the others to bolster the government budget. "He said he doesn't want to live like a king. A lot of it went to funding Avalon's first fiscal year."

"Yes, that too," Miguel sighed. "It is disheartening to see. But I think you will be good for him."

"The Philippines has pledged to offer any assistance they can give for our decades of friendship," another man named Rommel spoke up. "We hope our agimat can help repel some of the bad magic aimed his way."

"You have agimat too?" Of course they did. She should have thought about that sooner. The curse extended to all members of the Makiling clan, and they were exactly that.

There were a few chuckles. Rommel lifted a hand, and Tala could see the familiar glow of a shield settling around him, much like her own. One by one, the people sitting around the table manifested their own agimat, including Lola Corazon, whose curse settled and draped around her person like a shawl, at a level of proficiency Tala hadn't even thought possible. "Would you like to learn how to control your agimat like this?" Lola Corazon asked. "To wield it into any shape and form you would like, and—"

"Opo!" Tala practically shouted in her eagerness, and everyone burst into laughter.

"First," Miguel said, "what arnis style did your parents teach you?"

"Arnis style?"

"Balintawak Eskrima? Black Scorpion? Doce Pares?" He paused at the confused look on her face. "Lumina never trained you?"

"They did," Tala whispered, suddenly embarrassed. "But they didn't tell me what style it was supposed to be."

Another Filipino snorted. "Of course she would be confused. A white man taught her eskrima." Snickers met that statement.

"My father is good at it!" Tala said defensively.

"Really? A man who only took up the art because he is married to a woman who practices it? Do you think that someone who only started a couple of decades ago despite having lived hundreds of years would be more proficient than the people who have been using it to fight their whole lives?"

Tala looked down at her fish, not sure what to say. And who *was* she really, to say that her father was better at this than they were?

One of the women at her right, a doctor named Dolores Baet, sighed. "Pasensya," she said. "We Makilings do not like Kay Warnock. He worked with Maria Makiling in the past. He had the chance to save her, and he did not. But we do not want to make you feel uncomfortable either, trapped in the middle like this."

"You never saw any old videos of Maria Makiling back then?" Tala asked, remembering the Beast of Suddene's assertion that his father had sent a copy to the Filipinos decades ago.

Miguel snorted. "We have. It only proves that Maria should not have died then."

"Did you know," another Filipino said, a man the others called John Lloyd, "that Maria Makiling once boobytrapped a whole mountain and destroyed three Spanish armies without any loss of life in her own troops? Or that she once decimated an American regiment all by herself?"

"There is a mountain in the Philippines named after her," another of the warriors said. "Some legends say she survived the Americans and escaped to it, that she has found immortality and lives there to this day. We have so many stories about her. We will tell you everything we know about your history. Our history."

Miguel smiled. "Agimat first, for now. If you have nothing in your schedule today, we will be happy to teach you. I fight with the Doce Pares style of eskrima, which employs other arnis techniques based on your own preference and strengths. I think that would be a good choice for you."

"I use the Bakbakan style," Rommel said. "Dr. Baet is from the Garimot arnis school, and John Lloyd here prefers the Ensayo Tactical technique."

"It's saved my life many times," John Lloyd said.

"From his wife!" Someone farther down the table hooted, and everyone burst into laughter.

"It's a wonder he can get a girl to look at him, considering how oddly shaped his agimat is."

"It's not!" John Lloyd protested, and his agimat grew, the shield-like curse around him extending as large and as rounded as a minivan.

"Mine's bigger," a woman named Jennylyn countered, and her own expanded in response, now bigger than the man's, to even more mirth. Soon everyone was trying to outdo the others, expanding and shrinking their agimats in friendly competition.

"Pasensya na," Dr. Baet apologized again, though she was also chuckling. "They do this all the time."

"I don't mind," Tala said, surprised by how much she meant it. And then, on a sudden whim, she expanded her own agimat, outpacing most of the others in size.

"Do you see that?" Rommel chortled. "Hers is bigger than yours!"

The conversation shifted soon enough to other Filipino matters: insider gossip for the forthcoming Southeast Asian games the Philippines were hosting that year (mainly about a committee head no one in the group liked, who was being publicly slammed for his ineptness); concern over the potential floods brought on by the incoming monsoon season; some new transportation scheme by the Philippine's datu, Leonor Rizal to alleviate Manila's terrible traffic. Tala found that she was enjoying herself. For once, she didn't feel like the odd person out. For once, there was no assortment of spells clouding her vision, no need for her to have to control her agimat. For once, she didn't have to be so self-conscious about being the only person with a magic-negating curse.

For the first time in a long time, Tala relaxed and let go, no longer worried about having to tuck her agimat close around her for fear of disrupting nearby spelltech. Lola Corazon saw and grinned approvingly at her. She smiled back.

They didn't like her father or her mother for marrying him. But if they liked Tala well enough, then maybe they could learn to tolerate Kay for her sake, maybe even work toward patching up their relationship with Lumina.

And she could talk to these Filipinos about her agimat. Alex and Zoe and the others tried their best, but sometimes the only people who understood were the ones who'd gone through the same things she had, who understood what it was like to not feel normal. She didn't feel so alone now.

A loud ringing broke through the chatter. Lola Corazon took it, conversed quietly for a few minutes, then frowned, signaling the others to be silent. "They found a jabberwock by the Wonderland border," she announced in Tagalog. "Dead. His Majesty says his people are also detecting unusual energy at the southern border, near the Esopian lands. The Fianna are to investigate, and Datu Rizal is asking us to aid them."

The Filipinos rose to their feet, the meal forgotten. Lola Corazon paused, glancing down at all the uneaten food. "Tupperware," she ordered an aide, who went off to find some. "Normally, I would tell you to stay behind," she told Tala next. "But if your parents have been very remiss about your arnis instruction, then I would assume they have not shown you the extent of your agimat either. And the only way to learn is through observation and application. Would you like to come with us?"

"I would love that," Tala said eagerly, then hesitated. "As long as nobody tells my parents till afterward," she finally offered, sensing that this was not her mother's intention when she agreed to let Tala visit.

Lola Corazon laughed, a deep belly chuckle. "That I will not do. Come. Let us show you what it means to be a Makiling."

The Burn was exactly what its name implied. A wall of fire stretched across the horizon, black acrid smoke filling the air. A steel barricade separated them from the eternally scorching flames, more for their protection than as a means to help contain the blaze. Coming any nearer, one of the sentries told them, would be dangerous to their health. Tala didn't know much about it, save that it was the consequence of wild magic gone awry and that several American ministers had gone on the news blaming Alex for polluting the environment.

Several delegates from the Pirate Republic were also present. The fires extended beyond Avalon land into several miles of sea, and the *Jolly Roger* was docked within sight, by the small outpost set up to monitor the phenomenon. The *Jolly Roger* looked exactly like what Tala envisioned a pirate ship to be, complete with a skull-and-crossbones flag at its mast, flapping in the wind. For a warship that was purportedly several hundred years old, it was in remarkable shape.

Its leader, Captain Mairead Tattercloak, was scowling into the fires like they had insulted her somehow. "We could have the *Jolly Roger* shoot at it," she offered. "Most of my crew are already in place on board, waiting on my command."

"Not sure that would be wise, Captain."

"Probably not," the pirate admitted. "Offering our assistance is the least we could do, seeing that the *Jolly Roger* was responsible for that whole mess."

"How long has this been burning?" Miguel asked wonderingly. "I am not familiar with this part of Avalon."

"A powerful spell," Lola Corazon said with a shrug. "A result of the fight between Hook and Pan. It destroyed Neverland and separated the lands of Esopia from the rest of Avalon."

"Destroyed two-thirds of the *Jolly Roger* too," Captain Mairead said. "It's a wonder my predecessors even got it working again."

"Was it a bomb, like Wonderland?" Tala asked.

"Even worse. Hook was attempting to recreate your Nine Maidens. Pan was trying to steal it for his own ends." The captain shrugged. "Didn't end well for either of them."

"And there's no way to cross over?"

"Esopia has always been mostly desert," Dr. Baet said. "And it's not very likely that the few people who lived there could survive the harsh climate, much less the frost. Not even our agimat can affect it. The spells that created these flames were known only to Pan and the pirates."

"Not to the current pirates," another pirate, Zahid, disagreed. "We don't know how to fix this either. Those answers died with its original owner."

"So now we consider it our duty to use it to show love and kick ass instead," the drag queen—Tala remembered that her name was Seraphina—said. "Spread some chaotic good."

Not too far away from the flames was a… Tala could not describe it accurately, but it looked like part of the air was shaped like a hole, and that hole was wobbling. It was almost as if someone had gotten hold of a very thin, circular metal sheet that was also somehow three-dimensional and was enthusiastically making it flap up and down.

"What's that?" She gagged. The magic tasted like a mixture of raw meat and chlorine, and it was hard work, trying not to barf when she had a full stomach.

"An attempt at another port, similar to the one that erupted at that fancy party yesterday. This is why Avalon asked for us," Lola Corazon.

The Second Honor had arrived through another looking glass, and they greeted Lola Corazon and the rest of the group with obvious respect. "The energy patterns here are similar to the one we encountered before," said their leader, a tall man named Mak. He glanced at Tala and raised an inquiring eyebrow, but Lola Corazon showed no sign of wanting to explain her granddaughter's presence, so he continued. "The Gallaghers believe it is similar to the anomaly that brought the ice dragon into Lyonesse. We thought you guys might like first crack at it." He pointed to a small machine that some of the Fianna were also bringing out of the looking glass, a device that looked like a spiderweb except about ten feet taller. "The Gallaghers said we could use this to repair the vulnerability, but it will still take us another twenty minutes to achieve the energy levels needed to power it. I take it that's not enough?"

"You guessed right," Lola Corazon said with a grim smile. "Is there a reason why your machine takes so long to activate?"

"A consequence of the spell was to suck out the life force of everyone nearby. A longer charging duration instead of immediacy was the best compromise."

While the others examined the spiderweb-like spelltech, Tala approached the captain. "Miss Tattercloak?" she began.

The pirate laughed. "Miss or Lady is not my title, love. I answer only to *Captain*. But please call me Mairead."

Tala gulped and pushed on. "I'm sorry. I just wanted to ask how Ryker's doing."

"Ah, young Cadfael. Stayed with us for a night, a few days after your encounter. Rather sad. Moped a bit. Then he was off again and we haven't seen him since."

"He didn't tell you where he went?"

"Nay. I do know he was very honest about wanting to protect you. I don't know why he's refusing to cut ties with the Snow Queen, since it seemed to me he was all but ready to throw her off once he was done with his sulk. I suspect she's got something on him that's stopping him from making that final leap."

Tala's heart sank. "And you don't know how to contact him?"

"I can ask the *Jolly Roger*, but there are no guarantees. Maybe it'll tell me, maybe it won't. I can swear to send word as soon as it does. Would that be good enough?"

"Yes," Tala said quickly. "Thank you."

"Anything for Kay Warnock's daughter. You know, the *Jolly Roger* offered for your father too—decades ago, the previous captain told me. He refused. Said he needed to keep his feet grounded from here on out."

"Whoever is doing this distortion," Lola Corazon said, "is very good."

"Not just good. They're learning with every encounter." Mak scowled. "The portal at the Schaffers' opened quickly enough, but it was easier for us to detect it almost immediately. This one is slower and funnels shorter bursts of magic at a time. We almost didn't notice it, especially out here where the magic from the Burn can camouflage weaker spells. Might be why they chose this place. They're testing how well our defenses hold up. But why do this instead of putting everything they have into an all-out attack?"

"Slow or not, I want your people ready. There's no telling what might climb through. I predict about ten more minutes. It will be enough time to teach you the salamanca, hija."

"Really?" Tala asked, a little awed by her lola's unflappability.

"I will teach you to use your agimat as an offensive weapon rather than constantly be on the defensive. Watch." Lola Corazon's agimat grew until the old woman was surrounded by a perfectly spherical bubble. She pushed it forward, straight into the Burn's fiery wall, making a sizzling noise as it hit.

But instead of dissolving the fire spells like it normally would have, it sped the magic up. Parts of the flames encompassed by the elder's agimat seemed to burn even faster and quicker than the fires on either side of it, multiplying and ricocheting as the Makiling curse took effect.

Lola Corazon flung her agimat skyward, taking the fire along with it. It exploded noisily like fireworks above them, remnants turning into soot and ash as they fell back down to earth.

There was a small hole within the burning wall where Lola Corazon's agimat had taken out part of the spell. As they watched, the gap was gradually swallowed up again by the rest of the flames, as if it never even happened.

"This is the salamanca technique," her grandmother said. "Instead of dissolving and repelling magic completely, we instead hold it in place, jump-start it into levels that the spell can't handle."

"That was amazing," Tala breathed. "So you can overload spells and cause them to explode on their own?"

"That is often the result. Using it on ice spells makes them shatter. Lightning spells will turn the place into an electric storm, and so on. The trick is to find the point where the magic can be cut off from its source, to do with as you wish."

"It's like adding a kinetic pulse to the magic," Dr. Baet explained. "Your agimat functions like a supercharged battery that's stronger than the spell can handle if you put in enough strength and effort."

"Can I try?" Tala asked.

Miguel gestured at the Burn. "We have at least three more minutes."

Extending her agimat over such a distance was tiring work, but Tala managed to latch on to the flames, snagging a much smaller portion of the fire spells than Lola Corazon had.

"We will also work on pushing your agimat farther out," Lola Corazon said. "But for now, you are doing well—for a beginner. So instead of thinking to extinguish the flames, you must think about speeding them up, see the extent of their limits. Attack as hard and as quickly as you can. Picture your agimat like a sword that you slash with."

Tala did, lashed out like the agimat was a battering ram.

"Form your agimat thinner at the tip. You will expend too much energy if you hammer instead of skewer. Imagine your agimat to be as sharp as a rapier."

Her second attempt went better. The pointed end made it easier to focus on only one particular area of the wall, and soon enough, she felt part of the spell give, streams of magic coming apart with her agimat.

"Energy increasing!" she heard one of the Fianna yell. "Something's coming through! Get ready, men!"

"It's here!" one of the Avalonian soldiers yelled as something ripped through the air around the wobbling hole, tearing it open to allow shades to come crawling through. Leaping in from behind them were several ice wolves, howling for blood.

With a grunt, Tala yanked with all her strength. A portion of the Burn came apart, and she threw it as hard as she could at the approaching nightwalkers.

Shades and ice wolves exploded spectacularly.

"Sugod!" Without pause, Tala's grandmother latched on to a shade with her agimat. It chattered, trying to break free, then jerked, its movements suddenly spastic, as if caught in a seizure. The elder made a dismissive gesture, and with a panicked squeal, the shadow dissolved abruptly, torn apart by its own momentum.

All around her, the other Makiling clan members were doing the same, taking the shades apart with salamanca. An ice wolf attempting to attack Dr. Baet froze into place as the doctor brought her own agimat to bear on it. Cracks appeared along the creature's body, the increased pressure shattering it moments later.

The pirates were not idle. They drew out swords and spears of varying shapes and sizes, all glittering with spells embedded in the steel. Looks were deceiving; the bald accountant, Langsworth, skewered ice wolves with an almost graceful finesse, and a young girl who looked more like a pop idol than a pirate was ten for ten with her rapier. Captain Mairead was still using the same technique she'd wielded back at the American detention facility; her shadow rose from the ground and tore into other shades within range.

The skull-and-bones tattoos on the pirates' wrists were flaming a startling golden hue. But it was the *Jolly Roger* that shone the brightest, the whole ship lighting up like a fireworks display.

"Fire!" Mairead yelled.

Cannonballs packed with destructive spells shot out of the ship's hold, and every shade or ice wolf in their paths was promptly obliterated.

Tala shoved her agimat onto the nearest shadow and watched delightedly as her salamanca pulled the shade apart. She turned and did it again to another, and then another, and again to another. The Fianna and the Avalon guards were doing their best, but the ease with which the

Makilings ripped through their enemies was second only to the pirate ship's blasts.

Just like with the fire spells at the Burn, Tala focused on the strange magic layered across the hole in the air. She didn't know what would happen if she applied the salamanca to it, but something in her gut told her to try.

A shade tried to attack her from behind, but Seraphina was there, unwrapping her boa from around her neck and efficiently garroting the shadow with it.

The creases in the hole grew, a mass of spells crisscrossed over one another that amplified when Tala's agimat was brought to bear on them. She saw the lines disappearing, the nothingness in the air slowly being smoothed over, like ironing out wrinkles on a very magical shirt.

The hole fractured, almost like a mirror shattering into several hundred pieces. It sliced through the shades that were still in the process of climbing out, severing many in half.

"Now!" Mak shouted and flung a switch when one of the techmages gave him the all clear. The spiderweb spelltech activated, and the net-like spell flew, wrapping its threads around the hole and capturing it like a Venus flytrap might an insect. The spell fizzled out, and the cobweb dropped to the ground, magic steaming from around it, but the portal was gone, leaving only the dead shades and ice wolves, which were evaporating rapidly into the air.

Lola Corazon whirled to face Tala. If she had been either of her parents, Tala thought, she would have been furious. But her grandmother was smiling happily, looking both pleased and proud. "Now that's how a Makiling fights," she proclaimed, laughing. Her kinsmen were laughing and whooping.

"That was a very nice trick," Miguel said approvingly to Captain Mairead.

"The *Jolly Roger* don't work if *we* don't work it."

Mak was a little less enthusiastic. "She could have blown up the whole place," he growled. "We know almost nothing about shade magic and Beiran technology or how it would react if we bring Neverland spelltech in to fight it! Using an agimat on it directly could have made things even worse!"

"But it didn't. Your machine was taking a little too long, and your base would have been overrun. My granddaughter made a strategic decision, and it paid off. Sometimes it is necessary to take risks. You should be thanking her, not scolding her."

"I agree with the Filipinos," Captain Mairead said. The *Jolly Roger* powered down, the cannons no longer glowing. "We're in uncharted territory. Here be literal dragons and all that. We gotta take risks, clean up later."

Mak glared at them and threw his hands up over his head. "All right. Thank you. Let me report this to His Majesty. The Gallaghers will be pleased to hear the tech works at least."

"Astig, Tala!" Miguel chortled, surprising her with a one-armed hug from behind her. Laughing, the others surrounded her, fulsome in their praise and congratulations.

This, Tala thought, blushing, stammering, happy. *Is this what it feels like to belong?*

By the time Lola Corazon brought her back to her parents, Tala could barely stay awake. The unexpected lethargy had overtaken her on the way back, and it was hard to keep from yawning. Lola Corazon squeezed her shoulder. "A good night's rest will cure all that," she said. "You've had a busy day."

Lumina Makiling was already waiting by the time they pulled up. She took one look at Tala and then turned on her mother. "What did you do to her?" she snapped.

"She needs training, Lumina," Lola Corazon said calmly. "You seem to have neglected that."

"I wanted her to be a normal teenager! A normal student! I didn't want to fill her head with tales of Makiling superiority!"

"And what good did that do her now?" Lola Corazon squeezed Tala's hand. "I would love for you to come visit us again. Miguel is still adamant about teaching you the Doce Pares style."

"I'd love that," Tala mumbled.

Lola Corazon smiled, ruffled her hair, then left without another word to Lumina.

"She taught you the salamanca, didn't she?" Tala's mother said.

"I didn't get hurt," Tala protested. "You could have taught me that years ago."

"Utter exhaustion is the main side effect of the salamanca. The more you expend, the more it takes a toll on your body. And overexerting yourself can lead to even worse, more debilitating conditions! She didn't tell you about the limits, did she?"

Her mother sounded mad, but she didn't sound mad at *her*, which was good. Tala didn't have the energy to get into an argument this late in the day. "She said we had to become warriors," she said with another yawn. "We had to prepare ourselves, like Maria Makiling wanted us to."

A pause. A sigh. "I'll send a tray up for you if you're still hungry," her mother finally said, "so you can sleep this off. But we will be talking tomorrow."

Tala only nodded, too tired to argue further. She let her mother bring her to her room, tuck her in.

"Oh, Tala," she heard her mother sigh right before she drifted off. "Whatever am I going to do with you?"

17

IN WHICH KEN GETS HIS SHADOW INTO TROUBLE

I'm pretty sure I can pull this off on my own," Ken said. "The more people with me, the more dangerous it's gonna be. I brought Horse with me. It's waiting a mile out, in case I run into danger."

"What's your kelpie gonna do?" Tala asked dryly. "Kick people?"

"And the last time you went off on your own," Loki countered, "you destroyed a library."

"Well, sure. When you put it that way, it makes me sound bad."

"While I have no doubts that you can charm everyone all on your own, I'm sure you'll do just as good a job with us around," Nya assured him, keeping her voice low to avoid attracting the attentions of the two Avalonian ministers walking in front of them.

"I'm charming?" Ken's voice brightened considerably and then grew suspicious. "Wait. Are you trying to placate me, Rapunzel?"

She grinned briefly, and then her smile faded. "Of course not. Why would I do anything like that?"

Why couldn't she stop being so attractive for maybe just one second? They were better now since the Schaffers' party, though still not as tight as before. He knew Nya was trying to find a way to broach the topic and that it was his fault for constantly changing the subject whenever she made the attempt. He really didn't want to talk about it yet. If he had his way, he would pretend like he'd never even heard what her doom was to begin with. He could feel himself start to sweat, trying not to panic, at the memory of it alone.

He concentrated on his earpiece instead. "Say, Dex. You sure my shadow won't trigger any spells inside?"

"I'm pretty sure it won't," Dex's voice responded.

Their mission this time around was a bit more challenging: infiltrate OzCorp and find information about Nome's secret project that was apparently so powerful and costly that the CFO of one of the most lucrative companies in the world had to solicit funding from other potential rivals for it. Loki led the team, which also had Ken, Nya, Tala, Tito Boy, Tita Baby, and General Luna.

And Ken's shadow, if that counted.

Under the pretense of cooperating, OzCorp had agreed to a preliminary inspection from Avalon's Department of Trade at Marooners' Rock. In a stroke of genius, Alex had assigned the kind but bumbling Minister Fasshagh with his less well-liked colleague, Minister Ancilotto, to oversee the proceedings. Both were vocal supporters of OzCorp establishing a bigger presence in Avalon, which helped to head off any suspicions, and Alex had introduced them to the duo as his personal administrative team. Only the lightest number of glamour spells had been cast on Ken and the others, relying more heavily on traditional makeup and prosthetics as provided by Seraphina, one of the Neverland pirates. Tala's presence would handle the rest.

They had better reason to use the subterfuge now. The wildlife preserve that had offered to care for the baby jabberwock (their social media account had been posting videos, and people were cooing over it like it was a kitten) had performed a few quick tests to assess its health. That had given them their first real clue.

"Did you know that jabberwocks are related to dragons?" Alex had asked. "And that the reason Avalon hunted dragons in particular was because they provided additional firepower for the Nine Maidens?"

"What?" Tala gasped.

"With the Maidens, they can be used to conjure artificial but powerful creatures. Constructs that they can afford to sacrifice, because they could simply create another, and then another, until the dragon's life force runs out. It's a feature built into the Maidens as a defense mechanism."

"A construct like the ice dragon at the Schaffers' mansion," Loki said quietly.

Alex nodded grimly. "If OzCorp's responsible, then they're very good at copying most of the Maidens' schematics. And I'm willing to bet that the dead jabberwock you all found wasn't the first one they've hunted. But could the Snow Queen have created her own Nine Maidens? She was never able to before."

"Shardstones are mainly used for life engineering spells," Kay supplied, grim. "Shardstones aren't as versatile as spellstones, which won't break apart if the spelltech is too complex. They alone won't be enough to recreate the Nine Maidens. We… She was never able to make a working version in all the centuries I was with her. But she's desperate now. And after what she hinted at when she contacted me at Villeneuve, it's possible."

"Hypothetically speaking," Zoe asked Dex, "would her version be able to breach Avalon defenses?"

The techmage gulped. "There's a very good chance it can, Zo."

This was bad. If the one person who knew the Snow Queen best said it was likely, then they were in more danger than they initially thought.

And that OzCorp might have learned to reverse engineer their own Nine Maidens was a frightening thought. It explained Corvington's promise of a revolutionary spelltech to his investors.

And now, Ken wouldn't have recognized any of them, quite frankly. He himself wore a bald cap and looked years older, with pince-nez and a sudden protrusion of chin. Loki was deceptively androgynous, with a mop of red hair, a gray suit, and the tired expression of the overworked bureaucrat, which Ken suspected wasn't completely an act.

Tala was a mousy-looking blond, and Nya's glorious curls were now pulled back in a severe bun, and she had a suddenly hooked nose. Against all odds, even the Katipuneros looked boringly respectable.

The Second Honor were also accompanying them. It was an investigation disguised as a friendly visit. Nome and his representatives made no protest, even welcomed their presence.

If the ministers had any inkling that their staff were not who they appeared to be, they gave no notice. "I really don't see why His Majesty would have to insist on an inspection," Minister Ancilotto grumbled. "OzCorp's papers appear to be in order, and I'm not fond of this oversight."

"His Majesty is only erring on the side of caution," Minister Fasshagh said placidly. "And I for one would like to see OzCorp's corporate headquarters. I've heard stories about their recreation centers. It doesn't sound like any office that I've ever worked at before."

OzCorp's main headquarters was built on top of Marooners' Rock, just outside Lyonesse. It overlooked the glittering blue of the Ulster Sea, providing a fantastic view. It only made Ken's stomach plummet. The facility was built on a cliff heavily bespelled to prevent accidents, but looking down into the thousand-foot drop was unnerving to him all the same.

"You okay?" Nya whispered. Unlike him, she couldn't stop staring at the water, transfixed by the sight.

He remembered her telling him that she'd never been to the ocean before. How was that possible, considering she was part fish? Likely it was because the Ikpeans took their guardianship of the mine seriously, despite knowing the risks to themselves. Ken remembered the Beast of Suddene's revelation, that mermaids used to be hunted, and shifted nervously. "I am," he said. "Don't worry about me."

"I'm always gonna worry about you," he heard her mutter behind him, not realizing she was still loud enough to be heard, and it made him smile despite himself.

The first shock was seeing Ruggedo Nome himself waiting for them by the entrance, and Ken wondered frantically if they should have invested in spells for disguise rather than just the prosthetics. But the man simply looked them over and nodded, seeing nothing amiss. He was dressed in a lab coat and was just finishing up an interview with yet another reporter, turning to them with a beaming smile as the latter left. "Welcome to OzCorp, ministers," he greeted.

With him was another man he introduced as Jeremy Wyles, who was openly staring at General Luna and not bothering to hide his crush. The Katipunero had shaved off his mustache for this endeavor, revealing a surprisingly handsome face.

The third and final member of their welcoming committee was Vivien Fey. "It's an honor, ministers," she said pleasantly. "Will you come this way, please? I've instructed everyone from management to provide you with the information you might need. I would like to stress, though, that many of the products created and tested here are protected by confidentiality."

"I'm sure they know that, Vivien," Nome said heartily. "I'd like for them to be treated like good friends."

"We're more interested in the premises than your products actually," said Mak, the Second Honor leader.

"I know that the haste of the building's construction might give rise to some questions about the structural integrity of our headquarters," Nome admitted cheerfully as they filed through security, which checked their bags and scanned them. Ken held his breath as the guard passed a scanner around him, then waved them through, their earpieces and Tala's agimat going undiscovered. "We'll be more than happy to show you the permits and licenses we've applied for and received."

"Ah, well," Minister Fasshagh boomed. He hadn't a concrete reason on hand to explain their visit but now latched on to the man's apology like that was what he'd been here for all along. "I suppose OzCorp is very excited to do business with Avalon, hence the speed, eh?"

"Avalon is the most logical place for us to set up shop in my humble opinion. I've grown up with stories about the kingdom, and we're excited to see what working together here could mean for spelltech in general." They walked down a length of corridor, and Ken caught quick glimpses of rooms full of people working as they passed. Some were sitting before workstations, but some of the rooms were clearly for recreational purposes. They caught sight of a foosball game in progress and then a small conference room where people were simply sitting around, talking and laughing.

"I read that they've got a swimming pool here," Nya said. "Plus an all-purpose gym, a terrarium, several day cares, even a soccer field. No wonder everyone wants to work here."

"Heavy layer of magic, though," Tala said softly. "Barrier spells all around."

"They work with magic but aren't allowing most of their personnel here access," Loki murmured. "My guess is that this is the management wing of the compound. If they're creating spelltech, it's not at this level."

"This is very interesting decor, Mr. Nome," Minister Fasshagh said. "The fauna painted on some of these walls remind me of the stories of the strange creatures said to have inhabited Buyan."

The CEO laughed. "You are correct, Minister. I love the legend of Buyan, and it shows. It was my inspiration for founding OzCorp in the first place. We even have little fountains with Alatyr stone carvings, and our department wings are named after Buyan's four winds. Even our project team names celebrate Buyan creatures: simurgh, adarna, whitesnake… I'm on Team Adarna myself. You'll have to forgive my sense of whimsy. I've been looking forward to Avalon's upcoming fair as well. I'm hoping it will be a lot like the traditional festivals Avalon used to celebrate, rather than one that emphasizes modern spelltech."

"You'll be happy to note that our tourism minister strove to do exactly that." Minister Fasshagh chuckled. "I remember attending quite a few when I was just a young boy."

"Template 125," West was muttering to himself. "Template 126. Template 127."

"Our subordinates should be able to look through your paperwork and let you know if everything is in order," Minister Ancilotto said. "In the meantime, we'd like a tour of the place. I have heard nothing but good things."

Loki had prepared for this eventuality. The nimble-fingered Tito Boy had slipped a tiny tracking device on one of Minister Fasshagh's cuff links earlier under the pretense of helping him put it on. It should be enough to alert them of the ministers' return, giving them ample time to snoop.

"I've heard that you've all visited the Tangled Woods," Loki said evenly to Vivien Fey.

She nodded, smiling. "A simple mix-up. We've settled the matter satisfactorily with Avalon's Department of Environmental Protection."

"Spelltech research?"

"I'm afraid I can't divulge that just yet. I'm sure you'll find everything you need here," Vivien continued cheerfully, ushering them into a smaller office that nonetheless gave a breathtaking view of the sea, much to Ken's discomfort. "I'm afraid you'll have to excuse me, as I've got a meeting to attend. My assistant, Blake Lee, is currently at the staff cafeteria and will be more than happy to show you around. Mr. Jeremy Wyles here will be assisting your staff. But first, a very important question: are you vegans, carnivores, or omnivores? We have the best selection of every—"

This was going to pose a problem, Ken thought, as Vivien, Nome, and the ministers left. They weren't gonna be able to do much work if Mr. Jeremy Wyles was still with them.

"Landian mo," Tita Baby growled to General Luna.

"Ha?"

A flurry of heated whispering ensued, completed entirely in Tagalog, until finally General Luna grudgingly made his way toward Jeremy. "H-hi," he said, not very convincingly.

It worked. "H-how long have you been working for the Avalon government?" Jeremy asked, blushingly trying to make small talk. "This is my first job since graduating from Wharton, and I'm trying to make a good impression."

"We can talk…outside?" the general suggested and blinked his eyes rapidly in an attempt to flutter his lashes.

"Oh, but I should…" Jeremy cast a nervous look back at the others. "Sure."

"Leche," General Luna sighed as he led the man away.

"Fey put us here because she knows we won't find anything in this office," Loki said darkly.

"These look mostly like expense reports, proofs of permit, documents for licensing," Nya reported.

"How do you know?"

"My family runs a potions business. I know how this goes."

"Well, I think Miss Fey has underestimated us, because I've got this." Ken tapped at his ear, deliberately turning his back to the window. "Dex, we're in." A quick glance at Tala confirmed that she was already actively suppressing any of the listening devices and cameras in the room. "Ready?"

"Righty-ho. Whenever you are."

Ken clicked his boots together, then watched as his shadow slowly detached itself from his feet and slowly slid out underneath the door. "Tala?"

"They might claim that OzCorp's an employee-friendly company, but right now, there are two hidden cameras and one spell primed for recording conversations in this office alone. I don't see how the other rooms in this building would be any different."

"I'm putting up the blueprint we've acquired from the trade department on your specs," Dex reported, and a small image popped up against Ken's eyeglasses. It was slightly jarring and disconcerting because Ken was looking from two perspectives once again, his shadow creeping along the ceiling to avoid notice. It was strange to be looking at everything upside down and even stranger for Ken to realize that this was how a shade looked out into the world.

At his command, his shadow slithered up an elevator shaft, working its way to the top floor. The offices here looked a little more opulent, bigger than the ones below. There were fewer people as well, albeit more men and women in business suits. All the rooms were furnished, though some were empty.

"Sloan Gruffud," Ken reported, spotting a plaque on one door. "Now that's a familiar name we ought to investigate more closely."

"Sloan Gruffud," There was a pause as Dex called up his information. "Second officer, responsible for public relations."

"Hold up." Ken caught sight of Vivien Fey, not looking happy at all now, marching toward the man's office. "We may have something here."

Vivien stomped in without knocking, glaring at the man inside, who was eating lunch—Ken saw crab legs and an assortment of sashimi. A bottle of scotch had been placed near his right elbow, and the glass he held carried a thimbleful of the liquid.

"The high life," Ken murmured as his shadow found a cushiony spot in the corner.

"You went behind my back and approved the delivery," Vivien shouted at the man. "How dare you? This is *my* project! We need fifteen more tons of artificial spellstones from the Chinese, not ten! We're behind on Nome's deadline as it is!"

"Maybe if you'd been focusing on your responsibilities instead of falling behind on your own work, I wouldn't have to make the decisions for you!" Gruffud said calmly.

"Your incompetence and your compulsive need to constantly kiss ass are going to ruin the project! You even showed the Chinese part of the specs! What's gonna stop them from making their own prototype?"

"We've got a jabberwock, don't we? How can the Chinese replicate our work when they don't have jabberwocks in Asia? All they've got are the spirits of benevolent dragons or some shit like that that their ancestors worshipped. They're all just as extinct as Avalonian dragons are."

"Well, we all thought the jabberwocks were gone, but they're still thriving, aren't they? And who's to say they're not going to travel to Avalon and grab the few jabberwocks there still are for their own experiments? They'll find some way to screw us out of that contract, and I don't care how many times you can bespell it."

"What you *should* care about," Gruffud snapped, lowering his drink, "is that the order wouldn't have been placed at all if it wasn't for me. You were too busy looking after your precious little sister to even remember what you were supposed to do."

"I've been doing the jobs of four people since I started working here, with barely a paycheck for one!"

"Maybe you're not as good at this as Nome thinks you are then, Fey. *I'll* be taking charge of the basement delivery on Thursday. You don't need to show up. We're moving at eight p.m. Didn't you say you were gonna have to look after your sister that night anyway?" He smirked. "Which of us looks like we're doing our jobs now, Fey?"

The woman glared at him, then turned to march out of the room. "*You* better find a way to get another five tons of artificial spellstones from the Chinese in two days," she shot back over her shoulder. "Your name's already on the invoice, not mine, so everyone's gonna know it was you who screwed up the order."

"Bitch," the man growled after she was gone and downed his whole drink.

"Crap," Ken whispered. "So they *are* using the jabberwocks for their spelltech."

"How were they able to capture another jabberwock previously and bring it here without any of us knowing?" Loki didn't even sound surprised, though.

"That's what we're here to find out, right? I think Fey's heading to her own office."

Ken beat her there by a few minutes but promptly realized he wasn't alone. A young girl, probably a couple of years younger than him, was inside, rifling through a desk. There were enough similarities between her and Vivien Fey for them to be related somehow, but despite her age, she looked sallower and a little sickly, like she'd just gotten over a long bout with illness.

The girl must have found what she was looking for. She hurriedly pocketed something she'd taken from one of the drawers, and all Ken saw was a brief glint of something shiny before she hastily rearranged the papers on the table, straightening up and putting her hands behind her back as Vivien entered.

"Sorry it took so long, Abby," she said, her stern face softening. "Ready for lunch?"

Abby smiled brightly. "No problem, Sis. Can we go to that café they say makes the best boba in Avalon?"

"Sounds good to me!"

Ken tailed them, pausing only after they'd exited the main doors of OzCorp headquarters. "Well," he said, "that's that. Does this facility have a basement?"

"The blueprints say they don't have a basement," Dex confirmed.

"I think there is. Gruffud implied that there might be one." Ken entered the elevator again, bypassing it to plunge down the shaft. "And this elevator looks like it's still got levels to go past the ground floor."

"I think you're right, Ken," Loki said. "They didn't choose not to build their headquarters at the heart of Lyonesse because it was more expensive. They built their headquarters here at Marooners' Rock because they needed some way to smuggle in goods they don't want us knowing about."

"You might have something there!" Nya gasped. "Avalon hasn't completely secured their sea territory yet. OzCorp built this on top of a cliff that has no direct access point down to the sea. That's why we hadn't considered that a priority."

"The ministers are at the OzCorp cafeteria," Tita Baby announced. "I have seen Minister Fasshagh at a buffet before. We will have more than enough time."

"Let's test out the theory, then." Ken's shadow hit the bottom of the shaft and slipped out into a narrow, pitch-dark corridor. "Ha," he said triumphantly and scuttled toward a set of doors some distance ahead, slipping past it and—

He tried to move but realized he couldn't.

"Uh. I think I'm stuck."

"You're a shadow," Nya said. "How can you be stuck?"

"I wouldn't be asking if I knew the answer. Maybe a ward or something?" He could feel himself sweating. "I think you'd better start updating Avalon with some anti-shade barriers, Dex. There's some weird defenses here that even my shadow can't get through."

"What does that mean?" Tala asked.

Dex sounded very grim when he said, "It means someone is being very thorough. Might be the area's completely bespelled against all magic, no matter how trivial. That's a dangerous spell. Ken, you need to get out of there."

"Wait." There were voices, faint but audible. Ken was almost sure that one of them was Nome's. "Give me a couple of minutes."

"Very impressive, Mr. Nome," another voice was saying. "The Royal States could put these to very good use."

"They're still a bit rough around the edges, but they're functional and should serve your purpose well," Nome responded. "How many would you like us to produce?"

"How about enough for half of America's population?" the second man asked, chuckling. "That would shut down protests and solve all our problems. The first dozen or so you provided have been working quite well, though I would assume human thralls would be a lot more complicated to handle. How about a few thousand to start?"

"Our usual contract, then? I must warn you, Mr. Limler, to avoid places with heavy spell negators while using these. They can potentially snap the link between you and your thrall, and the backlash from that *will* hurt."

"Oh, we'll be very careful. His Majesty was beside himself with glee when you told us we'd be getting the first batch right off the production line. It's the type of spell he has been seeking for years."

"I do aim to please His Majesty. If you'll excuse me a moment—" For a second, the blackness disappeared, and Ken caught a very quick glimpse of bright lights overhead, the suggestion of some lab-like facility but in shades of gray and white, people in lab coats.

There was a majestic, sprawling *thing* at the center of the room, some strange sculpture made of glittering crystals that looked…off somehow, irregularly shaped clusters that looked disgusting to the human eye. And at the center of that contraption—

Ken saw bright yellow eyes glaring at them, leathery wings, and an elongated snout. It raised its head and roared.

Something slammed right into Ken's shadow, an overpowering counterspell that seemed enchanted to lash back ten times stronger than whatever it was built to counter, because despite all the magic barriers in place within the OzCorp building, every spell in the room they were in reacted to the attack. Some shorted out almost immediately. Others exploded more violently.

Ken made a rough, choking sound and slowly rose in the air, his hands clawing at his throat like something had taken ahold of him there. Something had seized his shadow in some kind of invisible vise, and yet it was also his physical body that was being strangled.

He heard Nya cry out, felt her grabbing at his legs to keep him from choking to death.

He saw someone in a lab coat and a mask that obscured half his features. The man's hands were curled, like he was gripping something unseen.

Dark eyes looked down at him. "Unfortunate," said Ruggedo Nome and raised his hand.

The force of his unexpected punch sent the shadow spinning into nothingness. It also sent Ken, despite Nya's best efforts to hold on to him, violently flying across the room, straight through the window. It shattered, sending him plummeting down into the sea below.

Something materialized beside him, keeping rapid pace, and he had enough presence of mind to grab on to Ruyi Jingu Bang lengthening beside him, slowing down his descent but not stopping it. He skidded down the full length of the building and then past the rock cliffs it was built on, the staff continuing to expand and keeping him from accelerating.

Until Ken hit the water. *Don't panic,* he thought in a panic. *Don't panic, don't panic, don't panic—*

Bubbles burst out of his mouth as he struggled, no longer sure which end was up—as if that made a difference, since he couldn't bloody well swim. The cold closed in all around him, and he thought to hold his breath before he could swallow more seawater.

His doom hadn't explicitly told him he would drown, but that didn't mean he wouldn't.

Something grabbed onto his shoulders, and Ken was propelled up without warning, breaking the surface before he'd even realized it, heaving in a grateful lungful of salty air. He started to sink back down, but the arm lodged underneath his armpits refused to let go.

"You really," Nya said breathlessly, tail flopping behind her, "should learn to float at least."

She kept him buoyant until a loud whinny told him Horse was near.

The kelpie dove and resurfaced with both Ken and Nya on its back, swimming briskly away from the cliffs.

He'd nearly died, and he still wouldn't stop blubbering. "Oh god. Shit. I thought for sure I was gonna—I owe you, Rapunzel. I—" He stopped when a particularly large wave crashed over him, his body freezing up.

"I'm here." Nya wrapped her arms around his waist, squeezing him tightly. "I'm here. I won't let anything happen to you."

"I know," Ken managed to say as Horse took them both away from the danger. "I know."

Nya was silent. By some miracle, Ken was also silent. It wasn't like he wanted to be in the same danger that the prophecy had foretold for them both to finally broach the subject they'd been avoiding for the last several days, but it was the unexpected icebreaker they'd been waiting for.

"I've never actually been to the ocean before," Nya finally said. "When I changed at Villeneuve Castle, that was the first time I'd done that. I don't think most people in Ikpe have ever transformed. We've been living on land for so long that most of us have never even seen the sea. I think it hurts people like my grammy, to know that we would not be welcomed back. But we all knew watching over the spellstone mines was more important than returning to the ocean."

"Do you know why your village decided to take on that kind of responsibility?"

"Yes." Nya looked down. "A couple of centuries ago, an ancestor fell in love with an Avalonian king. She convinced a sea witch to give her temporary legs to travel through the land to the king. She knew of the mines and took a spellstone from there, to wish herself completely human so she could marry him, even though the curse warned that it would cost her two kingdoms. She got her wish, but she gave up her most powerful weapon for legs—her voice. And so she became mute."

She sighed. "Not all the Avalon rulers were good people. Her people eventually declared war against the kingdom for the king's mistreatment of her, ironically using the same curse she used to bring about their revenge. The mer-queen opposed it, unwilling to incite more hostilities from the humans, and exiled them forever as punishment. Both sides took on heavy losses, but the war ended only after both the girl and the king were killed. My ancestors decided to protect the mines and remain. The generations after that were born with legs instead of tails—apparently proof of their resolve to stay."

Ken scratched the side of Horse's face absently and stared out into the sea, at the waves crashing against the shoreline the kelpie had dragged them to. "Her people must have loved her very much."

"They did. But they also realized that they could not be like the mer-queen, distancing themselves from the affairs of men while the world moved on without them. They thought they could make a difference, even if they couldn't for her. And so Ikpe was founded." Nya twiddled her fingers. "I'm sorry I couldn't tell you. There's prejudice against mermaids out there still. I know you won't tell, but I couldn't make that decision for the whole village. And then there were our dooms. What they implied. I—"

"Hey." Ken reached out, linked his fingers with hers. "No need for any of that right now," he said gruffly. "I know you were waiting to give me space to clear my head. There's not much inside my head to begin with anyway, so it cleared out pretty fast. But I'm not gonna be able to process any detailed explanations at the moment. Just…don't let me go, all right?"

Her hand tightened against his. "I won't. I really won't."

That was how Loki and the others found them, the cadet looking relieved. "For a minute, you had us worried," they admitted, eyeing their hands with cautious optimism. "Tita Baby got you a change of clothes."

"Thanks." Ken's cheek was already starting to look bruised. "I was not expecting the frigging CEO of OzCorp to punch me, that's for sure. What happened back there?"

"Minister Fasshagh was concerned but was mollified quickly enough once we told them you were safe. Minister Ancilotto was more suspicious, but he couldn't do much. OzCorp was apologetic, agreed to a more thorough inspection of their safety protocol, with a team of Avalon consultants on hand. They're calling it a faulty spelltech error, but as it is, they can't accuse us of snooping around without admitting that they've been using shadow spells themselves. Or that they've got an unauthorized basement underneath their headquarters. And we can't accuse them of the assault without evidence to back up our claims either." Loki scowled. "Fey was…smug. I think she realized who we were. She knew who I was anyway."

"So it's a stalemate, then."

"Let's get you guys warmed up first."

"What do we do about OzCorp, Loki?" Tala said.

Loki gazed into the distance. The OzCorp HQ was still visible from their vantage point. "I think," they said, "that I'd like to go rock climbing."

Ken toweled his face dry and looked down at his feet.

"Guys," he said, staring at his lack of a shadow. "I've got another problem."

18

IN WHICH THE GROUP
OPTS FOR A DIFFERENT
KIND OF HEALTH CARE

The International Charms Fair was a bigger event than Tala had expected, as apparently the whole town of Lyonesse would be participating in it. Stalls started at Maidenkeep grounds and wound through the numerous streets making up the heart of the city. It was only early afternoon, and already the streets were packed with both tourists and locals alike, exploring the hundreds of booths selling everything from homemade potions to bespelled fashion to homemade food selections.

Much to Tala's surprise, Alex had given them the day off without explanation. After the ice dragon and the Texas facility breach with Ryker, she'd been expecting him to double down on their duties. She knew Avalon was still getting flak from the media. The news on Royal States airwaves was full of gleeful opinion pieces on the lax security at Maidenkeep, along with speculation on where and when the next hypothetical dragon attack might strike next, and the fair was the clear favorite.

She'd tried to convince Alex that she should be by his side instead.

"That's what the Fianna are for," Alex had said with a laugh. "It's not every day that we can get a huge fair like this here. I think we all deserve a break."

Tala didn't believe him.

There was nothing in the news about the Texas facility breach, though. A few news reports had picked up on it initially, but interest died following an announcement that the facility had only been conducting emergency drills.

She'd told her parents everything. About Ryker and his past, about her run-ins with him at Avalon, about Alex's part in it. Despite her initial dismay, her mother had been warm and supportive.

That her relationship with Ryker even slightly mirrored her parents' was still a disturbing thought.

She'd failed at Simeli again that morning, which also contributed to her bad mood.

Several days ago, the Banders had decided to enjoy it as a group. But the dynamics of the relationships within the group had changed since then. Something had shifted between Cole and Zoe, and Zoe's apparent reconciliation with Tristan might have something to do with it. Ken and Nya seemed like they were finally back to being friends—still a step back from their previous relationship, but Tala was glad that they no longer looked as glum as before.

Loki was distracted. "I'm worried about what Fey might do next," they said, "but I'm also concerned about the firebird."

"The Dame of Tintagel said to trust in the firebird," Tala said, remembering her words all those months ago. Alex tried his best to be fair, but he had his own prejudices and was disbelieving when Loki had voiced their suspicions. The firebird had even yelped indignantly when asked, indicating with multiple gestures that it had only followed them for their own good. Loki was still unconvinced but had nothing else to go on.

Dex and West remained unaware of the tensions among the rest of the group. "Isn't that what friends do? Hang out together?" Dex asked happily. "We're what I believe is called 'work friends,' but does that make us friend friends as well?"

"Why do you act like you've never had a friend in your life before, Dex?" Ken asked suspiciously.

"Because I haven't. Not really. We've always been on the run like Alex, except we've been on the run as a family. Dad said people were always after us because they were gonna force us to build spelltech for them. I haven't stayed anywhere longer than six months until you guys got Avalon back. And, well, we have that memory problem."

"Ah," Ken said, visibly softening. "Well, in that case… Sure, Dex. We're work friends and friend friends. You don't even need to ask."

"So we can go around and eat food and watch the parade together like…I think the British term for it is a 'sausage fest'?"

"Speaking as your friend friend, Dex, I would recommend never saying those words ever again." Ken glared down at his feet. His shadow was still missing. One of Maidenkeep's physicians had examined him and assured them Ken remained in the peak of health and that its absence had no side effects, physical or magical. Still, this was Ken, and he liked to grouse. "Feels like everyone can see I don't have one," he grumbled.

Nya looked like she wanted to say something, but she settled back and took a long sip of her boba instead.

They were hanging out at Tea-ta's waiting for Cole, and Tala was a bit surprised by that. It was unusual for him to be late.

Ken coughed, taking great pains not to look at Nya. "So we're going as a group, right?"

"Of course," Nya said, also not looking at Ken. "We're going out. As friends. Nothing wrong with that."

"Of course." Ken took a noisy slurp of his matcha milk tea. He'd asked Tita Teejay for an extra shot of anti-jitters espresso, an unusual choice for someone who was usually so loud and happy. "Who said there was anything wrong with that? Not me."

"Good."

"Good."

Zoe looked from one to the other, obviously itching to say something. "At some point," she said instead. "we might have to spread out, make sure there aren't any suspicious-looking bags lying around or that no one's acting like Deathless."

"Alex said to take a break," Loki reminded her.

"You're not taking a break. Aren't you going to be one of the roving guards at the fair?"

"Yeah, because all the wannabe recruits get to do the most boring duties before they get to officially join up."

"Are we late?" Adelaide Nottingham entered the café and dashed toward them, long yellow hair flapping like a bird wing behind her. "I've never been to a fair before!"

Cole followed after her, looking a little irate.

"Mom said I could visit the fair if I went with him," the girl went on, oblivious to—or rather too accustomed to—her brother's scowls to pay them any attention. "I can come, can't I? Nicky said you won't mind?"

"Nicky," Ken echoed wonderingly.

"We don't have to go with them, Addie," Cole said brusquely.

"On the contrary," Zoe purred, offering her hand to Cole's sister, who happily took it. "I think we ought to stick together. There's gonna be a huge crowd today, and as things stand, it would be safer to stay as a group." She hesitated. "I can't stay long, though. I'm meeting Tristan at eight."

The door to the café opened again.

He was wearing an oversize hoodie that hid his face, but Tala would recognize Alex anywhere. He strode toward the group, ignoring the sudden, panicked silence that had stolen over the table, his hands folded across his chest and looking like he hadn't just turned their planned outing into Avalon's most hastily assembled security detail. "Well," the king said. "Shall we be going, or should I explain myself first before we do?"

⁓

"My parents are going to kill you," Tala muttered to Alex while the latter stopped by a vendor's stall to scrutinize a small vial that promised a cure for heartbreak. "And Lola Urduja too. Whatever possessed you to go out on your own without any protection?" She kept craning her neck, half expecting one of the Fianna to swoop in and drag him back to Maidenkeep. No one had recognized the king so far, but this was only upping her anxiety. "And where's the firebird?"

"Nearby but safely hidden." Alex wrinkled his nose and placed the potion back on the table. "I thought you guys would understand better. And you did say you wanted to stick by me, right?"

"Yeah, but back at Maidenkeep, not out here where you're a target for every Beiran or Royal States spy. The others are giving you a pass because you're their king, but that's not gonna work on me. You can't just ditch the Fianna, play hooky on the very summit you organized, all because you want to go and find a Baba Yaga at this fair."

"Not a Baba Yaga. *The* Baba Yaga." Alex tried on a small signet ring with a firebird emblem on it. "The same one that cursed me. She's here, and she wants me to find her. Her letter is proof of that."

"I'm sure my parents would have understood."

"They'd fill this crowd with undercover agents, make me wear every conceivable wiretap device known to man, and wind up scaring her away.

She'll know if I come with the force of Avalon at my heels. You guys are my best compromise. *I'd appreciate a visit to your fair lady.* The wording was deliberate. She's here. I know it."

"Well," Tala grumbled, "tell us first next time."

"I regret not giving you a heads-up, and I'm sorry. But I wasn't even sure I could get away. I knew you wouldn't tell, but I didn't want to put the others in a dilemma where they had to choose between ratting me out on principle and obeying me because I'm their liege if they knew beforehand." Alex glanced over toward the rest of the group. Ken and Nya were eating cheerfulness-inducing cotton candy, though it didn't look effective. Zoe and Adelaide were now best friends, their heads close together while they chatted, much to Cole's obvious unease.

As it turned out, West didn't do very well in crowds, so he'd temporarily shifted into a small hamster inside Loki's shirt pocket, happily feasting on some bits of chocolate the ranger smuggled in to him. And they nearly keep losing Dex, who, despite having crafted some of the most innovative spelltech in the world, kept lagging behind to ooh and aah over small Chinese finger traps and prank buzzers.

"See?" Alex pointed out. "It's not like I'm preventing them from having fun."

"So where exactly do you hope to find your Baba Yaga?"

"She didn't tell me the exact location. I assume she'd be along Fortune-Tellers' Row."

"We've walked through it, like, four times already." None of the booths had looked like something a Baba Yaga would be at. Half were staffed by either stereotypical fortune-tellers decked out in wispy veils and noisy golden trinkets clanking against their arms or severe-looking physician types calling themselves curse specialists, with a list of their degrees and qualifications carefully spelled out on the walls of their cubicle-like stalls as if they were doctor's offices. It was weird to see both together and know that they technically practiced the same profession.

"Wait," Ken said suddenly, staring hard at a piece of chocolate in his hand. "Loki, what exactly is in this?"

"Chocolate?"

"Yeah, funny. I mean, why does this one have a *Truth Serum* disclaimer stamped across it?" Ken waved the half-eaten bar in their face. "'May include spells to induce candidness, talkativeness, and truthfulness.'"

"Every vendor here had to submit a list of their products to the Food Department for approval. Besides, I don't detect even a whiff of a spell in any of these bars. They're likely placebos. Nya makes potions. She should know more than me."

Nya had been staring at her own chocolate bar, which was of the same variety Ken had eaten. "The ingredients listed include wheatrose and marigold stems. Those are common for affection potions."

"Affection potions?"

The chocolate vendor, a middle-aged woman in a flower headband, immediately began to protest. "If you're thinking that's illegal, I assure you it isn't! I use no censured spells for my love potions. It only reinforces the feelings you already have for someone else, but not to the point of aggression! My recipes have been passed down in my family for genera-tions. My great-great-great-grandmother was a Wonderlander, and we—"

"I'm sure they're fine," Loki said hastily, shooting Tala a look. She took the hint and tugged Alex away from the booth while the others fol-lowed her lead.

"Thanks a lot, Ken," Zoe said, rolling her eyes. "It's only chocolate with some harmless spells in it. What gives?"

Ken scowled and tossed the remains of it into a nearby trash bin. "It's fine. I'm sure it's fine."

"We should stop eating anything, just to be sure," Nya muttered.

"Good idea."

"Good."

"Good."

"What is up with them?" Dex asked, puzzled. "I thought they were friends again?"

"It's not always as easy as that," Tala sighed.

"If you're looking for a particular fortune-teller," Adelaide volunteered, "why not use some of those fortune-tellers' services around here? Maybe one of them is your Baba Yaga in disguise. Can we try, Nicky? Great-Grandma tells our fortunes all the time, but it might be fun to have someone else do it for a change."

"She has a point, Nicky," Zoe said innocently.

Cole grunted. It didn't take a genius to know that Adelaide was his weak spot, and Zoe was enjoying herself immensely. "As you wish," he finally said.

"Adelaide's right," Tala concurred. "The alternative is to just, you know, maybe just enjoy ourselves today and pretend like the kingdom isn't going to implode if you're not in charge for five seconds?"

Alex thought about it. "Maybe she *is* hiding among them. Can't hurt to try."

"That would mean she's gotta be good at what she does, right?" Ken asked. "So maybe we ought to start with the popular stalls."

That was the wrong choice. Every fortune-teller at the popular stalls told Alex he would be very happy in the future with a well-paying job and the girl of his dreams.

"The Baba Yaga wouldn't be this flashy," Zoe decided. "How about the ones with all the accredited degrees?"

That brought them to the curse specialists, who examined Alex with a stethoscope and asked him about his medical history and dietary habits, then told him he would be very happy in the future with a well-paying job and the girl of his dreams. They also prescribed him a number of natural supplements and, with one very gregarious doctor who apparently only specialized in a certain type of patient, a goodly amount of medical marijuana.

"I am going to have a very long talk," Alex said, "with the department official who issued these fools licenses for this fair."

Some of the other specialists were more competent. A few who inspected Tala were visibly perplexed, finally admitting that they couldn't give her a proper diagnosis. When West volunteered for an assessment, many were even more confused. "I don't understand it," said one doctor who'd come all the way from Norway, running a small whirring device over the boy. "How do you have *a dozen curses* running concurrently through you and yet still remain healthy?"

"Dad said those actually wind up negating one another," West volunteered. "So if we took out one curse, it might cause the others to run their course, so as long as they're all perfectly balanced against one another, he finds no need to excel...excern, exercise them? No, that doesn't sound right."

"Excise," Tala said.

"It must've taken generations for your family to achieve this kind of balance. Whatever happened to those who had only, say, half the curses?"

"They died, I think?" West said, scratching at his chin. "Mom said we inherited most of them this way. We get vaccines for even the rare curses, though, so that's why we're healthy. Rubin-x, Anti-Toad, the Antigone antidote..."

"The Antigone plague hasn't existed since 1769!"

"Better to be safe than sorry, right?"

"Thank you, but we have to go," Tala said hastily, paying the man and nudging West to his feet. Very few families had the particular blend of curses that the Eddingses had, and she didn't want the specialist figuring out who his patient was while Alex was still out of Maidenkeep.

"These don't even require prescriptions," Nya said after they'd all finally agreed that visiting more would be a further waste of time. She frowned at the pieces of paper Alex had accumulated over the course of a dozen visits. "You can buy all these over the counter. They're trying to look more legitimate than they actually are."

"I'm beginning to think that Fortune-Tellers' Row is made up of a few certified professionals amid a sea of quacks," Tala muttered.

Nya handed the prescription letters to Ken, and both jumped when their fingers brushed. "Here," she blurted out, all but shoving the papers at his chest, then skittering several meters back.

West, now back to avidly watching the proceedings from the comfort of Loki's pocket, chittered curiously.

"They gotta figure it out on their own," Loki told him.

"I have another suggestion," Adelaide spoke up timidly. "If you don't mind?"

"We don't mind at all," Alex assured her, and the girl blushed, dipping into a half curtsy almost without thinking.

"Well," she warbled. "My great-grandma's a seeress, as you guys know. You would think that would make her popular, but she's actually not. A lot of the fortune-tellers here read your dooms, but they're almost always dooms that people want to hear, which is why so many people prefer them even if they're fake. But my great-grandma doesn't tell fortunes. She tells the truth. So we should look for the ones without a lot of customers."

"That's good thinking," Zoe said. "I suppose having a seeress in the family brings a different perspective."

"I'm not sure someone would set up a stall at the fair if they know they're not going to get customers," Dex pointed out. "The whole purpose of selling your services at a fair is to make money."

"Not if that wasn't her reason for coming to the fair in the first place," Alex said grimly. "I've got an idea."

A call to mission control provided them with a list of all participating vendors, plus their locations. Even then, they almost missed it. It was a lone house on a street not yet occupied, most of the properties still under construction but temporarily suspended from work until the fair was over. It was the only residence on the block that had been completed—a small bungalow with one small window and a wooden door that looked like it would creak no matter how softly you pushed. It was a quarter of a block away from the nearest concession stand, but the sign in front of it that said INTERNATIONAL CHARMS FAIR—FORTUNE-TELLING SERVICES was not a mistake.

"If this was a horror movie," Dex said, "there'd be wax figures inside, and they'd turn out to be the bodies of victims that the serial killer placed as props. I know I've seen that movie before."

"I can't believe I'm saying this, Dex," Ken said, "but shush."

"I can't believe she actually applied for a permit for the fair," Zoe said.

"And then chose the one place that made it difficult for her to be found." Loki, easily the bravest of them all, approached the window and peered inside. And then, with a loud curse, they sprang away from the pane.

"What is it?" Ken asked.

"She's just...sitting there." Loki looked freaked out. "Just sitting there behind a table and grinning at me like a loon. Like she knew I was gonna look in."

That seemed to settle matters for Alex, who immediately marched to the door and pushed his way inside, which started a mad scramble as everyone rushed in after him on the chance that the king was walking into a trap.

There was no trap. The woman was exactly how Loki had described, the only light coming from the candle at her side. She was younger than Tala imagined. Definitely younger than Nya's grandma or the seeress of Tintagel or Lady Nottingham by half. Several chairs were formed in a semicircle before her—ten in all.

The woman's feet were propped up on the table, and she was thumbing through her mobile phone, cackling at a video she was watching there. Without lifting her eyes, she gestured impatiently at them all to sit.

"About goddamn time," she said, and she sounded nothing at all like the mysterious, fawning fortune-tellers at the fair or the clinical curse specialists or anyone else in between. She dressed nothing like them either; she wore faded jeans and an oversize shirt, no jewelry nor stethoscope to be seen. "My ass was getting numb from all this waiting. You were supposed to be here an hour earlier." She shot Tala a significant look. "Should've guessed. Hard to admit you're wrong when your reputation relies on always being right."

There was a rush of wind and a flurry of feathers, and the firebird was there by Alex's side, glowing until it lit up the whole room.

But the Baba Yaga only arched an eyebrow at it, unsurprised. "You're in a pickle, aren't you?" she asked. "Damned if you do, damned if you don't. It's a dirty job, little one, but you're the only one to do it."

The firebird hesitated. Then it pouted and settled ungracefully on Alex's lap with a loud harrumph.

"You're not her," Alex said. "You're not the Baba Yaga I met at Maidenkeep."

The woman lifted slim shoulders. "What gave that away? My youth or my charming personality?" The woman tossed the phone back on the table. "What I am, though, is a Baba Yaga with some of the answers you're seeking, though you may not like what I have to say." Her coal-black eyes wandered through the group. "Shall I start with His Majesty, or do I go through the lot of you first? Because believe me, you're gonna wanna know what the fates got to say about all of you too."

19

In Which the Baba Yaga Lays the Smackdown

It was warm inside the strange bungalow despite the absence of heat that wasn't from either the candle or the firebird. Tala could feel her palms growing damp as the Baba Yaga pushed her feet off the table, stood, and stretched, her joints making faint popping sounds. "The Russian scent is strong in this room," she noted and grinned. "Just a metaphor we like to say when shit's about to hit the fan."

"Why did you call me here?" Alex was never one to mince words. "Why not announce yourself at Maidenkeep?"

"Announce myself? At Maidenkeep? And have a hundred reporters shoving microphones into my face? No way. That would have involved far more Fianna in the room than I would like. You've all been busy little bees, focused on your own things, and I figured I'd gather you all in one place and have it out at once.

"Let's get the generalities out of the way. First, I respond to they or them, and willfully using another pronoun will get you a face full of warts. Just ask the last guy I went on a date with. Second—and I'm sure you all know this by now, so consider this a disclaimer before I start or a term of agreement if you will—I don't undo curses. Only a fool would try to undo curses. Even the smallest spells can backfire *spectacularly*. What I do offer, though, is mitigation. Every curse has a loophole, every spell a weakness. That's my specialty. You're gonna live a better life with a curse modified to be a tad more harmless than having a curse completely annihilated but with a hole through your stomach for your troubles. Third, let's save you for last, Your Majesty. Once we get started on you, I'm not sure we'll be able to get to anything else."

They turned to stare, irritated, at both Ken and Nya. "You know what? I'm going to start with the two of you first. If I don't slice up that tension quickly, you're both gonna start humping over my new rug."

Ken leaped to his feet. "We're not dating, okay?" he shouted. "We're not!"

Tala was expecting Nya to get mad or throw something at Ken, but she was right by his side and just as shouty. "We can't! It's too dangerous!"

"And it's not like I *don't* want to!"

"I know that he's kind of a jerk sometimes, and he talks too much and he does things on a whim that would send anyone into palpitations—"

"Hey! You're the one hiding that you're a mer—"

"—but he's a kind person and I like him, but that's exactly why we're doing this! I mean, *not* doing this!"

Everyone stared at them. The Baba Yaga sighed.

"Really the worst time for me to give up smoking," they muttered. "Has it ever occurred to you chowderheads that if this is what you both want, to maybe run with it, see what happens?"

"Absolutely not!" Ken snapped. "My curse says I'm marrying a monster!"

"And *I'm* the monster!" Nya said, at about the same octave as Ken. "And I'm supposed to marry a corpse!"

"And *I'm* the corpse! Can you not see the disadvantages that this situation implies?" Ken pointed at the floor. "I don't even have a damn shadow anymore!"

"A funny thing about shadows," the Baba Yaga said. "They say you can live vicariously through them. Peter Schlemihl did. Saved his life, even. If OzCorp didn't eradicate yours, I would imagine it's still somewhere about, living the high life." They chuckled at his glare. "You'll be just fine without one, Inoue. And causation isn't correlation. That you might one day wind up a corpse doesn't mean it's because you're marrying Miss Mermaid over here."

Ken floundered. "You mean—"

"There is a difference between searching for the symptoms of a disease you've convinced yourself you have and having a competent doctor make an actual diagnosis of your health." They snorted. "Not that I'm saying most of these specialists and fortune-tellers at this fair are competent."

"But my grandmother is a seeress," Nya warbled.

"Has she expressed any concerns about either of your well-beings? Any worries? Or was she quite nonchalant about the whole thing, once you'd discovered what your respective dooms meant?"

Both hesitated.

"I understand that Udeme has reasons to be secretive about your village's past, Miss Nya, considering their horrific history, but surely telling him would make things easier on you both." Their expression softened. "Make no mistake. There *will* be death. It has to happen. I have some theories about it that I'm sure your grandmother shares, but to tell you both would be to affect the outcome, and I'd rather not have to deal with that all over again. I've only got an educated guess about what might occur, same as she does. Anyone who tells you the absolutes is lying."

"Are you saying what we think our dooms are saying might not actually—"

"That's all I gotta say about it. Well, that was fun. Who's next?"

Tala felt cold. This Baba Yaga knew far too much.

The woman turned to Zoe, who looked ready to bolt out of her chair at any second. "What about you, Miss Carlisle? For someone who used to be quite the law-abiding straight A student, you've gotten yourself into quite a few messes."

Zoe blushed but said nothing.

"No, you don't need to say anything." The Baba Yaga whipped out a piece of paper and scrawled hastily on it for a couple of minutes before handing it to Zoe with a flourish.

"What's this?" Zoe asked, accepting it. "Tincture of sunrose? Five milligrams of sodium peorthide?"

"Peorthoxide," the witch corrected her, sounding irritated. "My handwriting isn't that bad."

"This is a prescription?"

"To help alleviate your preternatural mood swings. To keep you from throwing yourself into reckless endeavors because you have no other outlet to vent your feelings, now that you've given up your tears for warmth."

Zoe gaped at them. "How did you..."

"Hello. Do you remember who I am? Baba Yaga? Knower of things? Look, I could prescribe you some stronger stuff, but I would need permission from one of your parents. Fortunately for you, the curse you've taken on is easy enough to live with. It was a high-quality spellstone, for one, which makes both the spell *and* its consequences extremely potent, but you asked for the smallest repercussion possible. If you'd chosen anything else, it's likely someone would be dead by now."

Zoe squirmed in her chair. Cole was watching her.

The Baba Yaga tapped their chin. "The real solution to your problem, though, is a matter of willpower. It *is* possible to care about something hard enough to override the curse and bring you to tears. You're only gonna have to do it three times and *boom*—curse lifted."

"So you mean there's a way?" Zoe asked, looking suddenly, desperately hopeful. "Thank you."

"Don't thank me just yet. It's harder than it sounds, and the road to recovery will be a painful one." The Baba Yaga then turned to Cole and raised an eyebrow. They didn't need to speak. Whatever it was they would have said, Cole understood immediately.

"All right," he said shortly.

"If it eases your mind, I can tell you right now that Adelaide will not bear any permanent scars."

His younger sister leaped to her feet. "You have no right to tell him that!" she cried angrily. "I'm not going to shirk any of my responsibilities just because I'm a girl! Mom did it, and so can I!"

"That doesn't make my words any less true, Lady Adelaide. Your blue-eyed brother has quite a few more tribulations to go through, and you will share in some of those trials before long."

"He's not blue-eyed," Loki spoke up.

"Just another metaphor." The Baba Yaga looked toward Dex.

"Please don't tell me," the boy squeaked. "I still don't want to know."

They threw their head back and laughed. "All right. And you, Lord Eddings?"

"My mom said my doom was that I'm to marry," the boy said sheepishly.

"Your doom is that you will be wedded to a woman who will know your worth and that you will both be the catalyst to terrific things."

"I'm grateful," West said, face drooping a little, "but is that all? Won't I have a chance to, um, prove my worth by fighting ice wolves and ogres like my friends? Wouldn't my doom have said anything more if that was something I'll be—"

"Learn to be content with what you're given, Lord Eddings, and not ask for more than you can handle. And what about you, Laird Sun-Wagner? Ready to hear what I have to say?"

Loki leaned forward, their hands balled in their lap. "The Dame of Tintagel told me that I was going to break a scepter and give Neverland back its crown. What does that mean?"

"How the hell should I know?"

"But I thought—"

"If we knew what the bigger prophecies actually meant, don't you think the best of us would be running around, trying to right all the wrongs? We see symbols, intuition, quick glimpses of the future without context. You don't think we *want* to help you if we predict a doom that sounds like you're gonna die, mi'laird? My predecessor made it very clear that meddling in prophecies we ourselves don't understand always happens to our detriment. Be the change you want to see in your prophecy. That ain't on me."

Finally, the Baba Yaga turned to Alex, who had somehow managed to comport himself and wait, though Tala knew he was about ready to pop.

"Now that I've finally gotten your attention," he said, barely civil by that point, "why isn't the Baba Yaga who cursed me here? You wouldn't have gone through all this trouble just to tell me that."

"The original Baba Yaga is no longer in a position to help you."

Alex looked like he'd just been delivered a blow to the head. "You mean she's dead?"

"Her career is dead. She no longer possesses her abilities."

"But that's impossible. Don't all seeresses have theirs for life?"

"Yes," the young Baba Yaga said. "Until we break the rules and meddle when we shouldn't have. Excepting rare cases, no two seeresses see visions in the same way, but the consensus among us was that you should have died, Alexei Tsarevich, along with your family back in that throne room over twelve years ago. I do not know what my predecessor's visions told her, but I do know that whatever it was affected her so deeply that she was willing to break our laws and save you—at the cost of her own gifts."

Their words had taken all the fight out of Alex, who'd gone white. Tala sprang to his side, taking his hand in hers. The others looked stunned, also at a loss. "You really had to say it like that?" Tala snapped.

"No amount of dancing around it would change what I say. You were fated to die, but my predecessor saw something in you that was worth saving. And so here you are."

"So I've been living on borrowed time ever since then?" Alex asked. "So finding a cure is worthless because I'll die anyway?"

The Baba Yaga wagged a finger at him. "Didn't say that. For better or for worse, she's changed the course of history, shaped it to one where you're still alive, and the universe has bent to accommodate it. Would she really have cursed you if things looked bleak? She must have truly believed that there was a way and that you would be a force to be reckoned with."

"It's a damn frog's curse! How can she change so much with only a frog's curse? I could have still used the Nine Maidens without it!"

"The Avalon curse is of multipronged magic, layers upon layers of spells that must be addressed separately. Believe it or not, Your Majesty, the frog's curse *was* meant to protect you."

"From what?"

The Baba Yaga shrugged. "Unlike her, I prefer to keep my abilities, so I shall not deign to speculate."

"How am I to lift the Avalon curse if the only ways to do so no longer exist?" Alex interrupted.

"*Three main paths to Buyan lie, to claim what death can ne'er die.*"

Alex froze. "So that's it? Is this the confirmation I needed to hear? The only way to fix all this and lift my curse is to find a way back into Buyan?"

"There is a reason the Snow Queen would do anything to find it, Your Majesty. She cannot access it with her shardstones alone, and Avalon will never give her the spellstones she needs. But the world is changing. Other kingdoms are learning the ways of advanced spelltech. It is only a matter of time before she finds a way through their devices. If she finds the Alatyr again, Alexei Tsarevich, we will all lose."

"But it's no longer possible. The dragons are dead, the Seven Magical Wonders are gone, and using the Nine Maidens would kill me anyway."

"Perhaps the ways to the Wonders are hidden, just like Buyan. The old maps to such locations still exist. Here is what you will need: a lantern and a song, a herb and a flute, a jewel case and a bone. Find the mirror at World's End, and await your judgment."

They all stared at the Baba Yaga, who shrugged. "Hey, don't judge the messenger."

"World's End," Tala murmured, head spinning. Where had she heard that before?

The Baba Yaga drew close and clapped a friendly hand on Alex's shoulder. "The fate of Avalon, and perhaps of the world even, falls on you doing the impossible," they said, "And—I seriously cannot believe the words I'm about to say because, kid, I would read the *shit* out of this book—but the fate of Avalon, and perhaps of the world even, also falls on you getting a decent love life. *In shifting ice a prince you'll kiss, and the first shall be forgiven.* I cackled, seeing that the first time."

Alex turned a beet red.

"You needed to hear some hard truths before anything else, Your

Majesty, and I couldn't have done that in Maidenkeep. Avalon history is all about heroes and heroines finding their one true love, and for good reason—their enemies knew that was the easiest way to hurt them. Only right that the tradition continues with you. Session's over, loves."

Alex rose to his feet, still blushing. "Let's go," he snapped and all but marched out of the room. The others exchanged worried looks and hurried after him.

But Tala lingered. She had to make sure. "You didn't say anything about me," she said.

"You have an agimat. Far be it for me to make a prediction when it involves you."

"I somehow doubt that that would ever stop you."

They chuckled. "True enough. I figured it wouldn't be something you would like the others to know."

Tala nearly stopped breathing. "Thank you for that."

"You can't hide it forever." The Baba Yaga flopped back down onto their chair.

"I-I just need more time to figure out how to tell everyone." There was something different about the table now. Tala hadn't remembered it having carved claws on the base of its legs before. "Everyone who's ever wielded the sword dies. I don't want to die."

"I know. And that's why I'm not going to stop you. Hell if I'm gonna make the same mistake my predecessor did, however justified her reasons might have been. Oh dear. My spell's wearing off."

Those weren't carvings. They were real claws. No…real *talons*. Chicken's talons.

The candle was starting to flicker. They cast strange shadows on the Baba Yaga's face. "I hope this is the right decision for you," they said gently, and one of the talons curled up, tapped at the ground of its own volition with a very audible *click*, and began to scratch at the wooden surface. "And now, it's best that you leave. You might not like what you're about to see next."

Tala nearly ran into the leader of the Eighth Honor while trying to escape the Baba Yaga's shop. Slamming into Gareth Wildstone was like slamming your head against a brick wall, and he caught her before she could fall. "Easy there, milady," he cautioned gently.

The Fianna had finally discovered that Alex was missing. Fortunately, the partly abandoned block made things easier for the festival visitors to ignore them. Or it was possibly because of the sharp tang of smoky eucalyptus that Tala could detect in the air, telling her that someone had put up an invisibility barrier, masking them from view.

"Alex," Tala's mother said, looking angry and also disappointed, a devastating combination Tala had been privy to many times in the past. "Why would you leave without telling us?"

King or not, it had the same effect on Alex. He looked down at the floor. "I'm sorry, Aunt Lumina," he mumbled, "but I had to."

"Is the Baba Yaga still inside?" Not waiting for an answer, Gareth gestured at three of his subordinates to enter the house.

"I'm disappointed in you too," her mother continued, turning to Tala, who flinched. "Do you understand how much danger you've put yourself in? What do you think would have happened to Avalon if you'd come to harm, Alex? You could have put Lady Adelaide in harm's way!"

"That's okay, ma'am," Adelaide chirped, not really helping at all. "We're used to it."

"The Baba Yaga wouldn't meet us in Maidenkeep," Tala spoke up.

"And they wouldn't show up where they knew the rest of you would be. We had to take the chance."

"Don't blame Tala," Alex said sharply. "Don't blame any of them. They didn't know I was coming. They protected me anyway."

"We would have guarded him with our lives," Zoe insisted. "We've done it before."

Tala's mother groaned. "That's not the point. We can't have you meeting strange seers who may or may not be the Baba Yaga. How would you have known if they were a con artist? Or a Beiran agent?"

"Some things in the letter they sent us verified who they were," Alex said.

One of the Fianna returned, looking disgruntled. "There's no one inside," he told Gareth. "Bari and Flor are still searching, but I think they've flown the coop."

Tala shuddered, still thinking of the scratching sounds of those massive chicken feet against the floor.

"You nearly sent everyone at Maidenkeep into a panic," Lumina said and sighed. "What I'm asking is for a little understanding. There are scores of people working to keep you safe, and it's unfair to them for you to suddenly disappear like this. I know you want to find a way to lift your curse, but this isn't the way to do it. We'd all gladly destroy the Nine Maidens if we could destroy your bond with them as well, but since we can't—"

"I don't want the Nine Maidens destroyed," Alex said. "Even if it means I die."

"Alex!" Tala's mother exclaimed.

"I'm still expendable. I may be the last of the Tsareviches, but there are others who share my blood with a direct line to the throne. Heck, West could be king."

"I don't want to be king," the boy said immediately. "I can't even manage my own life, much less a kingdom."

"The Nine Maidens were the only thing stopping Beira from laying waste to Avalon. Imagine what would happen if we didn't have them. I wouldn't be standing here right now. The Baba Yaga told me that much."

"Perhaps we could talk about this back at Maidenkeep," Tala's mother suggested.

"You can't be serious, Alex," Tala said. "You'd really give up your life for that? Even after everything the Baba Yaga said? That their predecessor gave up her abilities for you?"

"*Especially* after everything the Baba Yaga said," he replied, voice weary. "I'm still not worth losing Avalon all over again. Maybe I'm only alive long enough to make sure that happens. I'll head back to Maidenkeep, Auntie."

"Do you want to come with us?" Tala's mother asked her.

Tala hesitated. "Can I hang around here a little longer?" She was furious at Alex, even though she understood why. The Baba Yaga's parting words were swirling in her head, making her guilt all the more acute. What right did she have, telling Alex what duty was supposed to be?

Her mother nodded, gave her a quick hug. "I'll be in my room."

"This isn't a very good sausage fest," Dex lamented after the king, Lumina, and the Fianna had left. "Do you guys wanna head back too?"

"I'm gonna go look for my folks," West decided. "They're hosting the readathon at the city library right now. They've got excellent catering. Charcuterie boards and caviar and chicken nuggets for the kids. Wanna come with me?"

"Oh, a readathon?" Adelaide asked, brightening. "Can we go, Nicky?"

Cole let out a low, long-suffering sigh.

"Thanks, Nicky!"

"I don't have anything else planned tonight," Ken said to Nya with deliberate care. "Wanna come with and see what the hell a charcuterie board is?"

"It's basically cold cuts," Nya said, blushing a little. "And I'd like that."

A man in a top hat and a dark-blue cloak brushed past them. Tala felt a small shock go through her body as her agimat came into contact with his gloved hand. For a moment, the man's figure wavered and disappeared, and a large cat stood in its place. And then that too was gone and the man was back, as solid as anyone could ever be. He winked at Tala, then walked on.

"Tala?"

"Sorry, but I'll meet you guys there."

The man had stopped before a nearby souvenir stall, waiting. It was only after Tala was standing beside him that he lifted his hat again, revealing a pair of bright-green eyes.

"Fancy a stroll with me?" the Cheshire asked.

20

IN WHICH THE CHESHIRE AND TALA BOND OVER COWARDICE

They were standing before a small booth that sold a variety of Avalon-related knickknacks: small plush dolls of the firebird, snow globes of Maidenkeep, shirts and tumblers and hoodies bearing the Avalon crest. The Cheshire picked up both the snow globe and a realistic-looking sword replica, turning the latter over in his hands.

"I think I'll take this one," he told the vendor. "Is there anything here that catches your eye, Tala? My treat?"

"I'm good," Tala said, her head filled with a million questions as she watched him pay the seller. "How did you do that?" she asked as they started walking away.

"Do what?"

"Pay the vendor. Have pockets. Use hands."

His laugh sounded like it was actually coming *out* of his mouth. "This spelltech was custom made specifically for me. The disguise is almost as real as you and I, as long as your agimat doesn't brush up against me again. Think of it as a CGI effect, except it's three-dimensional and as authentic as it appears on-screen."

"How much did it cost?"

"The price for the invention? Its creator owed me a favor and so asked for nothing. The price for the spell? The shape of my firstborn son."

"But you don't have a—"

"Even the strongest spells offer such loopholes. It's their investment in the future, so to speak, betting on human fallibility. But alas, that is not the case with me. I *had* a firstborn son." His fingers traced at the sword hilt. "I no longer remember what he looks like."

"Oh. I'm so sorry."

"Don't be. Did the Baba Yaga change your mind?"

"They said that it wasn't up to them to convince me."

"They're very wise. Would you like a sisig burrito? Cotton candy? My treat."

"I'm not hungry." Tala's stomach growled. "I am maybe a little hungry."

The sisig burrito was excellent and the picker-upper lemonade cold and refreshing. Tala took a bite of her sundae and gazed about the crowd. The charms fair was the kind of date she'd always imagined Ryker taking her out on, and a part of her wished that was still a possibility. Instead she was walking around with a human turned cat turned human who was kind but who mostly felt bad for her.

She hadn't wanted to return to Maidenkeep, but the Cheshire had promised that it wouldn't take long. She said nothing along the way, watching as the Cheshire turned the sword he'd bought over and over in his hands, admiring the craftsmanship.

It was only after they had passed the main gates of the castle and after the Cheshire had guided her toward the palace courtyard that Tala realized where they were headed.

"Don't leave," the Cheshire said quietly. "Like the Baba Yaga, I have no intentions of changing your mind."

The courtyard was empty for once. The Fianna had announced the area off-limits to the public while the fair was in progress, which meant the only people there besides them were a group of Fianna standing guard. The defenses around the sword were as strong as ever, and all the carefully controlled magic made even Tala's hair hurt.

The men and women keeping guard saluted smartly at the Cheshire. One stepped forward. "Will you be needing anything, milord?"

"We'd like a little private time if you don't mind. I haven't had the chance to look closely at this sword in almost…ah, three hundred years."

"Of course."

There was a faint buzzing noise, and the barrier disappeared. The Fianna withdrew to a respectable distance.

"Three hundred years?" Tala whispered. "How old are you?"

"Old enough." She wasn't expecting the undercurrent of sorrow in his voice. "When you've lived for as long as I have, sometimes the only thing you live long enough to have is regret." He let his fingers trail down the exposed part of the sword's blade. "I told them any security around the Nameless Sword was a waste of time. The sword chooses who it chooses. Even Anneliese the Snow Queen knew the folly of such an attempt. It's why she was more concerned with finding the firebird and controlling the Nine Maidens."

"Why bring me here?"

"Because a long time ago, I made the same choices you did." The Cheshire pulled, but the sword wouldn't budge. He relaxed his grip, let his hand drop.

Tala stared at him. "You…*rejected* the sword?"

"Not exactly the hero Avalonians say I am, eh? More like the coward and the traitor everyone else believes." The Cheshire drew out the replica sword he'd purchased, slowly slid the blade off its scabbard. He held it up to the light to admire. "It's almost like how I remembered it," he murmured. "Its maker must have done quite the research. Very few people know what the Vorpal Sword looked like beyond the few descriptions that survived Wonderland."

"The Vorpal Sword." Alice Liddell had drawn the Nameless Sword out of stone; from then until her death, it had been known by that name.

"Are you aware of her history?"

"Yes. She fought the Mad Queen, Elizabeth XXIV. She fought off Beiran influence in Wonderland. She…" Tala paused, not sure if she wanted to broach a subject that might be traumatic for him.

"She fought in the Wonderland Wars," the Cheshire finished for her. "And she fell into a shattered looking glass. They never found her body. I asked her to marry me."

"I'm so sorry."

"Not more sorry than I am. I drew the Vorpal Sword first, and I rejected it."

Tala could feel her heart speed up. "Like me."

"The sword must always have a wielder. Reject it, and it will only find someone else. Most people think prophecy is like a mountain, unlikely to adapt to the whimsy of humans. That's not the case. Prophecy is more like a river, filling in the spaces and crevices so it can continue moving in the direction it desires. And people forget that even mountains are impermanent."

"Are you saying that the sword found someone else because you rejected it? That the sword might find someone else because *I* rejected it?"

"I'm saying that there are consequences to rejecting the sword that you may regret later on. I rejected the Vorpal Sword, and Alice did not. I was horrified. She believed that it was her duty. She had always been more courageous than I was." The Cheshire gazed at the stone. "I've always wondered what would have happened if I'd wielded it instead. Would she have survived the war? I would have liked nothing better to have died knowing she would live to a ripe old age." He looked down at his hands.

"I do not even have that as a luxury. I had invested two centuries into not dying before I met her and realized what true strength really was."

"I'm afraid," Tala said.

"As well you should be. It is not a responsibility to be taken lightly, no matter how many foolish people believe it will give them nothing but riches and prestige. People believe that the spells we use, with their sets of bound laws and explicit repercussions, are what natural magic is made of. What they don't understand is that the wilder Wonderland magic is what magic actually is at its most basic form. It is the laws and restrictions we place that make it unnatural, and those are where our problems often begin. Every spell comes with a price, and that is the same for this sword as for everything else."

"Did anyone know about...?"

"Save for Alice? No one else. You are the first person I've told. I thought it would help ease your mind, telling you my story."

"What you're telling me is that someone else might suffer because of my choice."

"Do you really think that you'll be forcing anyone to take up the sword at this point? Did you think visitors are flocking to Avalon right now because of a summit? You are not responsible for their choices. I was not responsible for what Alice eventually chose to do. But it is normal to feel guilty. It is normal to reject the sword. Not all of us want the sorrow the Nameless Sword brings its users, despite all the fame they receive. Saying no when others say yes doesn't make it the wrong choice for you."

"Then what do you advise me to do?" Tala asked. "Do I try to raise the sword again?"

"Do you want to?" the Cheshire asked gently.

She took a deep breath. "No."

"Then that's answer enough, don't you think?" The Cheshire patted her on the shoulder. It felt like a real hand. "I asked Alice once if she would do it all over again, if she would take the sword when it chose her, despite knowing the grief that would come. She said she would always choose the sword. She asked me if I would make the same decision again, to reject it. I said yes. I was known more for my charm and my smile than for military skills or fighting prowess. I was an irresponsible git. I would have made a terrible hero. Countless more would have died under my care. Had I been one of the soldiers under my charge, I would have abandoned my post. Alice thrived where I did not. No, the countless needless deaths I would have brought about would have been worse on me. Alice forgave me. It was harder to forgive myself. We were meant for other things. But even today, I struggle." He smiled down at her, a wide boyish smile. "Forgive yourself," he said. "It'll be the hardest thing you'll ever have to do and also the best. Take it from me."

They made their way to the readathon in a strange, comfortable silence. As they approached, Tala spotted the Eddingses handing out books to children waiting in line, Loki, West, and Dex helping them. Nearby, a puppet play was in progress: another retelling of the Red Hood and the wolf king. There was even a small orchestra present, preparing to play.

"Kinda dark for a children's play, don't you think?" the Cheshire murmured.

"Only adults think these things are too dark for kids," Tala noted. "They're having the time of their lives."

He chuckled. "True."

Cole, Adelaide, and Zoe were also watching the show. Adelaide was frowning. "But that isn't right," she cried. "Didn't the Red Hood betray the wolf king first? Why are they all treating him like the bad guy?"

"You're biased to begin with, brat," Cole said, tone full of affection.

"Nicky should invite you to the wolf sanctuary our family's got," Adelaide told Zoe. "They're not bad like everyone thinks."

"If Nicky would invite me," Zoe said quietly, "then I would love to."

Cole paused, seemed on the verge of asking, and then turned back to the show instead. Zoe looked briefly disappointed but did the same.

Nya had somehow managed to gain an oversize teddy bear. Ken was beaming smugly at her, and they were actually holding hands. It was a good sign, and Tala was glad it looked like they were finally patching things up.

A crowd had gathered nearby, and West was the focus of all their attention. Once more in his dog form, the shifter was prancing around happily, obeying commands some of the delighted children were issuing to him and getting all the tummy rubs he could.

The orchestra began to play a slow, beautiful melody.

"'Smoke Gets in Your Eyes,'" Zoe said softly. She took another quick look at Cole, a little wistfully, but then glanced down at her phone. "I have to go," she sighed.

Adelaide watched her leave, then turned toward her brother. She hissed something at him, and they quietly began to argue.

Nya coughed. "Ken," she said tentatively, cautiously. "I know I turned you down at the party last time when you asked me to dance. I was wondering if I can make it up to you now, if you would like to—"

That was about as far as she got, because Ken had promptly scooped her up and was marching toward the empty space before the orchestra, Nya's delighted, embarrassed "Ken!" echoing through the air.

"You have good people at your back," the Cheshire said. "There was a reason I chose them to rescue His Majesty."

"I wasn't one of the people you'd chosen, though."

"No," the man acknowledged. "I wanted to honor your parents' wishes and give you a normal life for a little bit longer."

"I don't know," Tala said, "if I agree with my parents' wishes, then."

"Are you still angry at your father?"

"I want to be."

"West's parents have a staggeringly overextravagant catering service just for this event, Your Grace," Ken called out to them. "Would you like to join us?"

"I would be delighted." The Cheshire looked past her. "Would Mr. Cadfael like to join in the festivities as well?"

Tala whirled. Ryker stepped out of the shadows as soon as the Cheshire called his name, hands over his head. The tattoo on his wrist that marked him as one of the pirates was missing, again so carefully camouflaged that Tala couldn't detect it. "I didn't know how to announce myself without it being weird," he said nervously. The other Banders had tensed at the sight of him, as if anticipating a fight.

"What are you doing here?" Tala asked.

"Believe it or not, I thought I could enjoy myself too. I heard about this. Sounded fun. Then I learned the Eddingses organized it."

"And so you thought I was gonna be here too."

He nodded. "If you don't want me around, I'll go."

That would have been prudent, but Tala wasn't that. "Wait."

"Tala," Zoe said. "You sure?"

"Yeah, I am. He's not gonna pull anything. Can you give us a sec?"

Zoe nodded and the others relaxed, but it was Ryker who remained watchful, uncertain. Anxious. She'd always seen him confident and in control before. He also looked thinner and paler, like he hadn't been sleeping or eating much.

"Your Grace." Another man, slightly emaciated-looking and wearing a bowler hat, approached. "Lord Charming wishes to speak to you."

"All right, Hatter. I'll take my leave, then. Lady Makiling Warnock, Lord Cadfael, I sense you two have much to talk about without me intruding."

"What did you want to ask me?" Tala asked Ryker.

"How did you know I was going to ask you anything?"

"There had to be a reason you're seeking me out. Something must have happened since the last time I saw you. Plus, you look like crap."

He laughed, then grimaced. "Can't fault your logic. Wanted to warn you."

"About what?"

"The Snow Queen *is* working with Nome and OzCorp. I don't know what exactly she's planning but I know it's big, and she seems confident that she'll be able to sway Kay to her side if she pulls it off."

Tala stiffened. "But you don't know the details?"

"She hasn't told me any details. She hasn't told me anything for a while now. I had to eavesdrop to learn this much. She's been supplying them with shardstones. That much I figured out. I know the Snow Queen's got her eyes on the sword, even though she can't take it herself. She's going to sway whoever it is that wields it to her side. So I've been… keeping watch. Of a sort."

"Ryker," Tala began.

"I haven't told the Snow Queen anything about this. Or about how you've been helping me. Or how I've been helping you. She'd have my heart if she knew. Literally."

The nonchalant way he said it made her skin crawl. "Why don't you leave her, Ryker?"

"It's not that easy. I rescued other children before I even met you, Tala. I can't leave them behind."

"Tell us how to get to them. Help us save them."

"I—I can't. They won't want to leave. Mother treats them well, the way she used to treat me. It's not until they're older that she—" He hesitated, shook his head. "I can't."

"You can't promise to protect me and still follow her."

"When that time comes," Ryker said, "I'll choose you. But until then, I need to figure things out. Make sure people I care about back in Beira are safe. You're right. I'm not sure that my interests and Mother's align anymore. I found out some things. Horrible things. I'm not sure I want to stay in Beira any longer. But that's my problem, not yours."

"And if she finds out somehow?"

He flashed her a brief grin. "Then I'll probably die."

She shoved him. It wasn't enough to topple him over, but it was enough for him to stumble back, to send her a stunned look. "Stop treating it like a joke!" she snapped. She knew the others were casting worried looks their way but also trusted her enough not to intervene. "Stop acting like no one's going to mourn you if you—if you—" Suddenly, she understood her parents a little more. "You need to make the right choice, and soon. Staying neutral like this will put not just me but also Alex and the rest of Avalon in danger. And you know that isn't fair. Stop using me as your excuse to do the right thing. If you really are regretful and if you really do care for me, then you have to save yourself. Don't make me your redemption. I deserve more than that."

"You're right," he said gruffly. "I never seem to know the right thing to do. Sometimes I think about my mom and I—sometimes I wish I'd been with her, you know? Like I failed her when I was supposed to protect her. I do want to protect you, and not just because I care for you. I do want to live for myself. But I don't know how to do that yet."

Tala gazed out at her other friends, now waiting in line for the food. "A date," she said.

He blinked. "What?"

"A date. I want everything. A nice dinner, a stroll, maybe a movie or something if we've got the time. Conversation. Honesty. The works. I want to know who you really are, not who you're being forced to be." Over a year ago, their roles had been reversed; he was the dashing, confident jock who'd teased her into going with him to the Elsmore High bonfire. "You told me once that the main reason you liked me was because I made you feel normal. And that's what I need from you. For you to remember that you don't have to be a hero rescuing kids in cages or be some badass working for a powerful kingdom. Just someone who wants to play basketball professionally and loves spaghetti and K-pop and has wanted a dog since forever, if those are what you really like and not what you felt you needed to say to get close to me. But when that date happens, I want you to have come to a decision regarding which side you'll choose. I deserve to know that much."

"I see. I understand." He hesitated. "How did you know I like K-pop?"

"You're the only one who thinks you're singing along quietly when you've got your headphones on."

Ryker began to chuckle. It was a welcome sound. But shortly after, he began to hiccup, and then the tears falling down his face weren't from laughter.

Tala tugged him closer.

"Sorry," he said, voice scratchy. "Don't know why I started crying like that, like a—"

"It's okay." She preferred him like this, where he felt more like the boy she used to know. "Tita Chedeng and Tita Teejay have, like, a million and one dogs at this point. I think they're fostering a few. Wanna name one? What *would* you name one anyway?"

"Picard."

"Picard?"

"That's what I would have named mine, if I had one. You know. Picard and Ryker. I know it's supposed to be Riker with an *i* and not a *y*, but I'm sure people would get the context."

"This is, like, the *weirdest* time for me to discover that you're actually a *Star Trek* nerd."

"What the hell are you doing here?"

It was Loki, their voice hostile. Standing before them, smiling prettily, was Vivien Fey. She had a younger girl with her—Abigail, the sister, who was also the most exhausted-looking fifteen-year-old Tala had ever seen. She was pale and thin, with dark circles under her eyes and a faint tremor to her hands. She shrank back when she spotted Loki, and Vivien put an arm around her, pulling her closer in a sudden, protective manner.

"The fair is open to the public, Sun-Wagner," she said easily, though her eyes were hard. She glanced dismissively at Tala and Ryker. "Or is that reason enough for you to harass me?"

"I'm not harassing you."

"Given our history, I could easily make the case that you are. Look, you're scaring Abigail. Will you let me pass, or will I have to call the cops?"

Loki hesitated, scowled, let her pass. The Fey sisters swept past him toward the readathon.

She hadn't recognized Ryker. The boy had looked both confused and curious at the exchange between them and Loki, and Tala didn't think it was an act. Whatever Vivien Fey was involved in, he was at least not a part of it, which helped bolster his claims of innocence.

"I'm going to get her," Loki muttered, glowering after the Fey siblings. "I will." They turned their attention to Ryker and hesitated. "Loki Sun-Wagner," they finally said, extending their hand to him, to Tala's surprise.

A look of relief spread across Ryker's face, with a little gratitude mixed in. "Ryker Cadfael. I wanna, uh, apologize about Invierno. I had a lot of issues."

Loki raised an eyebrow and actually chuckled. "I'll bet."

It was Tala's turn to be grateful. "Thanks, Loki."

"Where've you been anyway? West said Alex's back at the castle."

"Long story."

Her phone rang almost at the same time as Loki's did. They looked at each other in trepidation as they reached into their pockets, hearing more phones go off among the rest of the Banders too. This didn't bode well.

"Should I go?" Ryker asked quietly, but Tala shook her head.

"The Gallaghers are detecting a disruption by the fairgrounds!" Her mother's voice was terse by her ear. "We'll be using a looking glass to port there immediately, but I want you close. The Fianna are already on-site to contain the intrusion."

"Where are they?"

"Right where we met you and Alex, in front of the so-called Baba Yaga's shop."

"That was my mom," Tala said, ending the call. "Something's trying to port into Avalon from outside the kingdom—"

"Again," Loki finished. "Same energy patterns as the one at the manor."

"A portal?" Ryker asked. "From outside Avalon?"

"Got anything you can tell us about that?"

"I think so." Ryker looked to Tala. "I don't know if it's the Snow Queen's doing," he said. "If it is, she never told me her plans. But let me try to help. Keep me under guard at all times if you think it's necessary."

"And if this *is* the queen's doing?" Loki asked.

Ryker met their gaze. "Then you do what you gotta do. That won't stop me from protecting Tala."

He understood, but he still wasn't choosing a side—not yet. Her parents had told her he would figure it out sooner or later, but the only thing Tala could muster at the moment was sadness. How much more damage would the Snow Queen have to do for him to admit his error?

He turned back to her and managed a small smile, as if he knew what she was thinking too. "Maybe a rain check on that date," he said lightly.

21

IN WHICH AN OGRE WANTS TO JOIN IN THE FESTIVITIES

The area had been cordoned off to keep the other festivalgoers from realizing anything was amiss, though Tala doubted that the spells would be much distraction if they didn't stop the portal, which was now half the length of a full-sized mirror, from growing. It kept flickering in and out of view, like it was a figment of her imagination instead of anything solid. Much to her surprise, Alex was already there. He was scowling at the empty lot where the Baba Yaga's house had once been.

"Bugger that," Ken whispered. "The whole place was a bloody spell?"

"The Baba Yagas in the old tales use walking houses for transportation," Loki reminded him.

Tala remembered the chicken feet and shuddered.

"What's he doing here?" Alex asked, eyeballing Ryker like he was a powder keg that might explode at any minute.

"I'm not here to start anything."

"He's the Snow Queen's right-hand man, Your Majesty" Gareth said. "We ought to take him in, if anything."

"Not really sure that's true anymore," Ryker said, "but okay."

"That won't be necessary. I think we can trust him today." The king paused, looking at Ryker. "You look like crap, by the way."

"Exactly what Tala said."

"We've got a room at Maidenkeep if you want to crash."

"Your Majesty!" Gareth exclaimed.

"Appreciate the offer," Ryker demurred, "but I'm not in the best place to accept that just yet. I'd assume Maidenkeep's an expensive place to stay the night."

"We accept credit cards and other forms of information as payment," Alex responded. "If you'd like to pay the deposit now, tell me more about whoever's using this to force their way into my kingdom."

Ryker squinted at the glowing portal. "That's not any of Moth—the Snow Queen's creations, Your Majesty."

"It's possible she has spelltech that you're not aware of."

"That's true, but no. I'm tempestarii. I can sense any nearby shard-stones. They're powering this spelltech, but so are spellstones."

"What?"

"Beiran tech is mainly biowarfare. Spells focused on control and sub-jugation. Avalon tech was built to repel that, so the spellstones have likely been added here to penetrate your wards."

"So what you're saying," Loki pointed out darkly, "is that someone has access to both the Snow Queen's Beiran tech *and* spellstones that Alex has never approved."

"You're saying there's a traitor in Avalon?" West asked. "Didn't the Dame of Tintagel warn us about that?"

"Either that, or someone's buying artificial spellstones as fast as China can make them."

Ken stared at them. "OzCorp," he said. "That conversation I over-heard between Vivien Fey and Sloan Gruffud. They mentioned some kind of shipment from China."

"Ryker said that the Snow Queen was providing them with shard-stones," Tala said quietly.

"We still don't know where this port's coming from," Gareth informed them tersely. "Severon's tracking it down, and he's certain it's not from OzCorp headquarters. We're setting up dampeners in place to slow down its progress, but anything can still happen at this point."

"Is there something I can do?" Tala asked.

"We're gonna need more than one agimat to counter a spell this big."

Tala concentrated, aware that Ken, Loki, and West had formed up behind her. Tentatively, she extended her agimat toward the flickering hole in the air and then recoiled at the sudden foul taste in her mouth, like burning garbage. Repulsive as that was, it was also familiar.

"An ogre," she choked. "There's an ogre trying to breach the barrier." And then she gave up and doubled over, dry retching on the ground. Ryker crouched beside her, rubbing her back soothingly.

"Merdam!" Gareth swore. "Elana, get as many Fianna as you can spare here immediately. We'll need to start evacuating people before this goes bad, and I want the next five blocks free of tourists and vendors. Tell them we're investigating unusual activity in the area and want to play it safe, but don't give them any more specifics than that."

"Seems like Mother really is trying to give Alex as much grief as she possibly can," Ryker said tersely.

"You would have been thrilled by that in the past," Ken pointed out.

"My priorities have changed since then."

A portal opened up behind them, and Lumina and the Katipuneros stepped through, followed by several more Fianna. The Makiling clan from the Philippines followed. From the look on Lola Urduja's face, it was clear she was bringing them along under protest.

"A powerful portal." Tala's mother was already making assessments. "It's not Avalonian technology, but I don't think it's Beiran either." She looked over at Tala, her hand moving to her arnis sticks when she spotted Ryker.

"I'm okay," Tala called out weakly. "He's trying to help."

"I really am, Lady Makiling Warnock," Ryker confirmed nervously.

"Any ideas regarding how many shardstones and spellstones it would take to power this?" Alex asked Dex, also hovering over Tala protectively while she fought to get her stomach back in order. The firebird was already itching to fight, as brightly lit as a flare.

"Far more than what even the most connected companies can get, that's for sure. The Native Californians have the second biggest mines, but they've only got less than a tenth of what we have. I haven't seen reports of any attacks on *their* territories, and they would never trade with Beira."

"Chinese bootlegs?" Lola Corazon suggested. "With artificially made spellstones and shardstones, it could work. They're cheaper to come by."

"Then that makes this even worse," Lola Urduja said tersely. "Artificial spellstones are unstable even in the best conditions."

"Why didn't our scanners detect this sooner?" Alex asked.

"That's what I'd like to know."

The portal widened. It was the only way Tala could describe it. The barriers the Fianna had set up were failing, and gigantic hands were pushing through the hole, ripping through it like it was a seam.

"Do everything you can to keep it from getting through," Alex commanded.

"Use your agimat," Ryker chimed in, raising his voice for all to hear, "and I'll try to freeze it, slow it down."

"Won't helping me get you in trouble?"

"I meant what I said about protecting you first."

The firebird abandoned its perch and soared into the sky, screeching angrily. The ogre had only managed to fit an arm through the portal, but a quick burst of fire from it set the limb aflame.

Without another word, Lumina and the Filipino spellbreakers raised their agimat and pushed them toward the slowly increasing hole just as the ogre stuck its head through and roared. Their combined abilities prevented the portal from expanding, though the monster held its ground. Ice began growing around the edges of the opening, though it was slow going; whatever magic was powering it was also melting Ryker's spells almost as quickly.

"Clever," he grunted. "It's made to withstand Beiran *and* Avalonian spelltech. Like they were anticipating having to deploy their magic against both."

Slices of wind cut at the ogre's face, and it roared. "Sige pa!" Lola Urduja ordered, and the Katipuneros obeyed, sending more sharp, cutting gusts to incapacitate it.

Keeping all this from the general public was a failure. The Fianna had set up invisibility wards but had failed to add soundproof spells. Tala could already see revelers running, frightened by the noise. Several Fianna were guiding the people out, toward the center of the city, calling for everyone to stay calm. She saw Nya among the group, helping the soldiers.

"This is very high-level spelltech," Lola Corazon noted through gritted teeth. "I can only imagine how many shardstones and spellstones they would need to power such a monstrosity, despite all of us working against it."

Tala added her own agimat to theirs, watched as the port slowly started to close, stopped for several seconds, and then widened again, only to shrink some moments later, then grow larger once more.

It was becoming clear, though, that the spelltech had not been created to withstand too much pressure for long. Sparks flew out from within the portal, and Tala's hopes lifted. Maybe if they held out long enough, it would destroy itself.

But Lumina's reaction was the complete opposite. "Put up more barriers!" she yelled to the Fianna. "Hurry!" The soldiers promptly obeyed without question.

Dark shadows slipped past the ogre, landing on the ground before them and displaying cruel, jagged rows of brown, decaying teeth.

"Shades!" Gareth hollered.

Ken tugged out both his swords, cutting down several that had just hit the ground. A flick of Loki's finger sent their staff slamming through a shade's head. Another tried to come up behind them, and Loki spun, kicking a hole right into its chest. The staff remained upright in the air on its own and continued to attack more shadows.

West had morphed into a large dog again and was making short work of many of the other shades.

But as Tala looked on in horror, people staggered through the portal; their eyes were wide and staring, their movements jerky. They were men and women and even children, all carrying knives.

"Deathless," Ken said grimly.

"We can't fight them," one of the Fianna said, aghast. "They're kids!"

"Kids that are under the Snow Queen's permanent thrall and therefore dangerous," Gareth said. "Sheathe your weapons when you face them. Take down, but do not kill. That's an order."

Ken switched direction, striking down the shade he'd been battling to confront the new threat. But as he swung, he shifted so that only the flat of his blade struck the Deathless at the back of their neck, and down they went. "Leave them to me," he said.

"Are you sure, Ken?" Tala knew he still blamed himself for what had happened at Ikpe.

"My sword won't harm the living." He took down another Deathless, then another. But he hesitated when a young girl no more than twelve or thirteen approached him, her face blank and her dagger raised. He lifted Yawarakai-Te, then lowered it again.

Calmly, Nya stepped in front of him and tossed the contents of a small vial into the young girl's face. She froze, suddenly immobile.

"Nya, what—"

"Here." She shoved another flask into his hands. "Paralysis. If you want to take them down, it's easier to use this."

Another portal opened up easily beside Tala, and this time it was her father who stepped out, a large battle-ax in his hand.

"Kay!" Lumina exclaimed. "You're supposed to be waiting at Maidenkeep!"

"Figured you can use all the help you can get." He swung the ax, bisecting three shades at once.

"It's been a while since you last talked to your former lover, Scourge," Lola Corazon said snidely. "Perhaps she's found some new tricks since you left."

Lumina glared at her mother, but Kay ignored the older woman. "How much weight can your segen hold?" he asked Loki.

"Probably a lot?"

"Does my weight count as a lot?"

Loki looked to him, then at the ogre's head pushing through the portal, then grinned suddenly. "I think so, yeah."

Alex raised an arm above his head, and the firebird made for it like a homing beacon. Magic swirled around as its form shifted and twisted until the king was holding a bow made of fire in his hand. Untouched by the flames, he pulled the string taut, and a shining arrow appeared against his hand, nocked and ready. There was an audible twang as he released it, and it sang through the air.

Every shade within the line of fire was promptly turned to ash, and still the arrow kept going. The shot found its way into the ogre's mouth and passed through its throat. It gurgled, tongue now torn.

The portal began to fluctuate wildly, the magic around it fading and returning. The erratic patterns seemed to influence the shades' behavior as well, and they began blindly flailing at anyone close by, shrilling wildly. Tala wasn't sure if it was because of Ryker, who'd frozen over half the hole by now but was running into trouble as the magic grew even more unstable, or if it was because the spelltech was coming undone before their eyes.

More arrows struck the shades, but they weren't from the firebird or Alex; they were shimmering with a different kind of spell, the sudden taste of fresh earth in Tala's mouth telling her it was elemental magic. Each arrow found its mark, hitting right in the center of the creatures' foreheads every time.

Another fresh volley skewered more of the shadows against the ground. Tristan Locksley continued to fire, arrow after arrow leaving his hand with deft skill as every shot landed, most of the creatures disappearing after the fatal strikes. Zoe was at his side, taking down approaching shades efficiently with Ogmios, the whip slicing them into ribbons.

Alex stopped. So did Tristan. The boys stared at each other, oblivious at first to the rest of the other shades approaching. "Alex!" Tala yelled, and both whirled around, standing back to back, firing shots effortlessly at the shadows around them once more, taking them down together.

The ogre's fist slammed down again, missing Lumina by about a foot.

Nya drew in a long breath and squared her shoulders.

"No!" Ken grabbed her arm.

"What are you doing? I could use my—"

"And reveal your secret to all the phone cameras recording this whole fight? Not on your life."

"Loki," Tala's father said.

Without any prompting, Ruyi Jingu Bang planted one of its ends against the ground and slowly bent itself backward, like a bowstring being pulled taut.

"Thank ye kindly," Kay said and then calmly stepped on the other end, balancing himself perfectly on it despite his heavy frame.

The staff snapped back, ricocheting Kay through the air straight toward the blinded but still snarling ogre. He lifted his ax high above his head and then brought it down as hard as he could.

The ax cleaved right through the ogre, severing its neck. Blood sprayed out like a fountain, and the dead creature sank backward, out of the portal.

"Ngayon na!" Lola Corazon shouted.

Every agimat user poured everything they could into the rogue portal, and Tala held her breath as Ryker's spells did their work, closing rapidly over the hole until, with a loud noise, it shattered, shards trickling down to reveal empty space again, with nothing to indicate a hole had ever been there save for the black blood and the ogre's lifeless head staring blindly back at them. The flow of shades ceased, everyone else making short work of those left behind. Several of the Fianna were already assisting Ken and Nya, cuffing the Deathless quickly.

"That was fun," Ken said, poking at a shade's still-bared teeth with his sword as the shadow melted into the ground. He turned to Nya, reddened. "Thanks for the help," he muttered.

"Thank you for—for telling me not to use my voice. Even after everything that I—"

"I understand better now. And we're friends, right? That's what friends do."

"I—" Nya looked down. "Yes. Friends."

"It's him!" a voice squealed. Now that the danger was over, a crowd had started to form, and several girls were pointing in Kay's direction with clear glee on their faces. Tala's stomach plummeted.

But then West trotted out from behind her father, still in his dog form.

"Good boy!" one of the women called out. "You saved those people from those nasty agents, and now you've saved us from the bad monster, didn't you?"

West froze, clearly startled, then inclined his head toward Loki to seek guidance. The latter merely shrugged and grinned.

Tentatively, West trotted toward his fans. Immediately they surrounded him, cooing and stroking at his fur, taking out their phones for pictures with him. West relaxed, and his tongue lolled up, clearly milking his time in the spotlight for all he was worth.

"Was there anyone hurt?" Alex asked, the firebird bow still in his hands. Now that there were no other targets, he was stepping away from Tristan, not even looking at him.

Tristan put his own bow away. "Alex."

"I don't have anything to say to you right now. Gareth, set up another barrier."

The Fianna obeyed, and a barrier popped up to shield Alex and Tristan from the onlookers. With a whooshing sound, the bow in Alex's hands transformed back into the firebird, who clearly did not look happy to see the other boy.

"I've been trying to talk to you in private, but you haven't answered any of my texts or calls," Tristan began.

"We don't have anything to talk about."

The firebird had planted itself between Tristan and its master. Alex sounded even-tempered, if a little angry, and hadn't reacted physically to the other boy's presence beyond folding his arms across his chest, but it seemed like the little creature was attempting to showcase the king's actual feelings through some kind of interpretative dance. It lifted its head haughtily and drew itself up to its full one-and-a-half-foot height, shook its feathers at Tristan, scuffed dirt in his direction, and punctuated Alex's words with a low, shrieking counterpoint made up of hisses and growls.

"Alex, I'm sorry," Tristan persisted.

"Sorry enough to stop using Zoe as your beard?"

Tristan froze. "You know I can't do that. You can't ask me to choose between my family and you."

Lola Corazon drew nearer to Tala, nodded at the two arguing boys. "You must do something about this."

"I don't want to intervene in their—"

"No, you *must*. The Tsarevich line mustn't die out. We cannot have the chaos from his successors fighting for the throne. You love him, don't you?"

Tala was taken aback. "Well, yes, like a—"

"Then it's about time you told him how you feel. We cannot have the next king marrying another man, susmaryosep."

Tala gaped at her. All the insinuations among the Makilings that she was closer to Alex than most. Lola Corazon's previous displeasure regarding his "lifestyle."

Lola Corazon patted her arm. "Think about it, mahal. You can do worse than becoming queen of Avalon." She turned to the other Makilings. "Search the area. Make sure there are no other attempts."

Ryker was still grinning, even after the old woman had left.

"Don't you say a word," Tala warned him.

"Wouldn't dream of it. Is she for real?"

"There's nothing else to talk about," Alex was saying. "Find me again when you've made that decision. If you care anything about me, then you better leave."

"Alex—"

"Goodbye, Tristan."

The other boy paused, looking like he wanted to stay and argue. But then he changed his mind and strode away, and despite himself, Alex watched him leave before turning to Ryker. "Thanks."

"That's for saving my ass back in Texas."

The firebird kept on delivering victory hoots until Tristan was out of sight; it then sighed and slumped down, looking depressed.

"I meant it. You could stay here," Alex offered. "Help us rebuild."

"No can do, I'm afraid."

"Are you sure this is the way you want things to be?"

"No. But I think I gotta learn to fix my own shit first before I drag more of you into it." Ryker glanced at the crowd. "Whoever's behind that portal's found a way to control shades too. I'd be on my guard if I were you."

"The Snow Queen—"

"This isn't her doing. When the spelltech failed, so did its control over the nightwalkers. Mother's hold would have been absolute." He turned to Tala. "I'm sorry that I can't tell you what you want me to."

"We'll wait until you're ready," Tala promised him, deciding to take the chance and trust he'd do the right thing before it was too late. "I'll wait."

"I know." His hands slipped from hers. She watched as he angled expertly around the group still fussing over West until the crowd swallowed him up.

"Any injuries?" Alex asked Gareth.

"We got everyone away from the area just in time, though I'm afraid we won't be successful at keeping the press from finding out about this."

He was right. People were still recording the scene, even taking pictures of the ogre's decapitated head. Tala wasn't sure how much of the fight they'd gotten on video, but she knew it was enough.

Alex nodded. "Let them, then." He stepped around the barrier so that everyone could see him. The firebird flew to its usual perch on his head and cooed.

The crowd actually cheered; the only thing preventing them from swarming the king were the Fianna now stationed in between him and his audience, keeping them from drawing closer.

"Your Majesty," Gareth said. "We've found some tech on the Deathless."

Tala followed the king, but her curiosity soon turned to horror at the sight of a collar wrapped around one of the enthralled children's throats. The spell lingering over it left a terrible taste in her mouth, like chlorine and syrup mixed together. "What is that?" she asked, but she already knew. It looked very similar to the collars used on the ice wolves they'd fought at the border.

"I'm not too sure," her mother said, crouching down for a better look, "but I've seen this before. It feels like—" She reeled back, looking repulsed.

"It's enchanted with thrall magic," Kay said quietly, moving to her side. "Mind control. The Snow Queen won't need it—the mirror shards she uses are enough to command their blind obedience without the need for artifacts."

"So the collars mean that someone else other than the Queen is controlling them," Lumina said angrily. "These poor kids."

"It's OzCorp," Tala said. "It has to be."

"I want a forensics team looking this spelltech over," Alex said, "and social workers with the most experience handling Deathless."

"That will be Ikpe, Your Majesty," Nya supplied. "I'll let them know."

"You must take better care, Your Majesty," Lola Corazon said. "You cannot put your safety in the hands of a terrorist, a newly formed police force, and two agimat users, with one only a minor. And an agent for the Snow Queen in the mix, sus mio! We want to offer our services in a more official capacity for the time that we are here in Avalon. I have already received express permission from Datu Rizal to do so."

"We are more than capable of protecting His Majesty ourselves," Lola Urduja said frostily.

"Di ba kayo nahihiya?" Lola Corazon demanded. Tala couldn't quite follow the rapid-fire Tagalog that followed. She only knew that her grandmother was making things a lot more personal. "Di nyo kayang protektahin sya. Aminin nyo na. Ang tigas pa rin ng ulo mo, Urduja, hanggang ngayon."

"May oportunidad kang protektahin si Alex noon. Tinanggihan mo dahil sa prejudice mo. Wala ka nang karapatang sabihin sa amin kung ano ang dapat naming gawin."

"You are nothing," General Luna tried again, "but a second-rate, trying-hard, copyca—"

"You will need more agimat users," Lola Corazon said, turning to Alex again. "It would be foolish to reject our offer, in light of everything that's happened. Our datus have a time-honored friendship with Avalon. If you will require vetting, then we would be more than happy to provide any information you need."

"Thank you, Lola Makiling. We may have to take you up on your offer soon enough."

"Call me Lola Corazon. We are all family here." The older woman smiled at him, ignored Lumina and the Katipuneros completely, and then moved to leave, the rest of her group following.

"Still as bigoted as ever," Lola Urduja muttered.

"Should I have turned her down?" Alex said.

"No. As much as I despise it, it is always good to have more agimat working for our side. They will not betray you, that much I will admit."

The king looked back at the crowd and sighed. "On the bright side," he said, "videos of the fight should at least improve our image somewhat on the world stage? Won't they?"

As it turned out, videos of the fight did not improve Avalon's image on the world stage.

22

IN WHICH THE NOTTINGHAMS HAVE STRANGE FAMILY GATHERINGS

Y ou'll be all right," Zoe assured the frightened crowd, trying to sound comforting. Maidenkeep's auditorium was the only place that could accommodate this many people, and the universal translator tech bespelled into the megaphone she held wasn't a hundred percent accurate just yet; the language wasn't common outside the eastern regions and wasn't in its database.

Wasn't common outside the eastern regions *they used to live in,* Zoe thought, unable to stop the familiar rage from building up again. Sanctuary at Avalon was the best she could offer.

She was tired. She'd accompanied Tristan five times to date—to two parties, a couple of speeches his father gave to science and art institutions in Lyonesse, and a family dinner. They had all been very awkward. She and Tristan hadn't actually spoken much to each other, smiling and posing only when there were cameras pointed their way. Tristan apologized frequently; he also asked about Alex often. Zoe learned to ignore the stab of mild hurt that still lingered, accepting that he was who Tristan liked, and answered as best as she could. *Yes, he is still mad. No, you're going to have to make the first move if you really want his forgiveness, buddy. No, I'm not getting myself involved in this. You two need to talk it out among yourselves without any input from me.*

The dinner had been the worst one of the lot; Tristan's mother, Valentina Locksley, had been gushing, clearly pleased that her son's girlfriend was one of the "Avalon Seven" that saved King Alex, and inundated her with questions about her mother.

Zoe was fairly sure that Valentina would not be so happy to learn what she'd been doing when she wasn't with Tristan.

She hadn't planned this mission. But the last several days spent helping grassroots organizations connect with Avalonian spelltech suppliers had finally taken root, and their reach had grown almost exponentially. A group of Nigerians were gaining traction, creating sustainable water tech to distribute throughout the region. Several health care cooperatives had taken some Ikpean patents and were manufacturing medicines quicker, at a lower cost. And now a Chinese minority rights group had, with Alex's permission, brought people they'd rescued from concentration camps in Asia here, to the auditorium.

Zoe had not been prepared for the awful reality of what they'd found at those camps.

She wanted to weep. She'd had all the prerequisites of a good cry: anger, despair, disbelief, anger, frustration, grief, anger. But the tears weren't coming, and that only led to even more anger. The people before her now had been forced to live in sties, beaten if they disobeyed orders, treated like animals. If she couldn't cry, having seen that with her own eyes, then she never would.

She wanted to blame the Baba Yaga. But now, after countless previous attempts to make herself cry and failing, it felt like this was all *her* fault. Like she didn't have enough willpower to break free on her own.

"You're all free to either stay in Avalon or opt for asylum elsewhere," she said, resisting the urge to march down the hallway, find the unused room at its end that she was used to visiting by now, and start punching the walls again. The universal translator changed the words the instant they left her mouth, turning them to ones she wasn't familiar with. But the group appeared calmer in their wake. "Please know that we will do our utmost to help, whatever your decision may be."

She handed the translator back to the minister of immigration, then turned when Yue Ying, one of the group's leaders, approached. "Thank you for housing us temporarily," the girl said. "Some of my family migrated to Avalon thirty years ago, but most of them have lived in Xinjiang for generations. I was very afraid."

"I can only imagine."

The girl shook her head. "I mean that I was afraid you would turn down our request. When they blocked our portal out of camp, I thought we were goners. Your techmages found our SOS and saved us. I know it was dangerous. I know His Majesty may get into trouble. If they find out..."

"Their government wouldn't dare say anything without incriminating themselves. I doubt they're going to draw attention to the escape. If anything, they'll do their best to cover it up." There was nothing in the news so far, and the biggest thing trending on social media was West again—this time videos of him attacking the ogre and the shades, often with headlines like Antifa Dog Still at It.

"Are you angry at me?"

Zoe was taken aback. "Of course not. Why would you say that?"

"Because you look so furious right now."

Because it wasn't enough, Zoe wanted to say. *Because you guys were successful at liberating this one camp, but there were still hundreds we couldn't get to. I want them all freed. How can one be enough for celebration?*

"Just a little stressed is all," Zoe said, breathing evenly, trying to control a new spurt of temper. "You did good, Yue Ying. We all did. And I'm proud of what we're doing."

The girl smiled back at her. "I'm going to talk to Mr. Peets. He said he's bringing other lawyers here to sort out their status."

"Do you have any idea of what they plan to do?"

"I think there'll be many who'll take you up on your offer, but there'll be others who'll want to return. To fight with us. I don't think they can live with the idea of being free if their family and friends aren't."

"I understand. I don't know how much support we can give them when we're not supposed to be involved, but Rongit has a list of patent-free spelltech they can consider, along with how to acquire the materials. I'll ask him to forward it right away, but they'll need to know what the magical repercussions for them are."

"I think that's a small price to pay for them at this point, considering everything. Thank you. I'll look for him now."

Zoe waited until Yue Ying had walked away before quietly leaving the auditorium, passing several of the lawyers she had mentioned and a group of Avalon's social workers, who all bowed before continuing on their way. Her role in this was the worst kept secret in Maidenkeep.

It was only a matter of time before the word got out.

But right now, she found that she couldn't be bothered to care.

She made for the punching bag the instant she entered the Hollows, striking it hard with a roundhouse kick. A flick of her Ogmios tore the bag's seams, and stuffing trickled out onto the ground.

"Arrrgghhh!"

"You're going to have to pay for that."

Nottingham lurked by the doorway, leaning against the frame with his arms folded across his chest. He'd discarded his jacket and was dressed in thicker clothes than his usual leather jacket and faded jeans.

"The bag," he said. "It's going to need repairs. You should invest in an actual gym membership."

"Exercising doesn't work. Screaming doesn't work. I feel like I'm going to explode, and this is the only way I can find release."

And by putting myself in danger. She knew that, and Cole knew that, and to his credit, he was saying nothing about it, though he had every right to. And while she was no longer exposing corrupt judges and getting trophy hunters in trouble, she was still taking huge risks to herself by helping organizations like Yue Ying's.

"Thought the Baba Yaga gave you a prescription to help?"

"I *am* taking it. This *is* me in a good mood. And you're not dressed up like a Latino James Dean today. What gives?"

"You think I look like a Latino James Dean?"

Zoe wanted to kick herself. *Those are compliments, you fool, not insults!* "Look, I'm ready."

"For what?"

"For whatever mission you're choosing for us this time. Isn't that why you're here?"

"Technically, you weren't directly involved in this one."

"I don't care. I still want in, or I'm gonna do something I'm gonna regret." She'd gone on a total of three missions with Nottingham since the beach cleanup. They'd planted trees in Brazil. They boxed up relief goods with several charities after an earthquake in Haiti. They even cleaned out stalls with an animal rescue group in Spain. They all required back-breaking, heavy labor, but the exhaustion helped Zoe forget her rage. She didn't want to admit it, but his ideas worked, and something good was actually coming out of them. "Where are we going next?"

Nottingham looked at her for a moment. And then an oddly grim smile spread across his face. "You're going to need to wear something warmer."

Everything was covered in snow. Zoe was glad she'd brought a fur coat to Avalon when she'd moved into Maidenkeep. "Where are we this time?" she asked. "Canada? Iceland?"

Nottingham pointed toward a castle in the distance, built atop a forbidding-looking mountain; the bulky, rocky fortress stood out starkly against the white landscape.

"Is that where we're going?" And then Zoe gasped. "Is this Nibheis? Your family's place in Greenland? You brought me to your family's ancestral home?"

"I'm not too sure I would call it home," Nottingham said evasively. "But my grandfather lives in the castle."

There were so many stories about Nibheis. That it was the most haunted place in the world. That it was the site of all sorts of dark and illegal magical rituals. "Does your family run some kind of charity?" Zoe asked tentatively.

"It could meet *some* of the requirements for charity." Already people were approaching—the Lady Nottingham and Nottingham's sister, Adelaide.

Zoe wanted to kick herself again. Of course. He'd been dressed for someplace warmer. They hadn't used the Red King; they'd used Maidenkeep's general looking glass, where all trips were officially logged. Of course he'd been planning to visit his family. Had he even *wanted* to bring her?

Did that mean he'd initially come looking for her not because he had another mission in mind but because he was concerned for her? Somehow?

She was touched. Even if she would never admit that. "I could have waited until you returned," she muttered, embarrassed. "You didn't have to bring me here just because I was being an ass."

"Zoe!" Adelaide squealed when she saw her and leaped forward for a hug. Zoe laughed; she genuinely liked his little sister, whose sunny, cheerful disposition was at odds with his own.

Lady Nottingham merely smiled and gave her a curtsy. Zoe released Adelaide and attempted a deeper one of her own. "I'm sorry I didn't give you any advance warning," she began, but the woman only chuckled.

"My son's friends are always welcome here, Lady Carlisle. Although knowing Nicholas, he told you nothing about today."

Nottingham shrugged. "Didn't want to influence her opinion beforehand."

"Well, I hope your opinion of us doesn't change," his mother sighed. "The procession will be along shortly, but we'll need to be at the graveyard before then."

"Did she just say 'graveyard'?" Zoe asked the boy as they followed his mother and sister down a winding path.

"You told me you wanted to know more about this." He indicated his Gravekeeper. He was tense, the hand wrapped around the hilt clenched tightly. He was nervous, Zoe realized, but of what?

Given the Nottinghams' history and wealth, she envisioned grotesquely expensive gargoyles and elaborate tombstones that proclaimed the graveyard's occupants' deeds and misdeeds. But what she saw were acres upon acres of emptiness. If this was a graveyard, nothing marked the tombs. Only the snow-covered ground offered up clues, the soil disturbed in places that suggested digging. The Nottinghams themselves gathered beside a freshly dug grave, its would-be inhabitant still missing.

Lord William Nottingham was there, every bit as imposing as he had been back at the summit. The patriarch was stoic as always, but his mother and Cole's great-grandmother, Anastacia Nottingham, were full of smiles. The seeress wore a thick furred coat that made her look like she would be more at home at a social gala than a funeral. Severe-looking men in black suits surrounded them, firearms displayed at their hips—no doubt family bodyguards.

The older man gestured at his grandson, and Zoe noted that the former's hands were shaking—not from fear or from any emotion but from what was apparently some kind of physical condition.

"You are Zoe Fairfax Carlisle," the dowager said. She took Zoe's hand in hers and squeezed. "Come with me for a moment. The procession shall arrive any minute, and it wouldn't do to distract the boys."

Zoe glanced at Cole, but he was already standing with his grandfather, watching the entrance to the graveyard. Gravekeeper was already reacting to something in the air, the dark tentacle-like energy wrapping around his wrist in constant motion.

"I am so very sorry that I was so discourteous to you at our last meeting," the Dowager Nottingham murmured. "I was very excited to meet you, you see, and I hadn't expected to be caught in another foretelling with Udeme and Elspen. But I knew you would return despite my behavior. I knew Nicholas would do the right thing."

"You asked him to bring me?" Zoe didn't know why that made her angry, disappointed, and sad.

"No. I didn't need to. I think you will understand soon enough. That is why I was hoping you'd come."

The procession was arriving. There was no coffin, only a thick human-shaped sack at the back of a wooden cart. The people who followed it were dressed in black, many weeping. Zoe was puzzled until they drew nearer and she could make out familiar faces. There was Baron Aleut, and the wine merchant Forange, who Zoe remembered from social gatherings with her mother in France. There was David Stolt, the head of the Hineski Banking company. And then there was the Duchess of Eléve and her two teenage daughters, and it was clear from their pale, strained faces who the dead person was to them.

But why was the notorious Duke of Eléve, from one of the world's richest families, being brought to his final resting place like he had no money to his name?

"The Nottingham line has had its share of rascals and scallywags, murderers and thieves," the Dowager Nottingham said calmly to Zoe. "One ancestor in particular, Morgan Nottingham, was an unholy terror even by our standards. He pillaged whole cities and looted villages and left nothing breathing in his wake. He was eventually struck down by an arrow, and in those last hours, he swore that he'd caught a glimpse of his final doom. Most Avalonians believe in reincarnation, Lady Carlisle, of endless cycles where we are rewarded or punished for our past lives, and he was one of them. He begged his son, Harry, to help him redeem his soul."

The cart stopped before the hole in the ground. Its driver alighted; two other men came forward to assist him in lifting the corpse.

"Harry was a worthier fellow than his father, whom he disliked, and felt it was his filial duty to carry out the man's last wishes. Unwilling to inherit wealth that was born from a lifetime of pillaging, he gave all his money and property to those his father had wronged. With his few possessions in either his pocket or his knapsack, he decided to travel the world, searching for a means to find redemption for a father who did not deserve it. He eventually came upon a church where a wake was in progress. There, he discovered thieves robbing the corpse. They claimed that the dead man was a cruel tyrant, evidenced by the fact that no one watched over him for his own burial. But Harry gave them all the money he had and himself held vigil over the corpse until dawn."

The men carried the dead body toward the grave, laying him down.

The deceased's widow stepped forward and formally scattered the first shovelful of soil into the hole.

"Harry resumed his travels and came upon a man who offered to become his companion. As it so happened, they stumbled upon a kingdom besieged by a sorcerer who could control the darkness. Ogres and shades and the undead were his to command, and no army could withstand his might."

The grave was shallow and was filled before long. Cole now stepped forward, and Zoe's eyes were drawn back to Gravekeeper, the tendrils around it writhing in apparent glee. The shadowy ropes sank into the grave as if of their own accord. The boy said nothing and waited, though his face was pale and his whole body was braced, like he was expecting an attack.

"Together, they defeated the nightwalkers, and the companion slew the wicked man where he stood. The king was grateful and offered Harry his daughter's hand in marriage. It was then that his companion told him he was leaving, revealing that *he* was the dead man the boy had kept vigil over, and this was his way of repaying him. 'Your father cannot be redeemed,' the companion told him, 'for only those who sincerely ask for forgiveness can be pardoned. I have knowledge of the sorcerer's spell, his ability to command the dead. If you wish to help redeem others who have wronged in life but repented only in their final hours, then use it. They will fight with you when the ultimate darkness comes. Only then can their souls be saved, as shall mine.' And as those final words left his lips, the companion dropped at his feet, dead once again. Legend says he was the first corpse that Harry buried in this graveyard."

Zoe saw them stealing across the horizon: countless shadows that resembled shades but were even worse. They were more corporeal to start, with bodies like the husks of the dead, with lidless eyes and faces stripped of skin, with teeth caught in perpetual, manic smiles. They crept toward Cole Nottingham, their eyes trained on the fresh grave behind him.

Zoe drew out Ogmios, but Lady Nottingham held her back. "I understand your worry, but you must not interfere," she said quietly. "This is something that the sword's wielder must face alone."

Gravekeeper was enveloped in a thick black miasma of its own making, and it looked like Cole was holding a darkness heavy and congealed, his whole arm enveloped in the thick mist. The horrifying undead were only a few feet away when he finally attacked.

The fog surrounding Gravekeeper expanded, the tendrils on its edges now sharp and deadly. Rows of creatures fell with every slash, yet Cole never stopped moving, cutting quickly. His dance with the devils lasted several minutes before the last of them had been dispatched, and corpses littered the ground before him.

"Burn them," William Nottingham said shortly, and some of the bodyguards approached the fallen shadows, guns trained. The shovels were soon put to work for a new purpose, transferring the burnt carcasses onto the cart the dead man had been brought in.

"They're not shadows," Zoe said, heart thumping madly.

"Harry Nottingham chose this graveyard not for the scenic view of the mountains, my dear," the Dowager Nottingham said placidly. "Nibheis borders World's End, the cradle from where nightwalkers spring forth, where men who dare to look past its borders go mad. So many wars had been fought over this piece of land for the potent magic that leeches into its very soil. The spells here encourage violence, allowing the demons to come and feast on the dead. We have claimed it for our own, ensuring that the magic would be used for redemption and no longer for greed or genocide. We welcome everyone who wishes for a second chance to redeem themselves to be buried here and await their judgment." She smiled dryly. "Of course, we do benefit from it. The more bodies we bury here, the stronger Gravekeeper becomes."

"And everyone who lies buried here will eventually rise up to fight beside Nottingha-Cole?" Zoe whispered. "Has anyone from history ever successfully raised the dead here?"

"None to my knowledge. My great-grandson may not be the first to. It may not even happen in our lifetimes. But it *will* happen. There is a darkness rising. An army will come, led by either the Snow Queen or one even worse. I believe we can even the odds with our own army of the dead to fight against them. This may seem strange to you, that we believe so much in what most people think of only as legend. But we know it to be true. We do all this because we know of the war to come. Do you not feel the strength of the magic in this place? The same magic that gives us our control of nightwalkers, of Gravekeeper?"

The dead will rise for you, girl. How many seers had told her this?

"Nicky screwed up our schedules when he was stuck in Avalon with you guys," Adelaide piped up. "We've had to keep a ton of the dead in freezers for several months, waiting for him to come back."

She'd berated him for going AWOL that month, and he'd never told her why.

Zoe really wanted to cry now.

Cole turned toward them, exhausted. The thick fog surrounding Gravekeeper had retreated, revealing the fresh lacerations that ran up and down his right arm, a few even reaching the side of his neck. As thick as his clothes had been, the tendrils had ripped through the material, and she knew he must be bleeding there too.

"Can I go to him now?" she asked, surprised that her voice came out so calm, because she felt anything but.

"We have physicians on hand to—" Lady Nottingham began, but her grandmother placed a hand on her arm.

"Please do," the older woman said.

Zoe ran toward Cole, just as he handed Gravekeeper over to his grandfather. He looked startled when she skidded to a stop, opening the bag where she stored some of Nya's medicine. "This is a noble thing, what your family's doing," she told him softly, adding a few drops of potion to the streaks on his arms. "It's a noble thing, what *you're* doing. Why would your family not fight for their reputations?"

"Lots of families had claims to this land," he said, watching her guardedly. "So we spent a lot of time and money presenting it as a graveyard to keep them away. People won't be happy to find out we've been growing an undead army on top of everything else. The worse they thought of us, the easier we could hide it."

"You're the only rich family I know to deliberately devalue your own property without expecting a profit." Zoe had to smile, but that faded when she glanced back at his arm. His wounds had healed, but there were new thin white lines crisscrossing his skin. The potion should have healed even those.

"It will always scar," Cole said quietly. "Not much of a duty if it doesn't leave a lasting impression on you."

"Thank you for bringing me here. I understand a little better now." He was taking on so much. No wonder he was always so pissed off. She was still holding his arm, realized it the instant *he* realized it, but made no move to let go.

He smiled at her then, that crooked half smile he always wore when something genuinely amused him, and her heart fluttered, just a little. "And I thought I was going to see some fancy Nottingham family crypts," she quipped lightly.

"This is the closest thing to a Nottingham family crypt that we've got."

"So your ancestors are buried here too?" There was nothing to mark which grave was a Nottingham and which wasn't. But after witnessing the Duke of Eléve's funeral rites, Zoe had an inkling that they would be just as cavalier about their own bodies.

"We're all going to be buried here eventually." She didn't know why Cole sounded so odd over that last word.

William Nottingham drew near and bowed low to Zoe, his gaze lingering on their hands. Zoe felt herself flush but stubbornly held on. "We will be having tea over at the fortress," he said politely. "I was hoping you would attend, Lady Carlisle? To see that there is more to us than just our strange burial customs?"

He probably intended to make it sound like a joke, but it came out an order all the same. "I would be honored, Your Grace," Zoe said meekly. "He's very intimidating," she murmured after the family patriarch moved away. The widow and her family were being comforted by Lady Nottingham and Adelaide, the group already walking in the direction of the Nottingham castle. An invitation to tea felt so strange to her in light of what she'd just witnessed, but she supposed that to the Nottinghams, this was just another Wednesday.

"I'm told it's a family trait," Cole said dryly.

"Lies. You've always been a sweetheart. Nicky."

He raised an eyebrow at her.

She raised one back. "Thank you," she said. She didn't know what exactly she was thanking him for. *Thank you for showing me a side of you that took trust to give? Thank you for letting me see you vulnerable? Thank you for entrusting me with a secret that would have made your family's property the most sought after in the world and not even asking me to sign a bespelled contract for my silence like Tristan had?* But she meant it with everything she had.

And then he did an odd thing: his whole face relaxed, and a soft, genuine smile broke over his lips, one not so very crooked at all, and despite the cold, she felt warm all over.

She really, really wished he'd asked her to dance at the fair. The orchestra had played "Smoke Gets in Your Eyes," and they'd both just watched the old film *Lovely to Look At* a couple of weeks before, in which Kathryn Grayson sang it. Cole had looked at her when the music had started, his expression strange, and for a brief moment, Zoe thought he might actually want to ask her, if she hadn't remembered she had to meet Tristan again.

"Nicky," the dowager said, appearing beside them. "The Duchess of Eléve would like to thank you. I would be glad to accompany Lady Carlisle back to the castle in the meantime."

Cole glanced at Zoe.

"I don't mind," she told him. "Please don't let me stop you from whatever else you need to do."

He nodded, gently taking his hand away from hers. The Dowager Nottingham wasted no time claiming it for her own.

"Most people would call us necromancers," the older woman mused as they began their trek back to the fortress. "Black magic users even. They question our loyalties, wonder if we have completely cut our ties to the Beiran queen. But what we really are, my dear Lady Carlisle, are priests and priestesses giving last rites and final absolutions to those everyone else considers damned. It is a heavy burden. It is heavier especially on Nicholas, given his doom."

A chill crept over Zoe, replacing the warmth she'd felt earlier at his smile. "Cole's always been reluctant to tell me about his. I would much rather wait until he was comfortable enough on his own to."

"And until you, too, feel comfortable enough to tell him yours?"

Of course the seeress would know about her own doom. Zoe bowed her head. "Something like that."

"Your fate is tied more closely to his than you even know. Keep him near, and protect him as much as he desires to protect you. Please. I speak not as a seeress but as a grandmother."

Adelaide had gone on ahead, finding her brother and linking her arm around his. Cole looked down at her and smiled.

The dead will rise for you, girl.

"I will," Zoe said.

23

IN WHICH LOKI
INFILTRATES A CAVE

The anti-magic barriers OzCorp had erected on their headquarters at Marooners' Rock also extended several miles out into sea, which made porting into the sandy area below the cliffs they were built on practically impossible.

Fortunately, Loki was an avid climber. A certain level of resourcefulness was still required, which meant doing things the old-fashioned way.

"I really think someone should be there with you, to back you up," Ken's voice said from his earpiece. "Alex got word back that some of those Deathless victims were families of OzCorp employees who had gone missing for a while. Kinda does suggest this is OzCorp's doing, but it's all absolutely horrifying. We should have brought the whole Fianna at this point. Or better firepower."

"Then what am I, hijo?" Tita Baby, who was hanging alongside Loki, demanded. "Chopped liver?"

"I meant from the Banders," Ken acknowledged, retreating rapidly from dangerous territory despite not being the one hanging hundreds of feet in the air. "Sounds like it would be good to have a couple more segen handy where you're going."

"I am worth at least two segen," Tita Baby said tartly. "And Chedeng and Teejay here are worth at least half a segen."

"That is not a compliment to us, *ate*," Tita Chedeng grumbled. The twins were scrambling down the cliffs at the same rapid pace both Loki and Tita Baby were—or that was what Loki assumed, at least, since they couldn't see anyone. The darkness helped to mask their presence, but they'd each taken a quick dose of an expensive invisibility potion they'd acquired from an Ikpean merchant, which worked for roughly ten minutes longer than Nya's dose. Tito Boy and General Luna were somewhere above them, making their own descents, and Dex and Ken were monitoring them from mission control.

"The whole point of this is not to use any segen unless they've backed us into a corner," Loki reminded them. "And not all the Deathless had connections to OzCorp. It makes them look suspicious, but it's not enough to outright arrest Nome."

"Just doesn't feel right, being stuck here at the lab while you're risking your life," Ken complained.

"Why are you in a bad mood? Is Nya avoiding you again?"

"Nobody's avoiding anyone. Rapunzel and I are cool. I mean, I kinda want things to be more than what we're at right now, but..." A pause. A deep sigh. "It's complicated."

"Sounds like there's something else bothering you."

"There is. Took another look at both Nya's and my dooms. There's a part in hers where it says that her husband's gonna lose his shadow. It's a little too much of a coincidence to say that it's not me?"

"The Baba Yaga thinks it might turn out okay."

"They're the one who said they don't even understand half the prophecies they make. And they're not the one who's supposed to be a corpse."

"Is this the only thing that's stopping you from asking her out again?"

Ken sighed again. "Maybe? I don't know. I mean, there's a reason why she didn't want to tell me all this in the first place. She thinks something bad's gonna happen if we don't just stay friends. And I'm thinking she might be right."

The boy's shadow was still missing, and nobody knew if it had been destroyed by Nome or was still inside OzCorp headquarters somehow. They'd considered asking Tala to join as well, but she was with Alex, monitoring some of the other detention camps, and Loki knew better than to ask when Ryker Cadfael might be involved.

The cliff was easily a thousand feet above sea level, possibly more. Loki had rappelled down higher places before, though, and it wasn't as difficult as it looked. Their last foray into OzCorp had shown that there was no way to access their basement through the usual means, and this was the next best option.

The grappling hook Loki had brought was of the good old-fashioned variety so as not to trigger any more OzCorp spells, and they all soon reached the bottom of the cliffs without incident. Deftly unhooking it with a jerk of their arms, Loki paused to survey their surroundings.

It was a very clever place to smuggle in contraband if one had a mind for it, and Loki could almost admire whichever OzCorp executive came up with the idea in the first place. The beach was shallow and small enough to be easily overlooked even by the Fianna. It was in a less popu-lated part of Lyonesse where very few people would notice any unusual activity, though OzCorp appeared to have spent a lot of money so as not to attract any attention anyway.

But any strange ships coming in would have been easily spotted, despite the remoteness of the location. Avalon coast guards would have detected them if the barriers in place had not. How were they able to ferry in spelltech this way?

They were disappointed at first. Loki had been expecting a cave, which would have been the easiest answer, but there was nothing here but the rocky stone cliff facing out into the sea.

"Well, that was a waste of time," Tita Teejay said, scrutinizing the cliff wall. "Nothing here but stones and seashells."

"Can't see anything from our scanners," Dex reported. "But it might not be accurate, given the amount of OzCorp defenses around here."

"Is that it, then?" Tita Baby asked, disappointed.

"Wait." Loki spotted the very faintest spark from within the solid-looking stone. It was gone as quickly, but they knew that hadn't just been their imagination. Their hands scoured the surface, but they could find no means to trigger an opening. They were gonna have to wait.

Loki checked their watch; it was 7:30 p.m. If they were right about how OzCorp smuggled in their wares and if Ken was accurate with his eavesdropping, then the shipment would be due soon, and they'd know for sure. "Time to find a place to hide," they said. "We've got half an hour."

Their potions were starting to wear off; oddly enough, it was Tita Baby's hair bun that first came into view, followed slowly by the night vision goggles they all wore, then her frowning face. The twins followed suit, dusting dirt and gravel from their catsuits, which Loki had pointed out weren't necessary and which they both insisted on wearing, anyway.

"How did you even grow it back so fast?" Loki heard Ken ask irritably once General Luna drifted into view.

"Ha," General Luna said smugly, caressing his mustache.

"Hair grower potion from Ikpe," Tita Chedeng said. "It will take the follicles from some other part of your body and transfer them to the place you prefer them to be."

Ken stifled a gag. "Yeah, Tita, I didn't need to know that detail. We'll let you know if we detect any strange ships."

"We could have done this the normal way," Tita Teejay said. "We could have just raided their headquarters and put everyone in prison."

"We don't have evidence for anything yet, Tita." Loki checked their gear. The other spelltech they'd brought had been a genius concept on the Gallaghers' part, and not for the first time, they thanked their lucky stars that family worked for Avalon and not against them. "And that's what we're here to find out."

"Incoming," Dex said abruptly, but Loki could make nothing out from the horizon. Tito Boy gestured at them to remain silent, then pursed his mouth, using it to point at the water.

They'd been expecting some kind of ship with an equipped invisibility shield, so it came as a shock to see a submarine slowly emerge from beneath the sea's surface instead.

And as they watched, the cliff's rock face slowly shimmered and disappeared to reveal the cave-like entrance Loki had been hoping for, from which several guards stepped out. There was a metallic, hissing noise as one whole side of the submarine detached, lowering to reveal a cargo hold. Already people were wheeling out several pieces of odd-looking mechanical equipment, followed shortly by heavy-looking crates. Nobody talked; everyone did their work silently, and it was clear that they'd done this many times before.

"About time you guys arrived," a guy in a suit announced, stepping out from the cave, vaping furiously. He winced, muttered a curse, and then kicked at the ground. "Why don't you guys come up with some spelltech to clear out the sand around here? You know how much it costs to clean this suit each time I'm out here?"

"You're the inventors, Mr. Gruffud," one of the men said, coming up to him with an electronic clipboard. "Sign here, please."

The man signed, grumbled some more, took a final drag of his e-cigarette, and then headed inside. Titas Chedeng and Teejay drew out their phones, already set to record. General Luna gave them the signal, and Loki popped open their flask and took another big gulp of the invisibility potion.

Now unseen, they moved toward the entrance. They could no longer see the titos and titas, hoped they were following close by, even as they tailed Sloan Gruffud, who was taking his sweet time.

OzCorp had done little to renovate the cave itself, save masking its entrance. The damp smell was strong, the constant rushing of waves from outside the only sound, quieting the deeper they went in.

"Can you see anything that looks like my shadow, by any chance?" Ken's voice was fainter.

"Sorry, Ken. Nothing yet."

"The Gallaghers say you don't need a shadow to be healthy, hijo," Tita Teejay murmured.

"I know. But if I were my shadow and I was still stuck inside OzCorp, I'd want out too."

After about five hundred feet or so, they came across another entrance, this one built from what looked to be steel, reinforced with spells based on the way it glittered. A magical barrier lay shimmering in between them, and it was clear they had to go through it first before they could access the door. A small console stood beside it, prompting for an ID.

Gruffud reached into his pockets and fished out a key card. The screen glowed green and the barriers slid away, granting him passage. The workers soon arrived, pushing trolleys full of heavy crates, and Loki quietly fell in line, holding their breath as they moved past the defense spell and relaxing after they triggered no alarms.

The first place they stumbled into was some kind of unloading area, where the crates brought in were being stacked into neat piles. The strange mechanical gears they'd noticed earlier were brought through another set of double doors while the boxes were quickly opened on the spot, revealing gleaming blocks of ice.

Except they weren't ice. As the men carefully lifted them onto waiting carts, Loki was quick to notice that none of the ice was melting, not so much as a drop on the floor even, while they were being transferred. "Shardstones," Tita Baby said, sounding closer than Loki expected, and they jumped. "Sorry, my dear. But this is all so very interesting."

"Interesting is an understatement." Loki tapped at their earpiece. "Ken. Dex. Can you hear me?"

There was nothing.

"Must be a lot of interference in here," Tita Baby said. "I do not need to detect magic to know it is everywhere inside this place."

"I can see that." There was barely enough light to go by, but it was too eerily bright to Loki's point of view. The air was practically sparking.

The shardstones were carted to a third set of doors. "I'm going in after them," Loki whispered. "Tita, you and the others try the other room."

Something grasped his shoulder, gave a squeeze, and then was gone.

Following the workers carrying the blocks of crystal led Loki into the largest lab they had ever seen. People in lab coats and protective gear were either hunched over tables, hard at work, or holding group meetings in the smaller rooms within. Various beakers filled with suspiciously gleaming chemicals were everywhere. Most of the scientists, though, were busy with more shardstones that were already on their worktables, running diagnostics over them. Other spelltech littered the area, though they didn't know what they were meant for. There were blocky cubes with wires attached to them, devices that resembled listening recorders, and others that were nothing more than a series of wires and tubes. Loki spotted several metallic rings hanging from hooks on one wall. They looked familiar somehow.

They hugged the walls, careful not to bump into the scientists walking past. They watched as the workers lifted fresh blocks of crystal onto the tables with a thump, sending some of the glass rattling. Quick sparks of magic sizzled against the air.

"Careful!" One of the scientists addressed them sharply. "They're worth more than a thousand times what they're paying you!"

"You'll have to pay me a thousand times more than what I'm getting for me to care, lady," the porter snickered but was more careful with depositing the next batch. Still grumbling, the woman turned her back on him, and Loki saw their chance. It took all of three seconds to filch one of the rings, and without anyone the wiser.

They returned to the unloading area, tried the other set of doors next, the one they assumed the Katipuneros had entered. In contrast to the pristine, sterile conditions of the lab next door, this was crammed full of construction materials and heavy machinery. A glass partition running from one length of the cave to its end had been set up in the middle of the area. People in hard hats and business suits were looking at computer monitors lining one end, no doubt their control station.

But past the glass wall was the evidence Loki had been hoping to find—and it terrified them. Looming above, in all its horrifying glory, was OzCorp's version of Avalon's greatest weapon. It looked like the Nine Maidens; it had large cylindrical columns constructed from stone, formed in a circle in the same way as the Maidens, with roughly the same height and width. But this version was constructed with Beiran shard-stones rather than with spellstones, and the result was nine crystal towers that shone ten times brighter than the light fixtures installed overhead.

Unlike the Nine Maidens, though, there was a giant rock, also made of crystal, in the middle of the spelltech, irregularly shaped and asymmetrical, with smaller crystals jutting out that made it seem almost repulsive to the eyes. It struck a dissonant note in something that had otherwise been carefully sculpted.

The platform they were building the shardstone towers over were made from a different material completely. Loki wasn't exactly sure what it was. It resembled spellstones but more brown than the black obsidian they were used to, and it sparkled far too much.

The Maidens-esque contraption was still incomplete; only seven of the nine columns appeared finished. Everyone beyond the glass barrier was in a hazmat suit, using some kind of levitation magic to bring up the necessary materials for them to fuse more shardstones onto the spelltech. Loki had seen that kind of magic back at the Earl of Tintagel's castle, though they had never thought about the potential use of domestic magic in this manner.

"Punyeta," they heard General Luna growl from somewhere nearby.

"This is impossible," they heard Tita Chedeng's voice next. "How could they do all this underneath Avalon with no one noticing?"

"We are in so much trouble," Loki murmured, staring up at this terrifying new prototype. Working with shardstones was a completely different matter than using spellstones. Shardstones were more rigid, with fewer limitations but stronger repercussions. Exactly how stable would this spelltech combination of shardstones and spellstones be, considering each had drastic polarizing effects on the other?

"What are you doing here?" Gruffud snapped. "I'm in charge for tonight."

"You told me I should be putting more hours into this," Vivien Fey told him sweetly. "And so here I am. You can swagger around and pretend to be more important than you actually are, but you know this will never work without me."

The man glowered at her. "You said your sister was—"

"I'll pick her up from therapy in a couple of hours. That's more than enough time to finish our tests for tonight. Sloan?"

"We're almost ready," a voice came up over the loudspeaker. "Stand down and clear the area. T minus one minute and counting."

People immediately retreated behind the glass barrier. Loki watched as a countdown continued, everyone else pausing their own work to watch.

"Shields up!" the loudspeaker blared, and the prototype began to shine, so much brighter than before.

"Tango down!" they heard next, and the giant rock at the center of the spelltech crumbled and disappeared.

In its place was a jabberwock.

Its loud roar echoed throughout the cavern. Its wings spread as it attempted to take flight, but it could only manage a few inches off the ground before the manacles encircling its front and hind legs yanked it back down. It looked around, snarling, and lunged at one of the nine crystal monuments surrounding it, then yelped when an electric spell hit it in response, the shocks reverberating through its body.

"Start the test!" Vivien ordered.

The crystal towers came to life, magic whipping from one monument to the other, entrapping the jabberwock in its own special barrier. The monster's body jerked in agony as more spells drove into it. Its movements became unnatural and strained, forced into jerking motions like something had taken control of its limbs entirely against its will. It reminded Loki of the Deathless, of how they moved while under thrall.

They edged closer to the group of suits, Sloan Gruffud one of them, all watching from one of the workstations. They saw data scattered on the screen, increasing and decreasing numbers that seemed to make sense to them but not to Loki.

"Twenty percent and rising," the seated operator reported. "Thirty. Fifty. Seventy..."

Something formed around the jabberwock, took shape, solidified—it was a dragon, made from ice.

It looked a lot like the dragon that had attacked the party at the Schaffers' manor.

The jabberwock twisted its head. The dragon juxtaposed onto it mimicked its movements. The jabberwock rose into the air again, still constricted by its chains. The ice dragon had no such restrictions and took immediate flight, soaring around the cavern in circles.

"We're reading an eighty percent synchronicity rate," one of the suits said.

"We'll need to get it up to at least ninety-five percent to satisfy Corvington," Vivien said. "See if you can keep control for another half hour. I want updates on towers one and five. See if they're in danger of breaking off like last time."

"They wouldn't be constantly breaking off if Beira didn't keep sending us substandard shardstones," one of the scientists muttered.

"Can't be helped at this point. But not even Beira will matter soon enough. Jake, can you push it up to ninety percent, see if it'll take?"

"You want to blow this whole place up?"

"We were on track to finish. The fuck was Nome doing, testing it on rich Avalonians? I thought we weren't cleared for that yet. Why not find some poor fucking village next time that won't make a blip on the news. Been a wonder we even got to salvage parts of it."

"You were in charge of security," Gruffud said, still determined to blame Vivien for as many problems as he could. "How'd someone start up the portal without our knowing? And to target the party with all those ambassadors?"

"Let me worry about that, Gruffud."

"How are we gonna test it without the firebird?"

Loki tensed. What was this?

"The firebird's not a problem. Let me worry about the firebird too. Have you gotten the orders for the extra spellstones yet?"

Gruffud snapped something Loki didn't quite hear. Vivien's reaction was immediate. Her hand lifted and crashed down on the side of his face. The man sank down, looking stunned.

"Don't you *ever* insult my sister like that again," Vivien hissed. "Or I will *feed* you to that dragon right now."

Sirens blared without warning, the whole cavern turning red as an alert system they hadn't realized existed kicked into gear. Loki swore and started running.

They made it past the barrier, shoved a startled porter out of the way, and kept on going until they'd exited the cave and reached shore before security could properly form up.

Already, their invisibility was starting to wear off. Loki could see outlines of their hands again and then spotted the other Katipuneros slowly shimmering back into existence. They all had another dose left, but Loki wasn't sure scaling up the cliffs would be the best way out, until a glowing portal suddenly opened up before them.

"Get in!" Dex yelled in their ear. "There's lots of interference, and I can only keep this up for so long!"

Shots rang out, and Loki hit the ground as bullets whizzed past. "Stop!" They could hear Vivien's voice ringing out from behind them before pain sliced through their leg. Tito Boy and all the titas had already jumped in, and Loki crawled the remaining distance to reach the portal, where a hand reached out from inside without warning, grabbed Loki by the scruff of their collar, and dragged them in before they could say a word. They turned back and saw Vivien Fey with her team of soldiers, panting and staring back at them, wild-eyed and murderous—

—and then they were tumbling into the familiar, comforting surroundings of the Hollows.

Loki rolled on the floor and was up on their feet in an instant, breathing hard as the spell wore off, the rest of their body regaining visibility though their right leg continued to throb. From behind them, General Luna leaped out, and almost immediately, the portal shrank and fizzled out before anyone from the other side could give chase.

"You shouldn't be wandering around so close to OzCorp property without telling anyone, Loki," Nya already had a first aid kit out, adding a pain reliever tincture to the wound on their calf. "Sit down. It only grazed you, but let's be safe."

"Here you go," Ken added, handing Loki a drink. "Ube boba tea with milk pops and a dash of calm. I think the Fianna will forgive you for drinking spells this one time."

"You made this?"

"I'm not a baby. Of *course* I can cook. Or, uh, mix drinks. Nya showed me how. Did you find my shadow?"

"No to that last one," Loki confessed. "And as soon as I saw the shardstones, that escaped my mind completely. We have to tell Alex. You saw it, didn't you? OzCorp is making their own version of the Nine Maidens. They created the ice dragon! We have all the evidence we need to get a warrant, halt all OzCorp operations in Avalon!"

"Oh no." Tita Teejay was fiddling with her phone, a look of abject misery on her face. "It didn't work," she said. "All our recordings inside the cave. All memory in this phone has been wiped out—all the data, including the video I took."

"Oh, crap," Dex groaned. "I didn't think about that! That's why our communications couldn't penetrate inside the cave. I'm sorry, guys."

"How did we trip the alarms?" Loki asked.

Tito Boy waved. "Was eavesdropping on a few other suits," he signed. "Heard them say they scan the place every hour for unauthorized body signatures. Couldn't find you fast enough, though."

"I don't think it would have mattered if we'd prepared for it, then," Ken said. "You think our word is enough for a judge to issue a search warrant?"

"I don't think so," Loki said with a wince.

"What if we take this Gruffud man and shake the truth out of him?" Tita Baby suggested.

"Tita!" Dex said, shocked.

"We must be civil now," Tita Teejay chided. "Alex is setting an example, and so must we. I shall seduce him."

"*Tita!*" Dex looked even more horrified.

"This is all above our pay grade, methinks," Ken said. "We'll bring everything to Alex and then let him decide what to do."

Slowly, Loki nodded.

Ken rubbed at the side of his head. "If anything, we've at least got more info out of this, even if it isn't concrete evidence we can show. We're close. We may not know how we're gonna get there, but we're close. I know it."

"We are." Slowly, Loki reached down and brought out the metal ring they'd stolen from the lab. "We may not have video," they said, "but we have this. OzCorp's gonna have a hell of a time explaining how a collar enchanted with a thrall spell—one very similar to what we took from those Deathless that attacked—made its way to their workshop."

24

In Which Alex Shares
His First Date and Ryker
Makes a Decision

S hut up," Tala said. Or rather, that was what she was supposed to say.
It came out as a very indignant *honk* instead.

Alex wasn't even bothering to be kind. The king was laughing his head off. Her father was doing his best to be stoic, but the side of his mouth kept quirking up.

"I mean it," Tala said, even though nobody could understand her. Being a goose *sucked*. There were too many disjointed thoughts, too many distractions on the ground, too many damn *feathers*. She was hoping her agimat would have kicked in by now, but apparently there was a required minimum time in this form that not even she could override.

She thought for sure she'd figured it out this time. She'd contained her agimat as best as she could and allowed the Simeli magic to complete the transformation. But then she'd promptly panicked when the change *did* happen and spent ages running around the Labyrinth without remembering where she was, what she was supposed to accomplish, even *who* she was, before the kindly custodian had come along with her trusty golf cart and taken her out of the maze. By the time her senses had returned, Alex was already staring down at her with the biggest grin on his face that she'd ever seen him wear.

She was finally, *finally*, turning back into a human. It was disorienting, feeling her wings lengthen and shed feathers, her face twisting and warping. How was West able to handle all this on a daily basis?

"Shut up," she said again, this time using human words. Alex was still laughing.

"Well," her father said diplomatically, "yer getting close, lass. Once you figure it out, it's easy."

"This still isn't funny," Tala growled. "Make him stop, Dad."

"It is a hundred percent funny," her so-called best friend chortled. But he did finally get a hold of himself and cleared his throat. "You're gonna do it. I know you will. You're gonna do it by the end of this week."

She was glad she could give him something to laugh about today anyway. King John and his entourage had finally arrived in Avalon yesterday, and the televised meeting was awkward, to say the least. Two hours after that, the Royal States king had gone on an unhinged rant about Avalon's lack of hospitality, mocking the lodgings they were offered, then made a big show of meeting Ruggedo Nome, treating *him* like he was Avalon's king. Alex had maintained remarkable composure throughout, though the first thing he'd done after entering the Hollows afterward was spend thirty minutes beating the crap out of the punching bag there.

That hadn't even been the worst part. INTERPOL had just ordered a warrant for the arrest of Kay Warnock, a.k.a. the Scourge of Buyan, a.k.a. Scotty Smith, a.k.a. Juraj Jánošík, a.k.a. Raibeart Ruadh, a.k.a. Rob Roy, a.k.a. Semyonich. Tala had been stunned to hear all the aliases her father had adopted over the centuries. King John had been gleefully parroting the warrant all morning. Avalon had yet to issue any official statement on that, mainly because Alex was refusing to.

Tala's father, on the other hand, didn't even seem bothered by the sudden pressure on him. It helped that he'd aged enough that no one knew what he looked like anymore—the forever young, handsome boy she'd seen in the Maria Makiling footage was what people recognized him as—but once people learned he'd lived in Invierno, it was only a matter of time before he'd be found out.

"Hah," Tala grumbled, still red-faced. But her father was right. She knew she was close. It was only a matter of—

A portal opened nearby, and one of the techmages at mission control, Aleena, poked her head out.

"Your Majesty," she said nervously. "We might have something."

The mirth quickly faded from the king's face. "What is it? Another attack?"

"Not on us, Your Majesty. But I've never seen anything like this before, and I thought you'd like to come and see for yourself."

"This is a trap," Alex said bleakly, scowling at the monitor. He'd been in a bad mood all day. The Apex news had taken footage of the fight against the ogre at the fair and spun video of the Fianna roughly handcuffing the enthralled prisoners as a human rights violation. That they were Deathless had been deliberately taken out of the narrative, which meant Avalon was once again under fire. Tita Chedeng was adamant about keeping Alex from viewing Avalon's social media accounts, though she had privately admitted to Tala that death threats were now a daily response to the kingdom's official social media posts. Even worse, the Gallaghers had just confirmed that the thrall spells were created with a master-slave encryption. "Someone else has another device controlling the thralls," Dex explained with a shudder. "Magic's law of equivalent exchange means someone would have to literally lose their minds to successfully create one of these master collars. I'm not sure I want to know how they're planning on mass producing them."

And now this was a cause for even further alarm. Several of the Royal States' concentration camps around Texas and Arizona had depowered most of their security spells without warning. It was not a site-wide failure or an accident; there were no alarms, no increased activity. The sites simply remained eerily silent, as if their staff were unaware of their very real vulnerability.

"No changes in work schedules," Aleena reported. "Trucks coming and going throughout the day, a few patrols out, guards still at their stations."

"The good thing about them disabling most of their spelltech," Lola Urduja said, "is the Gallaghers hacking into their security video feeds. And if they've detected the intrusion, they're doing nothing to stop this. Things *look* normal, if you consider working for a government willfully kidnapping kids normal."

Tala gazed at the monitors showing real-time footage of ICE agents and staff members at work, chatting with their colleagues, laughing.

"What are they playing at?" Aleena asked.

"They're baiting Ryker," Tala said, as sure of it as she could be. The red blips on the screen before them told her that while most of the spells were deactivated, the areas where they suspected children were being detained were not.

"We're not taking the bait," Alex said. "The question is, will Cadfael?"

Eyes turned to Tala, who flushed. It was foolhardy to think that no one else would know about her relationship with him, though no one had judged her for it. "I think he will. He knows that it's a trap to lure him in, but he won't back down from so obvious a challenge."

"Yeah. I think that too." Alex slammed a hand down on the table in frustration. "Why can't he just stay put and use his head for once?"

"And what do you intend to do about it?" Lola Urduja asked.

"Continue monitoring the facilities of course. Figure out the instant he tries to breach any of them. Try to bring him out of there if they surround him and succeed."

"There is another option," Lola Urduja said. "And that is to sit back and watch and do nothing."

"We're not doing that!"

"And why not? He was your friend, but he also works for the Snow Queen. He might have aided you both in the past, but you owe him nothing."

"You knew him too. He stayed over at our place, ate your food. You said you liked him."

"And still he was a betrayer. Understand that if you choose to rescue him again this time around, you are also risking the lives of everyone else taking part. Is he worth all that?"

"No," Tala said quietly. "He isn't. He'd be the first to tell you the same thing. But the children he's trying to save are."

"Children that he would then bring to the Snow Queen to be indoctrinated just as he was?"

"He won't. Every time we come to save him, he's quick to turn them over to us anyway. I think…" It was only a theory. But Ryker had expressed no desire to return to Beira. She didn't think he would bring anyone else back there either. "I think that he's doing it on purpose. That he's rescuing all these kids, expecting us to intervene, so he can turn them over to us. I know he's been having problems with the Snow Queen. I think he's looking at this as a way to get back at her. And maybe he knows now that they would be better off with us."

"That's a lot of 'I thinks' and 'maybes' to be devoting this much time and resources to a boy who once tried to ship us off to the very same agency he's now fighting against," Tala's mother said.

Tala looked up at her mother. Lumina didn't look disappointed or accusing. She only looked sad.

"Is this what you really want to do, Tala?" she asked.

Tala nodded. "Yes. He'll turn the kids over to us. I know it."

Lola Urduja exchanged glances with Lumina. "We have some undercover agents unknown to the Royal States on standby. At any sign of trouble, they're going in. You will not be involved this time around."

"I'm probably the most experienced person for this mission, besides Mom," Tala pointed out. "None of your other agents have ever entered their detention camps. And you can equip yourself with all the spell negators you want, but unless you've got an agimat, you won't be able to take on a whole facility that can power everything back on at a moment's notice. And you know that as soon as Ryker gets inside there, that's what they're going to do."

Lola Urduja nodded. "All the same, the agents have been trained for situations like this, and you haven't. I want Lumina on standby, not you."

"But—"

"I'll take responsibility for her, Tita," Lumina said quietly. "The spells they use to buttress their facilities are more than even one agimat can handle. I can use the help."

Lola Urduja sighed loudly. "You've always been too kind, Lumina. Very well, but if anything happens that would require sending the both of you in, the Katipuneros will be following after."

"Thank you," Tala whispered to her mother as the others turned back to the screen.

"I was just as headstrong as you. The more my mother forbade me to do things, the more determined I was to do them. It would be easier to be there with you than try and stop you. You're a little too much like me, love."

Tala gazed at the monitor, where a picture of a smiling Ryker was displayed alongside the map of the facility. "Was it like this with you and Dad?" she asked.

"Are you asking if I'm giving you more leeway than I normally would because Ryker reminds me of your father?" Her mother smiled. "Kay was a hundred times worse than Ryker. Your young man's crimes are nothing compared to what Kay's done."

"But you forgave him?"

"Did you forgive Ryker?"

"I don't know. I think could have maybe forgiven Ryker back in Invierno if he hadn't involved you."

"I think the one thing that most people assume and assume wrongly," Lumina said, "was that I've ever forgiven Kay." Tala gaped at her mother, who smiled sweetly back. "Every day when he can prove to me that he is a better man than he was in the past is his ongoing proof of his love for me. For every person he helps without my prompting, for every day when he can realize his presence will help someone—that is his continuing penance. I love your father, and he loves me. But with us, forgiveness is always an ongoing process. It's complicated."

"So it *is* a bit like Ryker and me?"

"You're both young still. From everything you've told me, it sounds like the relationship hadn't completely taken off before it ended, though it's clear your feelings for each other persist. I was older when I met your father for the first time. When you're a teen, everything feels newer, fresher. Better, somehow. I won't say that I'm not worried or that I trust this boy that you're fond of. But I recognize how desperate he is, looking for someone to save him, the same way Kay was."

"You've always told me you met Dad at work. You said he was injured and you nursed him back to health at the hospital."

"Partly true. I landed him at the hospital to begin with. Except there was also no hospital, because he didn't want to go no matter how badly I beat his ass."

"Excuse me?! Mom!"

"A war between the American, Russian, and Chinese kingdoms was ongoing, and we'd crossed paths, convinced one was a spy for the other. Neither of us realized our mistake until after we'd fought. Fixed his wounds as an apology."

"Mom. You're kind of a badass."

"Thank you, dear."

"Other mothers would have yelled at me, told me to never see Ryker again."

"I'm not like other mothers, now am I? I would like to, believe me. But that'd make me a hypocrite."

Tala hugged her. "Thank you for trusting me."

"Lumina?" Lola Urduja called. "Where would ICE most likely set the bulk of their barrier spells if they wish to go undetected by scanners?"

Her mother walked over to the older woman. Another shrill sound erupted from Alex's phone, which he promptly rejected. Tala moved toward him. She knew he was still dealing with a few other hostile countries. Certain kingdoms and a goodly number of corporations and insurance companies had not been happy to hear Alex calmly announce his desire to implement not only universal health care for Avalon but also child care and therapy, and several news outlets had been particularly vile and openly mocking about it.

"Don't have any royal duties today?" she asked.

"Not till later. West and his parents are covering my ass, entertaining the American delegation. They're better at it than I am, and West promised to sniff them out."

"Sniff?"

"Some of the OzCorp executives are there too. I told him to remember as many of them as he can by smell. Could be useful, once we get all the evidence we need for a warrant into OzCorp HQ. Last I checked, he was already on Template 300."

"You know," Tala said bluntly, "if you really didn't want Tristan calling you, then you would have kept your phone on silent. The only reason everyone is putting up with it is because you're the king."

"Tristan isn't calling me," Alex lied.

"Prove it. Hand it over."

He glared at her. "Fine. He's calling. I'm not going to answer. I just like hearing how desperate he's getting. It's the only thing keeping me in a good mood today."

"You're still a liar. You're trying to psych yourself up to answer his calls."

"Is this treason you're doing? I'm pretty sure this is tantamount to treason."

Tala rolled her eyes. "You know he's unhappy, you know he's using Zoe as a front, and you know he's still in love with you."

"He puts *everyone else* before me. His parents are the most self-absorbed, most completely condescending people on earth, but he still listens to what they say. He's still terrified about being outed."

"Look, I'll be the first to charge into battle with you and kick his ass. But you're not gonna know if he changed his mind if you're never going to talk to him, right? And you still haven't told me what exactly happened between you guys."

"You wanna know about this *right now*?"

Tala folded her arms.

"Fine. *Fine.* I'd been staying with his family for close to three months. I'd been madly attracted to him ever since we met, and I could tell he was the same but was doing his best to ignore it. I figured he's not going to act on it, and that's cool, his prerogative. So I ignored him. But in Reykjavik, he..."

He paused, his eyes suddenly soft. "It was a class trip from the Cerridwen School. I wasn't a student, but Tristan pulled some strings and talked the administrators into bringing me along, told them I was a cousin. He had a few more Locksley perks, like a room to himself. He was a different person when his parents weren't around. More open, less ashamed. He actually felt bad for me, being cooped up and in hiding for so long, and thought I could enjoy myself with them."

And then he colored. "On our last night there, we had this wild idea to live it up around town. It was a dumb idea. Nobody knew who I was, but we could have gotten in trouble all the same. I didn't care. I just wanted one day where it felt like the world wasn't a prison.

"We nearly blew it. An ice maiden was alerted to our presence somehow, sent shades to attack us. We fought them off. It was... I guess I got caught up in the moment, and after the danger had passed, we ended up kissing before I could tell him. You know what happened next."

"And people saw that?"

"One of the Cerridwen students saw, helped me cover it up before anyone noticed. He pretended to collapse, got everyone's attention so I could grab Tristan and his clothes and run. He's not someone who talks much or gives much of anything away." Alex chuckled. "He was also a terrible actor, but it did the trick. His family was of old Avalonian stock, and they knew about my curse. He knew who I was when he saw me turn Tristan into a frog. My cover would have been blown if he hadn't caused a distraction."

Cole, Tala thought, remembering the conversation she'd accidentally spied on back at Tintagel Castle.

"Got Tristan back to his place without incident, admitted the curse to him when he shifted back. He was understanding, and that brought us to a conversation about parents, responsibilities. He's the third son, so his parents have always placed too many expectations on him. He even admitted that he was tired of hiding who he was. One thing led to another. But the next morning, it was like his shields were back on. He was quiet the whole trip back, and he started avoiding me completely after. When I finally confronted him, he told me he regretted everything and that it would be better if I found another family to hide with. His brother rescued the Bluebeard heiress a week after that, and his mother was livid. She opposed the match, and things were a mess. It was going to put a giant spotlight on the family, so the Cheshire had to move me quickly anyway. Which brought me to Invierno."

"He treated you awfully," Tala said.

"So you do understand?"

"You said that he was terrified of being outed, of his parents finding out. But so are you. You're choosing not to out yourself for political reasons, but there's not much difference between you there, is there?"

Alex scowled at her. "You're supposed to take my side and be my best friend."

"If you ever need help with anything, including burying a body, you know I'll be there with a shovel. But I'm also gonna conk you over the head every time you're this willfully stubborn. He's calling you, and it's clear you want him to, even if you don't know what you're going to tell him. If he's ready to grovel, let him. Draw it out for as long as possible. Wring every bit of it from him that you can. And then afterward, sit down and decide what kind of future you have, if he's willing to go against his parents for you this time."

Alex stared at her and then chuckled. "If you ever do forgive Ryker, having you as his girlfriend might be punishment enough if you're that keen on the groveling."

"Just because I like him," Tala said, remembering her mother's words from earlier, "doesn't mean that I'm going to forgive him. Not this easily." And then she started giggling. "You ho."

"What?"

"You perv," Tala said, poking him hard in the ribs. "*One thing led to another.* You *slept* with him, and you never told me before? You're such a horrible best friend!"

Alex flushed a dark red. "It's not the big thing you're making it out to be."

"How? Like, how was it possible? Wouldn't he turn back into a frog again if, you know, while you were in the middle of it, you both were—"

"The curse was pretty clear that it had to be on the lips! Why am I even talking about this with you?"

"So if he kissed you, you know…somewhere else?"

"Tala!"

"He's there!" Lola Urduja announced.

Up on the monitor, Ryker was calmly freezing guards on duty, encasing them quickly in balls of ice and quietly dragging them out of view before continuing down the corridor. Every now and then, he would create smaller electric spheres of magic and toss them down on the floor before continuing on.

Ryker was skillful at avoiding incoming patrols. Still, Tala watched with her heart in her throat as he systematically disarmed and paralyzed guards and opened doors with ease, drawing closer to his destination. Surely, he knew by now that there was something wrong and that there was a reason why he wasn't coming across any worse obstacles?

Finally, he stopped at a set of doors where they thought the kids' detention was located, pushing past it.

"That's it," one of the techmages reported. "We don't have video feed of anything inside."

"Alex?" Lola Urduja asked.

The king turned questioningly to Lumina.

"Tell the Fianna to hold their positions," Tala's mother said promptly.

Just as she finished speaking, the map on their screen began to blaze red as, one by one, spelltech began reactivating all over the facility. The video feeds they had access to began winking out one by one as the defensive magic took effect.

"They know he's there!" Tala cried. "We have to help him!"

"Not yet," her mother said.

"Smart boy," Lola Urduja added quietly. "He brought more ammunition this time."

Tala wasn't sure what she meant until a gasp from someone from the control team drew her attention to another video feed they retained access to. One of the spheres Ryker had left behind had burst, and waves of ice wolves, snow bees, and shades were pouring out from it. There were shouts from the guards as they scrambled to defend the building.

But that didn't mean Ryker wasn't wounded right now, possibly surrounded by armed ICE agents. That didn't mean the children inside weren't injured. Tala had seen firsthand how the agents had no qualms about putting the kids in harm's way.

"Please be safe," she muttered under her breath. "Please be safe. I need for you to be safe. Please be safe."

"Your Majesty," someone from mission control called out. "I'm detecting a sudden surge."

"Where?" Alex asked. "Spells are erupting practically everywhere inside the camp."

"It's not coming from inside the camp. Someone's trying to send us an SOS, and it's coming from Greenland."

"What?"

"Punyeta!" Lola Urduja had seized command of one of the workstations, typing furiously. "A portal has opened up at Nibheis, the Nottinghams' domain. Someone there is doing their best to get our attention. I fancy that this is your Ryker, wanting to talk."

<hr />

"What are you doing?" Tala burst out the instant she stepped out of the looking glass, glaring down at Ryker. He was sitting on the ground, trying to look as harmless as possible, but that could also be in part because of the Nottinghams surrounding him, all of whom were quick to defend their territory. Tala spotted Zoe among them, looking sheepish.

There were a few dozen people with Ryker, children and adults alike—more people he'd taken out from the facility. Fire spells burned around them, keeping them warm, and thicker jackets were already being passed around by the Nottingham clan.

"Shall I run him through with my sword?" Lord William Nottingham inquired politely in the bland tone of someone about to extend an invitation for scones.

"That's all right, Lord Nottingham," Alex said. "He's a friend. Can you give us a little privacy?"

"But of course." Lord Nottingham bowed and sheathed his sword, and a quick inclination of his head was all it took for the rest of his group to withdraw.

Tala saw Zoe flash them a worried look, hesitating. "We're okay," she called out. "Tell you everything later."

Zoe relaxed and nodded. She rejoined Cole, who'd paused to wait for her, and took his hand.

"Am I really?" Ryker asked glibly. "Figured you'd appreciate neutral territory, since you don't like me traipsing into Avalon without warning. The Nottinghams welcome sinners of all stations, so I thought this was appropriate."

"Are you asking to be stabbed, Cadfael?" Alex demanded.

"Just making conversation. I just got myself out of a pretty tricky situation. Give me a chance to catch my breath."

Ryker hadn't needed their help. He'd faced down a facility full of ICE agents and had somehow managed to escape with the asylum seekers this time. He could have just ported out of the Royal States and back into Beira with new would-be converts to the Snow Queen's cause, and they wouldn't have been able to stop him.

But he'd contacted Avalon instead.

"Can you tell me honestly that you'll be safe in Beira, Ryker?" the king asked.

Ryker bowed his head. "Probably not. You've never been happy, knowing I was bringing these kids back to Beira. You think they'll just be more soldiers for Mother's army, made to fight more of the wars they fled in the first place. You're probably right. And I agree. They're better off with you."

"I never—I didn't deliberately ask you to—" Tala began.

"I know. I suck at deciding what's best for me, but I *know* I'm doing what's best for them. Are you going to arrest me now, Your Majesty?"

"I've got a lot of intelligent, logical people telling me that arresting you will be for both our good. But I've already got one wanted criminal working for me, and that's been more advantageous than just keeping them in prison. But the Snow Queen isn't gonna be happy with you when she learns about this new adventure."

"I know."

"You willing enough to turn against her and work for us as a double agent?"

Ryker eyed him carefully. "That's a far cry from the offer of food and lodgings from last time."

"Maybe what you need is a new purpose."

"I might be open to the idea, but you shouldn't be so quick to trust me. I wouldn't."

"You're going to have to pick a side, Ryker. Either you commit yourself fully to the Snow Queen, or come over to ours before it's too late for you." There was a pleading note to Alex's voice that he didn't seem aware of. "I know that she had you do terrible things. Stay with her, and you might not be able to get out at all."

"Thank you," Ryker said with genuine gratitude. "But you'll need to find someone else to save, Alex. I promise not to harm Tala. What choices I'm still free to make, I'll make with her in mind. But don't expect anything else from me. Not yet."

"We're opening a port for you to wherever you want to go. That's the best we can do. I'm sorry, Ryker. I can't have you staying in Avalon for the moment."

"That's all right. I know when I've overstayed my welcome. Greenland is neutral, I'd appreciate you dropping me off there." Ryker got to his feet. "And I'm sorry too. Despite what happened in Arizona, know that I genuinely liked you. Didn't want to, but I did."

"I know. I didn't have many friends there, but I thought you were one of them."

"I'm a disappointment, yeah. And thanks for looking out for me back at the facility. I appreciate it." Ryker turned to Tala, looking like he wanted to say more to her, but stopped. "Be well, Tala," was all he finally said as a portal slowly opened behind him. He stepped through, the hole closing up quickly before anyone could get near.

"You okay?" Alex asked Tala.

"He knows that we're using him," Tala said. "He knows that I'm using him. He's probably using us too. He won't give up the Snow Queen, but he won't fight us either. What game is he playing?"

"The same one we are," the king said heavily. "He needs something from her, but he doesn't want to tell us what just yet."

"I still don't trust him, but I don't want anything to happen to him either. Is that wrong?"

"No. If anything, that's how you know you're doing it right." Alex held out his hand. "Let's go, and maybe you can help me come up with another reason for Immigration to believe that we managed to get our hands on several dozen immigrants from *Nibheis*, of all places."

25

IN WHICH GENDER IS JUST A SOCIAL CONSTRUCT

Wolves!" Zoe squealed.

Nottingham had been infuriatingly secretive about this. It didn't matter that she'd put a firm halt on any more reckless missions. It didn't matter that this was feeling a lot less of an obligation she'd made to him and more like something she genuinely wanted to do.

She'd already begun thinking about scaling back anyway, lying low for a bit. The groups she helped were more than capable of handling things on their own now, once they had access to the tech they needed. That was good. Avalonians weren't better at doing things than people in other countries were; it was just that Avalon still had privileges despite everything that had happened to it. The others were just as good, probably even better, given the same opportunities and the same resources, and their successes were proof of that.

She also liked that a lot of the people they'd initially helped were turning around and doing the same. Some of the migrants they'd taken in after the first incident at the Texas border were now spearheading their own campaigns to rescue their countrymen and get them settled. Some focused on sex education and birth control. One had started offering free courses on both physical self-defense and using Avalon spelltech for protection. Another had started a co-op initiative for small businesses.

Oddly enough, Zoe didn't feel as frustrated as when she first started. She'd been so pent up about not being able to save everything and everyone. The missions they'd taken on hadn't been enough, and her secret solo attempts had only stoked those fires instead of dousing them. She was feeling the urgency less nowadays.

It was Cole. The damn ass had actually helped her successfully work out her stress with planting trees, cleaning up beaches and rivers, working at soup kitchens and shelters. Maybe it was because she could see the immediate effects of her hard work, from the grateful people who came in for food to seeing the before-and-after effects on places once riddled with garbage. And now watching other people advocate for issues they wanted to focus on, helping their own along the way, helped her peace of mind even more.

It was also odd to be spending days working with him and then nights attending some function or other with Tristan. It wasn't technically cheating, she told herself. What she had with Tristan was a farce. The problem wasn't just that she felt guilty but that it felt like she was cheating on Nottingham, weirdly enough, and they weren't even together. He didn't even want to, she thought sourly, his rejection of her springing back to mind. He knew about her and Tristan. He didn't know about the contract they'd made, but it didn't look like his feelings would change even if he did. It was a bit of a mess, and for someone who liked things neat and organized, Zoe seemed fairly keen on getting herself into a whole lot of opportunities for chaos.

The dowager's words were still rattling around Zoe's head, and she wasn't sure she wanted to explore the implications behind them. She didn't want to believe in prophecy, but if she did, then hers and Nottingham's seemed inextricably tied together, much like Ken's and Nya's appeared to be. Zoe was scared about what that could mean.

He hadn't told her much about his doom, and she hadn't wanted to pry. Sometimes she wished she'd let the dowager tell her, only to reject the idea immediately. Whatever it was, she wanted it straight from his mouth. That was the most important thing, that *he* make the decision to entrust her with the information.

She didn't want to think too much about the implications of why she wanted him to either.

And since when have you been so attached to his trust, Zoe? Why would you expect this from him when you won't even reveal yours to anyone else?

Nottingham hadn't wanted to tell her where they were going this time. He said it would be a surprise—a good one this time. She'd forgiven him by the time the snowy-white majestic creatures loped toward them, showing no fear, and the sight was one of the most magnificent things she'd ever seen.

Several other people were present, brushing the wolves' fur. "About time you showed up, Silva," one of them called out.

"You're a regular volunteer here?" Zoe asked.

"An occasional volunteer." A couple more wolves trotted over. She watched Nottingham crouch down as they nuzzled at his hands.

"We don't usually allow first-timers to handle the wolves directly," one of the staff members said to Zoe, offering her a metal brush. "But Silva vouches for you, said you've been around them in the past. And, well, his family practically funds this whole thing, so I guess we can relax the rules this one time."

Zoe watched most of the wolves make a beeline for Nottingham. He looked relaxed. He was smiling down at them, and it made her heart hurt, just a little. "Silva?"

"He doesn't want people associating him with the Nottingham name,

I guess. Goes by his dad's instead. We'll need you to sign a waiver, though. Protect our asses. Sorry."

"I'll sign anything," Zoe said. "They're gorgeous."

"Aren't they? Silva can communicate with most of that lot, so they shouldn't be any trouble. Just follow our instructions, and don't make any sudden moves. They're friendly, but it's important that they not be domesticated. Try and take out as many sticks and twigs as you can from their fur. This pack just had some fun at a bramble patch."

A few wolves approached her curiously. All it took was for Zoe to extend her hands for them to consider her a new friend, which they cemented by licking at her. One tried to nip playfully at her pinkie.

"No," Nottingham ordered.

The wolf sniffed, apologized by nuzzling Zoe's hand.

"You never told me how your family learned to communicate with them," Zoe said.

"My great-grandmother says it came with the land, an aftereffect of the spells still strong there. Live in Nibheis long enough, and most will pick it up eventually. And even without it, we have another notorious ancestor to thank."

"The wolf king? He's related to you?" She'd suspected it before, but it did explain Adelaide's annoyance with the Red Hood puppet show a few days ago. "When you guys said you had a lineage full of miscreants and villains, you weren't kidding."

"No tyrants in your family tree?"

"I don't know much about my father's side of the family, but I think a great-great-uncle from the Fairfax clan hunted Darquier down in Malaga and strangled him to death with Ogmios. It's probably not the same, though." Zoe waited several heartbeats, carefully grooming the wolf, before finally blurting out, "Silva."

"What about it?"

He'd told the sanctuary staff she was coming but hadn't told them not to stop calling him by that name. He'd wanted her to know. It was so much different from before, when he'd visibly tensed up when talk turned to families. "Your father's?"

"Yeah."

"You never really say much about him. Divorced, like mine?"

"Not exactly. Just estranged. For reasons you could probably guess at."

"You told me you lived in NYC."

"No, I said I lived in the Bronx." He grinned briefly. "We were happy there. Didn't have a lot, but that didn't matter. My mother married against my grandfather's wishes, so she rejected his wealth too." He scratched absently at the wolf's fur. "They were both social workers. We were all close. Highlight of the week was heading out to the nearest cineplex to watch the old movies they always had on for free."

Hence his knowledge of old Hollywood films. "But your dad was against the Gravekeeper tradition."

"He didn't want her to go back. He knew what it would do to her and to us. But then my grandfather collapsed when I was eight. He was getting older, couldn't handle Gravekeeper any longer. My folks argued, but Mom returned anyway. Dad kept us a little longer, till she was diagnosed with a chronic illness."

"How old were you when that happened?"

"Fourteen."

His mother had returned out of duty, to take up Gravekeeper's mantle. And when she could no longer do it, Nottingham had chosen to follow in her footsteps. Like mother, like son.

He'd been so young. That meant he'd started using Gravekeeper around the same time he'd been enrolled at Cerridwen, when they'd first met.

She looked down at his scarred arm, remembered that his grand-father's had been even worse. How long would he have to bear that burden before it permanently injured him too?

And if he failed, it would be Adelaide's turn. It explained why he was so frustratingly stubborn about accepting help sometimes.

"Two paths lie on the road you take," she said. "One way lies madness, and the other death. But the wolf will always outrun the deer. You will take the shire over the gest, the chaff over the grain, and they will laugh at your foolhardiness. But it is you who shall laugh long and loud, for in the end, the dead shall rise for you. How the dead shall rise."

Nottingham had grown silent, looking down at the yipping wolf nestled in between his hands. "That's your doom," he said.

"Yeah. *One way lies madness, and the other death.* That's the part that frightened me, because it sounds like things are gonna end badly for me either way. So I decided it wouldn't have any power if I just stopped believing in any of it. Because the more I talked about it, the more real it felt. The last part your great-grandmother said—the one about losing my tears and my way and all that stuff—that I didn't know. It scared me too."

He said nothing, processing her words even as his hands idly stroked at another wolf's fur.

"I always thought that maybe the wolf was a metaphor," Zoe continued. "Like the deer obviously is, since that's the Fairfax family crest. Your crest doesn't have any wolves on it, but Tristan's does." Back when she'd been foolish and nursing her terrible crush. Back when she thought Tristan was a different person, when she'd been more naive.

"You started dating him because you thought you were supposed to?" He was amused.

"More like me making up my own interpretation of my prophecy because that was the only thing about it that I wanted to come true. And even that's no longer the case."

"You're still going out with Tristan, though." Was there a hint of something else in his voice? Or was she deluding herself into thinking that again?

"It's not what you think it is. That's all I can say for now." She looked at him. "You never asked me about my relationship with him before."

"It wasn't any of my business."

"Wasn't it?" She wanted to wait for the right time. She wanted to wait until the terms of her contract with Tristan were over so she could explain everything. But it felt like the perfect time to finally say something else out loud, here in this beautiful sanctuary surrounded by the wolves he so obviously cared for. "Am I really none of your business? When it looks like our dooms are intertwined somehow? You must have suspected long before I did." She set the brush down and stroked at the animals' fur instead, and it rumbled contentedly. "I've been scared to tell anyone about my doom for the longest time. As a kid, my mother would announce it to everyone like it was some major prize I'd won, and I always had to endure the pitying looks because they thought it meant I was going to die young. But I'm telling you now, in the hopes that maybe your doom's got something to do with mine, or if mine might have any bearing on yours."

"Your doom," Nottingham said, "has every bearing on mine."

He looked sad, an unusual expression to see on someone who always took care not to let his emotions show, and resigned. Zoe wanted to reach out and grab his hand again. That was getting to be a habit with them, and it was safer than other options she could think of, like hugging him. Or kissing his cheek, maybe. Or…

She was staring at the ground, all too aware of how quiet everything was now, though Nottingham seemed comfortable enough without the need for words, hadn't noticed her ears burning. Even the wolves seemed to have sensed the embarrassment brought on by her epiphany, staring up at her with their tongues lolling out in laughter.

She liked him, didn't she? She really did like Cole goddamn Nottingham. And he would never let her live it down once he knew.

"I'm going to stop going on solo missions." Saying it out loud felt like she could finally hold herself accountable for it. "I want to keep doing stuff like this. With you. If you don't mind. I—"

A loud ringing broke through the silence. The wolves made a startled whine, backing away. Zoe gasped, her hands flying to her pocket.

"I'm so sorry! I forgot that I hadn't turned it off. I hope I didn't…" She trailed off when she saw that it was Dex's number on her phone's screen. She'd told him where they were going, so she knew he wouldn't be calling now if something wasn't wrong.

"Zoe!" The boy sounded panicked when she picked up. "I'm registering a really huge wave of magic from within the Royal States!"

"What? Is it another one of those mysterious portals?"

"No, it's much worse! I think someone's about to use a spellstone!"

Zoe froze. *She'd* used a spellstone months ago, an absolutely reckless thing to do, the consequence being her inability to cry. It sounded like a fairly tame curse to take on in exchange, but it had been responsible for every bad decision she'd made ever since. "It's not a spelltech?"

"Way too powerful for us not to have detected it earlier. It's got the same readings as the one I told you we spotted inside Avalon, back when it was still frozen! I've already called Alex, but he's in a meeting, and it's taking a while to get through!"

Zoe swore quietly, not wanting to scare the wolves further. "We're heading back right away. Keep track of it till we return."

Nottingham already knew. He was on his feet, gently nudging the wolves away and waving the staff over. "That bad?" he asked.

"Very bad," Zoe said grimly. *This is karma*, she thought, *coming back to bite me in the ass.*

It was only a matter of time before they were going to get caught.

Zoe's main worry had always been about the one person in the whole government whom she didn't trust, and that was the minister of trade, Fluvio Ancilotto. Alex hadn't listened when she'd voiced her concerns about him, and Zoe had hoped talking to Tala would help him change his mind. But Tala had only looked at her helplessly and said, a bit uncomfortably, "I know we have every reason to dislike him. But at this point, we have to trust Alex on this. I do."

The minister was waiting inside the Hollows, Dex pacing the floor. The latter looked relieved to see them, the former, scathing. "I'd expected better from you, Lady Fairfax," he said coldly. "Misusing government property to commit crimes is tantamount to a felony charge."

"I'm a little more concerned with Dex's discovery right now."

She was surprised when he nodded. "There will be a reckoning when you return, unfortunately. In the interest of fairness, I will be taking charge of sorting this mess out. The best-case scenario right now is to retrieve the spellstone without anyone the wiser. We need to wait for the Fianna."

"No. The spellstone could take out half the city by then. If the energy coming through is this strong, that means whoever's responsible has already activated the stone and is about to use it."

"And how do you know so much about the process?"

Zoe glared at him.

The minister set his jaw. "And I suppose none of you would listen to me if I said this was a foolish idea?"

"I don't think so. There's no time. Dex, can you track where it is?"

Dex had managed to single out one particular house in the suburbs, which was a surprise.

Zoe had insisted on going alone, not wanting to draw too much attention, and Nottingham had immediately vetoed that by insisting on tagging along, and she didn't have the energy to argue. They'd both been equipped with the Gallagher earpieces just in case. A quick exploration of the kitchen and living room turned up no one, and they were halfway up the stairs before they finally heard voices—one a low murmur and the other louder and angrier.

They found a girl towering over an older man who was groveling on the floor, a scenario that was the complete opposite of what Zoe had been dreading. There was stark fear in the man's features. In contrast, the girl was livid, furious, triumphant.

"You're Abigail Fey," Zoe managed to say. "Vivien Fey's younger sister."

The girl didn't even turn her head, still focused on the man. "Stay out of this."

"Would you like to talk about it first?"

"What's the point? My baby's still dead." The girl was practically shaking with rage, one hand pressed against her stomach as if in pain. "You destroyed my life, and even then, I would have let you if that meant I could have my baby. My parents kicked me out. Only my sister protected me from you."

Abigail was holding something in her hand. It was a small pebble-like stone, and it was glowing more brightly than was natural for a spellstone. It wasn't a pure, unadulterated spellstone, Zoe realized, but an artificial one.

The prototype Loki had seen at the secret OzCorp location had used artificial spellstones. Vivien Fey no doubt had access to some. And hadn't Ken mentioned spotting Abigail Fey inside OzCorp headquarters?

"Abigail," Zoe said slowly, knowing that Dex and the others could hear the conversation taking place, "it's not worth it. He's not worth it. Hand it to me, and I promise you everything will be all right." A quick intake of breath from Nottingham, who'd finally spotted the spellstone as well.

"You can't promise me that," Abigail wept. "You can't tell me you can bring her back. I tried, and it won't let me. I said I would sacrifice my life to have her back. But it won't work. If this is magic, then why won't it work for me?"

"Abigail," Zoe tried again as Nottingham began to inch himself over to the distraught girl, moving slowly so as not to startle her or draw her attention to him. "We'll make sure to arrest him, make sure justice is meted out."

"No," Abigail whispered. "Justice means my baby would be alive."

"I'll do everything in my power to make sure he goes to jail."

"No one ever believed me when it came to him. The police wouldn't do anything. What makes you think you're any different?"

"Because I am. Let me take the spellstone, and we'll wait for the—"

The sudden wail of sirens outside the house told her they had just run out of time.

Eyes blazing, Abigail raised the spellstone. "I'm going to be with her now, and you're not going to stop me. Now I'm going to ruin *your* life."

Nottingham made a lunge for her, but the stone in her hand blazed brightly, the glare so bright that Zoe had to look away.

When the light finally faded, Abigail was gone.

But the man was still there, unharmed and looking just as stunned as they were.

"Police!" someone behind the door yelled, followed by several sharp raps.

"Get a port down to our coordinates as soon as you can, Dex!"

Her earpiece crackled. "But—but what about—"

"There's nothing we can do for her now!"

A looking glass fizzled to life before them.

"Now!" Zoe cried, latching on to Nottingham's arm and flinging them both through the hole, just as half a dozen cops swarmed in, guns drawn and blazing. Zoe could have sworn she heard several shots, but by then, they were already tumbling into the Hollows, home free. There was another popping sound as Dex slammed the looking glass closed.

Nottingham grunted. For a horrifying moment, Zoe wondered if he'd been shot. "Hey. You okay?"

"Barely."

"Those fucking bastards!" She sprang to her feet. "Who the hell shoots at people running away?"

"American cops," Minister Ancilotto offered dryly.

Zoe stalked toward the deactivated looking glass, staring desperately at her reflection. "Did you see what happened to her?"

"No," Dex said, looking on the verge of tears. "It was like a firework had been set off in the room. By the time we could see anything, she was gone. I tried to run a scan, but I couldn't find anything. One minute, she was there, and then the next minute, she was just…"

With an anguished roar, Zoe punched the wall. Punched it again.

"Hey." Arms encircled her. Zoe tried to resist at first, then gave up, sagging back into Nottingham. "You're not going to do this again," the boy said quietly. "We've both worked too hard for you to regress. We'll talk to Alex, see what he can do."

"Alex is going to murder me and then salt the earth around my grave as a warning to everyone else."

"I think Alex already knows," Dex said. "There's a call coming through from him."

Zoe glared at Ancilotto.

"He needed to know what kind of trouble you're putting him in," the minister said calmly.

The monitor faded out momentarily, and then Alex appeared, just as angry as she had expected, but also worried. "Zoe?"

"Your Majesty," Minister Ancilotto said. "A spellstone was activated within the Royal States. I know that—"

"We'll get to what Abigail Fey has done in just a minute. Right now, there are American prosecutors on the other line, demanding that I turn both Zoe and Nottingham over for arrest. Something about trespassing, plus assault and battery."

Zoe stiffened. "They recognized us?"

"They recognized Nottingham. His family has a fairly bad rep, even in other countries. They mentioned a white brunette with him, so I naturally assumed it would be you. I told them that I was going to keep you both under house arrest rather than turn you over, but they're pretty insistent, considering that the first count they want to charge you with is a pretty minor one, and I'm not sure they can stick the second."

"I'll turn myself in," Nottingham responded promptly. "My grandfather will sort things out with them. We don't want Your Majesty getting involved—"

"Of course I'm going to get involved. You're my subjects, and I don't have that many of them yet to want to lose you two to the corrupt bureaucrats there. I'll talk to William, but you're staying in Avalon. I'm not going to have either of you killed while in custody, and I wouldn't put it past them to do exactly that."

"It's my fault," Zoe said. "Going in was my idea. Cole was just trying to look out for me. I'll cop to everything if they drop all charges against him."

"Carlisle!" Nottingham barked.

"They wouldn't be going through all this trouble if they didn't suspect a connection to the border raids or the concentration camp break-ins. I'm willing to bet they already suspect who has taken the asylum seekers from them," Zoe said. "They're waiting for Alex to turn me over on the minor charges, then slam me with the bigger crimes. I need to be the only person taking the blame for this."

The king sighed. "Some of the Royal States prosecutors will be arriving tomorrow to plead their case before the Avalonian court, and no doubt they'll be bringing a truckload of reporters too."

"I'm sorry, Alex."

"I gave you my blessing. I knew this was a possibility."

"Your Majesty!" Ancilotto exclaimed.

"Sorry to keep you out of that loop, old friend. There's a chance they might be bringing Marcus Abernathy in to testify if they can get him released from the hospital—"

"Who's Marcus Abernathy?" Zoe interrupted.

"The man whose house you allegedly trespassed in. He doesn't have a rap sheet, but he's got some interesting rumors surrounding him—and by that I mean interesting for our case but absolutely disgusting to other decent folk. They might use him as a witness despite his condition, at least until they can spring the other charges on—"

"His condition?" Zoe's head was spinning. "What condition? Abigail never even touched him. We didn't either."

"He started throwing up shortly after he was admitted. No one knew the cause until some enterprising nurse recognized the symptoms and suggested a completely different test." Alex rubbed his eyes. "And it came out positive. He's three months pregnant."

Stunned looks met that statement. *Oh no*, Zoe thought. *Oh hell no.*

26

IN WHICH WEST'S NOSE STARTS A FIGHT

I gotta admit," Zoe said, sounding almost cheerful. "I thought I'd be caught raiding detention camps or annoying more Worldenders. Not getting men pregnant."

Her father sighed. "Zoe."

"What's important is that you're due in court for your bail hearing in an hour," Mr. Peets said crisply. This was the first time Tala had even seen him, and he was a little person. Alex had told her he was a direct descendant of Queen Thumbelina, but she hadn't been expecting how directly descended he actually was. "You won't even have to spend a night in jail."

"That's one for the pro list, I guess," Zoe said. "The con, obviously, is that speeding up the hearing process means all the attention is on me and Nottingham. Am I right? ."

"Zoe," Jonathan Carlisle said again, even more reprovingly.

She winced. "Sorry, Dad. Are Alex and the others still listening in?"

"Yes, we are," Alex said dryly, looking up at Zoe's face on-screen. Tala, Ken, Nya, Loki, Dex, and West were gathered in the control room with the king. "In the interest of impartiality, I can't be there at your trial."

Zoe winced. "And the judge assigned to my case just so happens to be Judge Andrilov? A close friend of Ancilotto, the minister of trade?"

"I can't do anything to make it seem like I'm favoring you, Zoe."

"I know. It just sucks." She paused, hanging her head. "I'm sorry again."

"You should have told us earlier about the spellstone, Zo. I didn't know you'd already used one. Worst-case scenario, Mr. Peets can argue you were under undue influence."

"I didn't think it was important. I mean, all I was going to lose was my tears. Who would've thought that meant something more?" Zoe winced. "I might have broken my contract with Tristan, though. I wasn't supposed to be putting this much attention on him." The Locksley boy had come forward when he'd heard what had happened, had been open about the deal he'd made with Zoe as long as they could keep it from his parents, which Alex had agreed to. Tala didn't know much of Tristan's relationship with the girl, but she was relieved that he'd chosen to put Zoe first. And Alex had mellowed out considerably after finding out, though he'd remained just as abrupt and catty when he'd talked to Tristan.

"On the contrary," Mr. Peets said. "Your contract with the Locksley boy was focused on making your relationship believable to his parents. Your behavior has nothing to do with its terms. As it is, Locksley has already agreed to break the contract if you yourself agree."

"Yes. Damnit, *yes please.* Ending it early feels like the only good thing to come out of this. Where is Nottingham?"

"Doing a lot better than you. They granted him bail, and the news barely even covered it."

"The perks of being a Nottingham," Ken said, though with none of the rancor.

"They're not going to stick anything on him," Zoe said confidently.

"Are you really sure this is the defense you want, Lady Carlisle?" Mr. Peets asked. "It has its risks."

"Do you think we can pull it off?"

"It would depend if the Royal States' rancor for Avalon trumps their desire to protect themselves."

"Was it really that bad?"

"You haven't heard yet, I'm guessing?" Tala asked.

"Tell me."

Tala called up a news story Dex had recorded for them on the next screen. "—it's not yet clear what percent of the population has been affected by what they are now calling the Avalon curse," the newscaster was saying, "but hospitals all over the kingdom have reported sixty-nine confirmed cases with similar pregnancies. While there are still no verified accounts of cases outside the Royal States, Ohio, Texas, Arizona, Mississippi, and Arkansas are among seven states with at least one—"

"The *Avalon* curse?" Zoe all but shouted.

"They were originally calling it the Abernathy curse, but then some right-wing pundits opened their mouths."

Zoe could only sigh as Tala turned it back off.

"They've verified Marcus Abernathy as patient zero, so it's likely they'll be referencing that in your case," Mr. Peets said, pacing the table. "The American prosecutors will be throwing every charge they can at you, hoping most will stick. The objective for today is to prevent your extradition to their kingdom, as they may also know about your other... activities."

"I'm sorry, Dad," Zoe mumbled for about the twenty-sixth time.

The man patted his daughter's hand. "I won't say I'm not worried, but I'm glad to see you doing the right thing. Even given the circumstances you were under."

"It wasn't just because I wanted to do the right thing."

"You always sell yourself short, Zo. I may not always understand, but know that I'm proud of you, and I love you."

Zoe smiled, looking like she did want to cry. "I love you too, Dad."

"She's going to retaliate," Loki said quietly.

"Who is?" Tala asked.

"Vivien Fey. We haven't seen her since this all went down. You know she's attached to her sister. I don't know what she's going to do. Sir Mykonos said she has stopped reporting to work at OzCorp since her sister disappeared."

"I know. I've asked Titas Teejay and Chedeng to keep watch at OzCorp for any unusual activity," Alex said crisply. "That's the best we can do."

Mr. Peets checked his watch. "We'll need to head to the courthouse soon."

"We'll be there rooting for you," Ken said. "You'll beat this."

Zoe smiled worriedly. "Yeah. Hope so too."

<hr />

The courthouse was packed. Press reporters took up several rows, and a crowd of onlookers had gathered outside, eager to hear updates as they were happening. Even the Beast of Suddene was in the audience for support, though there was less focus on him. Tristan Locksley, too, was there, though he was alone. The Royal States had brought in not just their prosecutors but their representatives attending the summit.

Zoe looked slightly nervous at the size of the crowd but managed to keep her head up and remain calm as the Royal States prosecutors began to recite the litany of cases they were charging her with.

The judge had preemptively banned the use of magic inside the courtroom, but Tala's skin tingled all the same. People had arrived wearing minor spells, like acne concealers or caffeine substitutes—she supposed magic was too much a part of everyday life for it to be prohibited completely.

"Not guilty," Zoe responded firmly when asked by the judge how she wished to plead.

"Very well." The judge consulted his notes. "Be seated, all of you. I imagine this will take a while to go through, given the number of kingdoms involved."

The main doors opened again, and heads turned.

It was Cole. Unheeding of the startled looks and the sudden whispers, he strode forward and deliberately sat down in an empty seat beside Zoe, who gaped at him.

"What's he doing?" Ken asked. "His grandfather pulled a lot of strings to get him out without fanfare, and now he's planting himself back in the spotlight all over again."

"Oh," Nya whispered, eyes suddenly shiny. "How romantic."

"Romantic? This is a bail hearing. How can that possibly be romantic?"

"I punched you, and you said it was romantic."

"That's different. I'm a masochist."

"So is Cole, I think."

"Your Honor," the Royal States prosecutor began, "given the severity of the charges, we would like to request that the defendant be extradited back to the Royal States, as most of these charges were committed within our jurisdiction."

"The courts of Avalon would be more than adequate at meting out justice as well," the judge said coolly.

"Of course. We are not questioning the court's ability to carry out judgment, but we assert our right to try the defendant ourselves, to see justice for the victims."

"Victims?" Mr. Peets demanded. "What victims do you speak of?"

"There is Marcus Abernathy, the victim of a curse—"

"—committed by another girl. A curse my client sought to prevent her from accomplishing."

"Or so the defendant says."

"You understand just as well as I do that the laws of equivalent exchange mean that every powerful spell shall result in an equally powerful repercussion. Does my client look like she's been suffering the consequences of such far-reaching magic?"

"We would ask that the defendant be examined by doctors—"

"—which has already been done by court-appointed physicians we both agreed upon. They will testify that my client suffers no maladies resulting from this spell."

"There is the matter of trespassing—"

"I find it suspicious for the Royal States to come all the way to Avalon for a charge of trespassing, a minor offense punishable mainly with probation or mandated community service, and even then there are extenuating circumstances."

"The defendant had access to a looking glass that violated Royal States' laws—"

"The FBI and other U.S. agencies have an obligation to warn criminals about threats to their life should they come across such information. Miss Carlisle works in a similar capacity for Avalon and felt it was her obligation to warn Mr. Abernathy of the imminent threat to his life. If you will recall, Avalon has warned the Royal States through official channels of similar incidents in the past, only to be ignored."

"He's pretty good," Ken muttered to Tala and Nya.

The doors flew open a second time.

"What is this?" a voice cried. The woman who strode into view was a head turner, even without the dramatic entrance. She had long yellow hair that was artfully curled and big blue eyes that made her look younger than she was. She was dressed smartly in a blazer and pencil skirt, and she approached the bench with a grace that belied the five-inch heels she was wearing. "Why do you make such a mockery of your justice system?" she demanded in a strident French accent. "It is a travesty to me and to the king of France!"

There was a very audible clunking sound as Zoe's forehead hit the table.

"A travesty!" the woman repeated. "There is no rule of law to be followed here, and I am raging! Always I thought that Avalon would adhere to the law better than the other countries it often criticizes, but no! They follow the same inconsistencies!"

"Order!" the judge thundered. "You have no right to come barging in when court is in session, and I will not tolerate any more shenanigans while I am presiding!"

Mr. Peets cleared his throat. "Your Honor, while I agree with you that Lady Fairfax's entrance was unconventional, she has every right to protest."

"Lady Fairfax?" Tala whispered, and her mother nodded. No wonder Zoe was embarrassed.

"This is only a bail hearing, Mr. Peets," the judge said. "She has the right to a fair and speedy trial, but we're still a long ways from that."

"His Honor may be familiar with the trial process but not with French law." Lady Fairfax waved a blue folder in the air triumphantly. "My Zoe has been given special dispensation from the French government as part of her service to the Avalonian kingdom. The dispensation is still in effect for another two years and states that she has diplomatic immunity. My Zoe has performed admirably for the kingdom, risking her life while you all sit and connive to keep Avalon on ice."

"Does Zoe know about this?" Loki whispered.

"Judging from her face right now," Tala said, "probably not."

"There is still due process to follow—" the prosecutor objected.

"Oh, shush your mouth, Edmund. The charges should never have stuck in the first place, and you know it. Incidentally, my congratulations to your younger brother on his pregnancy. I wondered why your family chose not to announce it the way you announced your wife's—oh, was that supposed to be a surprise? My apologies."

Lady Fairfax turned a beaming smile on a row of cameras, not looking sorry at all. "Should you like to know about how my daughter and her friends saved the king? And are reviled as a result by the Royal States and their press—of which many of you are implicated—so I wonder how you shall be spinning this when you finally—"

"This is interference by a foreign state!" the prosecutor sputtered.

"Interference? Interference? And you are here to commemorate friendlier ties with the Royal States, yes? Ha! I spit on your claims of interference! Philip has approved of my interference! Neither the Royal States nor Avalon has conferred with us on this matter, and now we are exerting our right to request all charges be dismissed!"

The judge massaged his temples. "Lady Fairfax, Mr. Peets, Mr. Walters, please approach the bench, and let's get this sorted out."

"They're really going to let her do it?" Loki asked.

"What Zoe didn't tell the rest of you is that her mother is also the stepsister to the current king of France," Tala's mother said dryly. "Judge Andrilov is doing well not to step on their toes. Incidentally, she also happens to be a lawyer, though I wasn't sure if she had an Avalon license."

West was frowning, staring hard at the row of people closest to the door.

"Something wrong, West?" Tala asked. "Too many people?"

"A bit. There're too many different smells—but there's a familiar one too."

Before Tala could ask him more questions, the boy rose to his feet slowly and began to move among the crowd. Tala exchanged worried glances with the others. "I'll follow him," she said, getting up as well.

Despite the crowded room, it was easy enough to catch up to West. The shifter kept pausing to sniff curiously at people, many of whom reared back in alarm or scowled. One very nearly tried to start a fight, but Tala was quick to head them off, apologizing profusely. By then, West had already moved on, oblivious to the annoyed onlookers he was leaving in his wake.

"West," Tala finally hissed, grabbing him by the sleeve. "You're disrupting the court, and that's not what Zoe needs right now."

West shook his head. "This is what Alex asked me to do—to watch out for any unfriendlies while Zoe's in court—and I'm not going to let him down. There's something… I know I've smelled it before…" He was getting dangerously close to where the Royal States delegates were seated, the last group that Tala wanted to tick off.

"West," she pleaded. "Can't we do this later?"

"Trust me, Tala. I might not know a lot of things, but my nose will never fail me. And it's telling me right now that this can't be posit…post-pole…delayed. I won't be wrong. I can't be wrong."

Tala glanced at the still somewhat irate people they'd left behind, then at West. "All right," she found herself saying. "I trust you."

West smiled gratefully at her, and then his nose twitched and he was off again. Tala stuck to his side as they passed several more rows of onlookers. There seemed to be no rhyme or reason to West's methods. He simply let his sense of smell guide him for the most part, sometimes going back to the same area and circling it several times before seemingly moving on without finding anything of note, like a bloodhound.

"Excuse me," the judge called out, interrupting the prosecutor in midspiel. "You two, sit down. Please do not disrupt the proceedings."

Tala stopped, but West kept on. "I'm close," West muttered, paying the man no attention. "I know I'm close. I know that smell. Template 25? No, too salted. 31? 45? Where have I...?"

"Sir, if you don't sit down this instant, you will be charged with contempt and be escorted out."

West had paused by the Royal States contingent, staring hard at one of the young women seated there. "You," he said.

"Guards." Judge Andrilov's patience was wearing thin. "Please escort the young man out."

Men stepped forward, but West resisted. "It's her!" he yelled at Tala. "Blond Template 68! It's her! I mean, it's not her! She looks like Template 68, but she doesn't *smell* like her! She doesn't have a scent!"

For a moment, Tala was stumped, not sure what he was shouting about. While the others sitting around the woman were wearing minor, trivial spells, she could detect no magic coming off the woman at all. She felt normal. Blond Template 68 only looked puzzled by the commotion. Had West made a mistake?

No. That Tala couldn't find any suggestion of a spell at all from her, coupled with West's insistence that the woman wasn't right, was too suspicious to dismiss.

The guards started to lead the boy away. Ken and Loki had leaped to their feet in protest, but Lumina signaled at them to stand down, though she looked worried herself.

The trick was to find the point where the magic could be cut off from its source, to do with as one wished. That was what Lola Corazon had said.

Tala reached out with her agimat again, this time searching for the intersection where the absence of magic from the woman ended and the other spells around her began. While everyone else simmered with enchantments small and innocuous enough not to hide, the magic rebounded away when it drew close to Template 68, bouncing harmlessly off her like she had a personal shield or even her own agimat.

And the source of that barrier felt like it was coming from the woman's handbag.

"West," Tala shouted. "Shift!"

It was West's nature to be trusting without question, and rather than ask why, he obeyed. The guards jumped back as the now-canine West growled at them with his teeth bared. There were screams, chairs overturning.

Tala lunged. She latched on to the woman's bag and tried to wrench it away from her, though the latter was hanging on with unexpected strength. "Thief!" the woman shouted.

Tala dug in further with her agimat and found confirmation. There was a small device inside the woman's bag that felt no bigger than a mobile phone but was absorbing magic at an alarming speed, like it was a portable black hole. Avalon security measures were made to detect high concentrations of magic rather than the reverse. Tala would have walked by the woman several times and never caught on either if West hadn't singled her out.

Tala used her salamanca, pushing it onto the device, forcing it to absorb more magic than what it could afford to hold, her mind straining from the effort even as she felt arms pulling her away from the woman. At first, there didn't seem to be any threshold for how much magic the device could take in, and Tala feared that there may be no way to overload it. She doubled her efforts.

"Order!" the judge shouted. "You two are in contempt of—"

Tala hit the device's limit without warning. She could *feel* rather than hear it crack.

She was thrown back from the force of magic bubbling up when the spell failed. The woman rose to her feet. Her features had changed drastically, from the quiet-looking blond to a creature made from ice, her skin more glass than flesh. Black eyes looked out at them before the ice maiden let out a mocking laugh.

"A pity," she said. "I would have loved to stay long enough to see her convicted."

"Clear everyone out!" Lumina shouted, but the maiden had already begun her attack. A sweep of her arm turned half the courtroom into an icy prison, many in the audience promptly encased in ice. Tala blocked her second attempt, using her agimat to push back against the wave of frost, but she was already exhausted. The third assault sent her grunting, a chill enveloping her as her legs froze.

"So much for the Makiling," the ice maiden mocked and then raised her foot to stomp and shatter Tala's feet, but West, who had shaken off the guards, lunged forward and bit into her arm. With a shriek, the ice maiden shook him off, but her attempts to freeze him were blocked by Lumina's agimat. Tala's mother went one further and punched the woman hard across the face.

"Hold still," she instructed, and warmth returned to Tala's body as Lumina thawed the ice block keeping her immobile.

"Th-thanks," Tala chattered. "Mom, how did she get past us?" Avalon defenses were built specifically to keep ice maidens out.

"I don't know. But we're going to make sure this one isn't leaving alive to spread that information."

Ken was next to engage with the ice maiden, swinging Yawarakai-Te at her head, which she was barely able to block. Loki had joined the fray, working in tandem with Ken with their Ruyi Jingu Bang, but neither were able to stop her from blowing a new hole in the wall, though Loki's staff was enough to send her flying out of it and into the hall.

The hall, which had been filled to the rafters with people awaiting news, rapidly emptied as the fight continued from there. Another blast from the ice maiden destroyed another section of the building, sending the battle spilling out into the courtyard. The sword in the stone was nearly forgotten by all as the ice maiden sailed past it, regaining her balance just long enough to strike at her two opponents with a hailstorm that sprang out of nowhere. Tala's mother stopped the storm from expanding, the snow dissolving once she was within range.

"You can't keep this up forever," the ice maiden mocked her. "We are an army. We shall overcome."

"As far as I can see," Lumina said, "there's only one of you, and there're plenty of us."

"Mom," Tala whispered, because more people were now coming into the courtyard instead of fleeing, and it took her a second to realize that these weren't people. Not anymore. Because she recognized the jittery way they moved, along with the glassy-eyed stares and blank expressions.

"You might need a recount," the ice maiden said pleasantly.

"They're under another thrall spell," Loki said, planting their foot right at the face of one. They and their staff were fighting like a team, one covering the other's weak spots. "They've got the same collars on."

They were right, especially since the Deathless were each employing different tactics instead of attacking the same way: some more violent, others more cautious, choosing their targets with care. There were people controlling these Deathless from somewhere nearby.

Zoe ran toward the ice maiden, her mother right behind her. Nya reached into her pouch and extracted Ogmios, which she tossed toward the other girl. Zoe caught it easily with one hand. "You attended my bail hearing at the risk of being found out," Zoe said. "I'm flattered."

"And it would have been glorious. You and your kind killed many of my sisters. I would have liked to see you shamed and beaten before the kingdom you tried so hard to save before I kill you. And they will do nothing for you. All the people you'd saved. Everyone you'd helped. You've placed yourself in danger countless times for their sake, and they will still find a way to demonize you. They call you a criminal, twist your words." The ice maiden smiled. "Your service is meaningless. I wanted you to die knowing that."

Zoe ducked the spike the woman flung her way and swiftly decimated the next with her whip. "I do it because I know it's the right thing to do, and no one else can tell me otherwise."

"Tala!" Lumina shouted.

Tala knew before she'd even turned around. She felt the chill in the air that wasn't coming from the ice maiden, the familiar twinge in her stomach whenever someone was building up too much magic too fast. She'd felt it outside the Schaffers' manor and then again during the fair.

But this time, the hole in the air was growing much more rapidly than the previous attempts had, swiftly enough for a dragon's head to poke through before they could react, followed by two forelegs and a wing. It was made of ice.

"We need more Fianna!" Lumina shouted as the beast bellowed and a howling gale of ice erupted from its mouth, freezing every object within range. It sent both Nya and Ken sprawling back, the latter grunting as he caught the Nameless Sword against his side. Tala's mother grunted and dropped to her knees, part of her arm frozen. Tala dashed to her side. Her agimat held, but only barely. A company of Fianna took up the fight, armed with heat-bespelled guns, while Lola Urduja and the Katipuneros surrounded Tala and Lumina, ready to defend them.

There was an angry whinny. A horse with eyes as red as rubies and a mane like crashing waves raced into view, avoiding the dragon to reach Ken.

"We need to completely evacuate the premises," a Fiann named Marybeth barked.

In the chaos that followed, Tala's father appeared, ax in hand, gunning for the dragon with startling quickness for his size. He drove the ax right at the dragon's throat, and the creature screamed as the blade froze to its neck, having only cut halfway through. It opened its mouth again, but this time, only cold smoke wafted out.

The dragon lifted a wing and brought it down violently. It was enough to send more people tumbling away, though Tala, kneeling beside her mother, somehow managed to stay upright. The Katipuneros, as expected, simply dug in their heels and refused to bend.

"What about them?" Loki was keeping most of the Deathless at bay, Ruyi Jingu Bang whacking them on the head hard enough to bring them down but not enough to kill. Other Fianna were firing binding spells at the Deathless and springing on the ones who had fallen, cuffing their hands behind their back even as they, oblivious, continued to snarl and bite at the warriors.

Tala felt her mother's agimat push into one of the Deathless, the most violent of the lot. She felt the connection between them and the spell controlling them snap.

What she didn't expect was the loud, nearly inhuman-sounding screech that erupted from somewhere nearby. Her mother was relentless, slicing through the rest. One by one, the Deathless slumped over, unconscious and no longer under thrall.

The ax lodged in the dragon's throat bent and broke into two. It opened its mouth.

Another fresh hailstorm came slinging out of nowhere, avoiding Tala and her mother completely and striking the dragon full force, rendering parts of its muzzle frozen.

Tala knew even before she saw him. Ryker wore a hood that hid his face, but the sparks of magic from his hands told her all she needed to know about his identity. She hadn't seen him during the court session, but given the news, he would have known what the bail hearing was about. And he had come here to help them. He was directly confronting one of the Snow Queen's ice maidens for the first time, and he was no longer hiding his defection.

The ice maiden must have thought that too. "What are you doing?" she screeched, turning to face Ryker. "Mother will have your head for this!" She moved toward him but stopped when Zoe sent Ogmios flying, cutting deeply into her shoulder.

Ryker said nothing and simply sent heavy spikes the dragon's way again, pinning one of its legs to the ground. The beast groaned and pushed more of its body out from the portal.

"Don't let it through!" Marybeth shouted.

Ken appeared astride Horse, a whirlwind of swords. His first strike actually cut through the dragon, sending black blood spilling out of its stomach. His second and third slashed at the creature's wing and lopped half of it off. It shattered as it smashed on the ground. The dragon raked a claw at him, but boy and kelpie simply blurred from view, popped up several feet away, and continued the assault.

Zoe's whip wrapped around the ice maiden's waist. The woman grabbed at it, and ice enveloped the weapon. "That was a mistake," she taunted as the frost ran quickly across its length.

And then she jerked, eyes rolling toward the back of her head as she pitched forward. The sizzling sound of powerful volts coursing through her body, making her thrash uncontrollably on the ground, was audible.

"Big mistake," Zoe said, "to think that ice isn't a good conductor of electricity."

Ken was a one-man army. He sliced at sections of dragon, limbs melting as they came away. "Lord Charming," he said, "fancy giving us a toss up?"

The Beast of Suddene reached down and picked *both* Ken and his kelpie up like they weighed no more than a couple of puppies, spun a couple of times, and launched them through the air like they were a shot.

Ken soared through the air with the greatest of ease and aimed his sword. Sharp icicles hurtled out of the dragon's mouth but only passed through empty space, as Ken and Horse were no longer there.

Instead, they flickered back into view over the dragon, and Ken plunged his sword down, straight into the center of the ice dragon's head.

The dragon disintegrated promptly, and Horse landed back on earth with a grunt and a thump of a hoof. The portal immediately receded, shrinking swiftly until all traces of it were gone.

A peculiar change passed through the ice maiden. Her features shifted, stretched, and reformed, her whole body warping until it was the Snow Queen herself, standing in her subordinate's place.

"Kay," she said.

Tala's father hesitated. The Snow Queen shrugged off Zoe's whip with little effort and stepped toward him. Tala saw Ryker withdraw back into the shadows, but the woman only had eyes for Kay.

"I did it, Kay," she said. "For my love of you, I helped even the accursed Avalon. It was only a matter of time before OzCorp would have infiltrated Avalon's wards. So I cultivated a spy within their ranks. They used the prototype without Ruggedo Nome's knowledge to open all those portals into Avalon, knowing you would notice and investigate. You would have never known about Nome's plans otherwise."

"That explains it," Lumina muttered. "I was wondering why they would send Deathless the last time, knowing we could trace the victims' identities. She was counting on us doing that."

"Could it have killed you just to tell us instead of getting people hurt in the process?" Tala's father snapped.

"Would you have believed me if you hadn't seen it with your own eyes? Would you have preferred finding out about their ability to recreate dragons only after they had fully developed the spelltech?"

"*You* supplied them with shardstones!"

"It was necessary, to stay informed of their plans, to control their operations."

"This isn't what I asked for. I asked you to stand down, to forget your war with Avalon."

"That I will never do, and you know that. They took too much from us."

"Everyone responsible has been dead for a long time. We outlived them all. Isn't that good enough?"

"No! I will take the Maidens and the firebird and everything they've stolen! I will deal with Avalon the same way I dealt with Wonderland!"

Kay retrieved his ax. "Then I'm sorry," he said and swung.

The ax caught the Snow Queen in the stomach. She transformed almost immediately, back into the ice maiden, who staggered in surprise, clutched at her midsection, and melted, until not a drop of her remained.

"I'm sorry," Kay Warnock sighed, staring at the ground.

Tala looked around, but Ryker was already gone. She understood his reasons, though her heart felt heavy.

Her mother, arm now thawed, put it around her. "Kay," she said.

Tala's father drew nearer and hugged them both. And this time, Tala relaxed into his embrace.

"What was that terrible screeching, Lumina?" Lola Urduja asked.

Her mother let out a broken laugh. "The people controlling the Deathless had the spell rebound on them when I snapped their bond. You're not going to believe who they are. Though on second thought, you probably will. There's a huge group of King John's diplomatic team having a bad reaction inside their hotel right now."

"What the hell, Ken?" Loki laughed, stepping toward the boy. "How did you do that? I've never seen—" They broke off.

Ken turned, eyes glittering, glowing with fresh magic. Yawarakai-Te in his hand also shimmered—

No. Ken wasn't holding Yawarakai-Te or Juuchi Yosamu, because they were lying on the ground dozens of feet away.

Ken looked down at the sword in his hand—a plain broadsword. "Oh shit," he said and then cast a terrified glance over at where the Nameless Sword was.

It was gone. All that remained was stone.

"Ken," Nya said, her hands over her mouth.

Ken stared at the Nameless Sword in his hand again. And then he turned toward the crowd of onlookers who had lingered despite the danger, a good number of them from the media. Cameras and mobile phones were trained in his direction, still recording, still flashing.

"Oh," Ken said. "Shit."

27

IN WHICH EVEN HEROES NEED FAMILY TIME

Tea-ta's was closed to the public as an added precaution. Fianna had been posted outside to deter and at intervals escort persistent celebrity chasers out of the premises. Save for the Banders and their families, the Hollows was empty. It had only been an hour since Ken had drawn the Nameless Sword, and Tala was very tired.

Tita Teejay handed her a brown sugar boba and a Milo dinosaur chocolate drink. "You will have to talk to him sooner or later," she pointed out gently.

Tala winced. "I know."

A television monitor was tuned to the Avalon news channel, where the reporter was summarizing the events from the courthouse. Another screen was tuned to the Royal States channel, where the kingdom was dealing with their own fallout.

"I suppose it is very good," Zoe's mom said doubtfully, eyeing the drink she was given with curiosity. The Carlisle family was only one of several currently seated at the tables. Alex had invited their parents so he could talk to everyone without fear of being overheard by reporters, who were swarming every Maidenkeep wing.

"Even your parents, Tala," the king reminded her loftily, which was why Tala was dragging her feet. Her mother was running late, and she really didn't want to spend the next several minutes in uncomfortable silence with her father.

It was over. His confrontation with the Snow Queen had revealed his identity to the rest of the world, and people were already braying for blood.

"It doesn't have to be wine for it to taste good, Mom," Zoe said wearily.

Her mother took a tentative sip. She hummed, then put it down. "Why did you not tell me earlier, Zoe? All this sneaking around and hiding. Even with King Alex's approval, it could have gone much worse. I could have given you legitimacy." Tala wasn't planning on eavesdropping, but Zoe's mother didn't seem to care who heard.

"You could have vouched for me, but that wouldn't have protected everyone else," Zoe countered.

"You have always been like this, my Zo. Always saving people, always convinced that only you can save the world. That is not how life works, my love."

"Why?" Zoe blurted out. "Why do I have to get in trouble for you to visit me? You were off having tea with the British queen and playing tennis with the heir to the Swedish throne, and I'd been missing for six months. In all that time, you never even asked how I was feeling or if I was all right."

Her parents exchange glances with each other. "Sweetie," her father said. "Your mother only wanted to give you space—"

"I don't want space! I want someone who could actually be a mom to me! I don't want you two constantly walking on eggshells with each other just to appease me! I know you're never getting back together. I just don't want one of you always acting like I'm someone responsible who can look out for herself when I don't always feel that!"

"But, ma chérie," Zoe's mother said, "you *are* a very responsible girl, and we are very proud of you."

"No, Felicity," her father said. "That's not what she means."

"Ah. Sweetheart, you know you're free to yell at us if you have to. Cry it out if you must. Our breakup has never been your fault. And I am not very good at talking and changing diapers and gossiping. It would not be a stable life, to be with me."

"Changing diapers? Mom, I'm almost eighteen."

"I am not very good at being a parent, my Zo. Your father is better at it, and I decided he would be a steadier presence in your life. But I suppose I should do more than what I have. I am sorry."

"That's all I want." Zoe cleared her throat. "Um, well, since we're talking about crying…"

West was with his own family; his mother was doing all the talking, occasionally shedding tears of pearls, though apparently they were of happiness. William Nottingham was absent, but Lady Nottingham and Adelaide were sitting with Cole.

Conspicuous in their absence were Loki, Ken, and Nya. Loki, because they were on Fianna business with their fathers, and Ken and Nya, because nothing would have stopped the press from hounding them. Footage of the dragon's fight was replayed constantly over the airwaves. Two Worldenders had already accosted Ken, claiming he didn't deserve ownership of the Nameless Sword. Their attempt to wrest the weapon from him was caught on camera, and social media was now rife with mocking pictures of the two hysterical geese being chased by Avalon's Transfigured Animal Control, and nobody had tried anything else on Ken after that. The Nameless Sword, apparently, had its own protection spells built in.

The king was staring at the Royal States' channel. The firebird was on his head, grimly watching.

"—a very bad day for the monarchy," the pundit was saying. "There has been very little official word about the state of King John's health. He has not yet been charged with either possession of an illegal spell or attempted murder, though those in his official retinue to Avalon have not been so fortunate. As you know, there has already been controversy surrounding the bail hearing for Gregory Mints, director of communications, after his statement comparing his use of the thrall spell to a video game, and many have since called him out for what they say is a callous remark. His bail has since been revoked, and Mints will be awaiting his trial at the Eastward Prison in Arizona. Ms. Samantha Sacks, a spokesperson for King John, is also with us today. Glad to have you with us. Samantha, do you think judges will be considering more stringent bail hearings after this?"

"I think judges shouldn't let protests and complaints from the minority affect their judgments on cases. I feel that the original decision was fair and aboveboard. Twenty thousand dollars is not a low number for bail."

"It is if the defendant has investments in two toll companies and his own helipad," one of the several correspondents on-screen said dryly. "Would twenty thousand dollars be a good number for you should the king find himself in the same situation?"

"I'm not even sure that kings can be arrested and charged, Adam. That seems to go against everything America stands for."

"By holding someone accountable for their crimes?" another scoffed. "Does America stand against that? I'll tell you what nobody here wants said aloud—that you're so committed to the status quo of bigotry that King John espouses that he could sit back and let some queen from some distant snow country destroy our whole nation, and you would *still* fight to keep him in power. Oh, wait. He actually did that, and you're here defending him! One of his henchmen boasted about controlling those

Deathless like it was a game, and your response was not to censure and denounce him but to call for a video game ban!"

The panel promptly erupted into arguments, everyone talking over one another in their bid to be the loudest heard.

"Is that it?" Alex asked. "Their king was literally caught red-handed, and all they're concerned about is bail?"

"Didn't you tell me that the cruelty was the point?" Tala asked.

"I never thought a whole kingdom might actually give him a pass on it, now that there's actually evidence they were using those thrall collars on those poor people. The EMTs responding to their emergency calls *found* them while the curse was still backfiring. They've been filmed being loaded up onto ambulances, still twitching. Secretary of State Siskinger had lost so much brain function he requires permanent assisted living. Ken could probably testify about overhearing Nome and Siskinger's undersecretary, Limler, talking about the Royal States making those orders, but many of the others with King John are already confessing. Their own forensics confirm everything. Why are they talking like this is all circumstantial?"

"You lived in Invierno for nearly a year, and this still surprises you?"

"Maybe I'm just less of a pessimist than I hope to be." Alex stared hard at the screen. "What about Zoe's case?"

"The Royal States have dropped the charges. They don't have enough proof with the other cases, and technically, Abigail Fey is an American citizen. They're talking about proposing a new bill about this, though."

"Is it too idealistic to hope that it's for reinforcing everyone's rights to their own bodies?"

"What, you lived in Invierno for most of your life, and you're still expecting a decent law from those goons?" Alex sighed. "You're only half right. A bill to protect men should *they* get pregnant, and only who they consider men too. This is my surprised face. Wherever Abigail Fey is, I hope she's getting a kick out of all this." Alex looked back at Tala. "He's gonna wait for you as long as it takes, you know," he prompted with a quick look at Kay Warnock.

"I still don't know what to say to him."

"You've always known what to say to him before."

"Things changed."

"But he hasn't. Whatever you hate about him now, he's always been that."

Tala swallowed. "All right."

"Be happy you still have a parent to yell at. I would have liked the chance, even if my dad did things I disapproved of."

"Thanks," her father said after Tala had sat down and offered him the chocolate drink. "How'd you know what to get me?"

"This is what you always order," Tala looked down. "I'm gonna tell Ken I rejected the sword."

"You think it'll change things?"

"More about me not wanting to hide anymore."

"Ah." Her father took a sip of his drink. "Now that ye've mentioned guilt... I wanted to wait till yer mum was here so we could tell you together, but I think she'll forgive me for saying it now. I intend to turn myself over to INTERPOL."

Tala froze. "But why?"

"I think I've evaded justice long enough. The people I've harmed may have been gone a long time, but the damage goes down family lines."

"But they won't treat you well," Tala said desperately. "Why not just make a public statement, make amends financially or whatever else they want. There's nothing for anyone to gain if they put you in prison."

"Ain't that why ye were angry at me? Not just because we didn't tell ye, but because ye didn't want to think me capable of the things I've done? That I got away with it?" Kay bowed his head. "I doubt I'd ever be able to put things to rights, but at the very least, this will ease my conscience, give a bit more justice back into the world. It's for my peace of mind too. And for what it's worth, you inspire me to do better. And to be better, I gotta earn at least part of the time I was supposed to get."

"Dad," Tala choked.

"I'm sorry for adding another burden on you and yer mum. I'm going to dedicate as much time as I can to be with you guys till I've outlived my usefulness to Avalon. You understand, don't you, lass? I have to do this."

"I know. I love you, Dad."

"And I love you, my girl."

The looking glass shimmered to life, and Lumina stepped through, accompanied by a man who Tala didn't recognize at first and then did, because he looked like a much-older Cole.

The Nottinghams had already risen to their feet. The man exchanged a quick word with Tala's mother, then made his way toward them. He was smiling, and so were Lady Nottingham and Adelaide. Cole remained wary, though that guardedness faded when his father spoke to him, then clasped his scarred hand.

"Oh," Lumina sighed as she sat down beside Tala and saw their faces. "Kay, did you tell her?"

"You know me, mahal. Could never keep my trap shut for long."

"I'm gonna support him," Tala said, feeling a thousand pounds lighter. "I'll still be arguing about it with him every step of the way, though."

Her mother relaxed and smiled broadly. "I wasn't happy at first either. But Avalon's negotiating terms, and the other kingdoms seem amenable."

"I have to tell you something that Dad already knows," Tala said. "Before Alex got rid of the frost, I found the Nameless Sword at

Maidenkeep. I drew it out, but I also rejected it. Dad only knew because he was there when it happened. The Cheshire knows too, though I don't know how he did."

Lumina blinked, turning to her father. "Kay."

"You know me, mahal. Always keeping secrets I shoulda told ye in hindsight."

"Maybe Ken shouldn't be carrying the sword," Tala said. "It's my fault he has it."

"It was his choice to pull it out and accept it, same as it was your choice to reject it. I knew about your doom. I was worried, but when Ken pulled the sword out, well, I was relieved."

He didn't back down, though, Tala thought guiltily. He's being more responsible about it than she was.

"Do you plan to take it back?" her mother asked.

"I don't want to. But Ken should at least know."

"Tita Chedeng," Alex said. "The Fianna are ready."

The Katipunera quickly hit a button, and the television monitor switched to what appeared to be a body cam, recording in real time. "Anyone hear me?"

"Loud and clear," Loki's voice reported. "Teams One and Two on standby. Waiting for your signal."

The second television screen changed from the Avalon news channel to several split screens, all from the perspectives of several other Fianna also wearing body cams. All stood before the Red King looking glass.

"Are you sure you can get past the barriers?" the king asked. The other families had now crowded around the noble to watch.

"Yes, Your Majesty." Alex had asked him this about fifty times by this point, but Anthony Sun-Wagner's voice was still reassuring. "Tech analyzed the collars they used on the Deathless and pieced together the remains of the disguise spell the ice maiden used. We know how they've been trying to circumvent our barriers. Severon will stake his job on it."

Alex closed his eyes. "All right. Do it."

A quick bark from another Fiann and the portal activated. One team jumped through the portal and emerged at OzCorp headquarters, shouting at the startled OzCorp employees to put their hands up. The second ported into the cave entrance, the one Loki had first infiltrated, yelling for the workers there to do the same. Following the Snow Queen's revelation, getting the warrant needed to raid OzCorp's headquarters had been anticlimactic, and Tala was impressed at how quickly the Fianna had planned the whole thing.

Loki and his fathers were with the second team, at the Wake's request. It had only seemed fitting, he had said, since Loki had been the catalyst for the whole mission.

Alastor, the private security OzCorp had hired, gave up readily. A confession from one of them allowed a Fiann to gain access to the camouflaged entrance, and they all rushed in.

"Something's wrong," they heard Loki say. "The magic sensors are gone."

"Depowered?" Gareth asked. "Deactivated?"

"No, they're just…gone. There was an ID scan I had to get through before getting to this part of their lair, but it's not here now."

"Elana, see any possible signs of sabotage? Any of our devices detecting a bomb or similar in the area?"

"Negative, sir."

"Take all precautions anyway. Make sure your defusing devices are on standby. Let's not get careless when we're this close."

As Tala and the others watched, the main doors leading into the underground lab opened easily without further access codes.

"Impossible," Loki said, gaping. The cavern was completely bare. Broken pieces of what looked to be shelves had been torn down from the walls to hide the cave's true purpose, along with splintered furniture. "They couldn't have taken out their prototype so quickly without anyone else noticing."

"Search the area," Gareth ordered. "They could have left something behind."

"Not very likely," Alex said darkly. "They were given advance warning."

"We've got some happier news from the other team, Your Majesty," Lumina said. On-screen, General Luna was triumphantly holding up a pair of collars that looked like the ones the Deathless wore. "We'll be able to verify if they're the same devices. We've got them on that at least."

"Nome is not on the premises," Lola Urduja's voice reported. "Neither are Fey or most of the executive board of directors."

"I want an all-points search out for Nome this instant," Alex said. "I don't care if he's managed to find a way past the Burn, I want him in cuffs before the day is out."

"Of course, Your Majesty."

"What does OzCorp intend with their own Maidens prototype?" Lady Nottingham asked.

But Zoe was already thinking ahead, using one computer to call up the building schematics of the OzCorp facilities. "Based on Loki's report, the first prototype we found was here, at the outskirts of Lyonesse under Marooners' Rock. Since OzCorp avoided detection by bringing in their supplies and equipment via a modified submarine, I'd say they were able to take out their prototype the same way. They knew we wouldn't be able to monitor the whole sea even if we knew how they brought their artificial stones in the first time. That's a con for us."

"But bringing out a completed prototype would be very much different from bringing in parts and raw materials, Zo," her mother reminded her, springing up to pace alongside her. "That is a pro for the hypothesis it is still in Avalonian territory. That kind of magic will be more powerful than simply the sum of its parts."

"Did they use a looking glass to port it out, then? From their experiments with the ice dragon, it seems like they're getting better at it. Lyonesse is a big place, and there are parts of Avalon that aren't as populated as it is here. That's a con."

"Even so, any spelltech they attempt to smuggle at such a scale would be detectable in Avalon's systems even if the portal itself would not, is that right? They may send it to the remotest parts of the kingdom, but it will still be in the kingdom. We can detect those bursts of energy if they try to fire it up."

"True," Tala's mother said. "If they activate their spelltech anywhere in Avalon, we would all be alerted to it. That's why I'm worried."

"I'm not as well-versed as the others in Avalonian spelltech," Zoe's father spoke up, looking through the OzCorp blueprints. "But I think I might have found something odd."

"Please tell us," Lumina invited.

"It's not the buildings per se but their locations. I've done blueprints for New York companies, and one of the first things I look at is the land they plan to build on. OzCorp could have their pick of any prime real estate in Avalon, but they chose the worst kinds of land here." He pointed. "This kind of soil won't pass a percolation test, and it's built too close to wetlands territory for me to have recommended this particular spot. There seems to be perfectly good land several kilometers out where they wouldn't have this problem. The one near Ikpe isn't good either. With a spellstone mine in the area, sinkholes won't be unusual. Additionally, it's near swamps and on limestone karst terrain. I could give you more reasons for at least four of the other seven sites OzCorp owns."

"That is excellent work, Jonathan," Lady Felicity Fairfax said approvingly.

"Nome isn't a fool," Lumina said. "Why would he go out of his way to have his facilities built on bad land and spend an unnecessary fortune making repairs?"

But Kay had turned pale; he was already calling up more data on the workstation, the results displayed in the air before them. "This is why," he said, angry. "More fool I. Should have known. Pan and Hook tried to do exactly this. Hook made his own prototypes to use against Pan, Pan tried to wrest control, and their fight destroyed their own nation as a result. That's what they're doing now."

"What do you mean?" Zoe asked, but she was immediately answered when the locations of all nine OzCorp sites were displayed on a map Tala's father had drawn up. Each spot was positioned in an almost perfect circle, similar to the placement of each of the Nine Maidens.

"Lyonesse is at the center of their circle," Kay said grimly. "Wherever their prototype is, they intend to use it within the city."

"Syet," Tala's mother said. "They're attempting to recreate Pan's folly but using the whole of Lyonesse as their testing ground. That's why they wanted their buildings up as quickly as possible. They haven't built on those other locations yet, and which was why it wasn't obvious what they were doing. Beanstalking them when the time was right would have blindsided us."

"They'll need something just as powerful in the middle of that circle to use as a conduit," Kay said. "Hook used the *Jolly Roger*. What does OzCorp plan to use?"

"They'll put their prototype at its center and then put a jabberwock in the middle of *that* circle," Anthony Sun-Wagner's voice crackled. "They're going to use as much magic as they can draw, and they don't care if they destroy Avalon all over again to do it."

"But to do what?" Lady Margrethe asked.

"I remember something I watched on television." Slowly, Lady Nottingham crossed to the workstation and typed rapidly on the keyboard.

A search engine popped up, featuring several press interviews with Ruggedo Nome. Lady Nottingham clicked on one of them.

"…always been fascinated by Avalon legends," Nome was saying. "The myth of Buyan had always imbued my imagination as a child. A magical land where no one went hungry, where people could live forever, free of disease and vice. I grew up wanting to go to that place, and then, when I was old enough to realize there was too much divisiveness and inequality to make that a reality, I vowed instead that I would find a way to create that world myself."

"There's your answer," she said.

"Your Majesty?" It was Lola Urduja. "We found something."

"Nome?" Alex asked.

"No. We know where their fake Maidens prototype is. We gained access to their computers. The last portal they activated, twenty minutes before we arrived, was at Maidenkeep. At the Nine Maidens' coordinates."

28

IN WHICH BUYAN IS NO LONGER A MYTH

The towering form of the Nine Maidens loomed before them, black and forbidding as always, but it was the smaller but no less powerful ice-encrusted OzCorp replica that Tala spotted first. Positioned side by side, they looked very different and yet eerily similar in many ways, and the magic that crackled around them was so strong it made her nauseous.

The next thing Tala noticed was the Snow Queen, standing by another portal at the opposite end of the room.

Ryker and Vivien Fey were with her.

So was Ruggedo Nome. He had a gun, and it was leveled at Alex.

Nobody moved. Tala felt like her feet had been fused to the floor, the icicles that grew everywhere freezing her legs where they stood. She focused her agimat on them, trying desperately to thaw herself free, without success.

The woman raised a hand. "I wouldn't," she said calmly, "if you would rather not have your king harmed."

Alex's arms were stiff against his sides, his whole body trembling with a rage he couldn't more fully express. Loki, West, Zoe, and Cole were here with them. The firebird was by the king's feet, gazing back at the queen.

The looking glass portal they used should have brought Tala and the others to Ikpe, the next best place after Maidenkeep to protect Alex. The

Fianna and the Katipuneros were the ones who should have been here instead.

"They sabotaged our ports!" Zoe's whip did enough damage to the ice to free herself, and she ran toward the king. And leaped back, ducking a small fireball she only barely dodged. "What the hell is wrong with you?" she gasped, staring at the firebird.

"Because it's the traitor," Loki said angrily. "How could you? Alex trusted you."

The firebird shot them a bored look and sniffed.

"Don't be so hard on it," the Snow Queen said with a laugh as gentle as a bell chime. "It was my pawn long before Alex even existed. It had no choice. It *has* no choice."

"And what does that mean?" Zoe demanded.

"Ever wondered how the firebird could reconstitute itself after taking the full brunt of an explosion that decimated Wonderland?" Nome asked calmly. "Not even the strongest spelltech could withstand a Mock Turtle spell. I wondered about that, deduced that if it survived, it would be through the Snow Queen. Beiran spelltech specializes in longevity. Meanwhile, your Avalon king never even bothered to search for his prized firebird."

"We have a contract of sorts. It vowed to aid me, for as long as it would not directly harm any of the Avalon kings," the Snow Queen said. "If anything, it has always been loyal to you, Your Majesty. It would have chosen to die otherwise, and we couldn't have that."

"A work of art." Still keeping his gun on the king, Nome circled the Nine Maidens, his fingers running up and down the sides of the black towers. "As I expected, nothing OzCorp could do can match up to this masterpiece. Based on my research, when Buyan first began its expansion into other territories, it never foresaw its eventual estrangement from

Avalon. I knew that the Nine Maidens were built to share a link back to the Alatyr, and it is that connection I will exploit to open a path back into the hidden kingdom." He laughed. "You've had the key to it all this time, and none of you were intelligent enough to even realize it. Vivien, come here."

The girl obeyed. It was clear from her red eyes that she'd been weeping, but the look of fury she sent Nome's way was stronger than even her grief. "This hasn't been tested yet, Nome, and you know that. If you're wrong, we could blow up Avalon and all of us with it."

"You might have been working as a spy for Queen Anneliese of Beira over here, but I'm the reason you work for OzCorp in the first place," Nome shot back. "This was all my vision. My dream. You would never have thrived without me."

"Thrived? I built this prototype! I risked my life to find a Dormouse spell to power this, and my calculations are the reason it works! You merely funded it! I risked my health, even my sister's—" she choked off.

"That was all your fault, Fey. You were careless and let her take hold of an artificial spellstone. You spent more time with her than you ever did on the project. And you had the balls to ask for a raise?"

"You rerouted our looking glass too, didn't you?" Loki snapped. "You sacrificed everything for this jerk, and you're still going to help him?"

Vivien pursed her mouth and said nothing.

"You spent millions smuggling in shardstones and artificial spellstones to build your Maiden knockoffs, damaged property and injured dozens, and in the end, you're still after the original Nine Maidens anyway?" Loki's Ruyi Jingu Bang was quivering in the air, practically begging for a chance to strike.

"I wouldn't have needed the original if you Fianna hadn't stormed my facilities. It would have been perfect. I studied every document that

I could get my hands on regarding Hook's construction of his own Nine Maidens and how Pan attempted to reroute it. I know exactly how to reproduce it. Our Nine Maidens combined shall be enough to open a path into Buyan!"

"Tala." Her mother's voice crackled in her ear, to Tala's relief.

"I hear you," she said softly without moving her lips.

"What's going on? Half the Fianna have been ported into Scythia and the Esopian border. Someone's gotten into Maidenkeep's system, messed up the looking glass coordinates somehow. None of us can get at the Nine Maidens."

"*We're* at the Nine Maidens," Tala said softly, still staring at Ryker, who was making no move to acknowledge her. "The Snow Queen is here, as is the OzCorp CEO."

Her mother swore. "Is the firebird there at least?"

"Yep." Tala watched as the firebird slowly crossed the room, the tips of its feathers brushing against the light fabric of the Snow Queen's skirts. "Very much not siding with Alex or with any of us."

Lumina swore again. "They screwed up our comm. You're the only one we can reach. Keep us informed until we figure things out on our end."

"Please hurry with the figuring out. Things don't look too good here."

"It won't work," Zoe said. "Spellstones alone didn't make the Nine Maidens. Three of its heroines had to sacrifice themselves willingly to create it."

"Unfortunately, I couldn't find three people willing to do the same for mine." Nome shrugged. "It wouldn't even work if their families were, say, compensated for it financially. They needed to be completely dedicated to OzCorp's cause for it to have the same potency. Can you believe that shit?"

"Yeah, so few people are willing to be corporate slaves. How weird is that."

"And there were reports of OzCorp employees who've gone missing," Tala said. "You knew they had to be dedicated for this to work because you had already sacrificed them, didn't you?"

"They were necessary. For what we can do for the world. Avalon could have done so much more. Instead, you banned kingdoms from your most powerful spelltech. Where's your sense of altruism? Your so-called claims of wanting to help the less fortunate?"

"It's not the magic I don't trust to make the world a better place," Alex said quietly. "It's the people who think they have the right to it."

"A bold statement, Your Majesty." Nome stepped to the center of the Nine Maidens where he, with Vivien's reluctant help, attached a small black box to one of the towers. "By my scientists' calculations, not even the Nine Maidens on their own are capable of opening a portal into Buyan." Nome gestured at the small box. "So this will link your Nine Maidens to *my* Nine Maidens. A simple matter of overriding the safety functions so both spelltechs can work at their maximum potential."

"Override the safety functions?" Zoe cried. "You asses *overrode* the safety functions, and you think that's a *good* idea?"

"Destroying the Nine Maidens would benefit your king, lift his curse."

"No," Alex said grimly. "It's more likely I would be destroyed along with them, as I already share a link to the Maidens. It would also leave Avalon defenseless. Which is exactly why the Snow Queen chose to aid you." He turned to the queen. "You told Kay that you were aiding Avalon. But that's not the whole truth. You gave them access to Beiran shard-stones. You're using them to open Buyan because you couldn't."

The Snow Queen laughed. "I see that Your Majesty is not wanting for intelligence."

"Who's to say that we'd even need Avalon if we could have Buyan?" Nome's eyes were gleaming. "Isn't that what you want, Your Majesty? A world without sickness and pain, where everyone can live forever and no one ever goes hungry? Isn't that what we should want? Why would you allow a few greedy ancestors to close off this paradise from us, to dictate that we don't deserve it?"

"Because the problem was never Buyan," Alex said. "Do you seriously believe that people won't use Buyan for their own ends, subjugate others to gain more magic? Ever seen yourself in a mirror?"

"I know my own desires," Nome said dismissively. "I can control myself."

"Somehow, illegally siphoning magic to power an Avalon artifact you have no rights over doesn't strike me as controlling yourself," Zoe said.

"Let me prove it, then." Nome drew out a device from his coat pocket and pushed a button. The OzCorp prototype sputtered to life. So did the Nine Maidens.

"Stop!" Alex shouted, to no avail. The Nine Maidens were ignoring his control and slowly building up magic on their own—more than they should, flashing more dangerously than when Alex had used them.

The firebird spread its wings and leaped into the air. It shimmered and changed shape, until it was a glowing ball of light.

"Don't do it," the king pleaded.

"I've spent my whole life studying the Nine Maidens," Nome said and laid a hand on the transformed firebird. "You will need them, the firebird, and the sword to enter Buyan. I have two, which should be enough to test out some theories. Let's take them for a test run."

The Nine Maidens had not stopped glowing; now they flared up bright and red, like a star about to go supernova. Vivien gasped and scurried back, as far away from the glowing Nome and the Nine Maidens as she could.

"What's going on in there?" Tala's mother barked. "There's a storm sweeping through Lyonesse! People are reporting random spells popping up. People turning into animals and back again, or blipping out—"

"Nome's got control of the Nine Maidens," Tala said through gritted teeth. "You guys need to get here as soon as possible."

Some of the magic streams shooting above the Nine Maidens and the OzCorp replica intersected, growing larger until Tala realized that it was a portal in the making. Cracks appeared at the top of several of the OzCorp towers, bits crumbling down. The spells refracted, splitting into two beams once they passed through the nexus point; the first beam spun back around in an arc and rejoined the original stream, becoming a circle.

"You're going to destroy Avalon and everyone in it, including yourself, if you don't stop this," Tala screamed, watching faint cracks appear on the Nine Maidens as well. "Ryker!"

The boy's head jerked at her voice, but his hands remained balled at his sides, his whole body tense.

"Just as much a harlot as your mother," the Snow Queen said. "Fortunately, I have set him back on the right path."

Tala's heart sank.

"I think we're ready," Nome said. "Send him in, Fey."

A portal opened beside Nome, and Ken leaped into the fray with Nya right behind him. The Nameless Sword was in his hands, swinging down onto the OzCorp CEO's head.

Ice spiraled out from the Snow Queen. Nya swung her broom, deflecting the magic, but the force was enough to shove her and Ken several feet back.

"If you think your sword is such a responsibility, then prove it," Nome challenged Ken. "Will you be the boy who stopped humanity from gaining knowledge beyond our wildest dreams? If so, then come and kill me.

I'll be called a pioneer, a martyr, the damn hero you thought the sword was going to make you."

Ken hefted his blade. "Easiest decision I'll ever make," he said and started toward him again.

"Don't harm the firebird," Alex gasped out.

"It betrayed us just as much as they all did," Loki said.

"Don't harm the firebird," the king repeated stubbornly.

Ken hesitated, nodded. He ran toward Nome with the Nameless Sword aloft, but he stumbled when the blade sprang out of his hands, as if of its own accord, and plunged into the stream of magic tethering Nome and the firebird to the Nine Maidens and the replica.

The magic reacted horribly.

Ken was thrown bodily across the room. The Nameless Sword remained stuck in the air, suspended on its own between Nome and the Maidens. The magic was going *through* the blade and flickering violently coming out of it.

Nome laughed delightedly. "You never thought to question why we let you port into this room, didn't you? The sword, the firebird, the Maidens: we needed all three for Buyan. And you walked right into our trap."

"Hell," Ken growled, struggling to his feet.

"Ken!" Nya shouted. "Your swords!"

Ken drew both blades from behind him and stared in bewilderment at their glowing blades. He looked over at the Nameless Sword, still absorbing and amplifying the Nine Maidens' energy. "The Gallaghers said I could use shadow magic because of Juuchi Yosamu," he said, "and Yawarakai-Te can cut through anything that isn't living. Dad said they were about balance. Yin and yang..."

"What are you doing?" West asked nervously.

"An experiment!"

"Now is not the time to improvise, Ken!" Nya shrieked.

"Trust me!"

The noise both swords made as they hit the Nameless Sword was deafening in the sudden silence. It was like the whole room had been leached of sound, a strange ringing noise in Tala's ears all she could hear as she watched the Nameless Sword drop to the floor, no longer channeling the Nine Maidens' spells. But Yawarakai-Te and the dark sword had disappeared, fully merged with the Avalonian blade, which now sported a dark ash color on one side and a gleaming crystal surface on the other.

But the damage was done, the portal growing wider of its own volition. Tala could actually detect a hint of something within it—a suggestion of sparkling ocean, vibrant forests, and a bright sun.

"Buyan," Nome breathed.

His eyes grew wide and his mouth dropped open. Blood spilled out.

Calmly, the Snow Queen pulled her blade from his back and coldly watched the man fall.

Vivien Fey screamed.

Another portal appeared before them, and Kay rushed out, ax in hand. To everyone else's surprise, it was Tristan Locksley who followed after, a fire arrow already nocked. The port closed almost immediately behind them.

"Something's locking us out," Tala's mother said. "We can't keep the port open long enough to let in more than a couple of people at a time, and we need to charge up all over again before we can make another attempt."

"What are you doing here?" Alex asked, stunned.

"I want to help. And apologize. But help first." Tristan aimed for the ice around Alex's feet, firing rapidly and breaking off large chunks. "What *is* that thing?"

It took Kay only a moment to assess the situation before he was turning back to Ken, who was still staring down at his new sword in shock. "Follow my lead, lad!" he shouted, and that was enough to snap the boy out of his daze.

"Kay, my love," the Snow Queen called. "I kept my promise."

"I didn't ask you to kill him," Tala's father said. "I asked you to leave us alone."

"You know I can't do that. You know his death was inevitable. OzCorp was a threat to both our kingdoms. I only pretended allyship long enough for them to find a way back for us." The Snow Queen pointed to the portal. "It's Buyan, my love. My true home. Here is proof of my devotion. Finally, after so long, we can return! Come with me. Let us leave these humans and finally find our peace."

Kay stared at the opening. A look of longing and grief crossed his face, but only temporarily. His face hardened. "We both lost all rights to return. Home is where my wife and daughter are."

"But you will die here," the Snow Queen hissed, jealousy and anger twisting her face. "Not even Buyan can sway you? Even in Camelot, you longed for Buyan, so we could be together without Arthur's responsibilities on you. Are you truly that lost to me? You will die in the span of years when you could still have an eternity with me. Is that what you truly want, my love? To grow old and die a villain?"

"I will grow old, and I will die, loved by those I love."

The Snow Queen's eyes flared red. "Then you shall have nothing," she said, and the magic that firmed at her fingertips turned into sharp ice projectiles that scattered across the room, indiscriminate about who they hit.

They were met by an ice shield that had sprung up without warning, protecting not only Tala but everyone else. Tala's eyes flew to Ryker, who had not moved from his position. But the strained look on his face and the beads of sweat on his forehead belied the strength he was expending to keep the barriers strong and steady, even as more icicles slammed against his defenses.

"What are you doing?" the Snow Queen shrieked.

"Something I should have done from the very beginning," Ryker said.

With a shrill scream of rage, the Snow Queen flew at him, and Ryker barely had time to erect a shield of his own to ward her off. It was Tala's father who moved to block her, planting himself before Ryker.

"You've got a bone to pick with *me*," he said grimly. "Leave the lad out of it."

"He is nothing to you!" the Snow Queen shouted. Shadows formed behind her and twisted into shades. "Why would you go out of your way to save him?"

"For the same reason every father resigned to the matter would," Kay replied. "Because my daughter fancies him."

The Snow Queen's sword of ice sliced at him, and Kay countered with a swing of his ax. The distraction was enough for Tala to whip up enough of her agimat to melt the ice around her feet, and she rushed to help Tristan do the same for Alex and the others.

"We need to find a way to close the portal before things get bad!" Nya shouted. "Without anyone to control it, it's going to go nuclear in the next ten minutes, maybe!"

"The firebird's amplifying the Maidens." Zoe winced. "We need to disconnect the firebird and the Maidens from the replica! At this point, I don't think the firebird can free itself on its own even if it wants to!"

"I have an idea." Alex skirted around the ice shield, heading for the orb that had been the firebird. He grabbed at it and held on, ignoring the flames blazing up, burning his hands. Sensing an advantage, the Snow Queen summoned a large icicle and aimed it his way, but Alex didn't even bother dodging. The sound as the ice tore into his shoulder was horrifying.

"No!" Tristan shouted when Alex went down, barreling past the shields at his own risk so he could grab Alex and drag him back behind the barrier. "Are you trying to kill yourself?" he snapped. An ice arrow materialized in his hand, but instead of drawing it with the bow, he stuck the sharp end of it to the icicle Alex had been struck with.

"Aren't you supposed to be removing it from him?" West asked.

"I don't know if it hit an artery. He'll be in trouble if it melts, and this will keep it from thawing. What the fuck were you thinking, Alex?"

"It worked, didn't it?" Alex pointed out weakly.

There was a feeble coo beside him. The firebird had resumed its original shape, and the spells in the air were now limited around the Nine Maidens and the prototype, weaker but still dangerous. The creature was at Alex's side, nudging frantically at his hand with the side of its head.

"I know you're sorry," Alex told it, "and we can talk about that later, but right now, you know the best way to apologize."

The firebird nodded. Then it leaped up and aimed straight for the Snow Queen, who was still fighting Tala's father, and the woman had to turn and deflect the stream of fire headed her way as the battle turned into a fight on two fronts.

"I thought the firebird was under the Snow Queen's control?" Tala asked.

"Not anymore. The deal was to be broken if the firebird hurt an Avalon king, right?" Alex looked down at his burnt hands even as Tristan set to work wrapping them in gauze from the medicinal pouch Nya supplied.

Nya had approached the Nine Maidens again, her eyes on the conduit still strapped to the Nine Maidens' largest tower, linking it to the OzCorp replica.

"Absolutely not," Ken said. "The magic's still too strong. You're gonna dissolve the instant you step into that circle."

"I don't need to touch it to destroy it. You all just gotta cover your ears."

"What are you two planning?" Zoe asked warily.

"Just cover your ears, Zo! That goes for everyone else!" Ken was doing just that, and the others followed.

Nya inhaled sharply and long.

And then let out the breath she was holding in an earsplitting scream.

Tala could practically feel her brain rattling around in her head. Nya had directed the full impact of her shout at the conduit, but it rocked the room regardless. Even the Snow Queen had reeled back, looking stunned, and so did Kay. Only the shades seemed unaffected, hovering close to their mistress at first, then skittering forward again.

There was a large crack running down the middle of the OzCorp device, but it was still functioning. The portal had stopped growing, still not enough for a person to get through, but enough for Tala to see Buyan.

It was beautiful. There weren't any people that she could pinpoint, but she could make out slim, elegant structures in the distance that were presumably man-made. The port opened in the middle of a forest, and there were animals she recognized, like squirrels and owls and deer, and there were others she didn't, like strange snakelike things with a mane and legs draped on trees, or eagle-like creatures without beaks that seemed to be made of light.

None of the animals paid them any attention, save for a small bird not dissimilar to the firebird, alighting on a nearby branch. It stared interestedly through the opening, straight at Tala.

"You did good," Ken scolded gently. He was on the floor with Nya, and she was leaning on him for support.

"I can do a second one," Nya said weakly, practically whispering. "Just give me five minutes."

"I have an idea that might work," Zoe said, "and I think won't cost you as much strength."

"You promise?" Ken asked worriedly.

Nya reached out and touched his face. Without warning, she pulled him close and kissed him, then shoved him lightly away. "We'll figure something out. Now go and do whatever it is Avalon heroes are supposed to do."

"Yes, ma'am." Ken was grinning as he moved to confront the shades. Cole was at his side, Gravekeeper at the ready. West brought up the rear, shifting quickly into tiger form.

The first of the shades that had drawn too close was dispatched quickly by Cole, with the expected results. The shade he'd stabbed hissed, then turned on its kin. But when Ken stabbed his sword through another shadow, it simply paused, confused. Ken did the same to multiple other shades, and soon there was a whole swath that milled around one another, making chittering, puzzled sounds. And then, a final consensus having been reached, they all turned and, hissing, approached the Snow Queen, who disengaged from Kay and stepped back.

"The hell," Cole said, admiring. "How did you do that?"

"I'm not sure," Ken said, examining his blade and still grinning foolishly. "Dex said shades aren't good or bad on their own. It's just that the Snow Queen has a hold over them. Juuchi compels people against their will. So I assume Yawarakai-Te's influence on it is snapping them all out of her control?"

"If it does, you're gonna make my life easier from now on."

"Traitors!" the Snow Queen shrieked, flinging an army of shades away with one sweep of her arm.

"Let's put an end to this war," Kay said wearily. "Call off your army, your need for revenge."

"Never! They killed my father to gain his magic! These mortals are the same. They will take and take and take. Even if I concede, they will come, always, because they wish to take. Let's go back to Buyan, Kay. Leave them all behind. We can find peace there. I know it."

"I can't find peace there, knowing what's happening over here, Anneliese."

"Now!" Zoe shouted. The scream Nya directed at the Nine Maidens was lower in volume, more precise. It created a wall of sound that broke through the magic barrier spinning around the Nine Maidens, allowing Zoe to send the tail end of her whip flying through, wrapping around the conduit. Hundreds of volts of electricity sizzled through the link, and the device broke apart. The OzCorp replica fizzled out abruptly, large chunks of crystal breaking off from the towers.

The spells around the Nine Maidens stuttered but didn't stop.

"It might be too late for that," Alex said, struggling to his feet.

Tristan grabbed his arm. "You can't," he said grimly. The firebird belched fire at him, and Tristan jumped back.

"If you care about me," Alex said, "then you need to let me do this."

The firebird shone again, and it was once more encompassing Alex like a burning halo. More light surrounded them, the concentrated energy forcing the rest of the group away. More magic rose, and Alex directed it all straight into the center of the Nine Maidens.

The portal to Buyan began to close. With a shriek, the Snow Queen lunged at Alex, but Kay was there to block her, Ken, Cole, and West backing him up.

"They're drawing in more than they can handle!" Zoe shouted. "The safety features the Gallaghers installed are down! He'll die if we don't stop him!"

"Goddamnit, Alex!" Tala pushed her agimat out ahead of her to repel the magic spewing forth and crept forward toward the king. It was the world's slowest battering ram, but it was working. She could hear her mother shouting in her ear, but she could only mutter an apology and pushed on.

"What are you—" Alex uttered, but Tala didn't care to hear him either. She shoved her agimat at him, trying desperately to negate what she could. She was getting weaker, her vision swimming; it felt like her life force was draining alongside Alex's, and she wasn't sure if they could stop the stream without both dying first.

Ryker appeared by her side, thrusting his hand out toward the portal, ice freezing the opening. Tala grabbed at his outstretched arm and channeled salamanca, her agimat combining with his spell, their magic fusing together for the briefest of moments.

The world disappeared in a brilliant flash.

When it finally returned, Tala was on the floor, her hands still grasping both Alex's and Ryker's. The firebird was also splayed out alongside them, looking dazed.

The king groaned. "What the hell did you do, Tala?"

"Saved your sorry ass is what I did." Tala felt strange. It wasn't just the persistent ringing in her ears or her sluggishness or the way her head felt like it was packed full of cotton. The Nine Maidens were no longer activated. The portal to Buyan was gone.

"No!" the Snow Queen cried. "That was our chance, Kay!"

And then more portals opened around them. Lumina stepped through the first, and so did Lola Urduja, her mouth firm. Soon the room was full of Fianna and Katipuneros and even the Makiling clan and the Neverland pirates.

"It's over," Tala's mother said. "You're surrounded. Let's not drag it out further."

"This is our last chance, beloved," the Snow Queen said. "One last chance to come with me. Because if we meet again, then we will truly be enemies, and I will stop at nothing."

"My place is with them."

"Then you shall die with them as well." The Snow Queen turned to Vivien. "Your talents were wasted with that man. He took your ideas and gave you little credit for them. His disregard for anyone other than himself caused the death of your sister. I know your worth, and it was you and not him to whom I offered my friendship."

"Don't listen to her," Loki said. "She's using you just as much as Nome used you."

"It was my theory, my proposal," Vivien said. The tears were trickling down her cheeks, unabated. "My calculations. And yet he refused to give me a promotion or even a pay raise. Said I had to prioritize the company and I couldn't if I was constantly taking leave to look after my sister. And now Abigail's gone. I—I don't know what to do anymore."

"I will not make the same mistake as he. I will give you the respect and the accolades you deserve. Come with me. You will shine brighter than you ever will in his shadow."

Vivien hesitated. She looked back at all of them, then at Loki.

"Don't do it," they said.

But she was already turning, accepting the queen's hand.

A portal glittered to life behind them. The Fianna shot paralyzing bullets their way, but an ice wall materialized to bear the brunt of their shots, hiding the Snow Queen and Vivien from view. When it finally shattered, both were gone.

"How the hell did she get past us again?" Gareth barked.

"When OzCorp figured out how to bypass our security, so did she," Loki said quietly.

Ryker was sitting on his haunches beside Ruggedo Nome's body. He'd recovered quicker than either Tala or Alex and had already retrieved another small device from the man's clothes.

Mykonos leveled his gun at him. "You're under arrest," he said.

"I think not," Ryker said calmly.

"Stay with us, Ryker," Tala pleaded. "Help us fight her."

"Maybe someday. But not today. There's one last thing I gotta do."

"Let him go," Alex said.

"Your Majesty—"

"It's all right. Let him go."

Ryker pushed a button on the device, and a portal glittered beside him. "Sorry, Tala," he said and was through in an instant.

"Looks to me that there may not be much of OzCorp after this, though." Captain Mairead crouched down beside the fallen Ruggedo Nome and checked his pulse. "Seems like Avalon's gonna have another one of those full news cycles, huh."

"Unfortunately, the media doesn't need Nome to make us look bad." Alex was helping Tala to her feet. "Thank you, Tally."

Tala glared at him. "I swear, if you *ever* do that again, I'm gonna—" She moved to shove at him with her agimat, just to flush out whatever lingering spells were still on his person.

And felt nothing. The invisible shield she'd grown up with her whole life had vanished. She could no longer sense it around her.

"Tala?" Alex asked, seeing the stricken look on her face. Her parents were already dashing toward her, realizing something was wrong.

Tala was staring down at her hands in wonder. "It's gone," she said, blessedly numb, unsure how she was supposed to feel. "My agimat is gone."

29

In Which a Kingdom Goes On

Ken looked out at the throng of reporters and cameras surrounding him, undeterred. The Nameless Sword was on a hilt around his waist, front and center and difficult to miss. He stood, waiting calmly until people grew tired of shouting questions at him.

"Look," he began, "like every other guy out there, I thought I wanted the sword. I thought it'd make me look cool, plus *chosen one* looks really nice on a résumé. It took me drawing the bugger out to realize that was a pretty dumbass thing to hope for. I know about all the sore losers screaming about how this was rigged, because a scion of some rich family from wherever has once again been glossed over for the honor and how that isn't fair for some bloody reason. So."

He drew out the sword, and the circle of reporters retreated ever so slightly. But Ken simply turned and shoved the blade back through the stone.

"If anyone thinks they have a better claim than I do, here's your chance. I did do a really quick read of the sword's history, so I ought to warn you: side effects may include unwanted attention, threats, lack of privacy, political assassinations, *actual* assassination attempts, and death." Ken leaned forward. "So you lot better do your damnedest to take the sword before the day's out, because once I return and put my hands on it again, I won't be taking *crap* from any one of you. Come after Avalon, and I'm coming after you. Yeah, this is unknown territory. Yeah, nobody knows what the bloody hell is gonna happen next, least of all me. But you know what they say: better down the rabbit hole than up someone's arse—"

"Ken!" his mother shrieked from the audience.

"If no one else yanks it out by day's end, then I guess it's as good as mine. Thinking of calling it Kusanagi, in case some of you wanna start thinking about the headlines. That's all." Ken grinned and waved at the crowd. "I'm out. Good luck."

The flurry of questions shouted his way went unanswered as Ken sauntered away from the reporters, the Fianna by his elbow for security. "Well, you handled that well enough," Mak said. "Good of you to give them a sporting chance. Where to now? Maidenkeep?"

"No," Ken said. "There's someone I want to talk to first."

"Good show, Lord Inoue." Captain Mairead congratulated him. The pirates had shown up at the conference in a show of support; the threat of the *Jolly Roger* docked nearby was also a good incentive for the audience to behave.

"Thanks." Ken hesitated. "Captain, there's something I've been meaning to ask about, since…well." He pointed at the shadowless ground before him.

The pirate nodded. "So I noticed. Numerous Avalon heroes have used shadow magic in the past, as you may well know. Ralph Rinkelmann in his charities. Poesy hunted down corrupted shades with her own army of shadows. The famous botanist Peter Schlemihl was said to have survived death through it. Even Peter Pan used his own shadow as a weapon." The captain pointed at her own shadow, grinning. "I know a trick or two about it myself. If a way exists to get yours back, we'll help."

"Thanks." The solution to his and Nya's terrible prophecies seemed easy to Ken now. If he could get back his shadow, then he couldn't be the shadowless corpse-husband both their dooms had predicted, right? He was nothing but optimistic.

Captain Mairead clapped him on the back. "Consider us your servants, Lord Inoue. For nearly two hundred years, we've fought on behalf of Avalon's sword wielders. I won't be the one breaking the *Jolly Roger*'s tradition."

"Son," Kazuhiko Inoue said, he and his wife reaching Ken. They looked worried. Of course they would be. The Nameless Sword differed in ability and appearance each time it changed hands, but its owners all had one thing in common.

"You told me there might be something to why Juuchi and Yawarakai-Te are responding to me this way," Ken said. "And this is it."

"I know. But this isn't the answer I want. I am afraid, but I am proud of you."

"Arigato, Touchan." It was hard not to sound teary.

"Ken." His mother was openly weeping.

He hugged her tightly. "I'll do my best to be careful, Mum," he whispered into her hair. "I've got decades in me yet."

"We need to talk about this," Kazuhiko said. "Just to figure out how we go from here. See the extent of what your sword can do at least. Find a way to...keep things safer for you."

"I will," Ken said. "But I want you two to meet someone first. I mean, officially this time, since you've already met her."

"What's this?" his mother asked, wiping at her eyes. "Are you talking about a girlfriend?"

Ken rubbed at his face. He was suddenly nervous, more than he'd been at the press conference only minutes before. "I'm hoping," he said.

This time, Ken was alone when he ported outside Ikpe on Horse's back. The guards knew his face by now and waved at him as he passed. Ken kept going, past them and toward the tower looming over the village where he dismounted and told Horse to keep still. He cupped his hand and raised his voice.

"Hey, Rapunzel!" he yelled. "Let down your hair!"

There was the longest pause before he could make out her reply, her voice carrying down despite the distance: "Use the stairs like everyone else, you dolt!"

Grinning, Ken did just that.

Odd as it sounded, this was the first time he'd ever been inside the tower. She was on her hands and knees, wiping at the floor. She didn't even bother to look up when he entered. "Came here to gloat?" she asked tartly.

"Not really." Ken took off his shoes and planted them in a corner. Then he found another rag and joined her. The place looked like a library, which made him nervous all over again. The last time he'd been in one had been a disaster.

Nya blinked when he knelt down beside her. "You're the most powerful person in the world right now. What are you doing?"

"Powerful people gotta deal with cleaning every now and then."

"Yeah, with a bunch of maids and housekeepers."

He laughed. "My mom's got a title, and she mucks out horse stalls herself. You really think I'm gonna stop being me?"

"I suppose not." She paused. "How are Tala and the others?"

"Tala's still bummed that she doesn't have her agimat back." Ken scrubbed briskly at the floor. "The Cheshire says it might take a while. She deserves the rest, frankly. Loki's a bit down as well, but West's got himself the attention he thought he wanted. It's nice to see people finally

420

paying him notice. And Zoe… I really don't know what's up with her. I thought she was with Tristan, but apparently she isn't? And she's got a thing going on with Cole? *Cole*?"

"You're a bit clueless when it comes to matters of the heart."

"Seems like it." Ken looked down at the floor, where the absence of a shadow stared back at him. "I'm sorry about getting you in trouble."

"I decided you knowing everything was worth it." Nya winced. "I'm not gonna be let out of Ikpe till next month, though. They forgave me for what happened at Villeneuve, but getting grounded is my punishment for exposing myself at Marooners' Rock."

"Do you think that's a little excessive? It was an accident. And it's not like I'm gonna blab to anyone else."

"You won't, but secrets get out quick. There was a tabloid magazine yesterday that did report sightings of a mermaid off Marooners' Rock. That means someone might have spotted us. There could be more coming. If people knew mermaids still exist, they'll start hunting us again. Kill us and steal our voices. Doesn't matter that I didn't mean to."

"I didn't know about the risk you guys were taking. I was out of line trying to demand answers."

"You have a valid fear of water. And I got off pretty easy, considering. The council agreed that since we were"—she swallowed—"connected already and you would have to know sooner or later, it didn't warrant giving me any harder sanctions. They'd already voted and decided to tell Alex everything."

"Then I'm gonna stay here and help you with your chores every day till you're done with the punishment."

"You can't do that! You're the sword's wielder now. What if they see you like this with me?"

"I don't mind them seeing me like this with you."

Nya stared at him. "Ken. This doesn't change anything. There's still the prophecy. It's still saying one of us will die if we…"

"I already know which one of us is going to die. My knowledge of history sucks, but I know the names of every Nameless Sword wielder who lived to a happy old age, and the answer is 'not a one.'"

"Ken—"

"You know, I actually considered using the spellstone Alex gave me. Thought maybe it could change my prophecy somehow."

"Ken, you didn't—"

"Of course not. It's just that I felt helpless about mine for so long that I figured anything I could change would at least be something *I* chose. Never went through with it because I knew I was gonna make everything worse. And then the whole thing with Vivien Fey's sister happened, and it killed any lingering interest I had. Zoe's too. She's the most responsible person I know, and if even she could muck it up, then I'd be a million times worse. But you know what? Bugger our dooms anyway, Nya. They both say that there'll be death regardless of who we wind up with, even if it's not with each other. Maybe I can beat the prophecy. Maybe I won't. But even so, I don't wanna waste another second living with regrets. If you don't feel the same way, then tell me, and I can take it. I'm shooting my shot right now, because, well, I think *we're* worth it."

Nya laid the dustpan down beside her, looking sad. Ken steeled himself for the rejection that was coming.

Instead, she laid both her hands gently on his. "I'm still scared," she confessed. "But you're right. I want to be happy. And you make me happy."

This wasn't Ken's first choice for their first kiss (technically the *second* kiss, he amended), here in her grandmother's tower in the middle of cleaning. "What are you doing?" Nya squealed as he scooped her up.

"I think we've got a long-overdue dinner date waiting."

"But I'm not allowed to leave!"

"Your all-seeing grandma would have stopped me by now. So I'm gonna say she's fine with us playing hooky for today."

She wound her arms around his neck. "You *do* owe me a meal, since I *did* win fair and square."

"Wait, wait, wait. What? What do you mean, *you* won?"

"I finished the gauntlet first!"

"That's because *I* gave you a head start!"

They were still arguing as they cantered away from the village on Horse. The seeress of Ikpe watched them leave, her face a mix of sorrow and pride.

Revoking OzCorp's business licenses was easy enough, but Loki was helping coordinate a more thorough sweep of their headquarters at Marooners' Rock. All company personnel had been held for questioning, though most of the board directors had fled even before the Maidens incident. Still, most of the upper management in the know had confessed readily enough; their main fear had been gaining Nome's ire, and that had evaporated after learning the CEO was dead. Any further attempts to protest the man's death by OzCorp lawyers had been silenced with the admissions and with the body cam Loki had still been wearing when they'd burst into the Nine Maidens room, which had caught the crucial minutes documenting the Snow Queen's duplicity.

Avalon prosecutors were avid about pursuing the case. Ken's testimony regarding OzCorp's secret meeting with potential investors had been confirmed by several reporters already working independently on the story, and a bombshell report was expected any day now, which would indict more. Whether the people involved would actually be charged and convicted was another matter entirely. Loki had seen the lengths to which some governments would go and so wasn't holding their breath.

While their fathers watched, Loki conducted a thorough search of Vivien Fey's office. Ruyi Jingu Bang followed them around, hovering about protectively.

But Vivien had been too smart. All Loki found even remotely incriminating was a letter, and it was addressed to him.

Loki,

You won this round. So I shall lose gracefully and give you the people you need. Till we meet again.

Yours,

Vivien

With it came a list of names, safe deposit boxes, bank account numbers, transactions records—everything they need to make their case against the company even more airtight.

It had also obviously been written before she'd known what Nome's fate was going to be and before she'd accepted a fate she thought would be better than doing prison time.

Loki flung the letter across the room in disgust.

"I would call this a win, Loki," Shawn noted.

"It isn't that. It's just…"

"You're mad she got away. It doesn't feel like a complete victory, because she surrendered the information herself."

They nodded.

"All in a day's work for the Fianna, honey. You need to roll with the punches, get the frustration out of your system so you can get on with the next job. Every Fiann's got that one case they ruin their health trying to close, especially when they feel like it's personal. You can't ever make it personal, Loki. Know what I'm trying to say?"

"I do."

"And then there's your staff," Anthony added, eyeing Ruyi Jingu Bang. "It's never been so sentient, back when I was using it."

"You think the spellstone Loki gave the Gallaghers to use to repair it might have triggered some secondary ability no one else could access before?" Shawn asked.

"A bit of that, and perhaps something about Loki is calling to it." Anthony stared at the floating staff. "Do you promise to protect my child, Wukong?" he asked, speaking in Mandarin Chinese. "Are you worthy of them as they are worthy of you?"

The staff lengthened slightly and then easily bent itself in half like it was made of bamboo, bowing.

"But why me?" Loki asked.

"Historians and magic experts have studied it for years, and they have no answer to that. The staff does what the staff wants. And right now, it wants to serve you." Anthony reached out to hug them. "Good job. I just received word from Keer that he'll be more than delighted to have you join the Fifth Honor. Still up for all this?"

Vivien was still out there. So was the Snow Queen. "I am."

Anthony chuckled. "Just don't go around getting a second black mark on your record too soon."

"Well, well," Mykonos drawled when they finally walked out of the OzCorp headquarters. "Looks like we're starting our probation period, Sun-Wagner. Let's get going. We've still got to sweep the Esopian borders next. The Gallaghers are trying to reverse engineer the OzCorp devices to figure out how they keep getting past our ports, but till then, we gotta do what we gotta do."

Loki took a quick glance at their fathers, who grinned back at them. "Get on with it, cadet," Anthony said.

"Can I come with you guys?" West had popped up seemingly from out of nowhere, looking distressed.

"What's wrong?"

"There are girls chasing after me."

"I was wondering why there were more teenage girls hanging around the palace entrance than usual," Mykonos rumbled.

"Wasn't that the goal, Loki?" The Fianna's body cam video had been made public, and West's identity as the antifa dog had been revealed.

"They're asking for me." West sounded stunned. "Not me as a dog. Like, me as a *me*. With my face and everything."

"West," Loki said kindly, patting him on the shoulder. "I think one of the first things you'll discover is that it's not the looks that matter the most to a lot of girls but attitude. You're a good person, you're brave, and that's why you're lovable."

"It wasn't my attitude they said they wanted to grab," West said.

"Sakima, tell the Third Honor to be on the lookout for bands of roving girls around Maidenkeep," Mykonos ordered. "Warn them to behave, or they will be kicked out of the premises, as we don't take kindly to any form of sexual harassment. We would be honored to have you join us, Lord West."

"So," West said a lot more cheerfully as the Fifth Honor headed off to the Wake's office, where they would be briefed for their next mission. "Would you rather fight the Mad Queen of Wonderland using only a toothpick or Captain Hook using only a spoon?"

Loki reached up to place their fingers against Ruyi Jingu Bang, now tiny and nestled safely behind their ear. They could have sworn that it bent, just a little, into their touch. "I'd choose a toothpick every time," they said.

"So," Zoe said. "Once from frogs. That was back in the swamps, right? Before we entered Lyonesse for the first time."

They were at Tea-ta's. After the news broke, the boba café had become even more popular than before, people loitering for a chance to spot any of the Banders or even His Majesty himself. Titas Teejay and Chedeng were soaking up the notoriety, smiling and posing prettily for pictures with some of their patrons.

Zoe did not want the attention, especially so soon after her case had been dismissed. She stared at her salt and cream cheese boba. Nottingham's was a plain assam milk tea, and he was looking down at it without drinking either. It was nice out on the veranda, which had been closed off to everyone but them, and the Hollows' cedar tree loomed over the two.

"Once from fire and then once from winter," she continued. "That's what I have to watch out for, although it's so damn vague, it could mean so many things. And you'll have to watch out for poison and a sword and madness. Your doom really is a lot more specific than mine is."

"Carlisle."

"Should be easy enough. I gotta stay close to you, for one thing, so no more skulking away without telling me. I'm gonna promise the same. My contract with Tristan is done, so no more secrets. The prophecy *does* imply we'll both survive up to that point, so I'm counting it as one for the pro list."

"Carlisle."

"I'm not sure I even believe in prophecy. I mean sure, disbelieving doesn't mean I'm not worried, especially because that frog part was a little too on the nose, but I'm willing to admit now that it's not a coincidence. That doesn't mean the rest of it is as accurate as your great-grandmother thinks it is. This is why I hated people knowing about my doom. It's like I'm admitting to giving credence to it."

"Carlisle!"

"I know what you're going to say, all right? You're gonna tell me you believe in dooms because your grandmother's a seeress, and so you're going to die for me. That's absolute crap. I won't have it, you hear me? That's not gonna happen."

Ice rattled around inside Nottingham's boba cup. "This was why I didn't want to tell you. I knew you'd freak out."

He had finally told her his doom: *You will save them thrice: once from frogs and once from fire and once from winter. She will save you thrice more: once from poison and once from sword and once from madness. Eight shall fight at the end of the world, and only seven shall return. You will die so she can live.*

Of course she was gonna freak out. "Anyone would! I've already made several life-changingly bad decisions this year alone, and I wouldn't trust me to be in charge of another one!" Zoe said.

"A bad decision? Exchanging your tears for warmth?"

Zoe closed her eyes. "Of course not. I meant my...I dunno, misplaced vendetta that spilled out into other people's business. I don't know what I was thinking. I shouldn't have done that. It was like all logic flew out the window the instant the anger took hold. I'm going to feel guilty about Abigail for the rest of my life."

"It was her choice to make."

"I was so arrogant in thinking I was helping to save lives, and I couldn't even save one girl standing in front of me. I will always regret that. But I'm never going to regret giving up my tears to save you. I'd do it again."

"I'm not sure you should."

"How do you even know that this prophecy's talking about me? It could have been meant for someone else."

"It's not someone else."

She set her boba down and studied him. "How long have you known?" she asked finally.

"Since my fight with Tristan at Cerridwen."

"But that was the first time we'd ever met."

He looked away, almost embarrassed. "I knew as soon as I saw you. Still can't explain it."

And he'd acted like he had a bone to pick with her ever since. Getting all tough in class, countering her opinions, trying his best to dislike her because he was terrified he would give in, because giving in meant it would come true and that he was going to die. And the gentle, resigned expression on his face now, his previous attempts to help her deal with her anger, accepting his fate if it meant her well-being. There was a dam in her heart, threatening to burst. "This was the reason you asked the Cheshire to join the mission bringing Alex back from Invierno."

"He knew about the prophecy."

"You should have told me earlier."

"Didn't think it would matter."

"You think my feelings wouldn't have mattered?"

"You only had eyes for Tristan. And the prophecy was clear about what I felt. It said nothing about what you felt."

"So you thought it wouldn't matter because you were going to die anyway, and you wanted to spare me the guilt."

He had nothing to say to that.

He was convinced he was going to die. His prophecy all but stated that he was going to die because of her. He'd gone to great lengths to save her life, fulfilling part of his doom when he'd rescued her from the frogs all those months ago, and had asked for nothing in return. He had rejected her, but not because he wasn't interested. He'd rejected her because he was just as terrified as she was.

"Listen to me, Nottingham." She rose to her knees, her hands against his chest. A light shove sent him leaning back at an angle, one arm braced on the floor behind him. She moved closer. "I am going to protect you," Zoe said, forcing herself to believe her own words, pushing back against the wild panic fluttering inside her at all the ways she could fail at this too. "I've done it before, and I'm going to do it again. We're going to beat that prophecy. We're going to strategize. We are going to pro-con list the shit out of our dooms. We are going to spend as much time as we can together, whether it's brushing fur out of the wolves you're looking after, or watching a hundred more old movies together, or maybe officially introducing you to my parents—only if you're ready, of course. My mom is a kind person, but she takes some getting used to."

He looked perplexed. "Are you...asking me out?"

"Are you saying no?"

"I should," he admitted, suddenly hoarse.

"But you won't?"

Gray eyes gazed back at her. "I can never say no to you," he said.

She kissed him. This time, he didn't turn away. His mouth was softer than it looked, his arm around her gentle, like she was something precious to hold. She felt the tears prickle at the corners of her eyes, finally trickling down her cheeks.

She was terrified. But she was going to save him. She would.

Because she would break if she couldn't.

"Zoe," he whispered against her gruffly much, much later, holding her as she wept, and her name finally on his lips was the sweetest sound.

"Do me a favor," Tala said. "Never *ever* agree to a state visit from the Royal States ever again."

"I'm pretty sure the ministers are already planning one for next year."

"Fire all your ministers."

It was quiet in Lyonesse tonight. They were both dressed incognito, with sunglasses and caps and oversized jackets, and were sitting at the fountain at the park, watching people. Alex's shoulder was still bandaged, and he'd been complaining about the stiffness all day. The firebird was carefully hidden inside Alex's cloak, and for once, it was making no protest. Alex had been quick to forgive, though it was apparent it was having a harder time forgiving itself, since it had been downcast ever since its betrayal was revealed.

There were a few Fianna stationed unobtrusively nearby, pretending to be sightseers. The fair was over. Avalon was still in the news, though the emphasis had long since shifted to OzCorp and its shady business deals with a *lot* of other kingdoms, or so it seemed. Tala didn't doubt that the rich people involved were going to get away with it, because they were, well, rich people, but she was at least positive that none of them would be attempting another Nine Maidens replica any time soon, especially after the full story of Ruggedo Nome's death was released.

The Filipino delegation was gone as well. In the end, Lola Corazon hadn't even bothered to say goodbye to her. Tala found that she could live with that, considering.

"I thought you were getting along well with the Makiling clan," Alex said.

Tala debated about whether to tell him, then decided honesty was still the best policy. "It took me a long time to figure it out, because my mom felt like it wasn't her place to tell me, and also because I've been slow about realizing a lot of things, but Lola Corazon has some issues about you being gay."

"Really? She seemed pretty okay with it."

"She's fine with gay people. She's *not* fine with *you* in particular being gay, because then I wouldn't have a shot at being queen."

"Really?"

"Yes, really. I realized it back at the fair, after the whole ogre thing, but only got to confront her a day or so ago. Acted like it was my fault for pointing it out to her too." Tala understood now why her mother hadn't talked to *her* mother for years. To Lola Corazon, it was all about political connections. Her grandmother wasn't mad because Lumina had married someone who'd betrayed Maria Makiling; she was mad Lumina had married someone who had no clout for her to take advantage of. Someone who, in fact, had whatever the opposite of clout was. "Politicians suck," Tala said aloud. "Present company excluded, of course."

"Well, I *have* been thinking about renouncing my title."

Tala stared at Alex, who only shrugged.

"Hypocritical of me to criticize the excessive riches of other kingdoms without me following suit, right?"

"You're still a target. You're still the only one capable of controlling the Nine Maidens."

"And I'm still gonna need the Fianna for security. But I've lived almost my whole life in hiding. I don't need the fancy stuff. I'd rather put the money back into Maidenkeep's upkeep, improve our social programs. I don't need a golden throne to be good to my people."

"You're gonna get a lot of protests from your ministers for this again."

"If they don't like it, I can take up your suggestion and fire them." Alex chuckled. "We'll figure out a balance of what I want and what Avalon needs. What about you, though?"

It was strange to not have an agimat. She'd seen several physicians and been told that it would take time to return. It was odd to feel normal and not normal at the same time. "I'm good."

There was a muffled coo from inside Alex's coat. The king reached inside and petted the fire-colored, feathered head that popped out from beneath the folds.

"You've been way too lenient with it," Tala said.

"I know. But I do understand the situation it's been put in, since I've been in something similar myself." Alex stroked its neck. The firebird let out a happy, muffled squawk. "We need it for the Nine Maidens. It knew that. It had to choose between leaving us defenseless with its death and allying with the Snow Queen to give us a chance."

"Why didn't the Snow Queen take advantage of it earlier?"

"I suspect she'd been waiting for the sword to be discovered first. We need all three for…" Alex paused, frowned. "I don't even know if I *want* to open a portal to Buyan. I could simply take my chances here, avoid the temptation of using the Maidens. It feels like I'm putting far too many people at risk. I've been trying to tell the Cheshire and everyone that, but they won't listen."

Tala had been to some of those meetings. Meetings where people debated, argued, even got into shouting matches. Alex was in the minority of people who thought opening up Buyan was more trouble than it was worth. The majority were all for finding a way to access it again, to lift Alex's curse once and for all. The firebird had been particularly, violently *for* the latter argument and had nearly set fire to Ancilotto's hair when the discussion grew too heated.

The problem was that nobody knew how to accomplish that goal—short of blowing up Avalon, like Nome had attempted.

"Do you really want your descendants to suffer through the same thing you did?" she pointed out. "Finding the Alatyr can mean a permanent solution for the next generations of Tsareviches to come."

"It's not like I'm gonna be having biological kids."

"There are a lot of options. In vitro stuff. Surrogacy. Maybe Tristan won't mind getting pregnant, since that's a thing now."

"Tala!" Alex choked.

"Are you talking to him?"

"Yeah. Sort of. I still haven't forgiven him, but he promised to earn it. I don't know what that means. But we're talking."

"Good."

"Ryker contact you again?"

"Let's not talk about him," Tala said and meant it. Ryker had made his decision clear. So had she. "Stop changing the subject. Remember that email you told me about, the one snapped from the OzCorp internal servers? They mentioned stuff like World's End, which is what Lord Charming mentioned before when referencing the Seven Magical Wonders, and he thinks OzCorp knows more about this than they let on. He's got a whole team of historians on the case, analyzing everything they can get from OzCorp's internal files. They're also taking a look at Cole's doom, because that was mentioned too. If Nome thought there was something there, then maybe there is another route available to us. In the meantime, stop thinking of yourself as expendable, will ya? I'd be lost without you."

"You're frequently lost, even with me around."

"Shut up."

"I've got some of the mages focusing on a workaround for the male pregnancy spells."

"You're really gonna help them still, huh?"

"It's not the men I'm thinking about. It's the poor babies. You really expect the most toxic among them to not screw up their bodies because they're too manly for kids? Parker Sera, my health minister, is directing a team for birth control, potions to ease the pregnancy, help for labor, the works. They'd almost completed testing for the women's version of it, and she thinks it should be easy enough to implement for men."

"You're a good guy, you know that?"

"Not really. It's just about being decent. Are you really sure *you're* okay?"

"Honestly? Not really. I feel naked without my agimat. Which is weird, because for so long, I wished I never had it, so I could be as normal as everyone else, but now it's like part of me is gone. They keep telling me it'll return eventually, that I just temporarily shorted myself out, and that's the only thing keeping me from freaking out right now. But yeah. I'll be all right."

"Think on the bright side. At least your lola will have to indefinitely postpone her next attempt hooking you up with a gay king."

"Shut up, Your Majesty."

Bells sounded in the distance: different calls to prayer. People drifted past them, shopping, walking their dogs, biking. Despite all the anxieties and battles and life-or-death situations that felt so overwhelming during the last few weeks, no trace of those troubles remained. Avalonians were a hardy sort. After twelve years of loss and despair, there were people now: laughing, playing, living. Kids around them sang snippets of song, and life in the kingdom of Avalon went on.

Alex leaned back, tilted his head toward the sky, and closed his eyes. "This is what I want," he said. "This is what I want Avalon to be. If I have a legacy to leave, let it at least be this."

For a long while, neither of them spoke, content to listen to the sounds of those faraway chimes. The firebird nestled its head against the crook of Alex's neck and, like the children, started to sing.

It was dark in the courtyard when Tala arrived, and no one else was in sight. The sword still lay in its stone, gleaming and bright.

With trembling hands, she grasped at its hilt and pulled.

It didn't budge.

She tried again. Still nothing.

"Why?" she asked it, wanting to weep, wanting to rage. She should have shouldered its burden. Ken didn't deserve this.

"Because it's out of our hands now," the Cheshire said.

The man was gone; only the cat remained. It settled itself by Tala's feet and gazed at the Nameless Sword.

"Is that it?" Tala asked. "I'm no longer worthy? Just like that?"

"You have always been worthy," the Cheshire said gently. "It only means that we are destined for other things now."

30

IN WHICH TALA TAKES ANOTHER LEAP

On a bright spring morning in Avalon, Tala Makiling Warnock stood at the peak of the kingdom's tallest and most terribly cursed mountain and prepared herself to fall.

Her family and friends were with her. Nya and Ken stood, grinning and holding hands. Cole and Zoe were more subtle, comfortable together in a way that had not been there before. Loki was still in their cadet's uniform because they were set to go on duty in another couple of hours, and West had decided to go up a difficulty level, running the gauntlet in dog form, in anticipation of the throng of admirers waiting for him at the bottom of Simeli.

There would be cameras waiting for them at the mountain's base, Tala knew. Reporters eager to turn a regular outing among friends into the next splashy headline. It was inevitable.

But Tala was no longer worried.

She and the Cheshire had watched as Ken reclaimed what was rightfully his, pulling the Nameless Sword back out from the stone with a flourish. His parents stood by him, proud and also unable to hide their anguish, and her heart ached for them. Nya was by his side too, and she hadn't bothered to hide her worry.

Tala was going to tell him. After the news circus ends and the spotlight was no longer as bright on him, she was going to tell Ken, apologize, and ask what she could do to make things up to him, though she didn't think there was anything else left *to* do.

We were destined for other things, the Cheshire had said. But without her agimat and with the choice to wield the Nameless Sword finally, permanently taken away from her, Tala felt adrift, unsure of what her purpose was supposed to be.

It was General Luna who made the leap first, jumping off with a battle cry. Tito Boy followed, and then Titas Baby, Chedeng, and Teejay, diving down into the mists below like age was of no consequence.

"Same bet as before," Ken said to Nya. "Loser buys lunch. I'm thinking some really good sushi at the new omakase that opened up. Uni. Mackerel. Amberjack—"

Nya grabbed him by the collar, drew him closer, and kissed him. Then she turned and stepped into air, giving Ken a huge smile and a dirty gesture before she disappeared from view.

"Did you get that?" Ken yelled after her. "Amberjack? Mackerel?"

"You're still sucking at this," Loki said.

Ken grinned at them. "I love her," he said happily and jumped. With a loud, delighted woof, West leaped in after him.

"After you, Nicky," Zoe said grandly.

Cole rolled his eyes, but he was smiling when he stepped forward, Zoe close behind.

"You ready?" Loki asked.

Tala took a deep breath. "Yeah."

This was approximately her thirty-first gauntlet run.

And now she knew how to finish it.

Her father had helped her figure it all out without needing to tell her. She had felt calmer with him, had barely even panicked when she'd honked her way through the Labyrinth where, for once, she hadn't needed an old lady in a golf cart to bring her out of the maze.

He was right. Once she'd figured out the secret, it was easy.

"Are you sure you wanna jump, Tala?" Loki was even more nervous for her than she was. None of the others knew she'd successfully been through the gauntlet, but they did know there were media at the base of the mountains that would be recording her failure.

She only grinned. "You're gonna be late for your rounds, Loki."

They laughed. "All right." Still the show-off, Loki backflipped their way off the edge.

That left her family and Lola Urduja.

"Wanna do it together?" her mother asked.

Her father chuckled. "Won't make much of a difference. Never been able to beat your record, Lumina."

Tala took her father's hand, then her mother's. This was their last jump together. In another hour, Kay was going to turn himself over to the Iceland authorities. There would be backlash. There would be condemnation. Later, she knew she was going to curl up in her bed and have a good cry.

But for now, she wanted to enjoy the moment with her family while it lasted.

"Ready when you are," she said and felt her parents squeeze both her hands.

And then they took a step forward, into the great nothingness waiting for them below.

As before, Tala made it past the winds easily enough and then hopped from swanshirt to swanshirt until she reached the next stage. The jumping spider was a piece of cake, as was the wall. But now came the hard part.

The first rush of magic as the transfiguration spell settled around her had felt disorienting, and like before, Tala felt the initial onset of panic, the fear of losing her sense of self while contained in her fowl form. But instead of resisting the magic, she allowed it to wash over her, allowed it to change her arms into wings, her feet into talons. At barely a foot tall, the ground was closer than she was used to, and the desire to peck at it to hunt for bugs was hard to overcome. Without her agimat to help her resistance, she was more susceptible to those baser urges.

But she persevered. She hopped determinedly on, straight into the maze thicket. Brambles surrounded her, but the glint of light was all the guide she needed. There was a hole half-hidden by the thorns barely a few meters of the way in, one that an average-sized person would never have seen. The maze had been a decoy all along. The exit had literally been inches away this whole time.

She waddled her way through and this time encountered a different kind of spell warding the enclosed area, shifting her back into human form as soon as she made it past the exit. The final path leading out brought her into the Simeli main waiting area, which was now filled with cheering fans and the flash of news cameras. The rest of her friends and family were there, waiting for her with smiles on their faces.

"Congratulations, love," Kay said gruffly, extending a hand to her.

Tala was wrong before; *this* was what it felt like to belong. With people who didn't expect her to be anything else but who she was.

"Walang iwanan," Tala said to herself, smiling, and reached out to take his hand.

EPILOGUE

IN WHICH THE UNEXPECTED SEEKS SANCTUARY

I t was getting harder to breathe.

Keep moving, his mind screamed at him. *Keep moving, or you die.*

He was good at keeping himself hidden. Good at avoiding the patrolling Fianna moving up and down Maidenkeep's corridors. He tried to make a mental note, to tell them later that this was a flaw in their security that needed redressing. But his mind was a fog, and it was getting just as hard to think.

He wasn't even sure if he would still be alive for a *later* to happen.

He tried not to track blood onto the carpet, as a courtesy. Maidenkeep looked austere and forbidding at night. Was it because of the lack of fripperies on the walls? He wondered dimly if Alex was strapped for cash. Running a kingdom must be expensive.

He'd never gone so far as to step inside the palace proper before, the Nine Maidens control room notwithstanding. It felt disrespectful to his former friend somehow.

Why was he so worried about giving offense with his trespassing when he'd done so much worse, though?

Damned blood loss, maybe.

He knew where she was staying. Something pulled him to her, though he wasn't sure what connection between them made this possible. He only knew that she was the beacon shining through the fog about him. He was simply following her light.

And then he was at her door, somehow finding the strength to knock once. Twice. He faltered that third time, the sound all but inaudible as he staggered.

The door swung open, and she was staring at him, the shock clear upon her face. And fear. She looked like she'd been crying. He didn't like that.

"Ryker?" Tala whispered.

He smiled at her, a final effort. "I think," he managed to say, "that I will be taking Alex up on his previous—"

He collapsed. The dagger driven into his back glittered despite the near darkness, made completely, entirely of ice.

GLOSSARY

adobo: chicken or pork cooked in soy sauce, vinegar, and garlic

agimat: an amulet or charm

"Alis!": "Leave!"

anak: gender-neutral term used to refer to one's children

anak ng Diyos: son of God; also an exclamation similar to "son of a gun"

antipatika: someone unfriendly or disagreeable

arnis: Filipino martial art that incorporates stickfighting

ate (ah-teh): an older sister; used informally to show respect for older women

anting-anting: charm used to ward off curses

bagoong: shrimp paste sauce used as condiment in many Filipino dishes

bibingka: a baked cake made of rice, eggs, and coconut milk

boodle fight: a set of meals placed on a banana leaf–lined table for sharing, eaten using hands instead of cutlery

chicharon bulaklak: popular Filipino street food made of fried pork intestines

Diyos ko: "my God"; also spelled *Dyos ko*

dwende: mischievous dwarves of Filipino mythology

Heneral: general

kaldereta: meat stew made from either goat, beef, or pork

kulam: a curse

"Nakakamiss": translated roughly, "I've missed this."

"Natakot ba natin?": "Did we scare [them] off?"

leche flan: custard coated in a clear caramel sauce

lechon: whole roasted pig, cooked on a spit over charcoal

Lola: (formally) grandmother; also used informally as a term of endearment for older women, as Tala refers to Lola Urduja

lumpiang shanghai: fried spring rolls

mahal: "my love," one's beloved

mare (ma-reh): term of endearment to someone you're close to, of the same social class or age

pangitain: omen

pansit: noodles, often sauteed with vegetables

pinakbet: steamed vegetables cooked in shrimp sauce

punyeta: expletive to express frustration or anger

"Punyetang mga traydor": "Fucking traitors"

putangina: expletive literally meaning "bitch mother," but equivalent to "fuck this" in English

puto: Filipino steamed rice cakes

sisig: chopped chicken livers and pork meat (usually from pigs' heads), served on a sizzling plate with vinegar, chili, and calamansi

"Susmaryosep": mild expletive; slang for "Jesus, Mary, and Joseph"

takmon: mother-of-pearl sequin-like shells

tangina: derivative of putangina

terno: a stiff blouse made from abaca, often used for formal occasions in the Philippines

torta: omelet-style

"Umalis na kayo.": "You all better leave."

Acknowledgments

As always, all my love and admiration to the usual suspects.

Rebecca Podos, my agent, for having been there every step of the way, and for delighting in every weird idea I come up with no matter how strange the tale, and helping me make them a reality.

Annie Berger, my editor, for helping me through all the ups and downs that this series has taken me on and seeing everything through. Also to the rest of the amazing Sourcebooks team: Cassie Gutman, Sarah Kasman, Ashley Holstrom, Sabrina Baskey, Jackie Douglass, Nicole Hower, Beth Oleniczak, Mallory Hyde, and Ashlyn Keil for all their help, and to Jonathan Bartlett for the very beautiful cover! And, of course, to Dominique Raccah and Todd Stocke, for providing me with the opportunity for readers to find this book.

The last couple of years have not been kind, and so I've tried my best to find comfort in the little things. In my case, these are my two kids, Ezio and Altair—the two most chaotic children on the planet, the number one reason I no longer am able to sleep in, and also the two most lovable. Also my partner, Les, who is fine with living with all the monsters in my head, knowing they come with me as a package deal.

A shout-out to some of my closest friends who've been there since elementary school: my best friend Steph, Cham, NR, Jess, Kait, Charlie, Joanne, TJ, and Mercy—the last two also for giving me permission to use their nicknames for the twin titas, Teejay and Chedeng.

When I was younger and much more naive, I thought having magic would solve everything. Now that I am older and supposedly a bit more wiser, I now understand that doing the right thing is a lot harder. And as that struggle continues, know that I am grateful to each and every reader for letting me share my odd little worlds with them. Walang iwanan.

And also, because I have done this with most of my other books and I feel the need to be consistent, I would like to thank Tom Holland for many things, but especially for his contribution to the cultural zeitgeist with his "Umbrella" lip-synch performance. Cheers, Tom.

About the Author

Despite uncanny resemblances to Japanese revenants, Rin Chupeco has always maintained their sense of humor. Raised in Manila, Philippines, they keep four pets: a dog, two birds, and a husband. A former technical writer and travel blogger, Rin now makes things up for a living. They are the author of *The Girl from the Well*, *The Suffering*, the Never Tilting World series, and the Bone Witch trilogy. Connect with Rin at rinchupeco.com.

FIREreads
⑤ #getbooklit

Your hub for the hottest young adult books!

Visit us online and sign up for our
newsletter at FIREreads.com

 @sourcebooksfire

 sourcebooksfire

 firereads.tumblr.com